Re
PE.

The Uncertain Customer

"This was short, passionate and heartwarming… Just a fast, fun read that will make you feel all warm and fuzzy inside. I loved it!"

—MM Good Book Reviews

"Read this delicious historical novella. It is a delight!"

—Prism Book Alliance

"The story is light, amusing, and very sensual. I recommend it for a quiet afternoon when you want to relax and be carried away to another place and time. Thanks, Pearl, for introducing us to Wilcox and Church."

—Rainbow Book Reviews

'Til Darkness Falls

"A good story with a fascinating plot. I'd recommend this book for fantasy fans and romantics."

—Reviews by Jessewave

Burnt Offerings

"I found myself enjoying very much the relationship of Alen with his mother, so much that, in the end, I was almost in tears."

—Elisa - My Reviews and Ramblings

By PEARL LOVE

Burnt Offerings

Juicy Bits (Dreamspinner Anthology)

Men of Steel (Dreamspinner Anthology)

'Til Darkness Falls

To Be Human • To Be Loved

The Uncertain Customer

Published by DREAMSPINNER PRESS

http://www.dreamspinnerpress.com

to be
LOVED
Pearl Love

DREAMSPINNER
PRESS

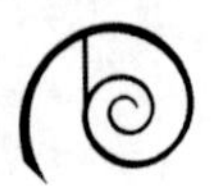

Published by
DREAMSPINNER PRESS

5032 Capital Circle SW, Suite 2, PMB# 279, Tallahassee, FL 32305-7886 USA
http://www.dreamspinnerpress.com/

This is a work of fiction. Names, characters, places, and incidents either are the product of author imagination or are used fictitiously, and any resemblance to actual persons, living or dead, business establishments, events, or locales is entirely coincidental.

ISBN: 978-1-63216-304-2
Digital ISBN: 978-1-63216-305-9
Library of Congress Control Number: 2014950608
First Edition February 2015

Printed in the United States of America
∞
This paper meets the requirements of
ANSI/NISO Z39.48-1992 (Permanence of Paper).

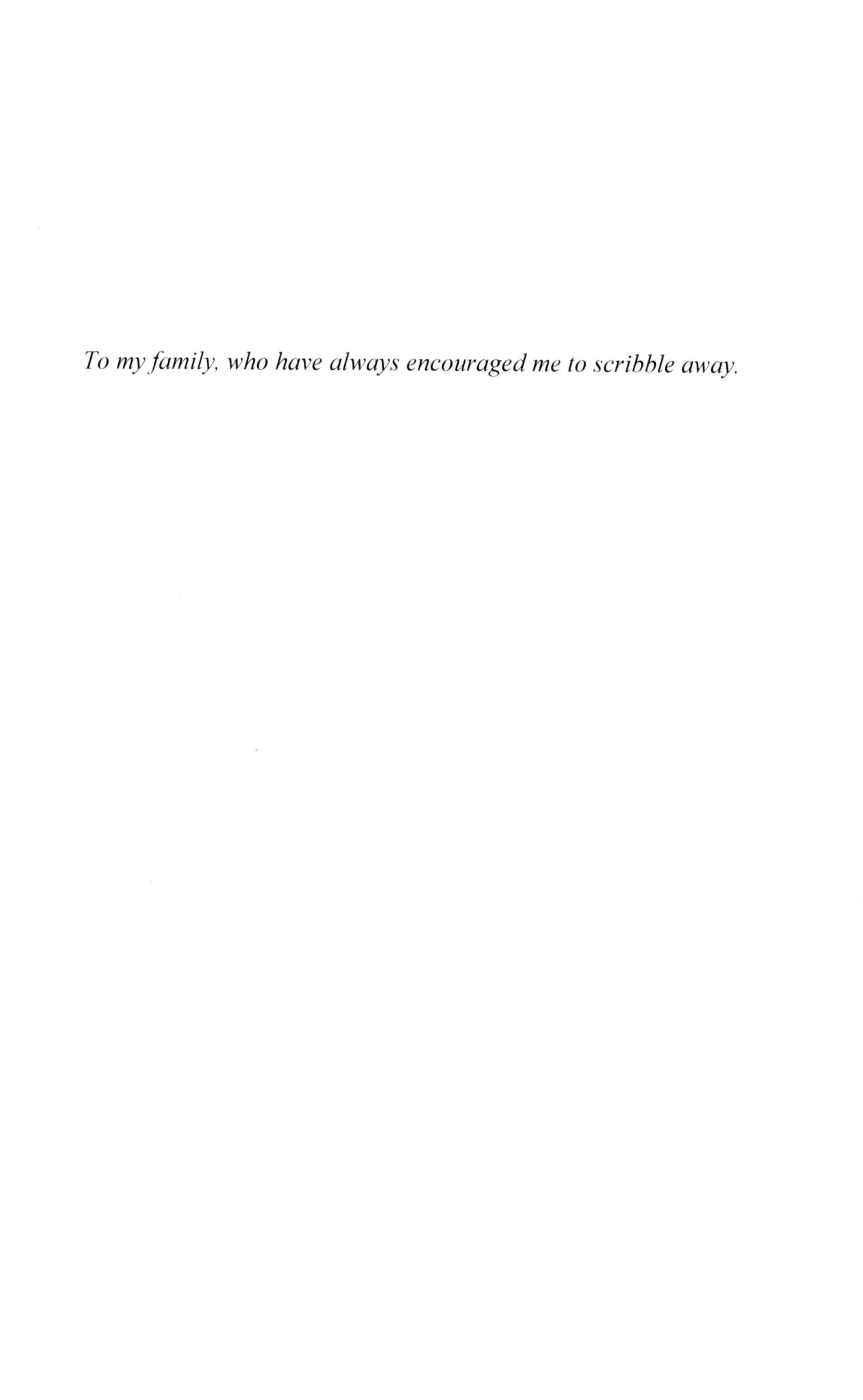

To my family, who have always encouraged me to scribble away.

PROLOGUE

INHALE. EXHALE.

One.

Inhale. Exhale.

Two.

Inhale. Exhale.

Three....

The unvarying rhythm of air rushing in and out of its lungs allowed it to track the passage of time. The helmet it wore was bolted down to the stiff collar ringing the neck of its suit, muting all external sound. The opaque visor blocked any extraneous visual clues. The lack of stimulus was of no concern. It had no other purpose than to await orders.

It stood completely still, save for the necessary expansion and contraction of its chest. Constantly monitoring its biological systems, it determined that it was running at peak efficiency. And even if it were under stress, the uniform it wore was made of a material that regulated its core temperature, enabling it to continue performing optimally no matter how extreme the conditions. The soft material rested so lightly against its skin, it barely registered the fabric's presence. It wore no body armor that might hamper the speed or agility of its movements.

It had no concept of how long it had been waiting. It had no memory of anything before the present moment. It was aware only of the darkness of the helmet's interior, the caress of the breaths that reflected back toward its face from the curved surface of the shielded polycarbonate, and the rigid feel of the weapon held in its grip. It identified the M16A2 assault rifle in its hands by touch alone, subconsciously aware that it would hit any target it aimed the weapon at without error. It accepted that it knew how to kill.

"TM 05637."

The voice came through the helmet's built-in audio system. Though it did not recognize the speaker, it responded instantly to the inherent authority in the man's tone.

"Sir."

"A terrorist cell has captured one of our diplomats. The group's leader is threatening to execute her unless we release certain prisoners being held by the *local authorities*."

It heard the subtle emphasis, understanding the term as a convenient euphemism for the government of the country in which it was currently stationed.

"If she dies, we will be forced to retaliate. Some of the locals are sympathetic to the cell and don't object to the group operating within their borders. Loyalties might get tested and agreements set aside. The conflict could get ugly. We need to avoid that contingency. Rescue the diplomat. Take any necessary measures."

"Understood," it replied, acknowledging the unspoken command to eliminate all hostile targets.

"We will extract you and your target once you have secured her. Failure is not an option, TM 05637."

Light burst through the visor as the polarization adjusted to transparency. Its heightened visual acuity allowed it to take in the details of its location in an instant. Sand stretched out for endless miles in all directions, broken only by the barren rises of stone that revealed the scoured corpses of long-dead mountains. The rocky outcrop it was currently sheltered behind was situated in a shallow valley between two distant hills. Although the area appeared devoid of life, it could hear the scurrying of small creatures living in the cool, shadowy places beneath the rocks. The wind blew grains of sand into gently whirling columns, though the occasional gust turned the granules into a force that had the power to ground rock to dust over the course of millennia. The sand repelled harmlessly off its helmet while its uniform, sealed airtight at wrists and ankles, did not admit a single grain. Though its feet were protected by heavy boots, its hands were bare, the weapon held securely in its strong fingers.

Detecting a faint sound carried on the wind, it adjusted its hearing to better distinguish the auditory input. It discerned numerous voices—men, women, young, old. Some gruff, some frightened. A detailed map of the area filtered up through the haze of its spotty memory, once carefully studied but somehow forgotten. The terrorists were holed up in a nearby village, obviously intending to use the inhabitants as living shields against any air strikes.

For all the good it would do them.

Judging from the volume of the voices, it determined the village was three klicks due west of its current position. A quick but thorough scan of its immediate surroundings revealed no humans in the vicinity. It rose from behind its shelter and, looking out over the sea of rock and sand, detected the outlines of its destination against the bright glare of the desert sun. The large canvas and cloth structures were well built and sturdy enough to repel the desert's relentless assault. The tent village was the semipermanent residence of a nomadic tribe—families bound together by blood, marriage, and arrangement, clinging to a vanishing tradition.

"Treatment of collateral targets?" it asked.

"Leave them unharmed. We need to keep the locals friendly lest they decide the terrorists are more to their liking."

"Acknowledged."

It set off with a sudden burst of speed. While a more cautious approach may have been desirable, the lack of shelter between the outcrop and the village limited its options. It covered the first mile in slightly less than three minutes, its breathing steady and the rate of its heartbeat remaining unaltered from the exertion. The shapes of the tents soon crystallized, allowing it to distinguish them from the smaller moving figures roaming among them. Several dozen horses and three times as many people were visible within the campsite, which consisted of tents arranged in a series of concentric rings. The humans were all similarly dressed in loose, flowing garments, practical for the harsh environment. But while most of the figures were clothed in overlapping layers of brightly colored cloth, a few wore drab robes of gray and brown.

The crack of flesh against flesh preceded a woman's sharp cry. She wailed a frantic plea, only the sound enduring as her words were blown away by the ever-present wind. A guttural voice answered with obvious displeasure and annoyed frustration. At this distance it could just make them out through the haze of blowing sand. The woman was shielding her head uselessly with her arms as a man loomed over her, gesticulating with the barrel of an ancient, yet still deadly, AK-47 rifle toward her face.

Half a mile out, it aimed the M16A2 at the man's head, its smooth stride keeping the weapon on target. The silencer muzzled the bullet's report, and the terrorist fell without warning, the projectile boring a neat hole through his skull. One of the man's compatriots looked over at his fallen brother, astonishment writ plain on his face as he grasped that the other man was dead. He shouted, raising the alarm, and pointed frantically out into the desert. The figures wearing colored fabric melted away among the maze of tents, leaving the terrorists to face the unknown menace alone. The woman likewise seized the opportunity to flee as the terrorists shouted at each other in confusion, crawling on her hands and knees until she disappeared into the shadows.

The midmorning sun was behind it, blinding its opponents. It was on them before they comprehended the nature of the danger they faced. Three pulls of the trigger, and several more of the extremists joined their fellows in death.

"Where is it coming from? There are no planes!"

"Someone is out there!"

The language was not English, but it understood the words without difficulty. Two more shots took out the speakers. By then, it had reached the outermost ring of tents, and any chance the terrorists had to pick it off in the open had vanished.

Pressing its back against the closest tent, it paused for the reinforcements the dead men had alerted to arrive. It fixed its gaze out onto the shimmering landscape, depending on its ears to warn of approaching hazards. It didn't have to wait long. A boot scuffing against rock from the left prompted it to whirl in that direction, weapon at the ready. A man, his head wrapped in a scarf to shroud against the heat, ran carelessly from behind the tent as he rushed to answer the summons for help. A pair of reflective sunglasses hid the man's eyes, yet surprise was evident in his gaping jaw when he came face-to-face with the barrel of the assault rifle. The man had no time to react and was falling to the ground, shattered glasses covered with blood, even as another terrorist appeared in his wake. Having no time to readjust its aim, it pivoted into a back kick, driving its booted foot into the man's stomach. The newcomer's dun-colored robe blew up, revealing the brown pants he wore underneath as he went flying. A crunch indicated it had broken several of the man's ribs. *Threat neutralized.*

Abandoning its position, it rounded the tent in the direction from which the terrorists had approached, pausing only to gun down another man running recklessly toward him. The circular arrangement of the tents created neat rows and columns that defined the camp's interior layout. The well-worn ruts between the tents indicated the duration of the tribesman's residency, their roaming consistently leading them back to this place. The nomads had likely only recently returned, their absence having unfortunately invited the rogue cell to infiltrate the village.

Cautiously, it eased its way down a passage made narrow by the close press of the tents. It could hear additional voices raised in anger coming from up ahead, the commotion likely originating in the clearing at the center of the camp. It was the most defensible position and was almost certainly where it would find its target.

As it neared the next intersection between the rows of tents, a rifle barrel emerged from around the corner of the canvas wall immediately to its left. It grabbed the barrel and gave a sharp tug, pulling the would-be assailant into a raised elbow. The man's nose spurted blood, breaking implosively against the hard curve of bone. Hearing a shout from the right, it wrenched the dead man's gun from his limp hand and used the newly acquired weapon to take out the attacker. The stolen weapon clicked as it emptied, the chamber spent. Dropping the useless rifle to the ground, it listened closely for signs of new danger. Catching nothing except the blowing wind, it continued onward. Before it could go more than a few steps, the sound of a piteous sob made it whip around. One of the terrorists stood there, using a young boy as a shield. He leveled a handgun, aiming at its unprotected chest, while his other hand held a knife to the boy's throat.

"Drop your weapon, scum, or the boy dies!"

The child was crying, his wails nearly overpowering the snarled order. It took no notice of the distraught boy. The difference in height between the man and his captive left the terrorist's head exposed, and before the echo of his yell had faded away, a bullet was drilling its way out the back of the man's skull. The child screamed as blood splattered down on him from his captor's shattered head.

"Hide," it said in an uninflected monotone. It didn't wait to see if the youth had complied before turning back toward its objective.

The next two minutes saw the death of five more of the dwindling group of terrorists. Their political goals were irrelevant. Nothing mattered but the mission. When it finally reached the center of the camp, it crouched behind one of the sturdy tent walls and peered around the edge. The remaining terrorists had gathered their frightened prisoners into a group to prevent any of them from escaping. The guards numbered slightly over a handful. Taking them all out would not present much difficulty, though it calculated several of the civilians would likely perish in the crossfire.

"If you'll just let me contact the State Department, I promise you, I can get you what you want—"

A loud slap cut off the woman's plea. Identifying her location as the tent immediately ahead and to the right, it backed away from the clearing and moved stealthily toward the gaping opening of the tent. Rescuing the civilians was not its concern. Its task was to secure its target—nothing more.

It found the slit where the fabric parted to grant access to the structure's interior and eased the tip of the M16A2 into the gap. The shifting position of the sun angled a ray of light onto its back, throwing its shadow into sharp relief against the canvas. Knowing it had lost the element of surprise, it burst through the tent opening, hoping to catch its enemy off guard before the terrorist could react.

The interior of the tent was dim, light entering only through an overhead flap designed to provide ventilation for smoke from the currently unlit hearth. Its enhanced vision adjusting swiftly to the poor illumination, it saw that its opponent had dragged his hostage in front of him to act as a barrier between his body and the surprise attacker. The diplomat wore a tailored suit of burnt orange, a choice that went well with her brunette hair and dusky complexion. The shoulder seam of her jacket was torn, as were her stockings, and whatever shoes she'd been wearing were long gone. Her captor, by contrast, was dressed similarly to his compatriots, though the loose material of his desert-appropriate garb was unable to hide the breadth of his shoulders and his impressive height. If the group could claim a leader, this man was clearly it. But whereas the other terrorists had worn scarves and eyeshades to protect them from the sun and sand, the leader wore only a scrap of cloth that hid his face from nose to chin, leaving his uncovered eyes in shadow.

"Oh, thank God!" The diplomat slouched against the terrorist's grip, her posture radiating naked relief. Her expression rapidly morphed into fear when the terrorist pressed a gun against her temple.

"Silence, bitch."

The man's voice was a low growl, soft yet compelling obedience. Tightening its grip on the M16A2, it stepped closer to the incongruous pair. Something about the man's intense stare was unsettling, and an unfamiliar jolt of emotion made its throat suddenly feel uncomfortably tight. It struggled to get a clear view of the man's eyes but was inexplicably unable to penetrate the dimness.

"Hurt her, and you die." An underlying quiver threatened the characteristic flatness of its tone. "Let her go, and my superiors will see your demands are met."

"What do you know of my demands?"

"Do not interact with the enemy, TM 05637." The commanding voice spoke through the helmet speakers, pitched so only it could hear. "Neutralize him and secure the package."

The leader wrapped an arm tightly around the diplomat's waist and pulled her firmly against him. For some reason, the sight of them standing so closely together interfered with its ability to breathe. It shook its head slightly to dispel the disquieting anomaly.

"Your comrades. You want them freed." It inched closer, never letting the aim of the rifle stray from the spot between the man's eyes.

As it narrowed the distance between them, it could suddenly see the terrorist's eyes. Their color was odd, not the common brown or occasional green of the other men it had eliminated. The leader stared at him with an unwavering gaze of deep, vibrant blue.

"They are not what I want." The man's voice was a low caress.

"TM 05637, eliminate the target."

Swallowing to wet its dry throat, it edged a foot outward, slowly erasing more of the space separating it from the mysterious figure. "Then what do you want?"

Show your face, it willed silently. As though the man had heard the unspoken plea, he reached up and pulled away the concealing piece of cloth, letting it drift toward the ground. The clatter of a round chambering filled the tent, a discordant counterpoint to the keening cry that rose from the terrified woman as the handgun dug into her skull. Though every instinct it possessed screamed at it to rescue the hostage, to complete the mission, it stood there frozen, transfixed by the impossible familiarity of the man's face.

"TM 05637! Kill him!"

"I want you."

The gun's report crashed into the stunned silence. The diplomat's lifeless body dropped bonelessly to the ground.

"No!" I screamed, staring down at the crumpled figure in shock before looking back up at the man who'd killed her. "David?" The whisper was as much a question as a plea, and I soon followed the dead woman into the darkness of oblivion.

ONE

"I LOVE you, David. In spite of everything, I never lied about that."

"Tim, wait." *Despite his pleas, Tim turned around and began to walk away.* "Tim, don't go!" *The slight figure began to blur out of focus, swallowed by an impenetrable mist.* "Tim, please!" *David tried to run after him, but the air around him was so thick he could barely move. His limbs were useless, equally weighed down by the mysterious fog and an internal reluctance he couldn't deny. Tim had lied to him from the moment they'd met, and now, even in the face of his departure, David wasn't sure he wanted to know the truth. But neither was he ready to let the kid he'd grown to love simply walk out of his life without a fight.* "Tim!" *he shouted again.*

"He's not yours. He's mine."

A large menacing shadow rose up in front of David, stopping him in his burdened tracks. The uniform the man wore was vaguely military in design, but the stranger's features were indistinct, save for the burning ice-blue eyes that glared at him. The man lifted his hand, and David's heart clenched in fear as the object the man was holding resolved itself into a deadly looking weapon.

"No, don't!" *he begged.*

The stranger peeled his lips back in a wolfish grin as he pulled the trigger. David screamed, his body jerking helplessly as electricity passed through him in excruciating waves....

"No!"

The terrified cry lingered in the air as David sat up with a gasp, his skin itching with the phantom memory of intense pain. He groaned, pressing a hand to his head as the ache focused into a vicious pounding inside his skull.

"What the hell?"

The question was barely discernible even to his own ears, his voice rusty as though he hadn't spoken in ages. His mouth felt disgusting, like something had crawled inside of it and died. David gave himself a moment before opening his eyes, but when he finally did, he instantly regretted it. A flood of light shriveled his pupils, sending fresh stabs of agony into his head. The sensation was instantly followed by an even sharper pain between his legs. Fear prompted him to open his eyes fully, despite the agonizing brightness of the light. He got the impression of a white room—floor, ceiling, and walls—with nothing to break the blankness except for a small sink and steel toilet sitting in one corner. The only other fixtures included the cot he was lying on, a stand holding an IV bag next to the cot, and the various items attached to his body.

The sight of the IV bag was worrying enough. It was filled with a clear liquid, which was dripping into his arm through the tube taped to his skin. David had been in the hospital before—a case of appendicitis when he was sixteen—so he wasn't wholly unfamiliar with having needles stuck into his veins. But the tube coming from between his legs and out from underneath the hospital gown he was wearing was new to him. Wincing at the twinge in his groin, he peered over the edge of the cot and stared at the bag full of yellow fluid hanging from a hook conveniently attached to the side of the makeshift bed.

"What the hell…?" he repeated queasily.

"Are you all right? You've been unconscious for some time."

David's head whipped up at the unexpected response. He regretted his curiosity when the room immediately started spinning. Grabbing the side of the cot to keep from pitching over onto the floor, he took a deep breath to tamp down the impending nausea. A second, more cautious inspection confirmed that he was, indeed, alone in the room. The voice was male and wavered with advanced age, but otherwise, David was in the dark as to the speaker's identity. "What?"

he asked intelligently, unable to marshal his thoughts sufficiently to ask the more salient questions of *where*, *how*, and *why*.

"I said, are you all right?"

"Uh…," David said, trying to figure out the answer to that question himself. He glanced down, flexing his arms and legs as he did. Nothing seemed to be broken, and nothing hurt, save for his head and whatever the heck was coming out of his groin. "I don't know," he replied. "There's, umm, this tube in my… er…."

"It's a catheter," the man replied, his tone calmly reassuring. "You've been here for over two weeks by my reckoning. They've kept you drugged up until now, so the catheter was a necessity."

David rubbed a hand over his face, the full beard that covered his jaw lending credence to the stranger's assertion. He cut his gaze toward the IV stand. "They're injecting me with something." He desperately wanted to know who "they" were, but the IV and the catheter warranted more immediate attention.

"I doubt it's a drug. Otherwise you wouldn't be awake. I'd leave it in," the stranger suggested. "It's probably a glucose drip. You haven't had any real food for a while now. You must be starving."

David's stomach reacted viscerally to the man's words, rumbling in instant agreement. The part of his body the catheter was penetrating once again expressed its disapproval of the invasion. "Okay, but this other thing has got to go. Hey!" he shouted for the benefit of whoever else might be listening. "Come get this thing out of me!"

"Save your breath. They'll come for you when they're good and ready, and not a moment sooner. But don't worry. You simply need to take it out."

"Take it out?" David had figured out the voice was coming from his right, and he looked doubtfully toward the wall in that direction. "I don't know. Shouldn't a doctor do that or something?"

The man chuckled. "I am a doctor. Well, more a scientist these days, but close enough. Trust me, it will be fine. Just ease it out slowly."

David was about to protest, but another spike of pain changed his mind. "Shit," he mumbled before reaching between his legs to take the tube gingerly between his first two fingers and his thumb. Drawing in a deep breath, he began to pull. “Ugh!” The plastic tube burned as it scraped along his urethra. David had no idea what damage he might be causing, but anything was better than leaving the damn thing in. After a long minute of pulling and cursing, the tube came free. Sweating and shaking, David threw it to the floor, ignoring the trickles of urine that dripped from the end of the tube onto white tiles. Unfortunately, his relief was short-lived. It was like the catheter had been holding back the tide, and once the dam had broken, the flood would not be denied. David nearly fell to his knees after he scrambled off the cot, his legs, weak from disuse, struggling to support him. Somehow he managed to drag himself and the IV stand over to the toilet before he could embarrass himself. Sighing with relief, he used the last of his energy to push on the flush handle before sinking to the floor, too exhausted to make it back to the bed.

“Thanks,” David said hoarsely as he braced his back against the wall separating him from his mysterious neighbor. “Now, tell me, where the hell am I? Who are you? And where is Tim?” He said the last without any hesitation, having no doubt his erstwhile lover was involved with him being wherever he was. As his mind cleared, David grasped that his dreams of Tim were muddled memories, which were becoming clearer with every passing second. He could still hear Tim shouting his name in the instant before the Taser had rendered him unconscious.

“You’re in a place called the Facility. This is where the boy—Tim, you called him? This is where Tim was raised.” A smile entered the man’s voice. “I like that name. Did you give it to him?”

Hoping further explanations were forthcoming, David forcibly pushed back the myriad of questions the enigmatic response had raised in his mind. “No,” he answered. “That’s what he told me his name was when we met.”

“And when was this?”

David thought back. “A little over three months ago.” Had it really been such a short time? David could hardly believe his life had been turned so completely upside down so quickly.

“Ah,” the man replied. “Then he wasn’t on his own for too long. That’s good.” A pause. “How much did he tell you about himself?”

It's not a he. *It's an* it. *TM 05637 is an escaped lab experiment, a rabid dog that got off its leash.*

David closed his eyes to dispel the memory of the grizzled soldier's taunting revelation. "Not enough, apparently." His arm twinged slightly, and he rubbed a hand over the site where the bullet had grazed him, feeling a dull ache but little pain. He raised the loose arm of the gown and saw only a pinkish scar, the stitches having already been removed. The stranger must have been right about how long he'd been there for him to have healed that much. David remembered how Tim had so expertly stitched up the gunshot wound. It had been one of the many mysteries surrounding the kid, though David realized now that he'd barely scratched the surface.

"Hmm. That's not surprising. The boy was trained from a very early age not to reveal his identity to anyone."

"Who are you?" David repeated more forcefully. He was tired of being kept in the dark and was desperate for any information that might help him make sense of his current predicament.

The man sighed. "A ghost. No, don't mind me," he continued when David scoffed at the odd response. "I'm just being maudlin. The privileges of old age. And heaven knows I carry enough guilt to be doomed to such a hapless eternity." The man took a deep breath, the inhalation audible even through the wall. "I'm Dr. Paul Anderson, Tim's creator."

Father Paul. David remembered the times Tim had talked about the man, and now, out of the blue, here he was. Not that the added qualification shed any light on the situation. "His creator?" David echoed, confused by the strange terminology. "What, are you his father? And aren't you supposed to be dead?"

Anderson chuckled. "Fortunately, I've so far managed to avoid that particular fate, though Tim couldn't have known I survived. And, yes, I am his father in every way that matters. Part of his basic genetic makeup is derived from my own DNA. But more importantly, I designed those parts of Tim no one else on the planet shares. The parts which make him special."

David's head began to throb again, as much from his inability to make sense of Anderson's explanation as from the lack of food and the drug still lingering in his system. "I don't understand," he said flatly, pain lowering his tolerance level for cryptic bullshit.

"Tim is human, but his genetic code was altered to give him enhanced abilities. He can see farther, hear better, and run faster. He is three times as strong as a man his size would normally be, and his rate of healing is five times greater than the average person's. He was trained and drilled in every advanced combat tactic the military could devise nearly from the moment he was born, including hand-to-hand fighting and extensive weaponry. In short, Tim is a genetically enhanced supersoldier possessing superior combat abilities, designed to execute covert infiltration, espionage, and target elimination. He is the perfect weapon, created to feel nothing, want nothing. His only purpose is completing his mission."

David's mind whirled at the startling revelation. Tim wasn't human? No, was more than human. *How could I not have realized it?* David asked himself. In hindsight, it should have been apparent that the strange kid he'd picked up off the side of the highway was simply too perfect to be real. David thought back to all of the incidents and moments with Tim he had found so confusing then, but which now made perfect sense. The way Tim had seemed so awkward when they'd first met. His cold and emotionless demeanor, like he had no clue how regular, everyday interactions worked. Tim's relentless pursuit of Bobby Wood, the young shoplifter who'd eventually become his closest friend, had been startling at the time, but suddenly didn't seem so crazy in light of what Anderson had told him.

And, of course, David couldn't help but remember Tim's thorough and brutally precise dismantling of Bobby's father, Don, the night they'd rescued the boy from his abusive parent. Tim had been merciless, the viciousness of his attack even more disturbing now that David knew for certain Tim had been utterly capable of killing that self-loathing asshole. But neither could he forget how, after they'd gone home, Tim had begged David not to hate him, pleading at first with words and then with his body….

David ruthlessly halted that particular train of thought, shying away from memories he couldn't deal with right then. "So, what?" he forced himself to ask. "You sent him out on some sort of training mission? 'Find some gullible dope and trick him into taking you in'?"

His stomach twisted into a knot at the notion that Tim had merely been using him. He swallowed past the lump in his throat, unaware until right then how deep his feeling of betrayal went. "Was that his objective?" He found he couldn't voice his real question. *Had any of it been real?*

"There was no mission, Mister…?"

"Conley." The people who had taken him captive probably already knew who he was, so there was no harm in being honest. "David Conley."

"As I said, Mr. Conley, there was no mission. You asked me if I am Tim's father. Well, I am, and as his father, I wanted my boy to be free. To know the world beyond the walls where he was warped into becoming a killer. What parent wouldn't want a normal life for his son?"

"You're the one who helped him escape from here," David guessed. "That's why they locked you up."

"Yes," Anderson replied bluntly. "The people in charge of this project, perhaps they meant well at the start, but somewhere along the way they forgot they were dealing with a living, breathing human being." He sighed heavily. "No, *we* forgot. I deserve as much of the blame as anyone, if not more. I was in charge of the research side of the project, responsible for manipulating Tim's DNA until he was precisely what we wanted him to be."

"Are there others like him?"

Anderson made a strangled sound. "No. None of the others lived. Tim was the first to be born alive." The scientist stopped speaking for so long, David was beginning to wonder if something had happened to him. When he began again, his voice was weak and tired. "I have committed so many sins I know I can never be forgiven for them. We recruited surrogates, hired young women to gestate the embryos I designed. Several of them died in the process, their bodies unable to cope with the aberrant chemical makeup of the children they carried. But after years of trying, Tim was finally born, and he was as perfect as I'd dreamed he could be. I did what I thought was right letting him go, but, of course, Talbot and the general disagreed," he added with a humorless chuckle.

The latter sparked a memory in David's mind. "The general?"

"General Woodard. I suspect you've met him already. He was in charge of retrieving Tim after I helped the boy escape. I had hoped Tim would be able to permanently avoid detection, to keep a step ahead of the search parties, but it seems I underestimated Woodard's determination."

He got caught because of me. David didn't voice the thought out loud, not sure how much he wanted to share regarding his time with Tim. He couldn't be sure Anderson's openness wasn't part of some plot to get him to reveal details about Tim's life away from the Facility. But if Anderson was telling the truth and Tim's unexpected entry into his life wasn't some ploy, then surely he had something to do with Tim's decision to settle down in Lubbock, at least for a while, rather than remaining on the run. Or so he hoped. The possibility that Tim's profession of love had been a lie was too painful to contemplate.

"You mentioned another name," David said instead, calling himself a coward but changing the subject all the same. "Talbot. Who is he?"

"She," Anderson corrected. "Coleen Talbot. She is the liaison between the military branch of the operation and the Company, the group which financed the project."

"The Company? The Facility?" David's bark of laugh held no amusement. "God, I feel like I'm in some shitty spy novel."

"You're not wrong." Anderson's smile was evident in his tone. "Talbot is just as dedicated to the success of TM project as the general. Perhaps even more so."

TM project. Tim. Even the name the kid had given him had been nothing more than a clever disguise. David waited for Anderson to elaborate, but after several minutes of silence, he realized the scientist intended to say nothing else about this Talbot woman.

"So, why didn't Woodard simply kill me back at the house?" he asked. It had been bugging him ever since he'd regained his memories of the night the general had barged so dramatically into his life and stolen Tim away. "What does he want with me?" David knocked his head back against the featureless wall in annoyance. "And what the hell is he doing to Tim?" He hadn't forgotten the way the scientist had previously dodged that particular question.

“I have my suspicions about Tim’s fate,” Anderson answered after a long moment, “and I fear it’s nothing good. As for why Woodard kidnapped you instead of eliminating you, I can’t say for certain. It’s likely you will find out soon enough.”

David could hear the concern in Anderson’s voice and didn’t like the implication. When he’d discovered he was alive, though a prisoner, he’d prayed his ordeal was coming to an end. Apparently that had been a naïve hope. “So, what now?”

“Now, we wait. Tell me, Mr. Conley, what are your feelings for Tim?”

Startled by the blunt question, David hesitated. What did he feel for Tim? Before Woodard had shattered their lives, he would have been able to respond immediately and with complete conviction. But now he wasn’t so confident in his answer. Even if Anderson was being truthful and his meeting Tim had merely been a fortunate accident, there was no telling if his creation shared his motivations. Tim may have simply decided to use his freedom to hone his skills by duping some unsuspecting guy into taking care of him. David’s lack of certainty began to color his own emotions, and he could only think of one thing to say that would be completely truthful.

“I loved him.” David winced at his equivocal usage of the past tense. Yet even his ambivalence failed to completely kill his lingering hope that, somehow, he and Tim could get out of this and go back to the way things had been before. “Is there any chance he could become something other than a soldier?” he asked, pointedly avoiding the other labels Anderson had used. Dozens of images of Tim—nervous, hopeful, shy, beautiful—floated through his mind’s eye. How could Tim have faked all of that? David still remembered how amazed and happy he’d been as Tim had slowly opened up. The kid had thoroughly become a part of their lives, his and Bobby’s and the other employees of Barry’s Bargain Warehouse, the large retail franchise David owned and managed. Not to mention the way his mother, Suzanna, had taken to Tim. He didn’t want to believe she could be so easily fooled, even if he had been. “Is there some way to save him?” David asked, the sincerity of the question catching him by surprise. Whatever his feelings for Tim, he couldn’t stand the thought of the kid being at the mercy of the cold-eyed bastard who had so cruelly put an end to their quiet life together.

“That depends on him,” Anderson replied carefully, “and on how much you care for him. I helped Tim escape from here so he might come to understand there is more to this life than what he was created to do. That he can be his own master if he chooses to be. But so long as Woodard and Talbot have their claws in him....” His voice wavered. “There’s nothing either of us can do.”

So help me get him out. Before David could voice the thought, he heard coughing through the wall separating them. “Are you okay?”

“My apologies,” Anderson managed before his words were disrupted by another harsh bout of coughing. “I’m afraid I’ve been unwell and need to rest these old bones of mine.”

David heard a stifled moan of pain and wondered if Anderson had been injured somehow. Accepting that their conversation was over for the time being, David made his way back to his cot, grimacing in disgust as he stepped over the bag and tube that had been emptying his bladder while he lay unconscious. He still couldn’t believe it had been so long, almost two weeks if Anderson’s guess was correct. His employees must be worried sick, not to mention his mother if she was aware of his disappearance. Had they called the police? Didn’t the Fourth Amendment have something to say about the military simply snatching people out of their homes?

Sighing at his pointlessly spinning thoughts, David tried as best he could to get comfortable. The drugs his captors had used to keep him under hadn’t completely left his system, and he realized he was exhausted as well as famished. Deciding sleep was the best way to deal with both problems, he closed his eyes, visions of gorgeous brown eyes and a sweet, bashful smile haunting him as he fell into slumber.

TWO

"YOUR OBJECTIVE is five hundred yards ahead, TM 05637."

It jumped over a rotted log and landed nimbly atop the saturated ground on the other side. The voice hissed through the speakers of its protective carbon-fiber helmet, which was bolted down to the neck of its close-fitting camouflage uniform. Dense jungle pressed in from all sides, but it moved easily through the undergrowth as it homed in on its goal.

"The drug runners kidnapped a group of Peace Corps volunteers working in a nearby village," the raspy male voice explained. "One of the females is the daughter of a US senator. Her father wants her back home safe and sound at all costs."

"Understood."

It dodged around a tree, using the long blade of a machete to cut through the gnarled tangle of vines along its path. The large knife was its only weapon, but it sufficed for the current task. The sun set quickly in this part of the world, and the jungle canopy nearly blocked out what light remained. It made use of the gloom, keeping to the shadows. Its opponents would find the sheltering darkness far more troublesome than it did. Still, the drug runners were at home in this terrain and knew how to take advantage of their chosen hunting grounds. It felt its boot hit a steel wire strung across the ground among the thick undergrowth and realized it had sprung a trap. Instinct told it not to hesitate, to keep moving. It threw itself into a forward roll, and the arrow whipped neatly past the spot where its head had been a mere instant before.

Angry voices speaking rapid-fire Spanish sounded through the trees, alerted to the presence of an intruder. Listening carefully, it identified five different speakers, and calmly assessed its options as the sentries descended on its position. Securing the machete in the sheath on its back, it leapt nearly ten feet directly upward. It caught the lowest branch of a sturdy tree and hoisted itself out of sight of the approaching men. Seconds later, two of the drug runners came into view. Each was armed with a semiautomatic Bushmaster M17 rifle, probably stolen from some hapless military convoy. Numerous knives were visible, strapped to the men's waists and legs, and their grim expressions bespoke their willingness to use them.

"Where are they?" the taller of the pair asked, examining the slackened wire. His gaze darted back and forth, straining to see through the darkness as his companion did the same.

"Whoever it was, they couldn't have gotten far."

Proving the shorter man right, it dropped down on him from the tree, knocking him to the ground. The other runner turned around at his companion's pained grunt, only to find his partner's knife buried in his belly. Its arm still outstretched from throwing the borrowed knife, it watched the dying man fall to the ground before glancing down at the one it had jumped. The man was unconscious, but that didn't stop it from swiping another of the runner's knives from his thigh holster, pulling the man's head back, and drawing the sharp edge of the blade along his throat. The first rule of combat—never leave an enemy at your back. It dropped the dead man's head to the ground, leaving him to bleed out into the rainforest's dark, nourishing soil. Retrieving its victim's semiautomatic Bushmaster, it stood to regain its bearings.

"Three hundred and fifty yards to target, TM 05637."

"Acknowledged," it responded flatly, unaffected by the two lives it had summarily ended. The enemy was simply a target to be neutralized. Nothing mattered but the mission.

It started off again toward its assigned terminus, deftly weaving among the ancient jumble of fresh vegetation and rotted husks. After it had gone a couple hundred yards, the snap of a fallen tree limb warned it of a threat approaching from the left. The new arrival shouted as he spotted the bodies of his fallen comrades. The man began firing wildly even before he had a clear line of sight around the trees and creeping vines. The bullets passed in front of it, wide of their intended target as the shooter carelessly wasted his ammunition. Rather than dodging, it stopped and aimed the stolen Bushmaster. It fired two shots, the first piercing the man in the heart and the second taking him through the throat.

Feet pounding against dirt, dry leaf litter, and twigs alerted it to the remaining sentries coming from the direction it was headed. The fastest of the drug runners burst into sight, only to be flung backward by the knife that buried itself in his throat. The second man appeared just as the first one fell. He skidded to a halt to stare in disbelief at his suddenly dead partner, and looked back up only when the blur of a slim figure in camouflage was nearly on him. Taking advantage of the man's confusion, it caught him with a spinning kick to the head and sent him crashing hard against the large trunk of a kapok tree. Rushing forward, it shoved a hand against the man's chest, pinning him to the knotted growth. It held the tip of the borrowed rifle under the runner's chin and brought their faces close together, the smooth lines of its helmet visible in the dark expanse of the man's dilated pupil.

"How many more of you are there?" it asked in fluent Spanish. It didn't blink as a glob of bloody spittle landed on the helmet's visor. The drug runner laughed harshly, his expression full of the bravado of a man who knew he was about to die.

"Fuck you, *cabrón*!" The man's laughter became a howl of pain as his kneecap splintered from the bullet fired into it at point-blank range.

"How many?" it asked again with no more emotion than if it had asked for the time of day. It dug the rifle into the runner's intact knee and slowly squeezed its finger on the trigger.

"Four! Four, you goddamn son of a bitch!"

It whipped the weapon upward. The next shot it fired passed through the soft underside of the man's chin and out the top of his head. It stepped back, allowing the body to drop to the ground before turning away to resume its prior trajectory.

"TM 05637, there are six captives. Don't allow any of them to be used as hostages."

"Distance?" it asked by way of response.

"One seventy-five."

Deftly avoiding the undergrowth that had given the dead runners away, it raced toward its target, devising, evaluating, and winnowing down the various scenarios that might present themselves when it reached its final destination. Surveillance and surprise would be paramount. The sun had completely set by then, night blanketing the jungle with a blackness so profound even it had to work in order to keep track of its surroundings. Suddenly, a glow appeared about a hundred yards ahead. *A campfire*. The thick, sturdy branches of the trees nearest the clearing were in full leaf. Sixty yards from the clearing, it slung the semiautomatic over its back by the strap attached to the weapon and climbed nimbly into the trees. Leaping agilely from limb to limb, it maneuvered through the canopy. It paused as the clearing came into full view. Hidden behind the thick growth of leaves, it looked down to assess the situation.

Five of the six captives—three women and two men—were tied to stakes stuck into the dirt. Two of the women were tied to one stake back-to-back while the other woman was secured with one of the men. The second man was tied on his own closest to the fire. He was shouting obscenities and threats in English, his voice hoarse from the effort. He strained against his bonds as he glared helplessly at the couple nearest the fire. Three of the drug runners were standing by their captives, their attention split between guarding them and enjoying the show as the fourth member of their group straddled a struggling redhead. She was lying on her back between his legs, her shirt ripped down the front, leaving her lace-covered breasts vulnerable to the barrel of the gun her captor was taunting her with. Her face was distorted with fear and tears, but her resemblance to her father was unmistakable. The senator's daughter. The girl's would-be-rapist laughed in her face before slapping her until her struggles collapsed into bitter sobs.

The man grabbed hold of his victim's wrists and wrestled her arms over her head. It leapt down from its perch in the tree at the same instant the runner popped the button at the waist of her denim shorts. Startled, the men on guard duty spun toward it as it landed lightly on the ground. They were still struggling to maneuver their guns into firing position when each was felled by several rounds to the chest. The surviving runner stared at the intruder that had killed the rest of his gang, his features hidden from view by the flickering campfire behind him.

"Stand up."

Silently the man did as ordered, his tall figure casting a distorted shadow, which stretched the entire distance between them. The sobbing redhead rolled frantically away from her assailant, her hands shaking as she held the remnants of her tattered shirt to her chest. She ran to her companions and knelt by the man who was tied up alone, burying her face in his shoulder as she wept. It saw her only in the peripheral of its vision, its attention completely caught by the man facing it. Even though they were veiled by shadow, there was something about the man's eyes that made its stomach clench. It began to circle around, forcing the man to turn toward the fire in order to keep it in view.

"Eliminate the target, TM 05637. He's still a threat."

But he wasn't. He couldn't be. I stared as I finally caught sight of his face. The firelight seemed to caress his familiar features, darkening the beautiful blue of his eyes to deep violet. I instantly felt my body react with a long-forgotten pang of desire.

"David," I whispered.

"Damn you, TM 05637. Kill him."

"No!" I threw down my weapon and tore at my helmet, desperate to see David without the obstruction of the visor. "No! I won't!" Trying to remove the helmet with one hand, I held out the other yearningly toward David, silently beseeching him to help. To explain. To do something to make this nightmare make sense. He simply watched me, his handsome face devoid of expression.

"Kill him, TM 05637," the voice growled, the underlying menace sending a tremor of fear through me. "Now!"

"Noooo!"

I was still screaming as everything began to fade from view. David, the hostages, even the jungle around us began to shimmer—the very air distorted as though by waves of heat. The fire began to dim as my visor turned opaque. And still I screamed, my fingers digging into the seam between the helmet and the neck of my uniform as I struggled to pry it loose. A loud roar filled my head until it drowned out even the sound of my frantic shouts, the noise grating against my sensitive ears until my cries changed from defiance to agony. Suddenly I couldn't move my hands. A sharp, antiseptic odor filled my nose, completely unlike the recycled air I'd breathed while in the helmet. When I discovered my eyes were closed, I opened them, only to be blinded by the glare of bright lights shining down on me from overhead.

"It's awake?" a familiar voice spat. The same voice that had ordered me to kill David. "How in the fuck is it awake?"

Dreadful recognition filled me, and I turned my head toward the speaker, straining to sharpen my vision so I could see the bastard's face.

"I-I don't know, sir." The young technician's voice cracked with nervousness. "The simulation is still running. The unit shouldn't have been able to break out before we released it."

"If this is your idea of retraining, General, your methods leave much to be desired."

I didn't recognize the female speaker, but her tone was as cold as the general's was irate. The ice in her voice sent a shiver down my spine. Distorted shapes gradually resolved themselves into distinct figures as my abused pupils finally adjusted to the overly bright glare. My restored gaze fell on the steel bands around my wrists, trapping me on the hard table where I was lying. The chill of the metal slab cut through the thin material of my black unitard, an outfit much like the one I'd worn from the day I'd first been given clothing until the day I'd escaped. I flinched away from the cold, the sharp movement causing my ankles to pull against a pair of tight-fitting restraints identical to the ones securing my wrists. Panic ripped through me. Had I only dreamed I'd escaped? Had everything about the last few months of my life been nothing but a cruel dream?

"David," I moaned, still remembering the longing that had filled me when I'd seen the man in the jungle. No, I realized. The setting may have been fictional, but David was very real. My every memory of him was so crystal clear it had to be true. The curve of his lips when he smiled, the way the corners of his eyes crinkled when he was worried, the gentle touch of his hand against my skin—that was no lie.

Latching on to those precious memories like a lifeline, my mind began to clear, and I looked around to get my bearings. The table I was secured to was surrounded by computers and complex-looking lab equipment. Men and women in white coats scurried about, some attending to the machines while others typed frantically at their workstations, entering data into the computers. Several of the monitors were situated behind me, and when I tried to tilt my head to look back at them, the suction pads attached to my temples pulled at my skin.

Brainwave monitoring.

Something cold and metallic pressed against my forehead and wrapped around to the back of my head. I identified the virtual reality projector from long experience. The jungle mission had been a training scenario, the same type I'd endured countless times before my escape. Relief swelled through me as I put the pieces together. I was profoundly relieved the image of David about to commit rape had been nothing more than a fabrication, even as rage filled me at the fact the general had devised something so twisted.

I felt a stinging twinge in my arm and cut my glance to the side to see that a woman had injected something into the IV line running into my vein. They were drugging me to keep me compliant. I had to act before the injection reached my system.

"Oh my God! What is it doing?" The technician goggled at me in astonishment as I began to strain against the steel bands around my wrists and ankles.

"Don't worry," one of her male colleagues observed. "There's no way it can break those restraints."

Woodard rushed over to the table, stopping in my line of sight. His gray-stubbled jaw was clenched in anger. "The hell it can't," he growled as the metal began to bend, the bands shrieking as the bolts fastening them to the table started to pull away. The general reached for the sidearm strapped in the holster at his waist.

Focused on my desperate task, I ignored the danger. I had to get free. I had to get away and find David. The steel dug into the soft flesh of my wrist as I pulled, but I merely gritted my teeth, ignoring the pain. More memories came flooding back as I struggled, fueling my desire to escape. I'd been so happy, especially after realizing my feelings for David went far beyond mere friendship. All the little things he had taught me, the pleasure of a shared meal, the feeling of pride in my work, the simple joy of an ordinary life. I wanted them back. I craved the touch of David's hand, the sight of his smile, the remembered bliss of his body surrounding me and filling me. The general had stolen everything away, but I refused to let the bastard win. The terror of watching David fall victim to Woodard's treachery came back to me in full measure, augmenting my already prodigious strength.

"Arrrggg!" I yelled as the band around my right wrist ripped free with a shriek of metal against metal, followed immediately by the one securing my left.

"Stop him!"

I sat up quickly, striking out at the figure who rushed toward me at the general's order to try and subdue me. The guard fell back, reaching up to stanch the blood flowing from his broken nose. I was scrabbling at the steel holding my left ankle down when I felt something being pressed against the back of my neck.

"You're not getting away from me again, you ungrateful little shit."

The guard had been merely a distraction to allow the general to sneak up on me from behind, but the realization came too late. I screamed as seven thousand volts of electricity surged through my body. Woodard kept the Taser firmly against my skin, not letting up even as I shook and flailed uncontrollably, narrowly missing biting my tongue clean in half. After what seemed like an eternity, he relented. I slumped to the table, my limbs twitching involuntarily as the current continued to dissipate through me. Despite the voltage, the stun had only rendered me immobile, not unconscious, though the drugs snaking through my veins were swiftly taking care of that. My vision began to blur, and the sounds of the laboratory echoed in my head as though coming from far away. I was lying on my side, half on and half off the table with my face angled down toward the floor, my still cuffed feet posing my body in an awkward twist. As a pair of black combat boots came into my field of view, my scattered thoughts mused on the fact that I'd never known the general to don any other type of footwear. High heels clicked across the bare tile of the lab floor, and a pair of sensible tan pumps stopped beside the general's boots. A line of drool crept from the corner of my mouth to pool on the stainless steel surface mashed against my cheek.

"This is unacceptable, General," the woman said. "It's even less under control than it was before."

Woodard growled. "Yes, I can see that, Ms. Talbot." He spat her name as though it left a bad taste in his mouth.

I could almost feel the woman's disapproval stabbing at me. "Care to explain?" She may have been addressing the general, but the technician who had drugged me spoke instead.

"We've been using the standard protocols enhanced with a derivative of scopolamine to increase the unit's susceptibility to suggestion. It should be responding only to your commands, sir. I can't explain why it's being so resistant."

"Increase the dosage," Woodard commanded.

"Or," Talbot interrupted, "we could stop wasting the Company's time and money and do what you should have done from the beginning."

The technician clasped her hands together at her waist, her knuckles going pale. "I'm sorry, Ms. Talbot, but I must advise against it. The serum is untested. It could do permanent damage."

Woodard exhaled sharply. "Look, I want the unit in the field as much as you do, Talbot, but it won't be of any use to us if its brain is fried."

"I hardly think that's likely," she replied in disgust, "but I will accept the doctor's advice. For now." The tan heels turned away but paused before walking off. "I'm running out of patience, General. If the unit isn't functional by next week, my superiors will not hesitate to pull the plug on this money vortex of a project. Neither of us wants that, do we?"

I watched as the heels clicked out of my line of sight. I looked down at Woodard's boots and the technician's soft-soled lab shoes, feeling helpless as my body refused to respond to my commands to move. My hands were still unrestrained, for all the good it did me. I couldn't even control my mouth. The line of spittle continued to flow steadily from my lips to the table. My desire to demand the general tell me what he'd done with David would have to wait for a more opportune moment. I felt two pairs of large hands close around my shoulders. The soldiers maneuvered me back into a recumbent position on the table and held me there as a third man resecured the steel bands, drilling new screws through the bolt holes on the restraints into the metal table.

"Put it under," Woodard ordered. "I don't want it conscious unless it's doing a simulation."

I couldn't even react when the needle pierced the side of my neck. In a disconcerting replay of the night I was captured, concern for David was the last thing on my mind before I slipped away. That and how very much I wanted to kill the general with my bare hands.

THREE

STARING AT the cell's blank white ceiling, David pretended he could see cracks in the concrete simply so he had something to count. His new beard itched, and he scratched at it absently. He couldn't be certain, but he figured three days had passed since he'd first woken up to find himself a prisoner. Someone had come to bring him food on nine separate occasions, passing the food to him through a slot in the cell door, and he assumed he was being fed three times a day. The guard who brought him his meals never said a word, not even when David demanded to be let go or begged for information about Tim. They had at least deigned to give him some better clothes after his first meal, though David couldn't say the puke green jumpsuit was exactly his color.

Only once did anyone actually come into the room with him. After his sixth meal, the door had opened to admit two soldiers and a middle-aged man wearing a white coat. The military men had towered over the scrawny doctor, if that's what he was. The smaller man could just have easily been some sort of research scientist rather than a physician, given what Anderson had revealed about the purpose of this place. The impression was reinforced when the man removed the IV from David's arm with all the finesse of a clumsy gorilla. Several meals later, and David could still see the bruise the needle had left behind. Neither the man nor his guards had been any more forthcoming with information than the people who brought him his food.

Sometimes David would speak with Anderson through the adjoining wall of their cells. For hours at a time, the scientist regaled him with stories of Tim's upbringing in exchange for him sharing tales of his and Tim's fleeting life together. The stories made David want to cry and impressed him by turns. He couldn't help but be fascinated by Anderson's detailed explanations of everything his creation was capable of, and the more he learned, the more he wanted to know. But the overwhelming emotion he felt when it came to Tim was a disturbing mixture of longing and ambivalence.

"David? Are you awake?"

David glanced over at the wall separating him from his companion in captivity. "Yes," he answered, moving toward that side of his cell so Anderson could hear him better. "I was wondering something."

"And what is that?"

"Why did you wait so long to set Tim free?" He hadn't meant to ask the question, but with Tim being so much at the forefront of his thoughts, it came out before he could rein it in. "Maybe if you'd acted sooner, he wouldn't have turned out so…."

"Dangerous?" Anderson said, finishing the thought David couldn't bring himself to articulate. The scientist sighed. "I'd like to tell you it was because Woodard kept him on a short leash and attempting to get him out would have been impossible, especially when he was young. But while that was certainly the case, it wouldn't be the whole truth."

Having no other options, David could only wait out the ensuing silence.

"To be completely honest," Anderson continued hesitantly after a long pause, "I simply didn't want to let him go." His tone was wistful, as if his words were as much of a revelation to himself as they were to David. "You have to understand, Tim is the culmination of my life's work. Everything I set out to accomplish from the moment I first began working in the field of genetics is manifested in him. Oh, I believed in the cause as well—protecting the free world from the terrorists and dictators who would destroy it—but my interest lay primarily in the science of making a being of singular perfection."

"But he was just a little boy," David said softly, his heart aching as he recalled what Anderson had told him about the impossibly rigorous regimen Tim had been subjected to day after day for nineteen years.

"At first he was nothing more than an experiment, the latest in a long line of failed attempts. But very soon after he was born, I began to see him as my own flesh and blood. As my child. My son." Anderson's tone was heavy with regret. "I'm not proud of what I've done, David, but I'd hoped that by helping Tim experience life outside of these restrictive walls I might atone in some small way."

David was angry the scientist had been unable to separate his quest for knowledge from his obvious affection for Tim for so long, but he supposed the man had paid amply for his sins. Anderson had explained what happened the night Tim had escaped, how he'd been nearly killed trying to protect his protégé from being shot. All the talk of familial bonds brought something else to mind David had long wondered about.

"So, what about Tim's mother? Or, rather, his other genetic donor," David clarified. Anderson hadn't said anything about Tim being a clone or something equally freaky. "Tim told me a story about getting her killed."

"Ah." Anderson suddenly sounded even more tired than he usually did. "He was referring to Karen. Or, at least, that's what Woodard called her. I never learned her real name. She was Tim's gestational surrogate, not a genetic donor."

If David expected Anderson to reveal the identity of Tim's maternal half, he was doomed to disappointment. "Karen was contracted only to carry the baby to term," Anderson continued, "but when Tim was born, she begged the general to let her stay and raise him in whatever limited fashion she could. She babied him as much as she dared, kissing his cuts and bruises, teaching him amusing little games and encouraging him to play like an ordinary child. Surprisingly, Woodard permitted it, but it was only later I discovered why he'd feigned such generosity."

"And why was that?" David asked.

"Though he wasn't thought to be capable of having emotions, let alone one so profound, it was clear to me Tim loved Karen in his own way. Unfortunately it was apparent to Woodard as well." Anderson's voice thickened with anger. "He used threats against her as leverage to force Tim to perform better in the drills and multitude of lessons heaped on him. Tim was far too young for all the combat and tactical training the general insisted he be put through, but Woodard was determined that the project be a success. I can't fault his motivations, but his methods…. Well, let's say they left a lot to be desired."

If the way Woodard had treated Tim the night he'd captured them was any indication, David shuddered to think of how unpleasant the man had been when Tim was a small, helpless boy. "So, what happened to her?" he prompted.

"When Tim was seven years old, Karen tried to break him out, much as I did. The general had been keeping them apart more frequently. He was convinced her involvement in Tim's life was preventing the boy from achieving his full potential. Thought she was treating Tim too much like a child and not enough like a weapon-in-training, despite her usefulness in keeping him in line. Karen thought she could thwart the general and save Tim from him. Alas, she failed in her attempt. After Woodard caught them, he promised he would allow her to spend more time with Tim. He lied," Anderson explained, his voice flat with anger. "Woodard lured Tim away from her and then ordered her to be shot. Tim watched her die right in front of him. That was the day he ceased being a child and began to turn into exactly what Woodard wanted him to be."

"A killer," David breathed, uncertain whether he was speaking to the other man or merely to himself. It was the first time he'd let himself speak the word aloud.

Anderson inhaled deeply. "As cold and remorseless as any weapon manufactured by man. You're right, I should have acted sooner, but I don't believe I was too late. After all, it seems he was able to make you care for him. Tell me," he added with some urgency, "did Tim come to return your feelings? Did he love you too?"

Whatever reply David might have made went unspoken as the door to his cell suddenly opened, revealing the very man he and Anderson had been discussing. The general's expression gave nothing away as he walked into the small room, save for the same arrogance he'd exhibited the last time David had seen him. The night Woodard had shattered his mundane life into so many broken pieces. Hatred flooded through him, even stronger now that he knew exactly who Woodard was and what he'd done to Tim. Abandoning his seat against the wall he shared with Anderson, David rose to his feet, his hands clutched into fists at his sides. It was all he could do not to punch the bastard in his smirking mouth.

"What do you want?" he growled. "And what the fuck have you done with Tim?"

"TM 05637 is no longer your concern. The unit is back where it belongs. That's all you need to know." Woodard looked David up and down with a penetrating gaze, as though sizing up all of his weak points at a glance. "You should be far more worried about yourself, Mr. Conley."

Having already guessed his captors knew who he was, David ignored the subtle taunt. "You can't do anything to me. It's not like no one is going to notice I've been missing for, what, several weeks?" David gritted his teeth, grateful he was tall enough to at least stand toe to toe with the general, even though he couldn't hope to match the older man's rock-solid physique visible even under his fatigues. "You have no right to keep me here. I haven't done anything wrong!"

"Now, that's where you're mistaken, Mr. Conley." Woodard moved over to the sink and propped his hips against it in an irritating display of nonchalance. "You have stolen government property. You have interfered with and obstructed a military operation. And you've had unauthorized access to a highly classified military weapon. Any one of those could get you convicted for espionage and treason." He grinned like a shark, showing all of his coffee-stained teeth. "We still do execute spies and traitors in this country, Mr. Conley."

David blanched at the threat despite himself, but hoping that Woodard was merely trying to scare him, he focused on the only part of the man's rant he cared about. "Stop talking about him like that. Tim is not some mindless thing for you to use and control!"

Woodard's laugh filled the small room and grated across David's nerves. "What did you think? That TM 05637 was a human being? That you could just take it home with you and keep it as your little fuck toy?" He shook his head as though he found David pathetic and not a little sad. "TM 05637 may technically be flesh and blood, but don't kid yourself. It's nothing but a tool, a living machine created by the nation's top scientific minds with one purpose and one purpose only. To keep this country safe."

Woodard's smile vanished like it had never existed. David stumbled backward as the larger man suddenly moved into his space, stopping so close he could feel the general's stale breath against his chin.

"TM 05637 can't feel. It can't love. And now that it's been fixed, it will follow orders like it was designed to do."

David went cold at that last part, both incensed and terrified at the unsubtle threat. "Fixed? What do you mean, fixed?" He paled as his imagination raced with innumerable scenarios of precisely what sort of repair Woodard had in mind, each more horrific than the last. "Where is Tim?" he asked again, agitation making his voice break like a frightened adolescent. "What have you done to him?" He shook his head, his brain suddenly unable to process the insanity of everything he'd learned. "Why are you doing this?"

"Because it's my duty," Woodard spat. "My duty to do what's necessary. From the moment that redheaded bitch squeezed him out of her cunt, TM 05637 has had one task, one purpose. To keep this country safe. And I'll do whatever it takes to make sure that happens." His eyes narrowed as he glared at David. "You're done acting out your disgusting faggot fantasies with my project, *Mister* Conley." He voiced the honorific like a warning, imbuing it with sarcastic emphasis to show David precisely what he thought of him. "Your usefulness is almost at an end, and when it is, you'll be dealt with however I see fit."

"My usefulness?" David asked through clenched teeth. "You still haven't told me why you brought me here." He glared at Woodard's back, irritated as the man turned around and moved toward the cell door without answering. Feeling decidedly out of control, he lashed out at the retreating figure. "If you're going to kill me, then just go ahead and kill me, you son of a bitch!" He stared at the door long after it had shut behind his unwanted visitor, his thoughts crashing into each other as he tried to separate the lies in what the general had told him from the truth.

"David, are you all right?" Anderson's concern was palpable, reaching through the wall separating them.

"How much did you hear?" David returned to the spot he'd abandoned when Woodard had interrupted their conversation and braced his hand against the smooth white surface.

"Everything," Anderson answered.

"Tell me," David said, struggling to breathe through his anger and rising fear, "how much of what he said was bullshit and how much was real?"

A long moment passed before Anderson responded. "I'm afraid he wasn't bluffing. While calling you a thief and an obstructionist is ridiculous, he is right that you have learned things which are classified at the highest possible levels." Anderson exhaled heavily. "Woodard might very well attempt to trump up some accusation against you."

"Well, if he does," David replied boldly, "I have plenty of witnesses who can vouch for me."

"Not if he has you branded as a terrorist. Thanks to certain laws enacted by our government, accused terrorists have almost no rights. Doing so is a surefire way to keep you firmly away from the legal system and any chance for due process. If Woodard wants to make you disappear, David, then he will find a way to do so."

It felt like all the air had been abruptly sucked out of the room. David slouched to the floor, his legs failing at the task of supporting him as he contemplated spending the rest of his life locked in this tiny cell. Not that his life might be all that long if Woodard had his way. "What did he mean when he said I was no longer useful?" David asked, grasping at any topic to distract himself from the thought he might not live to ever see the outside world again. "How have I been useful? All they've done is locked me up in here and, until recently, kept me practically comatose."

"That's not entirely true," Anderson replied. "When you first arrived, I heard quite a bit of activity in your cell, a lot of people coming and going. I can't be certain, but I have a feeling Woodard and Talbot figured out some way to use you in their efforts to reprogram Tim."

Too many questions were chasing around in David's head at the bizarre explanation, so he grabbed hold of the one shouting the loudest. "Reprogram him? What do you mean?"

"The general and his pet scientists—myself included—spent years not only honing Tim's skills, but also grooming his mind. What good is it to have the ultimate weapon if it won't obey your every command without question?" Anderson paused thoughtfully. "Woodard must be concerned the time Tim spent out of his control has weakened his grip on the boy's mind. And with good reason, I suspect."

David thought back to how violently Tim had tried to resist being captured by the general's men and how it had taken Woodard threatening David to finally make him give in. "Maybe," he said, not wanting to get his hopes up by reading too much into Tim's reaction. "But how could I have anything to do with whatever Woodard is planning?" Even as he asked, he wasn't sure if he really wanted to know. He had watched enough science fiction movies in his youth to think of half a dozen terrible ways the general's goal of reeducating Tim might be accomplished, and every last one of them caused his stomach to writhe queasily. "Is there any chance, any chance at all, we can free Tim and get out of here?" He kept his voice at a whisper, suddenly paranoid the cell was bugged and he would be overheard.

Anderson's voice was firm as he answered. "If there is a way, I swear to you we will find it."

FOUR

THE MOTORCYCLE roared as it opened up the throttle, pushing the machine to its limits. The tires slid across a patch of oil residue on the road surface, but it compensated easily, focused only on reaching the coordinates it had received. There was no distraction, no conflict. There was only the mission.

At the other end awaited the Sons of the Dawn, an organization of anarchists turned self-professed revolutionaries who had managed to get their hands on a highly dangerous chemical weapon. They claimed to be fighting to free their countrymen from a repressive government regime, but there was little politics in their actions. There was only destruction and chaos. The Sons were using the city as both a hideout and a shield, counting on the mass of innocent humanity to protect them from detection.

The motorcycle sped through a neighborhood riddled with the scars of years of unceasing conflict. Buildings housing the city's inhabitants were juxtaposed with corpses of structures blackened and weakened from explosions, their broken facades riddled with the holes of countless bullets. Using a spy satellite, its superiors had gained preliminary intelligence that the Sons of the Dawn were taking refuge in one of the abandoned units. It glanced up at the GPS map projected on the interior of its helmet's visor as it sped through the city, pinpointing its target.

Cla-chick.

It registered the unmistakable report of the sniper's rifle being primed, its augmented hearing easily distinguishing the noise from the city's background cacophony and the roar of the motorcycle's engine. Perhaps the sniper was merely a lookout, or maybe the Sons were aware of the operation. It didn't care. Security leaks were not its concern. It focused only on eliminating the immediate threat. The volume of the sound indicated that the shooter was targeting it from a mile away. Vision sharpening to laser focus, it sighted along the line of rooftops ahead to the east. The midday sun spotlighted the building where the sniper had set up. It could see the shooter clearly, as though they were only yards apart, but it felt no pride at its astounding visual capacity. Eyesight, hearing, strength, agility—they existed only to ensure mission success.

A high-powered range weapon was secured in a holster within easy reach of the motorcycle's steering grips. Maintaining control with one hand, it freed the long-barreled AR-15 with the other and aimed the rifle toward the sniper's position. It squeezed the trigger once before resecuring the weapon, not bothering to watch the sniper fall from his lofty perch as it sped on.

A moving green dot on the GPS display indicated its current location. It was abruptly joined by a large red X, which the map showed to be three miles from its own identifying marker.

"Awaiting location confirmation," it said, not bothering to raise its voice, confident the helmet would block out any external noise.

"Confirmed, TM 05637." The mechanical voice lacked any recognizable gender. "Positive identification of chemical residue achieved. Approach target and proceed."

"Roger that."

Following the shortest path indicated by the map, it took a sharp left at the next corner, followed by a right two blocks farther on. Its route went directly through the city center, and it was suddenly confronted with a large crowd—business people, shoppers, and families—struggling to go about their daily lives. They milled around with minimal caution, likely numbed by the unending violence of their country's internal strife. None appreciated the grave danger they now faced. The Sons had threatened to release the chemical bomb they'd stolen upon the populace if their demands were not met. Money, concessions from the government, the release of prisoners—it did not know what the Sons had requested, nor did it care. Its mission was simple—eliminate all targets and secure the weapon before the Sons could unleash the deadly toxin.

"Out of the way," it said calmly, a microphone embedded in the helmet amplifying the monotone command. Traffic blocked its path, and people screamed as the motorcycle jumped to the sidewalk. It ignored the pedestrians, expertly weaving among the throng. It took pains to avoid them only because a collision would slow it down. It didn't care if any of the civilians were injured. If it failed, none of the people fleeing from the oncoming vehicle would be alive to care.

The map showed a direct cut-through between a cluster of shops, and it took the turn at top speed, the motorcycle's tires squealing in protest. It revved the engine to announce it was coming through as it headed across an open shopping plaza. The square was ringed on all sides by storefronts and office buildings. It was late in the afternoon, but not yet time for the workers to head home for the day. As a result, the space was not as busy as it could have been, affording it easier passage. Still, there were idlers aplenty, and it took all of its skill to maintain its rapid pace as it traversed the plaza. A woman shouted frightened obscenities as she pulled her young daughter out of the path of the racing vehicle. It didn't register her ire, charged with saving more than the life of one woman and her child.

Aiming for an opening at the northwest corner of the square, it finally cleared the area. A set of stairs led back to the roadway, and it tore down them, barely skidding on the uneven surface. It came out on a street that ran directly toward its destination. Diverting its attention between the helmet's display and its physical surroundings, it located the building where the Sons of the Dawn were planning their act of mass homicide. The three-story, redbrick structure was on the cusp of being uninhabitable, an impression reinforced by the Caution! Demolition! signs posted on the fence that enclosed the building and kept the public out. It was ideal for an organization that wished to avoid detection.

When it was half a mile away, it abandoned the motorcycle and its loud engine in favor of approaching on foot. It saw no other sentries, and it realized it had killed the sniper before the man could signal a warning to his compatriots. It retrieved the rifle and took a moment to fit the barrel with a silencer before slinging it over its shoulder. A clock suddenly appeared in the upper right corner of the display.

"Countdown to dispersal of the chemical gas—fifteen minutes," the artificial voice announced.

"Copy."

Its breathing remained even as it approached the dilapidated structure at its top foot-speed. Six feet from the twice as high fence, it jumped and landed three-quarters of the way up the chain-link barrier. In a matter of seconds, it climbed upward and launched off its hands in a flip to clear the barbed wire stretched along the fence's top edge. Landing softly inside the perimeter, it paused to listen for any indication its approach had been noted by the clandestine occupants. Nothing stirred. The only sound was that of the traffic from the road over a mile distant.

"Countdown to dispersal of the chemical gas—thirteen minutes." The clock in the helmet's display confirmed the voice's information.

The front entrance loomed like a dark hole. The door that had once secured it had long fallen away to lie partially in and partially out of the doorway. It stepped carefully over the rotten slab of wood, the corroded knob jutting up from the ruined surface the only indication of its former purpose. The wood creaked beneath its feet, but otherwise there was silence.

"Recalibrate map," it whispered. The display obliged, a detailed image of the building gleaned from recent surveillance coming up before its eyes in blueprint form. The initial view of the building was top-down, the green dot showing its location in the entranceway. The image began to rotate to show the building's various levels and the red dot glaring several floors below. The structure's multiple subbasements would afford the Sons plenty of places to wait in ambush, but it was undeterred. It had its orders: find the bomb.

Holding the AR-15 high on its shoulder in firing position, it cautiously advanced inside. The room grew dim as the sunlight that penetrated through the open doorway fell away weakly after a few feet. The windows, which had been boarded up to discourage squatters while the city planners dithered over completing the structure's demolition, contributed to the darkness. "Switch to infrared," it ordered. The visor darkened, registering visible light only tangentially as it adjusted to read heat signatures. Following the map more than any visual cues, it headed for a room off to the right of the main entry hall. Apparently the building had once been some sort of dwelling. The room it entered was a large kitchen, the rusted remnants of appliances sitting forlornly along the walls. A huge table was situated in the center of the floor. There were no chairs, but the size of the table suggested the place had either housed a large family or had been some sort of boarding house, complete with a communal dining space.

Skirting the table, it headed for the far side of the room. It stopped before a narrow door and turned the handle, only to find that the door was bewilderingly locked. Pulling harder, it exerted a fraction of its full strength until the lock gave way, the bolt separating from the doorjamb in a shower of drywall. Behind the door was a dark stairwell. Seeing no movement, it took the first two steps slowly, instinctively calculating their depth. Relying mainly on touch, it rushed down the rest of the stairs quickly, the nearly total darkness doing little to slow its pace. Before it reached the bottom, a figure suddenly appeared, the size suggesting the male gender. The image in its visor glowed in gradated shades of bright orange to greenish blue, reflecting the heat differential in the man's body. There was a dark stretch across the man's face—goggles, it deduced—and the object the figure pointed at it was black in the infrared range. Cold. Metal. It fired without stopping its descent, the silencer reducing the noise to an almost imperceptible *snick*. The glowing image fell to the floor as the bullets from the AR-15 found their target. It neatly leapt over the rapidly cooling body and continued on.

The map led it across an open space matching the dimensions of the upstairs kitchen, and then into a maze of twisted corridors. It encountered two more lookouts about thirty feet into the concrete-walled labyrinth. Both men were also wearing infrared goggles, but it retained the advantage since the uniform it wore completely absorbed its heat signature, leaving it effectively invisible in the subterranean blackness. Running silently toward the closest of the pair, it jumped on the man's back and broke his neck with a sharp twist. The other sentry barely had time to react as his companion's body dropped to the ground before abruptly joining him, the knife that slid between his ribs penetrating and instantly stopping his heart. Retrieving the blade, it wiped the knife clean on its victim's clothing before returning it to the sheath buckled at the side of its thigh.

The green dot indicating its current position was directly above the red dot of its target, but it still needed to find the correct set of stairs leading down to the building's lowest level. It saw from the blueprints that the Sons had positioned the weapon right in front of a vent, which would carry the poison up to street-level to disperse through the air. After a bit of backtracking over rubble from the less than structurally sound walls, it found the stairwell and took the steps two at a time.

"Countdown to dispersal of the chemical gas—four minutes."

As soon as it reached the bottom landing, it noticed there was artificial light. With a word, it disengaged the helmet's infrared view, returning the visor to visual mode. The red dot was fifteen yards ahead in a room abutting the outside wall of the building. An ideal location for the vent. It had gone no more than a third of the distance when its path was suddenly blocked by a giant. The man's shoulders filled the hallway, leaving only a bare minimum of space to either side of them. He stood well over six feet tall, his head only a few inches shy of the corridor's low ceiling. A naked light bulb was directly behind the man's head, shadowing his face and concealing his expression.

It sized up the obstacle the anarchist presented, its concentration unmarred by feelings of fear. It never stopped moving from the moment the man came into view, determining the appropriate tactic in the seconds it took to close the distance between them. The man saw it approaching at a run and visibly braced for impact. Instead, it dropped to the floor, its momentum carrying it forward until it had passed through the man's legs. Reaching out, it grabbed hold of the man's right foot and yanked hard, pulling its opponent off-balance. The man stumbled, slamming his right shoulder against the corridor's concrete wall. Leaving the assault rifle on the floor, it pushed itself from its back to a standing position in one motion before bringing its foot around in an outward arch. The man's head followed his shoulder, blood spurting against the dark gray of the concrete as his temple impacted the unforgiving surface.

A meaty hand reached up and grabbed its ankle, holding its foot in place as the guard somehow summoned the strength to right himself. Cold eyes stared at its featureless helmet as the man tried futilely to penetrate the visor's opaque, one-way surface. Using its opponent's hold as leverage, it jumped off its free foot and bashed it into the man's face. The man grunted and let go, and it landed after executing a 180-degree twirl that left it facing the guard, ready to execute another attack. Before the man could recover a second time, it thrust out its hand, fingers flattened into a bladelike edge. It jammed its fingers into the man's throat, crushing his windpipe. The anarchist's hands flew to his throat as he gasped for air, but the next blow landed on his nose, breaking the bridge and sending fragments of bone into his brain. It quickly retrieved the AR-15 and was already moving past the dead man as the large body slumped to the ground.

"Countdown to dispersal of the chemical gas—one minute, forty-five seconds."

It pelted toward the far end of the corridor, encountering no further resistance. It destroyed the door blocking access to its destination with a flying kick. Landing in a crouch, it took in the scene with a quick glance. The room was deserted save for the lone figure bending over something sitting against the back wall. There were no lights in the room, but the darkness was broken by the bright glow emanating from the device the man was tending. It snapped the rifle to its shoulder and moved slowly into the room.

"Step away," it ordered evenly, "and put your hands in the air."

The man ignored the command and continued to work, his fingers moving deftly over the bomb.

"I said step away." It aimed the AR-15 at the back of the man's head. "If you don't, I will shoot."

"Countdown to dispersal of the chemical gas—one minute, five seconds."

"Disable sequence?" it requested.

"Cut the wire that triggers the release of the gas canister, and then disconnect the timer from the detonator."

It stared at the man's back, startled, not only by hearing him unexpectedly explain how to stop the device, but by the uncannily familiar sound of his voice.

"Who are you?" I demanded, my voice containing more than a hint of pleading.

"Countdown to dispersal of the chemical gas—fifty seconds."

The soulless announcement snapped it back to itself. It sidled closer to the last surviving member of the Sons of the Dawn and repeated its warning. "Move away, or you're dead."

"You won't kill me."

"Countdown to dispersal of the chemical gas—thirty-four seconds."

"Those are my orders." The mechanical voice was a constant drone in the background as it ticked off the remaining time until the chemical weapon released the deadly gas. Not even the strange feeling that it knew this final enemy could shake its resolve to see its mission completed. "Move away," it repeated, "or I will shoot you."

"Countdown to dispersal of the chemical gas—twenty seconds."

The man suddenly spun around, the device's readout reflecting dully off the surface of the gun in his hand. It dropped into a forward roll, passing inches below the bullet's trajectory. Stopping at the man's feet, it kicked away the gun from its crouched position and yanked the now unarmed man hard to the ground. Tossing the AR-15 to the side, it slid out the knife from its thigh holster.

"Countdown to dispersal of the chemical gas—ten seconds. Nine. Eight."

Its attention was fixed on the device as it slammed its fist into the man's jaw, dazing him as it searched the device for the first wire.

"Seven. Six."

It gripped the knife tighter as it found the canister trigger and quickly located the one for the timer.

"Five. Four. Thr—"

The voice ceased its count when it slashed the wire, stopping the device's countdown.

"Eliminate the target with extreme prejudice." The mechanical voice had been replaced by that of a gruff, authoritative man.

It wasn't concerned that the anarchist was no longer an immediate threat or that he had been summarily condemned by its superiors. Its only function was to obey. Gripping the man's hair, it positioned the edge of the knife against his throat. The hair felt silky in its hand as it held the man securely for the deathblow.

"Please, don't."

I jerked as the voice pleaded with me. It sounded so familiar I found myself struggling to place it.

"Eliminate the target, TM 05637."

Shaking my head, I gritted my teeth and clenched my fingers tighter around the strands of soft hair.

"Please—"

"Shut up!" I inadvertently shook the man's head, and the motion brought his face within the circle of light from the display of the inactivated device. The hair in my grip was dark blond, and the eyes gazing up at me were a deep, poignant blue.

"Eliminate the target, TM 05637."

I shook my head violently as bile rose up the back of my throat. "David. What? How?"

"Kill him, TM 05637!"

"Nooo!" I screamed. I released David's hair like it had burned me, a flood of horror filling me at what I'd almost done. The rush of emotions was immediately followed by nausea as some unknown force assaulted my body. Hot blades of pain sliced into my brain, and I gripped my head with both hands against the unrelenting torment. Slowly, the blades moved down into my body, tearing at my lungs and stabbing at my heart. My stomach was ripped open and my limbs flayed until my skin hung off me in ragged strips.

"Complete your mission, TM 05637," the voice soothed, "and the pain will stop."

I gasped at the abrupt cessation of the torrent of agony battering my body from head to toe. I sucked in frantic lungfuls of air, relieved for a brief moment until my scattered thoughts congealed enough for me to understand the ultimatum. Kill David and go free. Refuse and face more of the excruciating torment. Like there was really a choice.

"Fuck you!" I shouted into the darkness.

The sight of David's emotionless visage fading from view was the last thing I remembered before the pain consumed my consciousness.

FIVE

DAVID WAS picking at the remnants of his fourteenth meal when the door to his cell opened without preliminaries. Knowing who it had to be, he glared down at the congealing mass of gravy and noodles in lieu of acknowledging his visitor. It may have been a petty victory, but after so many days of being locked up, he'd take what he could get.

"Mr. Conley—"

David let his fork clatter to the tray as he cut the general off. "How much longer are you planning to keep up this farce?" He gritted his teeth and looked up at the general, unable to resist directing an angry stare toward the unwelcome figure. "If you were going to charge me with something, you would have done it by now. So, what in the hell do you really want with me?"

Ignoring David's outburst, Woodard walked calmly over to the toilet and sat on it after glancing down at it to make sure the lid was closed. He propped a foot over his opposite knee and leaned back against the wall behind the toilet, looking for all the world like he was settling in for a friendly chat. "Tell me about yourself, Mr. Conley. I'm aware that you're a businessman and a sexual deviant, but I'm ignorant of the finer details of your life. Are you a God-fearing man? Do you have any close friends? What about family? Besides your mother and father, that is." Woodard leveled a hooded gaze at David. "We know all about them, of course."

"What the fuck do you want?" David repeated in a heated growl, trying to ignore the implied threat even as his stomach clenched in fear.

“I’m simply trying to figure out what makes you tick.” Woodard wrapped his hands around his raised ankle, his fingers interlocking. “I want to understand why my biological weapon went through so much effort to try and protect you.”

I love him, you bastard!

David looked away from Woodard’s piercing blue gaze, a lump growing in his throat as he thought back to Tim’s impassioned declaration in response to that very question. Woodard hadn’t bought the explanation then and, apparently, he still refused to accept it as even a possibility. “Where is Tim?” David asked again, the memory increasing his desperation to see him and make sure he was okay—or as okay as he could possibly be given the circumstances.

Woodard hummed thoughtfully. “Answer my question first, and then I’ll answer yours. Why did TM 05637 go through so much trouble to protect you? What did you do to him?”

David bristled at the impersonal designation, hating the reminder that Tim was nothing to this man but a thing to be used. “Nothing. I didn’t do anything to him.”

“Come on, you must have,” Woodard replied testily. “TM 05637 was trained to be concerned only with completing whatever mission we assigned it. It was taught that the mission is everything, and that nothing else matters. Not even its own well-being, let alone that of a total stranger. Just because its misguided creator decided to let it off its leash shouldn’t have changed that basic reality.” His expression gave no indication he was aware Anderson was in the adjacent cell and was, in all likelihood, eavesdropping on their conversation. “When we came for the TM unit, you became a liability, Mr. Conley. It should have been willing to sacrifice you to facilitate its escape. Those were the protocols we drilled into its supposedly perfect brain. But, instead, it tried to help you. To save you,” he said through gritted teeth. “From me.” Woodard leaned forward, the genuine curiosity that shone on his grizzled features doing little to hide his underlying ire. “I want to know why.”

David thought back to all of the moments he and Tim had spent together. Since waking up trapped in this small room, he’d entertained plenty of doubts about whether their relationship had been real or merely a fiction that Tim had fostered for his own purposes. Nothing else about Tim had turned out to be real. Why should the kid’s so-called feelings for him be any different? But, contrary to Woodard's likely intent, the reminder of how Tim had struggled to keep him safe that night helped strengthen David's faith in one truth. Tim had sacrificed himself to try and save him. That fact was undeniable, and it gave David the hope he needed to continue defying Woodard now.

"Like I said," he repeated, "I didn't do anything, except treat him like a human being." David looked the general straight in the eye. "Which is something you obviously know nothing about."

Woodard returned David's gaze evenly for a long moment, the glacial color of his eyes making his direct stare even more disconcerting. "You seem to be mistaken about one very important thing, Mr. Conley," Woodard said finally. "I am not the bad guy here."

David snorted, unable to suppress the incredulous outburst. "And how exactly do you figure that?"

"Let me guess what your typical day is like," Woodard said evenly. "You wake up, eat breakfast, and drive to your store. Once there, you spend your day engaged in mundane managerial tasks before calling it quits in the late afternoon. Afterward, you drive home, maybe stopping somewhere first for a bite to eat, and then settle in for an evening spent watching boring sitcoms in front of your respectably midsized television." He raised an inquisitive eyebrow. "How am I doing so far?"

David stared down at the tray of cooling food, unwilling to acknowledge how on the money the assessment had been. His life in a nutshell. At least until he'd picked up Tim off the side of that highway. Everything had changed after that.

"Hmm," Woodard breathed, correctly taking David's silence for affirmation. "And why do you think your existence is so damn boring?" He paused as though waiting for an answer. "Because," he continued when none was forthcoming, "it's allowed to be."

David glanced up and met Woodard's mocking gaze, not understanding what he was getting at.

"Your life is mundane and ordinary," Woodard continued, reading the confusion on David's face, "because you don't have bad men with guns beating down your door in the middle of the night endangering everything you care about."

David sighed, frustrated with the general's vagueness. "Enough with the bullshit. Get to the point already."

Woodard chuffed. "Okay, then. We are the ones who keep you and other dull little shits like yourself safe from all of the big bad lurking outside the blissful walls of your ignorance. We are the ones who keep the terrorists at bay, the gunrunners, the drug cartels. Everything that would gladly see oblivious citizens like yourself dead for some fucked-up notion of God, country, or riches." Woodard glared at David as though offended by his very existence. "But the threats are never-ending, Mr. Conley. They're just getting bigger and more dangerous, and one day soon, law enforcement and the military as it exists today won't be enough to protect you."

David finally grasped where the rambling soliloquy was headed. "That still doesn't justify whatever you're doing to Tim. Just because you people created him doesn't mean you can control him and use him however you want."

"That's precisely what it means," Woodard snarled. The general's reasonable demeanor had begun to lull David into a false sense of security, and the abrupt return of the man's rancor took him aback. David's shoulders hunched in instinctive defensiveness when Woodard suddenly pushed himself to his feet and began to pace across the cell's meager floor. "It was created to do a job. No matter how you delude yourself, TM 05637 is not a person. It's a means to a very important end. And once the unit has been deployed in the field, I need to be certain it won't suffer any unexpected lapses in obedience." His tone had returned to normal even though he continued to pace. "My weapon must be in perfect working order. For your sake, Mr. Conley, as well as mine."

"What have you done to Tim?" David asked again, deliberately contradicting the general's insistence on referring to Tim as a thing rather than a person.

"Do you really want to know?" Woodard sneered.

David hadn't seriously been expecting an answer, so when Woodard turned to him with a chilling smile, he was unprepared for the uneasiness that twisted his gut. He couldn't help but envision a gruesome tableau of Tim stretched out on a gurney as shadowy figures tortured him with neurological probes, causing his slim body to writhe in agony. *Too many late nights spent watching dystopian sci-fi thrillers*,

David chided himself as he fought through the disquiet making his heart pound in his chest. He nodded in silent response, not trusting himself to speak.

"Like I said, it is critical that TM 05637 follow any order it is given without question or hesitation. When lives are on the line, there's no time for second guessing or inconvenient crises of conscience." Shaking his head, Woodard chuckled, the raspy sound making David's skin crawl. "I have to give the crazy bitch credit. It was all her idea."

David didn't ask the general to clarify who he was referring to. He was too busy trying to keep himself from strangling the man for being so deliberately cryptic. Luckily, Woodard needed no urging to continue, clearly enjoying David's confusion.

"She was the one who suggested copying enough of your neural activity so the virtual reality simulator could produce a realistic facsimile of you."

"Virtual reality simulator?" David repeated in a daze. "Realistic facsimile?" Apparently his likening of the situation to a bad movie hadn't been so far off the mark after all.

"History has proven it to be the most efficient method of instruction. The system can produce an endless variety of scenarios without risking either the unit or the soldiers we'd have to send against it in a real-life training exercise. For the past few weeks, we've run TM 05637 through every type of mission and environment the computer could devise. But although the simulation varies, the goal is always the same." The glance Woodard slid toward David was equal parts sly and menacing, the crude replica of a grin lending him a sharklike aspect.

"Which is?" The question broke free seemingly without David's permission.

"Why, to kill you, Mr. Conley." Perversely, Woodard's smile grew more sincere as the color drained from David's face. "And, let me reassure you, TM 05637 has performed admirably every time."

"B-Bullshit," David stammered. Denial screamed through him, every cell in his body rejecting the very notion. But an overwhelming fear that the general was telling the truth made his throat close until he could barely breathe. "I don't believe you," he whispered in feeble defiance.

Woodard shrugged, unconcerned. “That’s certainly your prerogative, but your opinion doesn’t negate the facts. To TM 05637, everything in the simulation is completely real, and it has destroyed you many times without the slightest hint of remorse. TM 05637 is a killer. That’s what it was created for, and that’s all it will ever be. It’s time you accepted that, Mr. Conley.” Woodard turned to leave. He rapped on the door, but as it slid open, he paused and glanced back over his shoulder. “There is nothing left of the boy you thought you knew.”

It was only after Woodard had been gone for what seemed like an eternity that David realized he was trembling. Awareness returned to him in time for him to hear his name being called anxiously through the wall.

“David, answer me. Are you all right?”

He stumbled over to the wall he shared with his neighboring prisoner and slid to the floor. Leaning his head against the cool surface, he tried to quiet the nausea roiling his stomach. “I’m okay,” he replied, the lie tasting as bitter on his tongue as the bile that was crawling up the back of his throat. “Was he telling the truth about the simulations?”

“Well, he was right that Tim was frequently trained using virtual scenarios.”

David exhaled sharply in exasperation at the blatant dodge. “No, not that. Was he telling the truth about putting me in them? About… about Tim….” He couldn’t finish the sentence, but fortunately the scientist took pity on him.

“I’m afraid I don’t know,” Anderson admitted. “But I wouldn’t put it past either Woodard or Talbot to do something so drastic.” He groaned, the weight of the exclamation seeming to convey the depths of his exhaustion. “My God, Coleen, what have you done?”

David recognized the name of the woman Anderson had mentioned before. The liaison between the project and its financial backer. His numbed brain latched frantically on to the inconsequential piece of information as a distraction from the horrible possibility that the general hadn’t been lying after all. *No,* he silently chastised. *Stalling won’t do you any good. You need to know the truth.* No matter how the scientist might protest, David hadn’t missed the horror that had crept into his voice. “Be straight with me, Anderson. You think they’re using me like Woodard said, don't you?" David forced himself to ask. The lengthy pause before Anderson spoke was all the answer he needed.

"They must be drugging Tim to keep him compliant."

David clenched his fist, annoyed at Anderson's refusal to speak plainly. "Dammit, you know what I mean!" He took a deep breath in reaction to the wave of nausea that abruptly swept over him as he struggled to give voice to the unspeakable thought. "Would Tim really kill—"

"No," Anderson said firmly before David could finish asking the painful question. "Even under the influence of hallucinogens, I can't believe Tim would be capable of something so contrary to his heart. He loves you, David. I have no doubt about that. Not after everything you've told me."

Can't believe, not don't believe. The distinction was subtle, but David couldn't help mulling over the scientist's equivocation. No matter how much Anderson wanted to think his creation could never kill something he supposedly cared about, he was clearly uncertain. But David was equally adamant in not wanting to believe it. He vastly preferred remembering the expression of intense affection that had suffused the kid's beautiful face as he and David had made love. That was far preferable to imagining Tim staring at him with the same cold expression he'd leveled on Bobby's father in the instant before he'd tried to rip the man's head off.

"Okay, Doc," David mumbled, gratefully accepting the lifeline of denial. The general might find it amusing to mess with his mind, but he wouldn't give the son of a bitch the satisfaction of letting the morbid insinuation get to him. "Whatever you say."

SIX

"GENERAL, I must counsel against this."

"The last drug you tried didn't do shit. The unit is still showing resistance."

"But burundanga is too dangerous. Even the CIA uses it only for interrogations with subjects who have been approved for termination."

"The unit is strong." A woman's voice. "It will survive. And if it doesn't, we'll know once and for all that the project is a failure."

I could hear the voices, but they were indistinct and faint. It was like I was underwater, going deeper and deeper until the pressure against my ears blocked out all sound except the beating of my heart.

No, not "I."

It.

"Help. Help me."

The cry was weak, as though every word was a struggle. The first thing it noticed after opening its eyes was that its face was exposed. The concealing helmet was missing. Looking around with naked eyes, it instantly detected a flaw in its visual acuity. Everything appeared indistinct, like it was trapped inside a thick fog, though it was uncertain whether the problem lay with its vision or the environment. Its head felt heavy, its thoughts sluggish, suggesting it had somehow been compromised. Considering the possibility that it was being held captive, it blinked rapidly, trying to clear its vision. The haze began to clear, but when it looked down, it noticed it was wearing the same black unitard it had worn nearly every day of its life. An outward visual scan revealed that it stood in a large room full of equipment and monitors as well as toys and games. The incongruity of the scenery sparked a memory and, suddenly, it knew exactly where it was.

"Help… me."

I spun around, my gaze searching Father Paul's lab for the source of the plea. How long had it been since I had last been here? Weeks? Years? There had been a time when I'd spent many hours of every day in this room. This is where Father Paul had instructed me, where he'd snuck me pieces of cake on my birthday, where he'd cared for me when I was injured. This is where Father Paul had raised me. And it was where he had hatched the plans for my escape.

Wrong. Not "I."

It.

"Help me!"

The image of Father Paul falling into a pool of his own blood flitted through its mind only to be instantly scattered away. "Dr. Anderson," it called out, "identify your location."

"Over here. Please, hurry!"

The cry came from the small room housing the scientist's office. Now that it knew where to listen, it could hear the telltale sounds of a scuffle. The hard sole of a shoe squeaked across the linoleum flooring, and a stack of papers rustled as they were knocked off some surface onto the ground. It picked up the sound of something banging against a piece of metal and remembered the tall filing cabinet where the scientist kept all of his important hard copies. It sprang toward the door separating the office from the main part of the lab, fighting against the inexplicable sluggishness that pervaded its body.

My limbs felt like they weighed a thousand pounds, but I had to keep going. Father Paul was in danger.

"No, let me go!"

"Not until you give me back what's mine."

I opened the office door as the stranger spoke, only it wasn't a stranger. I knew that voice as intimately as I knew my own.

Error. "It."

No. *I.*

"David," I whispered as I took in the sight of him holding Father Paul in a headlock, his strong arm fixed tightly around the older man's frail neck. I shook my head in disbelief when I saw the gun he held pressed to Father Paul's temple. David wore jeans, sneakers, and a collared shirt, looking every inch the retail store manager he was, and not at all like anyone who could hurt a fly. "David, why are you doing this?" My voice was choked with disbelief. An instant later, a wave of intense dizziness and nausea caught me as the cells of my brain seemed to be trying to battle against each other. My consciousness was divided down the middle—on one side was emotion and anguish and on the other, stillness and clarity. In desperation I probed the latter, and the queasiness vanished as though it had never been.

The gaze it leveled on the interloper was cold with deadly purpose. "Release Dr. Anderson immediately or be eliminated."

Father Paul whimpered as the gun dug painfully into the side of his head.

"They stole you from me," David hissed. "You were mine, and they just took you away!"

"It was never yours," the scientist growled, anger seeping through the fear. "TM 05637 was made for a reason. To keep this country safe."

The wrongness cut through the calm in which I had immersed myself. Father Paul had always called me "my boy," refusing to use my assigned designation. And my creator had certainly never referred to me as "it." I was not an "it."

"I have a name," I said uncertainly. "Don't I?"

"Yes," Father Paul croaked, "you are TM 05637."

I shook my head, the violent motion making the room spin. "No, that's not it. That's not right." My voice grew stronger even as the pounding in my head began to build once more. "I have a name!" The nausea returned in full force, knocking me to my knees as my stomach cramped, threatening to expel its contents all over the lab's pristine floor. The emotional part of my consciousness surged back into control, overwhelming the false, calculating facade. I felt unequipped to handle the onslaught of foreign sensations, of… feelings. They were too new, leaving me raw and exposed. But I had learned how to handle them once. Anger. Concern. Affection. I had known them all. And one other.

The most important of all. If only I could remember it, everything would make sense. Somehow, I understood the man threatening my mentor had all of the answers I could ever need.

"David," I begged, "what is my name?"

David stared at me, his glacial blue eyes burning into me with ice instead of heat. "Monsters don't have names."

The vile words cut deeply, but I refused to believe David would ever speak to me so cruelly. We had shared something once, this man and I. I simply had to remember what it was.

"He's going to kill me, TM 05637." Father Paul's brown eyes were wide with fear. "You must stop him!"

"No." I shook my head. "David would never hurt you. He couldn't."

David's stare bore into me, calling me a liar. "You don't know anything." The muscles along his jawline bunched as he clenched his teeth. "Your beloved Father Paul is right," he said, spitting the scientist's nickname like a curse. "You were never mine. Before I even met you, they had already stolen whatever we might have had." David shook his head, his expression twisting between rage and hurt. "I tried so hard to pretend you were nothing more than a kid who needed help, but you never were just a kid, were you? I wanted to believe you were normal. That you were someone worthy of love. But when I saw how you tried to hurt Bobby, how you almost murdered his father with your bare hands…." David spat out a laugh devoid of amusement. "I knew you were beyond redemption."

Each word cut like a knife, stabbing me in places I could never hope to protect. "Please, David, you don't mean that. I—" In a flash, the truth came to me, spreading through my mind and heart in a brilliant glow of warmth and joy. How could I have ever forgotten what David meant to me? I swore I would never forget again. "I love you, David." My body seemed to move on its own as I instinctively sought to erase the distance between us. "I love you!"

David's smile was a cruel thing. "I could never love an abomination. Everything about you is wrong. Evil." He tightened his hold around Father Paul's neck and cocked the gun.

"David, please," I sobbed. "Don't do this!"

“Help me!” Father Paul’s face matched the unblemished white of his lab coat.

An authoritative voice cut through the tense stalemate, booming out over the lab’s PA system. “Eliminate the target, TM 05637. Protect Dr. Anderson at all costs.”

I shook my head. “No. You can’t ask me to hurt David,” I answered, staring rebelliously at the speaker located in the corner of the room, near the ceiling. I didn’t know who had given the order, but something about the voice made my blood boil with pure hatred. “I won’t do it. And that’s not my name.”

“I’m begging you, TM 05637,” Father Paul sobbed. “Don’t let him kill me!”

The PA system crackled. “Eliminate the target, TM 05637.”

“You shouldn’t exist,” David growled. “Neither should anyone who had a hand in creating whatever the hell you are.” His finger began to squeeze down on the trigger.

“No, David! Stop!” For the first time, I felt the gun in my hand, and I aimed it at David’s head, struggling to focus through the tears running down my cheeks. My hand shook, the gun trembling in turn as waves of indecision buffeted me from every side. How could I let the man who’d given me life die? Yet how could I take the life of the man who meant everything in the world to me? I searched frantically for a way out, for some way to save Father Paul, to convince David we could still be together. “David, please. Listen to me.”

“Help me!”

“You’re wrong, David,” I continued, deafening myself to Father Paul’s frantic plea so I could concentrate on making David see reason. “You’re wrong about me. Maybe I did start out as a monster, but you changed me.” I stared at him, desperately trying to convey everything that was in my heart.

“Eliminate the target, TM 05637!”

“You made me better,” I continued, ignoring the terse order. “You showed me how to be human.”

David’s dark expression didn’t waver, and his gaze was filled only with disgust. “No. I failed.”

The gunshot rattled the walls with deafening finality.

The primal scream came from a place deep inside of me that, ironically, hadn't existed before David had brought it into the light. Rage warred with disbelief as I watched Father Paul's body fall lifelessly to the floor, rivulets of blood dripping down from the gaping head wound, staining his long white coat. My finger tightened on the trigger, the desire for revenge warring with howling despair. Yet still I faltered. It was David's fault that my creator was dead, but I was the one who had turned the man I loved into a killer. David's face went out of focus, dissolved by an interfering screen of tears.

"Eliminate the target, TM 05637."

It was time to give up my self-indulgent exertion of free will. I was tired of trying to process the buffeting assault of emotions. I had no experience dealing with them. I was only good at one thing.

Not "I."

It.

Abandoning itself to the command, its vision abruptly cleared as the tears stopped. The shooter's features sharpened, and it firmly pulled the trigger.

The scene collapsed along with David's body, and it found itself lying on a metal table, its hands and feet secured to the platform with steel bands. Its head was pounding and felt as though it had been stuffed with cotton wool. It licked at cracked, dry lips with a tongue that felt too thick for its mouth. Something was touching the skin around its forehead, temples, and torso, and it recognized the distant beep of the equipment being used to monitor its neural activity and vital signs. The lights shining on its face were too bright, but its eyes adjusted rapidly, enabling it to see the bustling laboratory. A shadow fell over it, blocking out the glare. It looked up at the large figure looming over the table. The man wore simple fatigues without any insignia, but it knew without asking that he was the person in charge. As its brain function came fully back on line, it abruptly recalled the man's name.

"General Woodard," it said with a voice hoarse from disuse.

The general's lips pulled into a pleased smirk. "It's a start, TM 05637. It's a start."

SEVEN

THE NEXT time Woodard showed his face, David was ready for him. For the past seven meals, he had been turning the man's taunt over and over in his mind. Anderson had insisted that Woodard was merely trying to get a rise out of him, but David couldn't let the stomach-churning thought go. He didn't doubt that Woodard would attempt to trick Tim into killing him just to prove some sick point, but he refused to believe the bastard had been successful. Like he'd told the general, he was confident Tim would never hurt him, not even in a virtual simulation. David was tired of the mind games. It was time to end this charade, once and for all. If only he had a clue how to go about it.

The door of the cell had barely opened before David was on his feet, facing the man entering the room with a scowl. Woodard stepped in and stopped immediately inside, taking in David's determined stance and clenched fists with a raised eyebrow. "Well, Mr. Conley? It looks like you have something you'd like to say to me."

"Nothing you haven't already heard. You know what I want. I want to see Tim, and I want to see him now." David ground his teeth in frustration. "Keeping me here like this doesn't make any sense. Maybe you did copy some of my brainwave patterns to use in your mind games, but that was weeks ago, right? What else do you want from me?"

"Do you really want to see TM 05637?" Woodard grinned evilly, as though he'd used the designation simply because he knew how much David hated hearing it. "Fine. I suppose a short visit would be okay.

What's one more breach in national security? You already know more than enough to justify me putting a bullet in your head."

David wanted to call the bastard's bluff, to tell Woodard to go for it if he wanted him dead so badly. But he held his tongue against the counterproductive gibe since it looked like he was actually getting what he'd been hoping for all this time. Woodard stood aside and gestured for David to precede him out of the cell. David glanced at him suspiciously, but save for the chilling smile, the general's expression remained conciliatory. Two guards wearing military fatigues were stationed outside of the room. Each one of them easily outweighed David by at least twenty pounds of sheer muscle. When he emerged from the cell, they moved to flank him, each taking one of his arms in a viselike grip. Woodard walked past them and turned left to start down the corridor.

Having been unconscious the last time he'd come this way, David looked around curiously as he was frog-marched behind the general. They were at the far end of a hallway as white and featureless as his cell had been. He counted at least twenty doors identical to the one opening onto his cell along either side of the corridor, leaving him to wonder why Woodard had ordered he be put in the one next to Anderson's. He'd have thought Woodard would have preferred to keep them from being able to communicate. His attention was diverted from the riddle when they reached the thick metal door at the end of the cellblock. The door was painted white to match the rest of the unimaginative décor. Idly, David wondered if they called it a brig even though they weren't on a ship. Or at least he didn't think they were. Not that it mattered. Letting his mind wander in an attempt to ignore the nerves knotting his stomach wouldn't get him anywhere. As unlikely as it seemed right then, an opportunity to escape might come at any moment, and he needed to be ready for it. David forced himself to pay attention as Woodard bent to align his left eye with the scanner in a panel next to the door. A green light flashed, and the door slid open.

The part of the compound beyond the cellblock was far different from where he'd been held, though the sight did nothing to inspire confidence. Instead of relentless white, the walls, ceiling, and floor of the corridor the guards maneuvered him along were a dull gunmetal gray. Soldiers walked along in tight patrols, but there were also people hurrying along dressed not in fatigues, but in regular clothes or in white lab coats.

The civilians scurried past the four men, coming and going in all directions, several people glancing curiously at David as they did so. While some of the nonmilitary workers darted into doorways that opened off the hall, most seemed to be headed generally the same way.

"Where are we going?" David asked when he realized his small group was following the herd. He didn't know what awaited him at the end of this journey, and the suspense was killing him.

Woodard spared David a brief glance over his shoulder. "To see TM 05637, as promised," he replied blithely.

Irritated at the general's false bonhomie, David was glad when Woodard turned his attention forward once more to navigate down the bustling corridor. They turned left off the hallway and then left again at the next corner before taking a quick right. After half a dozen more turns, David was hopelessly disoriented, having long ago lost his bearings. He wondered briefly if Woodard was merely toying with him, and whether the next turn would find them right back at his nice, cozy cell. David was working up the nerve to protest the apparently pointless stroll when they came upon a long queue of scientist types waiting to get through a single narrow door. Curious at the cause of the unexpected crowding, David noticed each person had to submit their eye for scanning before being individually let into the room. The general walked unhurriedly to the front of the line, the lab workers giving way before him as he peered into the scanner. When the door opened, Woodard took hold of David's arm and personally escorted him through into the room beyond.

The laboratory—for clearly that's what it was—was enormous. At a glance, David guesstimated there were over fifty people currently present. Most appeared to be scientists, though a handful of soldiers stood guard in various corners of the large space. One group was stationed in front of a bank of monitors, typing furiously on keypads as they logged incomprehensible streams of data. Others were busy maintaining the vast amounts of technical and medical paraphernalia—EKG and EEG machines, consoles, machines hooked up to IV bags containing fluids in a variety of hues—while still others were hovering around a raised platform situated in the center of the room.

The gathering inexplicably drew David's attention, and at first he couldn't see what was on the table that the white coats found so engrossing. Through the mass of figures, he caught only glimpses of something black and flashes of olive-toned skin. Suddenly David realized he was looking at a body lying recumbent on the platform, wearing black clothing. His heart throbbed painfully in his chest. *Please God*, he prayed silently, *don't let it be him*. Out of the corner of his eye, he saw Woodard nod toward the hub of activity, his lips crooked in a twisted smile as he took in David's obvious distress.

"There you are, Mr. Conley. Consider your wish granted."

"Tim," David whispered as though speaking louder would make it true, but there was no denying it. The slight figure reposed on the cold metal surface was unmistakable. And yet he was so different from the last time David had seen him as to be almost unrecognizable. Tim's skin held a grayish tinge beneath its permanently dusky hue. The slender yet muscular limbs he'd spent so many hours ogling looked thinner than he remembered, appearing more fragile still as he took in the steel bands that bound Tim to the table.

Still, David managed to hold it together until his gaze finally landed on Tim's pallid, lifeless features. Sensor pads covered Tim from forehead to chest. Wires sprouted from them like macabre vines, conveying information from the sensors to the monitors arrayed around the platform.

David's breath hitched, his throat tightening and allowing little air to pass. He grew dizzy as he struggled to find his voice. "Wh-what have you done to him?" The question came out garbled as he tried futilely to repress a sob.

"I believe I already told you. We're drilling the unit using VR until it's ready for real world operations." Woodard gestured to a bank of video monitors on the wall immediately behind Tim's head. "This gives us a visual representation of what the unit is currently experiencing, so we can ascertain whether the training is having the desired effect."

David squinted at the screens, unable to make sense of the chaotic jumble of images. All he could see were swiftly moving shadows and strange flashes of light. "What is he doing now?" David looked back at Tim's face, dismayed at what he saw. Tim's eyes were open but obviously blind to what was before him. His gaze darted back and forth, rapidly following what only he could see. He was completely absorbed in his task, as though the outside world didn't exist, his expression a blank mask.

"I believe this is another desert drill," Woodard answered nonchalantly. "The simulations represent the various types of environments and conditions TM 05637 will be expected to face when it's finally deployed." Woodard watched David for a few minutes as he struggled to accept what he was seeing. "So, Mr. Conley, are you satisfied? TM 05637's rebelliousness has been dealt with, and soon I will once again have my perfect soldier."

"Stop calling him that," David growled, sending Woodard a heated glare. "He is not a thing, damn you. I don't know what you think you *created*," he continued sarcastically, "but that's not the Tim I knew. I lived with him for months, and I can tell you, he's as human as anyone else in this room. Maybe even more than a few I could mention." He sneered, doing nothing to hide the insult's intended mark.

Unfazed, Woodard merely returned David's angry stare with a self-assured smirk. "Is that so? You're a stubborn man, Conley, I'll give you that. Believe it or not, I respect that type of loyalty." He chuckled in a show of grudging admiration. "But, son," he added, pretending not to notice when David bristled at the unwelcome familiarity, "I'm afraid it's misplaced. I wasn't planning on showing you this, but I think it's something you need to see." Woodard led David over to a group of monitors on the far side of the lab, taking care to keep as much distance as possible between them and the platform on which Tim was lying. "We maintain records of all of the simulations TM 05637 completes, but these are by far my personal favorites. I had them saved separately from the main database so I could enjoy them at my leisure." Woodard noticed David was hanging back hesitantly and raised a mocking eyebrow. "Take a look, Mr. Conley. You say you're confident in your opinion of what TM 05637 is and is not capable of. Here's your chance to prove it."

Reluctance filled every inch of his body, but David felt his legs propel him forward seemingly without his conscious decision. When he looked down at the monitor, the screen was displaying an image of Tim making his way through a maze of tents surrounded by sand, ruthlessly killing anyone foolish enough to get in his way. When he reached the centermost one, he entered to find David holding a woman at gunpoint with an evil expression that looked completely foreign on his face. Before David could shoot, Tim took him out with a bullet between the eyes.

The scene changed rapidly from desert to jungle, and Tim was running through dense forest, eliminating the hostiles attacking him with a minimum of effort. In a clearing, Tim found a group of young people sitting tied to posts stuck in the ground. David saw himself holding a girl to the ground at knifepoint as he tore her shirt open. With only a single word of warning, Tim struck, burying the blade of his own knife in David's eye socket.

The images of the jungle faded, only to be replaced by a cityscape and a figure—obviously Tim—on a motorbike. Tim cut a skillful path through a panicked crowd before making his way to an abandoned building. Inside, he worked his way through the maze of passageways, dealing with various assailants as he headed for the lowest subbasement of the abandoned structure. When he reached his goal, David was there, sitting hunched over some sort of machine. Tim attacked without preliminaries, trapping him with a knife to the neck. He slid the honed edge of the blade over David's skin, slicing it open to release a torrent of blood.

"What the fuck is this?" David croaked. A rising tide of bile choked him as his stomach heaved, and for a frightening moment, he thought he was going to be sick in front of the crowd of curious onlookers.

"This, Mr. Conley, is what TM 05637 has been trained for. To eliminate all threats to national security, no matter what form they take and no matter where they arise. Casting you as the villain was to ensure the unit still possessed the proper level of obedience. As you see, it has performed admirably."

"Then why am I still alive?" David asked, feeling exhausted, as if the wind had been knocked out of him. "You've captured my… whatever for your damned simulations. Why do you still need me?"

Woodard grinned in his trademark sharklike fashion. "For one final test. The ultimate test, if you will." He gazed intently over at the figure lying motionless on the platform, his expression bordering on pride. "TM 05637 is nearly ready to begin resuming its physical training. That means running it through actual scenarios rather than the virtual ones it has faced up until now. How better to inaugurate TM 05637 back into reality than by having it eliminate a traitor?"

David couldn't even feign shock. From the first moment he'd watched Tim virtually shoot him, he'd known what Woodard was planning. What he'd seen on the monitor was undeniable. Tim had killed him more than once in a variety of gruesome manners. Would doing so in truth really be so different? But even as despair threatened to swallow him whole, something deep in his heart refused to abandon all hope. David prayed that, maybe when Tim saw him with his own eyes rather than through images pumped into his brain, the kid would remember what they'd shared. Maybe, once they were face-to-face, Tim would spare his life.

Turning his back on the general, David moved deliberately over to the platform. Dazed, he only peripherally noticed the guards who started in his direction, but they abruptly backed off at an unseen signal from someone behind him. The scientists looked at him nervously, but they merely watched him approach the motionless figure without protest. David's gaze roamed helplessly over Tim's body. The black spandex bared his arms and was cut high on his thighs. Where it did cover, it hugged him like a second skin, hiding nothing. If he'd been in full possession of his wits, David might have been disgusted at the way his heart raced and his groin tightened at being so close to that tempting body again after so long. But all he could think of was how perversely beautiful Tim looked as he lay in a mockery of peaceful repose, like something out of a fairy tale. David shook his head, not seeing how this story could have a happy ending. He sure as hell wasn't Prince Charming. In lieu of a kiss, David reached out and touched Tim's cheek. His skin was clammy and ice cold, and David recoiled despite himself, unable to dispel the disquieting impression that he'd touched a corpse.

"What have you done to him?" David demanded. He noticed Tim's pupils were completely blown, the liquid brown of his iris nearly swallowed by fathomless black, and turned to shoot Woodard a look of pure venom. "You've been drugging him."

"TM 05637 was being, how should I put it, recalcitrant. The unit spent too much time away from my control and proved somewhat difficult to reprogram." Woodard clasped his hands at the small of his back, standing completely at ease. "But thanks to a drug protocol Dr. Anderson developed, we have been able to resecure TM 05637's complete tractability."

David flinched at the mention of his cellblock neighbor but refused to rise to Woodard's obvious attempt to distract him. "What did you give him?" David demanded hoarsely as he stroked a finger over Tim's slack lips.

"It's called burundanga, if you must know. A nasty little drug developed by our friends at the CIA. It lowers inhibitions and the ability to resist suggestions, preparing the subject to accept a new reality." Woodard smiled at David indulgently. "You should be proud of yourself, Mr. Conley. However you managed to convince my project that it could pass as a civilian, your efforts were quite successful. It took far more effort than I'd anticipated to break TM 05637's attachment to you. But make no mistake," he continued, the pleasant expression vanishing as the general fixed David with a hard stare, "break it, we did. TM 05637 is now completely free of independent thoughts or desires. It lives only to obey and follow orders." Woodard bared his teeth in a parody of a grin. "And if I removed those restraints and ordered it to kill you, you had damn well better believe it would."

David turned away, unwilling to let the bastard see how much anguish his words had caused. Not for the first time, David had to admit he was afraid of Tim. But this time it was far worse. Because now he was fully aware precisely what Tim was capable of. Still, it tore his heart out to see the kid like this, bound like an animal and drugged to the gills, at the mercy of the mad general and his underlings. Though deep down he knew it was useless, the stubbornness that had gotten him through the past few weeks of captivity without losing his mind refused to let him give up without one last fight.

David bent low over the recumbent figure and spoke directly into Tim's ear so none of the onlookers could hear. "I'm so sorry, kid, for everything. For not being there for you when you needed me. For what's being done to you in this horrible place." He swallowed the lump in his throat and forced himself to gaze into Tim's sightless eyes. "I wish to God I could get you out of here, but I'm not like you. I'm only a man. Weak and helpless," he added, his voice breaking as he was flooded with a futile mix of anger and despair. "If—if you can hear me even a little, I hope you'll remember me. I hope you'll remember what we shared." David reached down to take Tim's slack hand in his, being careful not to press Tim's wrist into the metal bindings. "I hope you'll remember that what we had… it was real."

"David?"

He almost missed the sound of his name over the beeping, hissing sounds of the lab equipment. The voice that had uttered it was soft and weak, but so beautifully familiar. David gasped. He glanced quickly around to see if anyone else had heard, but the lab technicians had all turned away in disinterest. Woodard was still standing near the monitors where he'd forced David to watch his own murder on an endless loop. David was almost afraid to look down, but when he did, he found himself staring into a mesmerizing pair of fully aware brown eyes.

"Tim?" he breathed, almost afraid to speak lest he accidentally wake himself from the dream his nightmare had suddenly become.

Tim blinked, his eyes widening as his chapped lips formed a loose *O* of surprise. "My name. Is that my name?" He tightened his hand around David's. "Please, say it again," he begged. "Say my name."

David smiled, reminded of the night they'd made love when the kid had made the very same plea. The memory was even more bittersweet now that he understood what Tim had really been asking of him. Tim looked at him with the same bemused expression he'd worn the first time he'd told David he loved him, as though he couldn't believe this was actually happening. David understood the sentiment perfectly.

"Tim," he repeated, his smile stretching as the kid's face lit up in recognition. Unable to resist, David bent down and pressed his lips on the tempting curve of Tim's lips.

Woodard had finally cottoned on to the fact that something wasn't right. "Mr. Conley," he barked, "step away from the table."

"Tim," David said fervently, ignoring the strident order. "Tell me what I can do to you help you. What do you want me to do?"

"Take me home?" Tim looked so young and frail, it broke David's heart.

"Okay," David replied, not knowing how in the hell he was going to keep that promise but determined to figure something out.

"How is it moving?" A male lab tech standing closest to the platform was staring at Tim, bemused. "We gave it enough burundanga to incapacitate an elephant."

"There's too much about the unit's physiology we simply don't know," the woman standing next to him opinioned, looking frazzled and uncertain. "And without Dr. Anderson here to explain—"

"Conley, I said move away!"

David turned toward Woodard, noting that the general was the only one in the room who looked furious instead of completely stunned. The general had unholstered his sidearm and was aiming it steadily in David's direction. Realizing the time he had left to do something—anything—was running out, David tried frantically to think of a way to stall. He glanced back down at Tim, hoping for a bolt of inspiration, but the look of hatred on Tim's face took him aback until he realized he wasn't the one at whom the kid was staring daggers.

"Be ready when I say," Tim mumbled.

David blinked at him in confusion. "Ready for what?"

"Conley, goddammit, this is the last time I'm going to tell you—"

"Now!"

David didn't know what Tim had in mind, but something told him to duck. He crouched down next to the platform, nearly falling on his ass in his haste to make himself as small a target as possible. An animalistic growl emitted from Tim's throat as he broke the metal restraints holding his wrists away from the table. The bands around his ankles soon followed, and David could only watch in amazement as Tim leapt gracefully to his feet. Unable to process what had just happened, David stared dumbly up at the figure standing protectively above him.

"Stop him!" Woodard shouted, the slip in his terminology revealing that his fury had finally won the upper hand over his reason. His gun was still drawn, but before he could fire it, Tim hurled one of his former bindings at the general's head. The metal band glanced off Woodard's temple, spoiling his aim and dropping him to the ground.

Tim reached up and impatiently pulled the sensor pads off his skin. The monitors embedded in the walls of the lab went dark. Finally realizing their peril, the scientists began to flee the room en masse, like rats leaving a sinking ship. While the gaggle of white-coated figures clambered to get out through the single entryway, the guards moved to surround the escapee, positioning themselves just out of Tim's reach.

David waited for one of the guards to pull his weapon and gun Tim down, but when none of them did, he noticed they were all unarmed. He couldn't imagine why, but he refused to question their good luck. Tim didn't give them time to formulate any sort of strategy to subdue him. The other wristband landed squarely against the forehead of the soldier standing across the table from him with a loud clang. The man fell like a ton of bricks, and David winced as he saw the knot already forming at the site of impact. Figuring he would only get in the way, he crawled under the platform to give Tim room to maneuver.

Tim was looking at the men positioned directly in front of him, but from his vantage point, David saw the guard to his left nod at his partner standing across from him. "Tim, look out!" he managed to shout before the two men rushed at Tim from opposite sides at the silent signal. The idea man was slightly faster, reaching Tim first. David grimaced, betting the man regretted his haste as Tim grabbed hold of his outstretched hand and used his own momentum against him to slam him into the other soldier, sending both of them sliding across the room to crash into a bank of monitors.

The remaining guards didn't hesitate as their less fortunate colleagues scattered equipment in the wake of their unintended flight. They came at Tim head on. Tim sank to the floor to catch the rightmost of the pair around the legs with his own. Legs entangled, the man stumbled. Tim rolled forward, knocking the soldier down, before coming up in a handstand to slam his foot into the other guard's chin. Tim completed the maneuver by springing off his hands to land neatly on his feet. David gaped at the speed at which Tim had disabled his opponents, awed by his grace and power. If Tim was like this when he was as weak and malnourished as David had ever seen him, what must he be like at full strength? A brief flash of Tim's deadly fight with Woodard's men the night they were captured ran across his thoughts, but it suddenly morphed into an image of Tim glaring at him with a cold, murderous gaze. David closed his eyes, trying not to see the gun aimed at his head, trying not to watch in helpless terror as Tim slowly pulled the trigger. Shaking his head, David dispelled the false image, silently cursing Woodard for showing him those damned videos in the first place.

"David."

David looked up and found a hand in front of his face. His gaze traveled up along Tim's arm, stopping only when he met an urgent gaze.

"It's time to go."

"Can't argue with that," David quipped, recognizing his inappropriate humor as a coping mechanism for shock. In moments, he'd gone from fretting about how he would ever free Tim from his sanitized prison to watching while Tim rescued them both. Thinking absently of gift horses and mouths, David took the proffered hand and let Tim pull him from under the table and to his feet.

"Stand down, TM 05637!"

Tim froze, and David watched in disbelief as Woodard rose unsteadily to his feet. The general viciously swiped away the blood at his temple while his free hand leveled his retrieved sidearm between Tim's shoulder blades.

"If you think I'm simply going to let you walk out of here a second time, then your brain is more fried than those eggheads feared." Woodard stumbled for a moment, his wits clearly scrambled by the hit he'd taken. David braced himself to take advantage, but Woodard's moment of weakness didn't last long. His aim was steady as he edged closer. "Now, we're going to do this nice and easy, TM 05637, so I don't have to blow a hole through lover boy's chest."

David gritted his teeth as their window of escape diminished. Somehow, he doubted Woodard would be as easy for Tim to dispatch as the guards. The general might be significantly older than the men Tim had just dismantled, but he had experience on his side. Not to mention, he was fully aware of Tim's capabilities. Even David recognized it would be foolish to underestimate him. Experiencing a flash of clarity, he realized there was no way they could both get away. Alone, Tim had a chance. David feared he would only slow him down. Facing his own death wouldn't be so hard if only he could be certain Tim regained his freedom in exchange. Giving himself no time to think it through, he grabbed Tim and spun them around so he was standing between the general and his target.

You're a sweet boy, David, but it's going to get you into trouble someday.

David couldn't help the wry smile that crossed his lips as his mother's favorite admonition ran through his head. *Well, Ma, it appears as though "someday" has finally arrived.*

"Go ahead and shoot, Woodard," David said, surprised at the evenness of his tone. "It doesn't matter what you do to me, but Tim is done being your lab rat."

The general's lip turned up in a sneer. "Have it your way."

David jumped in spite of himself as the gun went off, but rather than the agonizing bite of a bullet, he found himself facedown on the floor. Glancing up in confusion, David rolled onto his back to look up at Tim.

"No!" he shouted as he saw Tim stagger and reach across to press a hand to his left side. David's mind went blank with dread as a wet stain spread across the dark material of Tim's unitard. A drop of blood fell to the floor, but before it could hit, Tim was already gone, closing the distance between himself and the general in the blink of an eye.

Woodard's face reflected stunned disbelief as Tim stopped mere inches in front of him. Moving faster than David could follow, Tim struck out and punched Woodard in the face. He grabbed hold of the general's uniform, taking advantage of the larger man's bewilderment to maneuver him so they both faced David, a dazed Woodard in front with Tim standing behind him.

"Why in the hell did you take that bullet for him, TM 05637?" Woodard demanded, his tone reedy from shock and pain. "It goes against every shred of your self-preservation protocol!"

Tim answered directly into the general's ear, enunciating every word carefully as though he was speaking to someone too stupid to comprehend normal speech. "You wouldn't understand even if I told you. And my name is Tim!"

David watched as Tim placed a hand on either side of Woodard's head, leaving a bloody handprint on the general's cheek. Tim braced himself, his face a mask of ruthless determination. David guessed what Tim was about to do, and even though Woodard had intended to kill him, the thought of the man's imminent death made his stomach clench. Still, David couldn't bring himself to speak out in protest. He tried to tell himself the general deserved it after what he'd done to both of them, and to Anderson for that matter. But he couldn't help the feeling of revulsion that rose in the back of his throat, threatening him once again with the nausea he'd barely resisted after watching Tim kill him in those damn simulations.

Though David remained silent, something of his ambivalence must have shown on his face. Tim stared directly into David's eyes, his face ravaged by the same horrified self-awareness as the night he'd nearly killed Bobby's father. But like the trained soldier he was, Tim quickly shook off his hesitation, the confusion in his expression disappearing in the next instant. He chopped the side of his hand against Woodard's neck with an audible *thwack*, rendering the man unconscious for a second time.

"I'm not a monster," Tim said, meeting David's gaze steadily.

David smiled at him. "I know. Now, let's get the hell out of here."

EIGHT

I STUMBLED over to the console behind where the general was lying. The searing pain in my side made it difficult to breathe, but I fought through it, pressing my hand to my side to stem the bleeding. I'd experienced worse under Woodard's tender care. As I typed one-handed on the inset keyboard, David came up close behind me. The warmth radiating from his body did much to alleviate the throbbing sting of the gunshot wound. How long had it been since we were together? Weeks? Months? I'd been sedated almost constantly since the moment of my capture, so I couldn't be sure of how much time had passed since then. It seemed like forever. Now that I was fully awake, I realized I'd felt David's absence like a physical ache. If only our reunion could have been under less traumatic circumstances.

"What are you doing?" David asked, scowling at the red smear my fingers were tracking across the keyboard.

I shivered as the words caressed the back of my neck. "Setting the self-destruct sequence. Father Paul taught it to me some time ago. All the research conducted here is top secret, so in case the Facility is ever compromised, authorized personnel are instructed to destroy the base to prevent any information about the TM project falling into enemy hands." I spoke briskly, trying to pretend I wasn't referring to the project responsible for my very existence. I frowned as the words "Access Denied" flashed across the screen in red. "Damn," I mumbled, "the code's been changed."

"Are you all right?" David was staring pointedly at the blood on my fingers. "You're still standing, so I guess the bullet only grazed you, huh? First me, now you." David shook his head with a humorless chuckle, clearly remembering when Don had shot at him. "Maybe there's some guardian angel looking out for us."

"It hit me full on," I snapped, my anxiety spiking as I remembered being terrified that Bobby's misguided father had killed David. "A rib must have stopped it. It's still in my side, but I'll be okay long enough to take care of this."

David gasped, his eyes widening with fear and concern. "Are you kidding me? We've got to get you to a doctor, or a hospital, or something!"

I shook my head. "Later. Right now, this is more important. Besides," I added, glancing at the unconscious Woodard, "we still need to get out of here."

"Yeah, okay." David exhaled, his expression tight with uncertainty. "But, are you sure you should do this? What about all of the people here—"

I wondered at David's abrupt cut off, but kept my focus on trying to hack into the Facility's security system. My fingers flew across the keyboard as I worked my way methodically through the system's firewalls, studiously ignoring the blood seeping uncomfortably down my waist and hip. A pool of red had begun to form next to my left foot as the material of my uniform became saturated. I knew anyone else would have likely been unconscious by now, and for once, I was grateful for my altered physiology.

"Once I commence the sequence, an alarm will sound. All personnel will immediately abandon the base." I turned to look behind me at the men I'd incapacitated. "As soon as someone discovers the general isn't among the escapees, they'll come looking for him." Woodard would doubtlessly survive, and I wasn't quite certain how I felt about that. "If I don't do this, they will never stop hunting me. Most, if not all, of the records about me are in these computers. Keeping any data off-site would have been too risky. By eradicating them, I can wipe every shred of information about the TM project that exists. The general and the Company will find it impossible to start over, especially with Father Paul gone. Even if they manage to recapture me, it won't be enough. Reverse-engineering my DNA would be impossible without his help."

The monitor beeped an accepting tone, and I nodded with grim satisfaction at the resulting green-lettered announcement granting me access to the system. With a few keystrokes, I entered the necessary instructions and backed away from the console as an ear-splitting klaxon cut through the air. Flashes of blinding orange warning lights glared from several recessed panels in the ceiling. An authoritative female voice spoke over the PA system, barely audible over the sirens.

"Self-destruct sequence initiated. Countdown commencing. This location will self-destruct in fifteen minutes."

"That doesn't leave us much time," David said tensely.

"I remember the way out," I replied. In the next instant, I slumped to the floor, my knee landing hard in the puddle of my own blood.

"Tim!" David cried.

I tried to keep David's face in focus as he knelt in front of me, but my suddenly blurry vision made it nearly impossible. I had been so focused on destroying the Facility, I hadn't registered the sheer amount of blood I'd lost. The severity of my weakness caught me by surprise. If we didn't get out of here soon, we'd be found by whoever came to save the general. Calculating the likelihood of success given my compromised condition, I made a decision and struggled to meet David's anxious blue gaze. "You've got to leave me before someone finds you."

David followed the direction of my gaze as I looked meaningfully toward Woodard, his features instantly freezing into a stubborn mask. "No," David barked, emphatically shaking his head. "Not without you. Besides," he added, placing the palm of his hand against my cheek, "I'd never find my way out of here alone."

I wanted to argue the point, to say I could draw David a map or tell him where to go and make him memorize the route. But there wasn't time, and my willingness to be left behind was not as unequivocal as it should have been. After everything that had happened, the thought of being separated from David again was unbearable.

"Okay," I breathed and held up my right arm. Taking the hint, David came under it and wrapped it around his shoulders to help me to my feet. I winced at the stab of pain in my side, but having David beside me empowered me to dig into my deepest reserves of endurance. All thoughts of self-sacrifice vanished. I wanted to get out so David and I could finally be together again the way we'd been before this nightmare began. To do that, I needed to survive. Taking as deep a breath as I could manage to steady myself, I nodded, ready as I would ever be.

The going was slow as David carefully guided me out of the lab, justifying all of his concerns about the amount of time we had left. But just when I began to think we might be safe from being discovered by the general's rescuers, David dropped a bombshell large enough to reduce the Facility to rubble ten times over.

"We have to get someone," David said hesitantly.

I fixed him with a bleary gaze. "Whaddya mean?" My speech was already beginning to slur.

David paused to brace me more firmly against his side. Visibly girding himself, he looked directly into my eyes. "Dr. Anderson, the man you call Father Paul, is alive."

"This location will self-destruct in twelve minutes."

I barely heard the update. *Father Paul is alive.* David's words rang through my head more loudly than the alarms warning about the base's impending annihilation. "How?" I breathed.

"I have no idea." David glanced down the corridor stretching away from us. "All I know is he's being kept in the brig, or whatever it's called. The same place they were holding me. Do you know how to get there?"

Gasping for breath, I nodded and pointed toward the end of the hall. "That way, then take a left when you reach the end."

David started off without waiting for further clarification, apparently understanding the effort it was taking me to speak. Even though David was half carrying me, he moved rapidly in the indicated direction, spurred on by panic as the voice announced the eleven-minute mark. Between the blood loss and the impossibility of what David had told me, it was all I could do to stay conscious. If I'd been injured like this on a mission, I would have been equipped with the first aid resources to patch myself up enough to continue. Now, I had neither the time nor the means. All I could do was lean on David and trust in him. Trust had never come easy to me, not when my entire life had been about suspicion and deception. But David had broken through the walls of my harsh, inhuman upbringing, teaching me what it meant to have faith in another person. I relaxed and let him lead the way, knowing in my heart that he would never let me down.

"This location will self-destruct in ten minutes."

With judicious expenditures of my rapidly flagging energy, I managed to direct David toward the fastest route to the detention area.

"I knew that son of a bitch was just trying to confuse me," David mumbled cryptically. "Okay, I definitely remember this." He quickened his pace as we approached the door that led to the cellblock. He stopped in front of it and smacked his hand against the keypad controlling the electronic lock. "Fuck! I forgot. We can't open it without an authorized eyeball."

"'S open."

"What?" David asked at my slurred response.

"Protocol for the—the self-destruct sequence. No locked doors to prevent anyone from being trapped inside."

David's brow furrowed in confusion, but he tried pushing at the release latch recessed into the door. Sure enough, it immediately slid open. "Huh, will you look at that," David remarked. He threw me a relieved smile, but it was short-lived as he took in my rapidly deteriorating condition.

"Don't w'rry 'bout me," I uttered weakly. "Just help Father Paul."

David's face tightened, obviously fighting to keep his opinion about my apparent lack of self-concern to himself. Pressing his lips into a tenacious line, he hauled me with him as he started down the row of cells. I could hear David mumbling to himself sequentially, counting off the number of doors as we went.

"Eight." David paused before a featureless white panel to the right side of the corridor. "I counted when Woodard took me out of here. I was in the ninth, and given where the adjoining wall was, he should be in here." David placed his hand flat against the door. "Damn, there's no handle." He tried to slide it using nothing but his hand, but it wouldn't budge. "Why won't it open? I thought you said—"

I swallowed to moisten my parched throat. “Protocol doesn’t apply to prisoners.”

“That’s fucking great!”

“David, is that you?”

I froze at the sound of the beloved voice. Even though I’d had no reason to think David was lying to me, I’d convinced myself he was somehow mistaken. After all, how would David know if he were really speaking to Father Paul as opposed to someone who had simply assumed his name? It would be just like the general to set up such an elaborate deception to trick David into revealing something he shouldn’t or to give him a false sense of hope about his chances of rescuing me. But I couldn’t disbelieve my own ears.

“Father Paul,” I whispered before I succumbed to the shock. The sound of a terrified voice calling my name was the last thing I heard before I gave in to my debilitated body’s demand for rest.

NINE

"TIM!" DAVID shouted again as the slim body went limp in his arms. Heedless of the blood now covering them both, he hugged the slender figure to him as his heart crashed against his ribcage. He couldn't lose Tim now, not after everything they'd just been through. Not after he'd finally gotten him back. "Come on, kid," he sobbed, burying his face into the sweat-soaked mop of black hair. "Don't do this to me."

"David, what's wrong?" Anderson demanded. "Who set the self-destruct?"

"I can't open the door," David replied absently, his mind grasping on to the detail to avoid the reality that Tim was dying in his arms.

Anderson was silent for a moment. "David," he continued in a soothing voice. "Do you have Tim with you? Is something wrong?"

"He's been s-shot," David answered, his voice catching on the last word. "He's not moving. Oh God," he added in a panic, "I think he's dead!"

"Put your fingers on the side of his neck, right under his jawbone. Do you feel a pulse?"

David hastily followed the instruction, trying to ignore the gory prints his fingers left on Tim's pallid skin. His breath rushed out in a gush of relief when he felt a surprisingly strong flutter against them. "Yes," he replied.

"This location will self-destruct in six minutes."

"David, we need to get out of here," Anderson said, his tone steady but firm.

"How do I open the door? There's a keypad, but I don't know the code."

"Tim can open it."

"Tim?" David said incredulously. He glanced down at the unconscious figure in his arms. "I don't think he's going to be much help." To have come so far only to be done in by the very trap Tim had set to protect them. David felt like yelling at the unfairness of it all.

"David, listen to me," Anderson said. "You need to wake him up."

"But—"

"It would take a lot more than one bullet to kill him. Especially if it didn't do the job right away. His body was designed to heal at an enhanced rate. It's gone into sleep mode to help speed up the process. Go ahead," Anderson urged, "take a look at the wound."

Skeptical, David ripped open the hole the bullet had left behind in the spandex and gaped as he saw the flesh around the gunshot already beginning to close. He shook his head in disbelief. "That's incredible." A troubling thought occurred to him. "But Tim said the bullet is still inside of him."

"I'll get it out once we're clear of the building. Now, wake him up."

"Tim," David said sharply, resisting the urge to speak softly. This wasn't the time for niceties. Swallowing his reluctance, he struck Tim across the face as hard as he dared. "Tim, wake up!"

Tim's eyes flew open at the reinforced command. He blinked up at David in confusion, but David noticed the kid's gaze was clearer than it had been before he'd passed out.

"Welcome back," David said, not bothering to stop the crazed grin that spread across his face.

"Father Paul," Tim croaked.

"He's in there. He said you could get him out?"

After glancing up at the door, Tim nodded. "Help me to the keypad."

"What are you going to do?" David asked, bewildered. He rose to his knees and pulled Tim up beside him, using his body as a support. "Do you know the code?"

Instead of answering, Tim pressed his hand to the access panel. He took a moment to catch his breath, staying upright only because

David was holding him securely from behind. Gathering himself, Tim curled his hand into a fist and drew it back. Then, uttering a pained grunt, he struck it against the panel as hard as he could. David's jaw dropped as the keypad exploded into dozens of pieces and fell to the floor.

The cell door slid open, the power source controlling the magnetic lock destroyed. David looked up at the elderly man who stood in the now open doorway. He appeared to be in his late seventies, if not older, and was gaunt and unshaven, the green jumpsuit he wore emphasizing the pallor of his skin. The gray whiskers sprouting from his chin matched the surprisingly thick tangle of hair on his head. A pair of dingy white socks covered his feet. Smiling gently, the man looked down at the spent figure in David's arms with a kindly gaze the same shade of rich brown as Tim's.

"Father Paul?" Tim asked, his expression dazed from blood loss and shock.

"Hello, my boy," Anderson said softly before cupping Tim's cheek with his hand. His smile was almost proud as a tear spilled out of the corner of Tim's eye and ran down to his fingers.

"I thought you were dead." Tim sounded tired and younger than David had ever heard him.

"Not quite yet," Anderson replied wryly.

"This location will self-destruct in four minutes."

"Sorry, you two," David said hastily, "but the family reunion is going to have to wait."

"Family reunion?" Tim asked.

Anderson shook his head at David. "Later. Where are Woodard and Coleen?" he asked. "Are they here?"

"The general was in the lab with us," David replied. "Tim said someone would come for him before the countdown finished. I never saw the woman."

Anderson looked relieved. "She must be away from the Facility. Coleen would never have let you anywhere near Tim. A justified reaction, wouldn't you say?" Chuckling darkly, Anderson glanced down at Tim. "Can you carry him? I don't think he's up to running right now."

David released Tim and turned so his back was facing him. "Can you hold on to me?"

Tim nodded.

"Then climb on, kid."

Anderson was already heading back to the door at the end of the cellblock as David secured Tim against his back. Placing his linked hands beneath Tim's bottom, David stood, hoping Tim was strong enough to keep himself from falling. He pointedly ignored the wetness against his back, not wanting to think about how close Tim might yet be to dying, Anderson's reassurances aside. Instead, he focused on the comforting weight of the dark head pressed against his shoulder. When he caught up with Anderson, the scientist was peering cautiously out into the adjoining corridor.

"All clear."

Anderson's in-depth knowledge of the base's layout bespoke his long familiarity with the place. He led them unerringly to safety, deftly avoiding the remaining groups of civilians and military personnel likewise fleeing from the imminent destruction. Every time they rounded a corner, David feared the general would be there waiting for them, but either he'd already left or Anderson was merely that good at anticipating his movements. They continued on unmolested, and soon David could see a huge opening at the end of a hall, with a large group of people pouring hastily through it.

"This location will self-destruct in three minutes."

They hung back for a long, nerve-wracking moment until the crowd had dispersed. With a nod, Anderson urged David to follow him. Tim must have fallen unconscious again, because he was deadweight against David's back. Concentrating on not dropping his increasingly heavy load, David focused all of his attention on simply moving his legs and not giving in to the stitch in his side. He swore to himself he would start working out as soon as this madness was over. He was so busy simply trying to breathe as he struggled to keep up with the unexpectedly spry scientist, it was a moment before he realized he was running on loose, bone-dry dirt.

Glancing over his shoulder, David was confused by the desert vista that spread out in nearly all directions. It was nighttime, but even if there had been light, there was little to see, save for one building that stood alone against the darkened sky. The structure looked to be a hangar of some sort, but it wasn't nearly big enough to be the Facility. When he looked for the door they'd come out of, he could barely see it behind a large rocky outcrop.

"Where did we come from?" he asked breathlessly.

"The Facility is mostly underground—easier to hide from both visible and electronic detection." Anderson pointed to a gigantic boulder situated between the partially obscured door and the building. "Come on," he urged.

"Tim," David tossed over his shoulder. "Hey, kid, you awake?" He received no reply. As they settled behind the boulder, David eased Tim off his back. He carefully examined the still figure for signs of life, his shoulders slumping in relief when he saw Tim's chest expand on an inhale. Reassured that Tim was still breathing, David glanced up and saw Anderson staring at the odd structure. "What is that place?"

"A garage. It's where all vehicles for use by Facility personnel are kept. We need to commandeer some transportation."

Raising an eyebrow at the choice of terminology, David shot the scientist a glance. "You mean steal a car."

Anderson grinned. "That too." After another few seconds of watching, the flood of people leaving the base slowed to nothing. "Okay, we need to get to that building."

"I don't know," David said uncertainly. "There are a lot of people over there."

"Trust me, the only thing they'll be thinking about is getting away from here, which is what we need to do."

"But the general—"

"Is long gone. All high-ranking officials would have been evacuated first."

"This location will self-destruct in two minutes."

"Get Tim, and let's go," Anderson ordered.

Having no other choice, David gathered Tim into his arms. He trailed behind Anderson as he darted out from behind the boulder and ran toward the hangar. Though even more slender after his stint as a prisoner, Tim was still heavy, but adrenaline gave David the burst of strength he needed to cover the distance without his heart bursting out of his chest. When they reached the side of the building, they encountered a gaping double door. Anderson flattened himself against the structure and edged toward the opening, the fine sheen of sweat on his skin the only indication that he'd found the sudden burst of physical activity at all objectionable. David did the same as best he could. He juggled Tim gently to get a better grip on the still figure in his aching arms. Anderson peered around the corner into the interior for a second before gesturing with his head for David to follow.

Anderson had guessed correctly. The few people who were left were madly scrambling for the remaining vehicles and didn't spare them a glance. The scientist headed for a nearby Jeep, and David followed him closely. After laying Tim on the backseat, he hopped into the passenger's side. Anderson settled in the driver's seat, and David watched with amazement as he ripped some wires out from under the steering column.

"Don't tell me you know how to hotwire a car."

Anderson tossed him a grin. "I wasn't always a geneticist."

David just shook his head and turned to look back at Tim as the engine roared to life. He took his eyes off the motionless form only when Anderson stomped on the gas pedal, shooting the Jeep out through the open doors and into the desert night. David hung on for dear life as they bounced along, dirt and rocks spinning from beneath the tires.

"Maybe you could slow down a little. Tim's hurt enough without you crashing us."

"There's nothing for us to run into," Anderson said, shouting over the wind as the open-air vehicle sped away from the hangar. "Besides, we need to be as far away as possible before—"

A titanic explosion aborted the explanation. David spun around in his seat to stare at the fireball that seemed to erupt from under the earth, thrusting hundreds of tons of dirt into the sky. Black debris filled the air, only to be quickly blown away by the strong desert wind. When the sky had cleared enough, David could see that the ground that had once hidden the base had sunk in, leaving behind a gaping chasm spanning several acres.

"Holy shit."

"Like I said, escaping was imperative."

"Yeah, okay," David said weakly, unable to argue the point. Soon the scene of devastation was lost in the distance, and his mind turned back to more pressing concerns. "What are we going to do about Tim?"

"First, I have to get that bullet out of him so he can finish healing."

"And then?" David prompted when Anderson was silent for a long moment.

"What comes next won't be so easy." Anderson shot him a glance. "You said before that Tim didn't tell you who he really was. I'm also guessing he didn't tell you about his infirmity."

David shook his head in confusion, as well as in answer to the question. "What infirmity?"

"As I'm sure you've gathered by now, Tim is quite valuable to certain, less scrupulous sectors of our government."

"Yeah, I got that," David said dryly.

"Although we trained him to be unfailingly obedient, Coleen wasn't satisfied with that." The muscles in Anderson's jaw worked as he clenched his teeth. "She insisted I build a trapdoor into his genetic code. I curse myself every day for acquiescing to her demands."

"A trapdoor?" David asked. "What in the hell is that supposed to mean?"

"Did you ever see him taking some blue-colored pills? I'll take that as a no," Anderson said when David only gave him a confused look. "The pills were to remedy a flaw I deliberately built into him. Something that would render him unable to function away from our control."

"And what was that?"

"Tim has a severe case of Addison–Biermer anemia."

David stared at Anderson blankly. "I'm afraid I left my medical degree in my other pants."

The scientist quirked his lips wryly at the humorless joke. He stared directly ahead as the Jeep sped across the flat expanse. "I designed him so his body is incapable of processing vitamin B12," Anderson began, squarely accepting the blame. "But it's far more severe than a mere deficiency. Whereas you or I could simply take supplements or eat the right foods, Tim's body is incapable of extracting the necessary amounts of the vitamin from external sources. He lacks the necessary gastric parietal cells, which secrete an essential protein that enables the body to absorb the nutrient. The resulting deterioration can be slowed by flooding his system with the vitamin, but to function normally, he requires a special metabolizing agent I created."

Lost in the technical jargon, David struggled to sift out the most important parts. "Wait a second. What do you mean by 'deterioration'?"

Anderson shot David a glance, his expression slightly impressed. "You listen very well, especially given the circumstances." The scientist's expression grew grim. "Addison–Biermer can present with many different symptoms. But, at the very least, the deficiency will hinder his ability to recover from his injuries as quickly as he should."

"That's the *least* of his problems?" David asked incredulously, his face twisted with concern as he looked back at the sleeping figure. "Then what's the worst case scenario?"

"Neurological failure and cardiac arrest," Anderson said baldly.

David stared at the scientist in disbelief. "Are you serious?"

"Unfortunately, yes."

"How in the hell could you do that to him?" David yelled as loudly as he dared so as not to wake Tim. "He's your son, for fuck's sake!"

"You don't have to tell me that, Mr. Conley." Aside from Anderson's sudden formality, the only sign David's jab had hit its mark was the sudden whitening of his knuckles as his grip tightened around the steering wheel. "I'm not proud of it, but what's done is done. We can only move forward from here."

"So, how did you keep him alive all this time? With that drug you mentioned?" David's gaze moved uneasily over Tim's uncharacteristically pale skin. "I mean, I lived with him for months and never suspected anything. Well, other than the fact he really seemed to love certain types of foods."

"The more meat the better, hmm?" Anderson guessed. He nodded at David's affirmative grunt. "It was his attempt to compensate and overload his system with B12-rich foods. The pills I gave him were formulated to artificially stimulate growth of parietal cells in his stomach so his body can extract the vitamin from food. They would have kept him alive for a while, although, as I said, the effects only last for a few days per dose."

David stared at Anderson darkly as he worked up the nerve to ask the obvious question. "Would have kept him alive for a while?" he echoed.

Anderson fixed his attention where the Jeep's headlights illuminated the terrain, his silence confirming David's morbid supposition. David clenched his hand into a fist, wanting nothing more than to slam it into the old man's face. He didn't bother asking how long "a while" was. It didn't matter, he thought, drowning in the realization that all the dreams he'd had of spending his life with Tim had been doomed from the start. Ever since he'd accepted how deeply he cared for Tim, David had been thinking about what it would be like for them to grow old together, convention and laws be damned. But all along, Tim must have known they were destined to have only a limited amount of time. The fleeting moments of sadness David had seen cross Tim's face toward the end now made perfect sense. He'd been a fool, wishing for something that could never be.

"How long does he have?" David finally made himself ask.

"Let me answer your original question instead," Anderson replied. "How did we keep him alive for so long? The pills were created for him to use while away from the Facility on missions. They were based on a variety of the medication I gave to him when he was a child. As he grew, the lower dosage form was no longer adequate, so I developed a stronger version of the metabolizing agent for him to take through intramuscular injections. Back at the base, Tim received the treatment on a weekly basis, enabling him to function normally."

"But he's no longer at the Facility," David noted dryly.

"No, and he doesn't have the pills anymore either."

David could feel himself grow hot with helpless anger. "So, what? You're just going to let him die?" The look Anderson shot him was indecipherable, but it made David shiver. It was obvious his perception of the man as nothing more than a kindly scientist was extremely misplaced.

"No, David. I am not going to let him die." Anderson's tone was as cold as his expression. "With the Facility gone, there are no easy options, but that's not to say there is no hope. We can delay the effects of Tim's condition by saturating his system with B12. It's not a permanent fix, but it will at least help with the healing process." Anderson glanced quickly over his shoulder at his unnatural child. "Under ideal circumstances, Tim would only need a day or so to recuperate from his injury. Even the significant amount of blood he lost wouldn't present too much of a challenge. But in his compromised state, his recovery will take much longer." *If it happens at all*, he left hanging in the air, unspoken.

"How do we do what you suggested? Saturate his system."

"A massive, intravenous infusion of B12 will maintain him for a while. Let's focus on that for now, and then we can talk about more long-term measures."

David wanted to discuss it then, but the flat, thin line of Anderson's lips warned him not to push. "Okay, so what's the plan?"

"I have a friend who works as a doctor on a reservation up near Greer County."

"In Oklahoma?" David asked.

Anderson looked at him briefly before turning his attention back to the road. "You've heard of Greer? Ah, finally," he added, pulling the Jeep onto a two-lane highway. They passed a sign, but it was too dark for David to read it.

"Yeah. I grew up in the northeast part of the state. We took a school trip down to the reservation one spring when I was in junior high."

"Yes, well, my friend isn't too fond of governmental authorities, so she won't feel duty bound to report Tim's gunshot wound to the police. Not that I plan to let her discover it," Anderson elaborated. "It's best she know as little as possible for her own sake."

David nodded, unable to think of a response over the conflicted storm raging in his head. Part of him still wanted to kill Anderson for what he'd done to Tim, but for now, he needed the man to save Tim's life. Besides, whatever the scientist might have been in the past, it was clear he loved Tim like a father. David also doubted Woodard would be as defeated as Tim had thought, especially considering Anderson was still alive. With the scientist's help, willing or not, Woodard and his people could use Tim's genetic code to create more like him. No, the likelihood the general would merely give up the hunt was slim to none. They would end up facing the man one day, David was certain, and they would need Tim as healthy as possible when they did. Of course, that imminent confrontation wasn't the only reason David was anxious to see Tim recovered.

Reaching into the backseat, David took hold of Tim's hand, which was resting limply at his side. David winced at the chill in Tim's skin. He squeezed, trying to impart some of his warmth. David didn't fully trust Anderson, but if the man wasn't lying and there was some way to save Tim from his genetic trap, he would do everything in his power to see it done. As he gazed at Tim's slack features, David marveled at how beautiful he was, even though he was so gravely injured. If nothing else, Anderson had gotten that part very right.

An image of Tim's perfect face etched with deadly intent flittered across David's mind. The roar of a gun firing filled his ears, and he flinched, almost as though he could feel the bullet drill a gaping hole in his forehead. Closing his eyes against the disturbing vision, David silently cursed the absent Woodard anew, and continued to hold Tim's hand as the Jeep sped eastward.

WOODARD SAT motionless in his seat as the vehicle slid to a halt on the loose, parched dirt. He stared fixedly at the glow erupting in the distance. A wave of dizziness washed over him, but he ruthlessly ignored it, his icy gaze never faltering from the scene of his defeat. He had to hand it to Anderson. The man had proven himself a master of manipulation and human psychology.

It had been Talbot's idea to capture a neuro imprint of Conley's brain to use in the simulations, but Woodard had been the one to place the doctor and Conley in adjoining cells, which were bugged on his orders. By listening in to their conversations, he'd hoped to gain some insight into the best way to turn TM 05637 against Conley. More importantly, he'd planned to use Conley as a means to dangle Anderson's success at giving his creation a soul in his face while at the same time letting him know he had ultimately failed in that very attempt.

Instead, it was that son of a bitch Anderson who'd gotten the upper hand. Anderson had told them the unit wouldn't allow itself to be controlled forever. Woodard blamed himself for not heeding the warning. Not only had it proven extremely difficult to coerce TM 05637 into killing Conley even in virtual reality, but after finally doing so, the unit had still been affected by its lingering feelings for the man.

Woodard swore to himself that he'd never underestimate any of them again. But he would find them—Anderson, Conley, and TM 05637. And when he did, they would sincerely regret ever daring to defy him.

"Sir? What are your orders?"

Woodard didn't bother looking over at the dark-haired woman seated next to him or at the large man standing in the rear well of the vehicle behind her. Instead, he kept his attention on the glow, which was all that remained of the last two and a half decades of his life. Though it was too far away to actually feel, he let the imagined heat of the conflagration fuel his sense of purpose. "Use the new tracking unit we implanted in TM 05637 to locate it and the other fugitives."

"We don't have any of the equipment needed to locate the signal, sir," the woman said matter-of-factly. "Everything was in the base."

Woodard smirked grimly. "That's what I like about you, Lieutenant Farley. You're always on hand with good news."

Sergeant Cooper held his silence. He had been the one to find Woodard and single-handedly carry him to safety with moments to spare before the Facility had exploded. Farley must have been in contact with Cooper because she'd been waiting right in front of the entrance with a Jeep. They had nearly been swallowed by the sinkhole that had opened as the self-destruct sequence reached its inevitable end. Woodard owed both of them his life, but it was not his habit to show gratitude. Besides, they had merely been doing their jobs, and he never offered praise for what should be expected without question.

"There's no point in driving aimlessly in the dark hoping we stumble across them. The search will have to wait until morning. Lieutenant," Woodard continued, finally turning his gaze in her direction. She looked back at him steadily, her attractive green eyes expressionless as she waited for his command. "Contact Ms. Talbot at Company headquarters. She left for there this morning. Arrange for her to send us some portable tracking equipment ASAP." He swore under his breath. By the time they got the gear, his quarry would have gotten a significant head start. Still, the range on the newer, more sensitive tracker would allow him to find the TM unit anywhere in a one-hundred-mile radius. He would send several teams out in the most likely directions and hope they came in range before the fugitives could slip too far off the grid. The endeavor was all too reminiscent of the last search for TM 05637, and it left a bad taste in his mouth.

"Sir, if we take advantage of the Company's systems, we can boost the range of detection. Ms. Talbot should be able to find the unit if it's anywhere in the Lower 48."

Woodard stared at her for a moment, impressed despite himself. "Do it."

Farley was instantly occupied setting up a satellite phone so she could place the call to the Company in White Plains, New York. Woodard tuned her out, knowing she would carry out his revised instructions to the letter. Yet again she had proven herself to be an invaluable asset. It was time he started thinking of giving her a promotion. After the TM unit was secured, he vowed. In the meantime, she could damn well help him salvage this sublimely fucked-up situation.

Woodard knew his real opponent was Anderson. TM 05637 was capable primarily of following a narrowly defined set of mission parameters, and Conley would be completely clueless. The old man would be the one running the show. Woodard's challenge would be figuring out how to best outthink someone who was, by any measure, a certified genius. He had a high opinion of his own abilities, but he knew where his strengths lay. If the search came up empty, he would have to employ different tactics.

"Tell Talbot to stay available in case we need her assistance with the recovery mission," he said.

Woodard gritted his teeth as the lieutenant faithfully repeated his statement. He couldn't stand the overbearing woman who oversaw what he'd always thought of as his project, but neither could he discount her resources. And surely there was no one on the planet who knew Anderson better than she did. Anderson and Talbot had been married for well over two decades, and while he hadn't been privy to the details of their breakup, no one could be together for so long without coming to understand each other intimately.

For the first time since the unit had defied all of the logical dictates of medical science and shaken off the CIA's best mind-control drug like it was a bad hangover, Woodard felt a miniscule sense of optimism. He would recapture both his runaway project and the man who had created him. And this time he would crush them both, Talbot and the Company be damned. The country could solve its problems like it always had, with hardworking human men and women. It was time to stop messing around with freaks of nature. Rabid beasts were nothing but a nuisance, and he would gladly put this one down personally.

Woodard turned his attention back toward Farley as she completed her call, the sergeant waiting like a silent hulk behind them. "Fall back to the rendezvous point at Clovis. We'll wait for the equipment there."

The trio was quiet as they headed off into the night, leaving the glow of destruction behind them.

TEN

"PLEASE, DAVID. Let Father Paul go." *I stared earnestly into the blue eyes I'd come to love so much. The gun trembled in my hand.* "You made me better, David. You made me human."

"Then I failed."

I cried out as the bullet bored into Father Paul's temple, my mentor violently jerking once before dropping heavily to the floor. David stood over the body without an ounce of emotion on his handsome face as Father Paul's life blood spilled out onto the white tiles.

"Eliminate the target, TM 05637."

"David," *I whispered, my eyes filling with tears. David's image grew fuzzy as I pulled the trigger. Right before the bullet reached him, his features came into stark focus and blue eyes stabbed me with hatred....*

I jolted into consciousness, ingrained habit causing me to make the transition without giving myself away. Tendrils of fire radiated out from the place where I'd been shot, but even as I noticed it, the burning began to ebb away.

"There, that should get it. It's okay, my boy. I know you're awake."

Recognizing Father Paul's voice, I instantly opened my eyes. He was looking down at me with a gentle smile, his graying hair haloed by the streetlamp hovering directly overhead. I was lying in the backseat of an open-air vehicle with my head pillowed on something firm yet comfortable. A flash of vivid red caught my attention, and I looked at the switchblade he held poised over me. The tip of it was slick with blood. In Father Paul's other hand lay a gore-covered bullet.

"What happened?" I asked, the question a hoarse rasp. My mouth was so dry, it was difficult to speak. "Where are we?"

"Here, drink this."

The request came from above me, and I looked up to see David's face. He had never worn a beard in the time I had known him, and the growth lent a new, fascinating dimension to his face. I quickly figured out I was lying on David's lap, and a weak grin spread helplessly over my lips as relief surged through me. "You're still here," I sighed.

David's mouth quirked in response. "Yeah, kid. Now, here." The opened top of a bottle suddenly appeared at my lips. "Drink."

I gratefully obliged, stopping only when my thirst was fully quenched. The angle was awkward, and several rivulets of water escaped to run down over my chin. I heard David's chuckle a moment before he dabbed the wetness away with the sleeve of his green jumpsuit. "Thank you," I said shyly. I glanced back at my creator. "What happened?" I asked again, suddenly remembering the last time I was awake. "Did we make it?"

"Yes, we did," Father Paul answered, patting me carefully on my leg. "You did it, my boy. You blew that place to high hell. We're free, thanks to you."

"Do you think they'll come looking for us?" The scientist's continued survival had changed all of my calculations.

"Don't worry about that," Father Paul soothed. "Right now we need to concentrate on setting you to rights."

I sat up gingerly, the twinge in my side indicating I hadn't fully healed from my injury. Or rather, the removal of the bullet only moments before had reopened the wound. David moved closer to help me, and I rested gratefully against his broad chest as I studied our surroundings. We were in one of the Jeeps I assumed came from the Facility's vehicle pool. It was currently sitting in the middle of a nearly deserted parking lot in front of a twenty-four hour convenience store.

"We stopped here for first aid supplies," David explained, his expression perturbed. "I still can't believe the clerk bought that lost credit card story. Whose card number did you give her?"

Father Paul chuckled. "I can't give away all my secrets."

I glanced meaningfully at the bloody bullet. "Thanks," I said, looking up at Father Paul.

"My pleasure. But you're not out of the woods quite yet, my boy."

"I lost the pills you gave me," I said, immediately grasping Father Paul's unspoken meaning.

"I know, which is why we're going to find something to help stimulate your healing factor."

I nodded as my eyelids began to droop. "S'rry," I mumbled, slumping even more heavily against David.

"You rest easy." I felt the press of gauze against my skin along with a sharp sting. The smell of a strong antiseptic burned my nose. "David and I will take care of everything."

As deft hands secured the gauze with medical tape, the steady beat of David's heart against my back began to lull me further toward the border between wakefulness and sleep.

"Are you sure he's going to be okay until we reach Greer?"

I could feel the deep rumble of David's voice against my back. I sighed, savoring the sensation of the fingers riffling tenderly through my hair. A cautious touch brushed softly along the edge of the gauze. "He's starting to bleed again. I thought you said he would be okay once the bullet was out?"

"He's already started to heal, but he won't be able to do so fully until we get him that injection of B12." The Jeep's engine roared to life. Gravel crunched beneath tires as the car began to move.

"We're still a couple hundred miles away from Oklahoma," David said worriedly. "Lubbock is a heck of a lot closer. We've been on the road for several hours already," he added tightly. "We could have been there by now. I know we can't go back to my place, but surely we could find somewhere to hide while you take care of Tim."

"Absolutely not. It's the first place Woodard would search for us."

David exhaled gustily. "Yeah, I know." His fingers continued to card through my hair absently, as though he was drawing comfort from the contact. "It's just, he looks so weak."

I remained as still as possible, not wanting to belie David's assumption that I had fallen back to sleep.

"I've never seen him like this. He's always been, I don't know, so full of life."

"Don't worry, David," Father Paul said soothingly. "He'll be fine. Like I told you, he was designed to be hard to kill."

I felt the growl vibrate through David's chest more than I could hear it over the sound of the wind whipping past. "You keep telling yourself that." The low-pitched remark reverberated with anger. "You know, Anderson, you said you don't think of Tim in the same way General Woodard does, but you sure seem to be goddamned blasé about his life."

Father Paul didn't speak for a long moment, and when he did, his tone was an icy counterpoint to David's ire. "You are quite mistaken, Mr. Conley, and I apologize if I ever gave you that impression."

David groaned. "Shit. Look, I'm the one who's sorry. That was uncalled for."

I struggled not to react to the tension I could feel thrumming between my companions, concentrating instead on the thumb gently caressing my cheek.

"I just can't get the image of him getting shot out of my head."

"I'm afraid this isn't the first time." Father Paul sighed, clearly bothered by what I suspected he was about to reveal. "A few years ago, when Tim was sixteen, the general and Talbot wanted to test precisely how quickly he could heal from various types of trauma. They subjected him to many tests, some of which caused pretty significant injuries."

David's shock was evident in his unsteady response. "Y-you mean they shot him? On purpose?" *And you let them?* The accusation remained unspoken but hummed in the ensuing silence.

Father Paul didn't bother to answer, letting his silence confirm David's horrified conjecture. I didn't often let my thoughts drift to that time, but now the memory of the endless, torturous trials came rushing back. In addition to being shot, I'd been stabbed, nearly drowned, electrocuted, and strangled. Each time I'd been certain I was going to die, but I always bounced back. I never asked Father Paul why he was letting them do all those awful things to me, thinking only that it was my duty to fulfill whatever command I was given. Looking back from David's perspective, I could see how sick the whole thing had been. Still, just as I had then, I trusted Father Paul would take care of me. I wished there was some way to reassure David I would, indeed, survive this, although I was perversely enjoying his concern too much to say anything right then.

"At the time," Father Paul said after a long while, "I thought it was necessary. You have to understand, the project was very important to us. To me, the general, and Coleen."

David gamely accepted the conversational gambit. "She's that Talbot woman, right?"

"Yes. Coleen and I met at university while I was earning my postdoctorate and she was getting her Master's degree in government studies."

I stiffened slightly, my mind filling with images of a stern gaze in an odd shade of green that had always seemed to look at me with profound distaste.

"She was the most beautiful woman I had ever seen," Father Paul continued wistfully. "It took me over six months to work up the courage to ask her out, and I almost thought she was putting me on when she actually said yes." His voice warmed. "We were married a year later. Those were the happiest years of my life."

"You two were married?" David asked.

I felt him shift uncomfortably even as I gasped quietly in surprise at the revelation. I had sometimes wondered about the relationship between Father Paul and Ms. Talbot. There had always seemed to be so much unspoken between them, I suspected their connection went beyond the project. But I could have never guessed the startling truth.

Father Paul was quiet for a moment before continuing. "You may find it difficult to believe, David, but once we were nothing but young, wide-eyed idealists. She wanted to change the world, and I wanted to save it. At times it was a struggle—neither of us made a lot of money when we first started out—but eventually my research got noticed, and she began to rise in the ranks of the government defense contractor where she worked." Father Paul paused as the Jeep sped over the smooth pavement. "And when Cody was born less than a year after we were married, we thought nothing could ever get in the way of our joy."

"You have a son?" David asked quietly. "Where is he?"

I fought to remain silent, willfully repressing the astonishment that jolted through me. Father Paul had a child? I could hardly believe it. Why hadn't Father Paul ever mentioned him? I was abruptly struck with how inappropriate my nickname for my creator was. If he had a real son, then it wasn't right for me to usurp his place, though I'd been unaware of the other boy's existence until that very moment.

"He's dead."

No emotion accompanied the blunt statement, but I could feel David tense against me as I struggled likewise not to react.

"How?" David asked sympathetically.

"He was on a school trip to Israel." A hint of sadness crept into Father Paul's tone as he explained. "Cody had become fascinated with history. It was his favorite class. So he was thrilled when the opportunity arose to visit a land so steeped in it. Coleen was reluctant at first. Due to her position, she was more aware than most of the scale of the continuing conflict endangering the region. But Cody wore her down with my help." Father Paul's voice suddenly sounded tired. "She tried not to cry when we put him on the plane, but she failed miserably. Cody hadn't been in Tel Aviv three days before the hotel where he and his schoolmates were staying was destroyed by a suicide bomber. He was only fourteen years old."

"My God," David breathed.

I dug my fingers into the car seat beneath me, hoping the darkness hid the gesture.

"Cody's death destroyed her. It was like he took a piece of her soul with him to the grave. Afterward, she seemed incapable of having feelings for anyone, including me. We divorced shortly after we buried our son, but that wasn't nearly enough closure for Coleen. She became obsessed with ensuring nothing so painful would ever happen to any other parent. Thus, the TM project was born. And, I have to confess, at the beginning I was as determined to ensure its success as the rest of the team. No matter what the cost." The vehicle shot forward for an instant, as though its driver had accidentally jammed a foot on the accelerator, before slowing again. "Back then, nothing mattered to me except the project, not the dubious ethics of what we were attempting and certainly not the suffering we inflicted."

David's arms tightened around me. "What changed?"

"Tim was born. He was perfect, even more beautiful than Cody had been. From nearly the moment he entered the world, he was clearly fully aware of his surroundings. He looked at me with those big brown eyes and wrapped those unnaturally strong baby fingers around mine and squeezed. I had given him his life and his strength, and in that moment, I wanted nothing more than to see him grow up. I can't say I didn't think of Tim as a substitute for the son I'd lost so tragically, but I soon came to love him in his own right." The Jeep jerked again in a reflection of Father Paul's agitation. "Even so, I was still intent on fulfilling my obligations to the project. That is until the day of Tim's nineteenth birthday when he came to me for the bit of cake I smuggled to him every year. He was covered in horrific cuts and bruises from one of the general's training sessions, and I suddenly reached my breaking point. It was only then that I fully grasped the depravity of what I had done, and I became just as determined to end the TM project as I had once been to begin it. That's why I promise you, my boy, I'll do everything in my power to make certain Woodard can never use you again."

I gave up the subterfuge when I realized my deception had failed. I opened my eyes and stared intently at Father Paul's profile, willing my creator to look at me. When he did, his gaze was full of sorrow.

"I forgive you," I said, instinctively knowing what Father Paul wanted to hear. "I'm grateful to you for being like a father to me all of these years."

Father Paul chuckled without humor. "Oh, Tim, if only that were true."

I didn't understand his response, but I was too tired to try and make sense of it right then. Though they came far more naturally to me now, I still considered myself a mere student of human emotions. But the jealousy burning deep within me was easy enough to label. I was ashamed of resenting a boy who had been dead for so long, but I couldn't help it. While I might call the scientist my father, there would always be someone else more deserving of the privilege. The realization pained me, but even so, I was contrarily pleased that I was capable of the sentiment at all.

I didn't have to pretend this time as I closed my eyes and let David's warmth and the quiet whine of the tires against the road lull me into true slumber.

ELEVEN

DAVID HELD Tim close during the remaining three-hour drive to Greer, as though he could impart some of his own body heat to him by osmosis. Neither he nor Anderson did much to break the silence following the scientist's stunning revelation. While David could understand how such a heartbreaking experience could warp a man, he wasn't sure he would ever be able to accept the path Anderson had taken in trying to channel his grief. Still, the so-called "TM project" had given him Tim, so David supposed something good had come out of it. He simply couldn't fathom how anyone could treat another living thing the way the general and this Talbot woman—and Anderson, for that matter—had treated the creation they'd professed to care so much about.

A large sign came into view in the distance, suspended conspicuously over the road. They had cut across the Texas panhandle on back roads, avoiding the interstate. Anderson had recently taken a right off Route 83 past Wellington and was driving east on the 203. The road changed to Oklahoma-9 as the sign welcomed them to the Sooner State, the green and white of the state's official colors muted by stingy lighting along the road. David wasn't sure how he felt being back in his birthplace after so long. He hadn't set foot in Oklahoma since leaving his parents' home to attend Texas Tech. It had to mean something that he'd ended up back here when his life had been turned so completely upside down. He just didn't know what.

"We'll be there in less than an hour," Anderson commented without preliminaries.

"Where exactly are we going?" David asked, watching the side of Anderson's face from his vantage point in the backseat.

"Magnum, the county seat. My friend is on staff at the hospital on the north side of town."

The conversation dwindled again, and David glanced down at the sleeping figure lying against his chest. Tim's skin felt less clammy, but he was still far paler than David had ever seen him. He wished he could somehow teleport them to the hospital so Tim could get treated without further delay. Since that was impossible, he dug deep for his tattered store of patience. To his credit, Anderson was driving much faster than he should be on the dark road, obviously feeling the same sense of urgency, no matter how often he'd professed confidence in Tim's elevated healing capabilities. David gently spread the ripped fabric of Tim's unitard so he could see the bandage covering the gunshot. The bleeding had finally stopped, but given how much Tim had already lost, he couldn't have much more to spare.

The old man was as good as his word. It was only forty-five minutes before they began to see signs of increased civilization. Anderson drove a little way past a gas station before abruptly pulling off the side of the road.

"What are you doing?" David asked, startled by the unexpected detour.

Anderson brought the Jeep to a halt and killed the engine. Before David could repeat his question, the scientist got out of the car and opened the back door to climb in next to Tim.

"Ruth is a good friend, but she's also the nosiest woman I've ever met. If I explain that Tim needs a blood transfusion, she's going to want to know why."

Anderson repeated David's earlier gesture and examined the gauze over Tim's wound. Instead of stopping there, he went further and peeled back the medical tape. David hissed as Anderson pulled the bandage away, expecting to see a raw gunshot wound, but there was only a pinkish circle of newly healed flesh to indicate Tim had ever been injured.

"Incredible," David mumbled.

"Indeed, but it presents a problem. Ruth is never going to believe Tim is so bad off he needs blood if he looks no worse than this."

Anderson pulled the switchblade he'd gotten at the drugstore in New Mexico out of his pocket. He took hold of Tim's arm before looking David directly in the eye. "You're not going to like this, but I'm going to have to cut him."

David reacted viscerally to the suggestion. "The hell you are!"

The shout woke Tim, who blinked up at the two men with curious, sleepy eyes. "Is something wrong?"

Anderson smiled down at him, never releasing his hold on Tim's arm. "We're almost to the hospital. You need a transfusion, but we need to be able to give the attending physician some excuse she'll believe."

Tim glanced down at his freshly healed skin and then up at the knife. His face smoothing in comprehension, he nodded his acquiescence to the scientist's plan.

"Now wait just a minute," David said hastily as Anderson positioned the point of the blade immediately below Tim's elbow. "I mean, come on. Is this really necessary?" His stomach churned at the thought of Tim being hurt again.

"I'm afraid so." Anderson stared into Tim's eyes. "Ready?"

Tim nodded, his expression betraying nothing as the knife cut a deep gash lengthwise down his arm from elbow to wrist. Blood immediately began pouring out of the jagged cut, and David blanched. Anderson grabbed David's hand and balled it into a fist before placing it at the crook of Tim's arm.

"Press here as hard as you can," he instructed. He bent Tim's arm up and lifted it so it was above the level of his heart. "Hard as you can," he repeated before leaping spryly from the backseat and sliding quickly back behind the wheel. He restarted the engine and jerked viciously at the stick shift, jamming the Jeep into gear, then tore off south on Route 34.

They hadn't gone two miles before David could see the bright lights of the hospital growing closer. "What if your friend isn't on duty?" he yelled over the noise of the wind rushing past the open-air vehicle.

"She's always on duty."

The enigmatic explanation was all David got. Minutes later, they were pulling up to the emergency room entrance.

"Wait here," Anderson ordered as he got out of the car. "It won't do any good for all of us to go in there together looking like rejects from some demented Halloween party."

Given that both he and Tim were covered with blood in various stages of drying, he couldn't argue with the characterization. Anderson disappeared through the sliding doors of the emergency wing, and David forced himself not to fidget while waiting anxiously for him to return. He kept as much pressure as he dared on Tim's arm, trying not to think about the warm stickiness oozing over his hand.

"It'll be okay," Tim slurred. His head flopped back, and David noticed the unfocused look in Tim's eyes from the additional blood loss. "Father Paul will take care of everything."

"I wish I could believe that, kid," David said under his breath. He held Tim tightly with his free arm and stared at the hospital entrance, mentally willing Anderson to reappear. His prayers were answered less than a minute later when the scientist came rushing back outside with a diminutive woman in tow.

The lady doctor wore a white lab coat and baby blue scrubs. Her bone-straight hair was pitch-black, though liberally streaked with strands of gray. Coppery skin a half shade darker than Tim's and the roundness of her face proclaimed her Native American ancestry. When she reached the Jeep, David could see the intelligence and concern sparking from her warm brown eyes. David found himself wondering if she, or someone who looked like her, had been Tim's maternal genetic donor, so striking were the similarities in their appearance.

"Is this him?" she asked, her tone full of competent urgency.

"Yes," Anderson confirmed.

The woman turned as a couple of orderlies emerged from the entryway with a gurney. "Set him up in Trauma 3," she said briskly.

The orderlies snapped to attention, and Tim was soon vanishing through the door, secured on the gurney. David scrambled after him, following behind Anderson and the doctor.

Anderson made hasty introductions. "David Conley, Dr. Ruth Marcus."

"Pleasure," she said, giving David a nod in lieu of shaking his bloodied hand. "Is any of that yours?" she asked, her keen gaze raking over the dark red stains on his jumpsuit.

"No," he replied. "It's all Tim's."

"How did he get hurt?" she demanded of Anderson.

"There was a problem with the car, and Tim thought he could fix it. He did, but managed to cut his arm pretty badly on a piece of jagged metal under the hood."

David marveled at the ease with which the man spun the probable tale. He couldn't help but wonder how such an eminent scientist could have learned to be so damn devious.

"I'll give him a tetanus shot too. Just to be on the safe side." With that, Marcus dismissed both David and Anderson from her notice as she orchestrated the necessary equipment and personnel to get Tim's blood transfusion going as rapidly as possible.

"Did you—"

"I already mentioned the B12 issue," Anderson reassured, quietly cutting David off. "I suggest we get out of her way and let her work. Ruth knows what she's doing, trust me. Besides," he continued, giving David a once-over, "I think we could both stand a shower and a change of clothes. The hospital deals with a lot of poverty cases, so they always keep items on hand for anyone who might need them."

David couldn't argue with that. He caught a glimpse of Tim lying on the bed he'd been transferred onto. He was surrounded by staff and monitoring equipment, and David had a disquieting flashback to earlier that evening when he'd first seen Tim in the Facility lab. Had it only been a few hours? It seemed like a lifetime had passed since they'd escaped. Though it pained him to leave Tim's side for even a few minutes, there was nothing he could do for him right then. Anderson's doctor friend was barking out clipped orders, and in less than five minutes, Tim was hooked up to a fresh supply of blood. David wondered briefly what Tim's blood type was and whether anything the hospital had on hand would be compatible with his altered system. *Of course it would*, he berated himself. Anderson would never have allowed his creation to be so easily detected.

The scientist led him to a storage room where the donated clothes were kept. Given Anderson's familiarity with the place, David figured he must have been here many times before. "How do you know Dr. Marcus?" he asked as he rifled through a bin of men's clothing, looking for something in his size.

"She was my research assistant after she graduated from medical school. She'd considered getting her doctorate in the field of genetics, hoping to use the knowledge to combat the various conditions for which certain Native Americans have a specific genetic predisposition." Anderson pulled out a couple of shirts and pants for himself before turning to a bin full of used shoes. "She was a stellar researcher, but after a couple of years, I convinced her to focus on practicing medicine. I could tell her heart wasn't in lab work. She's been much better off caring for patients, and they've been lucky to have her. Before I got so heavily involved with the project, I used to come here to consult with her on cases on a fairly regular basis. But I haven't seen her in person since before Tim was born." He shot David a glance. "The project kept me rather occupied."

Humming absently to keep from saying something he'd regret, David completed his own search. He easily found everything he needed, even underwear. A thought occurred to him, and while he waited for Anderson to finish, he pulled out a few items for Tim. Anderson didn't take much longer and, clean clothes in tow, led David to a room lined with lockers on one side and inset shower stalls on the other.

"This is where the medical staff comes when they need a refresher during a long shift," Anderson explained.

David gratefully stripped off the ugly green jumpsuit and tossed it in a medical waste bin as he headed for the nearest stall. The pressure was strong, and the hot water felt wonderful as it pelted down onto his head. He closed his eyes and just stood there for a long moment, letting the wet heat ease the tension in his muscles. He had no desire to watch the gore from the injuries Tim had sustained, both accidental and purposeful, streaming down the drain. Grabbing a helpfully supplied bar of soap, he proceeded to scrub away the grime of his long captivity as he pondered the mess they were in. Getting to the hospital had been the immediate goal, but it was only the first step. Woodard would surely be looking for them, and if the relentless way he'd hunted Tim down before was any indication, the man wouldn't give up easily. Anderson seemed to have some sort of plan for dealing with the situation, but his caginess was making David nervous. He still wasn't sure how far it was safe to trust the scientist, but for now he didn't have much choice.

When he was as clean as he was going to get, David turned off the water and retrieved a couple of towels off a conveniently placed shelf. He wrapped one of them around his waist and stepped out of the shower while rubbing the other briskly over his sopping hair. Anderson was already out and mostly dressed, save for socks and shoes. He glanced pointedly toward a small item wrapped in plastic, which sat on the bench where he was changing.

"I thought you might also want to shave."

David noted that Anderson's gray whiskers were nowhere to be seen.

"Go ahead. It will take some time before Tim is finished with his transfusion," Anderson explained. He sat on a bench to pull on his borrowed footwear. "In the meantime, we should get something to eat."

"Okay," David agreed, his stomach growling loudly at the mention of food. After taking care of his unwanted beard, he hurried to get dressed and followed Anderson to the hospital cafeteria, carrying a second set of clothes for himself and the items he'd chosen for Tim. Dr. Marcus was already there, the two extra cups of coffee sitting on the table in front of her revealing that she'd been waiting for them to join her. David took one of them gratefully and found himself subjected to a pointed, dark-eyed stare.

"Mr. Conley, was it?" she asked.

"David," he corrected. She nodded at his insistence on informality.

"No problem finding what I asked for, Ruth?" Anderson inquired.

Marcus took a sip of her coffee before shaking her head. "No. Setting up a B12 glucose drip was no problem. Addison–Biermer, you said?" She tsked. "That's nasty. So, who is this boy to you, Paul?"

Obviously she wasn't one to beat about the bush. David found himself admiring her forthright nature and wondered what sort of story Anderson would spin.

"He's my son," the scientist said to David's surprise.

Marcus was equally stunned. "Your son? But—" She frowned. "I thought Cody was your only child."

"I adopted Tim after Coleen and I divorced." Anderson chuckled self-deprecatingly. "Perhaps not the smartest move, seeing as I was still reeling from losing Cody, but I don't regret it for a second. He saved my life even as I gave him a better one."

Son of a bitch, David thought as he listened to Anderson weave the incredible yet completely plausible fiction. The old man was one hell of a liar. But even if the doctor was buying Anderson's story, it made no sense why she was being so unquestioningly helpful to them now. However close Anderson and Dr. Marcus had been in the past, they hadn't seen each other for at least twenty years. It made her easy acceptance of their sudden appearance at her hospital even more remarkable.

"Well," Marcus said, "I'm just glad I can finally pay you back even a little bit for everything you did for me. So much so that I'm not even going to ask why you were running around in those janitor rejects when you got here."

It was clear from the look on her face that she was dying to do just that. David admired her restraint and was glad, since he wasn't sure if even Anderson could come up with something that wouldn't sound crazy.

Anderson ignored her quip and covered her hand with his. "How is Isabelle?"

"She's fine," Marcus replied with a wistful smile. "Or rather, she has her good days and her bad days. But that she has any days at all—" She inhaled deeply, her dark eyes gleaming in the harsh florescent lighting. "I don't think I'll ever be able to thank you enough."

David had no idea what they were talking about, but he could tell he was a third wheel. Besides, he was eager to check on Tim. "Dr. Marcus, is it okay if I sit with Tim for awhile?"

"Call me Ruth." She glanced over at him with a curious expression. "Who are you to that young man?" she demanded impolitely, clearly taking her position as Tim's caretaker very seriously.

"I'm—"

"David is Tim's boyfriend," Anderson blurted out.

"Oh?"

The look she gave David had him fighting back a blush. He wondered if he should curse Anderson for outing him to this stranger and silently girded himself to deal with any homophobic bullshit she might throw his way.

"A bit old for him, aren't you?"

Her smile completely threw David off his footing. He gaped at her, trying to think of a response. "Tim's over eighteen," he settled on, lamely.

Dr. Marcus laughed. "I'm only messing with you, David. I don't mind if you keep him company. I'm sure he would appreciate a friendly face." She glanced toward the food bar. "There's salad and hot stuff over there. Pick out something Tim might like and take it to him. Food will do him as much good as that transfusion will."

David didn't wait for further instructions. He gathered up the spare clothes and made his way over to the food bar. Grabbing two plates, he filled them with what he hoped was a healthy assortment of mixed vegetables, something resembling beef stew, and steamed rice. He had to ask directions from a passing nurse for how to get back to the emergency ward, but once he was there, he found Tim's assigned quarters with no problem. It was obviously a slow night, and besides Tim, only two other beds were occupied. David maneuvered his way past the half-open curtain separating the makeshift room from the rest of the ward. He dropped the clothing out from under his arm onto a chair and settled in another that was closer to the bed.

From the moment he entered the room, David could feel Tim's gaze on him, but he waited until he was seated before he returned it. He told himself the tightness in his chest had nothing to do with the fact this was the first time they'd truly been alone together since the night they had first made love. When they'd been on the run from the lab, he hadn't been able to think of anything besides finding Anderson and getting the hell out of the base before it exploded around them. Now there were no other distractions. Thinking back to that fateful night, David could still hardly believe how it had gone from being the happiest moment of his life to such an unimaginable nightmare.

When he finally looked, Tim was biting his lip, his own nervousness ill concealed. The pallor of his skin and the loose fit of the hospital gown he wore all conspired to make him look even younger than his nineteen years. But, strangely, the sight of Tim watching him so uncertainly eased the tenseness that had knotted David's shoulders ever since he'd realized just how badly Tim was hurt. In its place he felt a surge of protectiveness, though the feeling was tainted by an undercurrent of something much darker.

"I liked the beard."

David blinked at the offhand remark before realizing Tim had apparently said the first thing that had come to mind to break the silence. "It itched," he said with a smile, explaining its absence. "I'm not used to wearing one. How are you holding up?"

He handed Tim one of the plates while he struggled to place the unsettling sensation. Tim reached for it with the arm Anderson had cut. It was wrapped with sterile gauze. David's stomach clenched as he remembered the knife digging into Tim's skin. Still, it was in some ways a far better sight than Tim's other arm. David frowned as his gaze landed on the needle taped to Tim's left arm. A tube ran from beneath the tape, and he traced it upward until it split into two. Each led to different bags hanging from an IV situated close to the side of the bed. One was filled with what was obviously blood, while the fluid in the other was clear. The sight reminded David uncomfortably of the first thing he'd seen after waking up in the detention cell at the Facility.

Tim shrugged. "Better. Dr. Marcus told me they're giving me vitamin B12 along with the blood." He glanced at David from beneath his lashes. "You know why." It wasn't a question.

David nodded. "Yeah. Anderson told me everything about your, um, condition. Why did you lie to me?" He knew his own expression likely mirrored the surprise on Tim's face. He hadn't planned on blurting out the accusation, but it had been building up in him ever since he'd first woken up in that godforsaken cell. David schooled his features into neutrality, forcibly ignoring the image that flashed through his mind of Tim pointing a gun at his head.

Though it seemed impossible, Tim's complexion lost even more color. His eyes were huge in his face, and David suddenly understood what Anderson had been going for in creating Tim's appearance. No one could ever stand a chance against such a blatant show of devastating innocence. And, dammit all, he was no exception.

"I'm sorry, kid," David sighed, accepting defeat. "I didn't mean it."

"No," Tim said hastily. He swallowed nervously and licked his chapped lips. "You have nothing to apologize for."

Shifting in his chair as his body reacted to the unwitting tease, David could only laugh silently at himself in disgust.

"You're right," Tim continued. "I did lie, but how could I have told you the truth about myself? You never would have believed me."

David wanted to protest, but Tim was right. He wouldn't have believed such a crazy story. Genetically engineered supersoldiers and secret government labs? Even though he'd seen it with his own eyes, he still found it hard to accept. "Yeah, you've got me there, kid."

"Besides," Tim said in a rush, as though not wanting to give David any further chance to interrupt, "I wanted to leave all of that behind me. Father Paul had given me the chance to live an ordinary life, and I did, thanks to you." Tim stared at David intently, clearly willing him to understand. The hands curled into fists at Tim's side reflected his inner turmoil. "When you picked me up off the side of that highway, you saved me. Not my life maybe. I would have been able to survive on my own. But you saved Tim," he said, jerking a thumb toward his chest. "Not TM 05637. *Me*."

David stared as heightened emotion forced color back into Tim's cheeks and sparks into his eyes. *So damned beautiful*, he thought for the thousandth time. "Take it easy," he began, wanting to calm the kid's agitation.

Tim shook his head, his dark eyes flashing. "No, I'm glad that I can feel upset, that I can experience any emotions at all. You gave me that too, David. Before you, I didn't know what it meant to feel things, but I do now. That's what frightened me the most—that I would never fully be able to leave behind that part of myself that was taught emotions are a weakness. And I wanted to so badly. Not because of what Father Paul wished for me, but because of you. You deserve to be with someone who knows what it means to care about other people." The color deepened into a blush. "You made me want to be someone who knows what it means to be in love."

David had to clear his throat before he could speak around the lump that had formed. Since they were being completely honest with each other, he asked one of the more pressing questions that had been festering in the back of his mind. "Are you really gay? You said you loved me, but…." He swallowed his reluctance to learn the potentially painful truth. "Were you just pretending? Trying to blend in like you were… like you were trained to do?"

Tim dropped his gaze to the cooling plate of food in his lap. His shoulders were hunched, every line of his body revealing how much he didn't want to answer. David's heart sank. He'd hoped he was merely being paranoid, but having his suspicions confirmed hurt more than he'd thought possible. Resting his own neglected plate on the floor, he stood abruptly and turned his back to the bed.

"You don't have to answer that," David rasped. He closed his eyes against the sudden sting, refusing to admit he was so close to crying from a goddamn broken heart. "It doesn't matter."

"David," Tim said after a long moment. "I promised myself I wouldn't lie to you anymore."

David heard the sound of Tim taking a deep breath but still didn't turn around.

"I realized shortly after we met that you were attracted to me. The way your pulse raced when you looked at me, the way your pupils dilated slightly, how you'd get a little bit sweaty. Everything gave you away."

David wondered if it was possible to die from humiliation. "Jesus," he breathed, wiping his hand down his heated face.

"I'd been trained to use any advantage I could to complete a mission. That's all it was at first, a mission given to me by Father Paul to live in the outside world. So when I discovered how you felt about me, I thought I could use it as a way to bind you to me, to keep you loyal to me in case I needed your help in hiding from the general, or if I needed you to help me fight against him if he found me. But it wasn't long before my feelings completely changed."

Fighting back his mortification, David forced himself to listen. "What do you mean?" he asked, keeping his gaze firmly directed toward the floor. He was well aware that he'd be unable to resist whatever expression Tim wore to match the earnestness in his voice.

"Whenever I looked at you, I started experiencing those same symptoms myself. My body temperature would rise and my heartbeat quickened. My palms would get sweaty, and I would get a funny feeling in my stomach and… in other places."

David reacted instinctively to the husky litany, his body doing all the things Tim had just described. Well, he'd never tried to deny the instant attraction he'd felt from the moment he'd first laid eyes on Tim.

"At first, I thought it was merely a physical reaction. But the night you rescued me from that nightmare, that's when I realized I saw you as far more than a simple expedient."

"The nightmare," David interjected, grabbing on to the lifeline he'd been unexpectedly offered. "I never did ask you what it was about." He heard the bed creak as Tim shifted.

"It was about my mother," Tim began slowly, clearly uncomfortable with the topic. "My surrogate mother. I was dreaming about how she died."

"Anderson told me about her," David offered.

"She always encouraged me to think of her as my real mother, so I did, even though I knew she wasn't. She was very kind and would spend as much time with me as the general would permit. She had the most beautiful red hair," Tim said, his voice soft as he recalled the woman who had raised him for several years. "One day, she tried to break the two of us out of the Facility. The general caught us, of course, and he convinced me that if I went back with him, he would spare her. But he didn't."

Even though he'd already heard the story, David winced in sympathy. His body strained with the need to comfort Tim, and after a moment of struggling against himself, he gave in to it. Turning back around, he moved closer to the bed. *Romantic fool*, his rational mind mocked. Maybe he was, but his heart ached at the sight of Tim sitting on the bed looking so very fragile and alone.

David placed a tentative hand on Tim's head. "It wasn't your fault."

"If she hadn't tried to help me, she'd still be alive."

"Maybe, maybe not. But she did what she did because she loved you." David gently petted the dark mop of hair. "Because you were worthy of her love."

Tim looked up at that, his eyes desperately seeking reassurance. David smiled at him gently and sat carefully on the side of the bed, taking care not to disturb any of the IV tubes. "I know you could never hurt anyone you truly cared about. And I know you are capable of caring very deeply." He moved the cooling plate of food from Tim's lap and took hold of his unencumbered hand. "Look at how hard you tried to protect Bobby when he was in trouble. What you did to his father, I understand it now. Yeah, it was rough, but your heart was in the right place."

"Was it?" Tim's voice was nearly inaudible, as though he were posing the question only to himself.

David opened his mouth to offer encouragement, but he was waylaid by another intruding image of Tim in the simulation video, his expression cold and hard as he aimed his gun, fully prepared to take David's life. He'd looked almost exactly the same when he'd single-handedly demolished Don Wood one piece at a time. Shaking his head to dispel the unwanted memory, David was trying to think of some way to disguise his lapse when Anderson suddenly rushed in.

"We have to go. Now." Anderson checked the IV bags and grimaced. "Damn, we need more time." He pressed his lips together thoughtfully for a moment before coming to a decision. "We'll have to take these with us."

David stood and looked at him in confusion. "Why? What's going on?"

"I should have known," Anderson mumbled to himself as he began to unclip the bags from the IV stand.

"Should have known what?" Tim seemed equally bewildered, but he scrambled out of the bed quickly, reacting to Anderson's air of urgency.

"Four military vehicles just pulled up outside of the hospital," Anderson spat. "Woodard must have implanted another tracking device in you." He gazed at his protégé sharply. "Tim, can you feel where it is? Concentrate."

Tim closed his eyes, turning his attention inward. David couldn't fathom how he would ever be able to find something hidden inside his own body.

"I can't," Tim said after a moment, looking pensive.

"Concentrate." Anderson's voice was reassuring as he continued to fuss with the IV bags. "This one is probably a lot smaller than the one they implanted in you before." His lips curved in a humorless smile. "I'm sure Woodard was less than thrilled about how easily you were able to remove it the last time."

David watched as Tim went completely still. Nothing moved on him, not even his chest to show he was breathing. It was like he had gone into some deep trance. Anderson glanced over at Tim, his expression grim, before turning to stare intently through the parted curtain into the ER. David looked too, half expecting that, at any moment, the ward would be filled with armed soldiers.

Suddenly Tim's eyes flew open and he stared at Anderson triumphantly. "I need a scalpel."

Anderson retrieved one from a nearby supply drawer, unwrapped it, and placed the blade in Tim's hand. David let out a sputtering croak of protest when Tim raised his gown, baring his left hip, and slid the sharp blade across his skin. Tim narrowed his eyes, but David suspected it was more in concentration than from discomfort. Squeezing the gaping edge of the cut, Tim eased a tiny, smooth-edged cylinder out of the incision.

"How did you find it?" David asked, amazed.

"He's been trained to be hyperaware of his body as well as of his surroundings," Anderson explained.

Tim shot David a look that made him instantly aware of the double entendre lurking beneath Anderson's words. David pointedly ignored his own body's untimely reaction while Tim carefully balanced the tracker against the safety railing that encircled the hospital bed. He took the knife from his dinner plate and used the butt end of it to smash the tracker against the rail, crushing the electronic device into dust.

"That's a handy talent," David remarked, still trying to wrap his mind around how extraordinary Tim really was. He stood back while Anderson helped Tim get dressed. Unable to put on a shirt over the IV, Tim simply draped it over his shoulders, leaving his chest exposed. David told himself not to ogle the bared expanse, instead making himself useful by scoping out the area beyond the curtain. Nothing looked out of place that he could tell. "Are you sure you saw something?" he asked.

"We both did," Dr. Marcus said, startling David as she swept past him into the room. He was still trying to figure out how he hadn't seen her coming as he turned to watch her stalk angrily toward Anderson. "They've staged themselves far out in the parking lot so as not to draw attention, but I don't know how they think they can hide so many vehicles in one place. And all painted in camouflage." She shook her head in disgust and glared at her friend. Her patience had clearly reached its limit now that her domain was being threatened. "You still haven't told me what all of this is about, Paul."

"And I'm not going to," he replied. "Believe me, it's for the best. Just stall them when they come asking about us and give us a head start." When her expression remained mulish, Anderson paused in his efforts to secure the IV bags. Shoving them at Tim to hold, he walked over to her and pulled her arms out of their stubborn posture so he could take her hands in his. "I'm sorry, Ruth. You're simply going to have to trust me." He pressed his lips to her cheek, and she crumbled, but not without rolling her eyes to express her irritation.

"Fine. But next time I see you, you'd better be prepared to spill everything."

Considering how long it had been since their last encounter, David knew the threat was an empty one. Still, he couldn't help but admire her willingness to help a friend while not getting so much as an explanation in return. Pushing Anderson aside, Marcus moved over to Tim. In less than a minute, she had bandaged the wound on his hip and had found something to hold the half-empty bags of blood and B12-laced glucose.

"Take care of yourself, young man. You hear me?"

"Yes, ma'am," Tim answered, his tone an uncertain mix of military precision and shyness.

She nodded and glanced at David. "You too."

"Yes, ma'am." David repressed a smile, her exasperated expression reminding him not a little bit of his mother when she was fed up with him.

"Here, you old coot." Marcus thrust a wad of bills into Anderson's hand. "It's not much, a few hundred dollars. You're lucky I hit the bank before I started my shift. And take this too." She followed the money with a set of keys. "I have a feeling you don't want to keep whatever you arrived in. It's the dark blue Civic in the employees' lot. Leave yours where you parked it." Without warning, she wrapped her arms around Anderson's waist and gave him a frantic hug. "I don't know what you're mixed up in, Paul, but please, keep yourself safe."

"I promise," Anderson replied.

David couldn't help but think that was a lie.

Anderson led the way as they hurried out the back corridor Dr. Marcus directed them toward. David kept a firm hold both on Tim and on the bags of life-giving fluid still being pumped into his veins. He hoped the ill-timed activity wasn't putting too much strain on Tim's still-healing body.

The metal emergency door at the end of the hall opened onto the employee parking lot. Dr. Marcus's car was right where she said it would be, and Anderson used the remote on the keychain to open the doors as they reached it. As before, he took the wheel, leaving David to hustle Tim into the backseat.

"Keep the bags higher than his shoulder," Anderson instructed.

Sitting lengthwise on the seat, David pulled Tim against him, settling the slim body between his legs. He propped his arm up on the back of the passenger seat to keep it from getting tired as he held up the IV bags. Tim tilted his head to look back at him. "Relax, kid," he murmured, smiling at Tim's upside-down face. "I've got you."

Anderson eyed the bags critically. "They should be empty in a couple more hours."

The scientist pulled out of the lot and headed toward the street that passed in front of the hospital. He was forced to drive uncomfortably close to the military vehicles, but the soldiers who had arrived in them were too busy invading the hospital to pay them much mind. David was saying a small prayer of thanks when he noticed that one woman had held back. She was also wearing fatigues, and her dark hair spilled out from beneath her matching cap. The woman was speaking intently into the radio pressed against the side of her face, and David guessed she was the one coordinating the action. She turned to look at their car as they passed about twenty feet beyond where she was leaning against one of the Jeeps. David's heart stuttered when her gaze sharpened for a moment as she studied the borrowed sedan, but she couldn't see through the windows in the predawn darkness. She looked like she was about to move in their direction, but something on the radio caught her attention and she turned away, dismissing them.

David exhaled in relief and settled back against the rear passenger-side door. "Where to now?" he asked.

"Now we put as much distance between us and the search team as possible. It won't take long for them to discover the broken transmitter. Then they'll know we're on to them."

"What about Ruth? Will she be okay?"

Anderson chuckled. "They'll have more luck getting information from a turnip. That woman can be a sphinx when she wants to be."

David hoped he was right. Either way, there was nothing they could do to help her now. He glanced out of the front window and watched the lights dwindle as they headed out of town.

TWELVE

A GENTLE hand skimmed down my chest, brushing against a peaked nipple and making me shiver. I moaned, wordlessly pleading for more. Blue eyes gazed down at me with amused affection.

"You like that?"

"Mmm-hmmm," *I breathed. The affirmation turned into a groan when the hand was replaced by nibbling lips.* "Ahh! Yes!"

"You're a greedy boy, you know that."

The caress of soft breath from my lover's chuckle only served to inflame me further as it blew over the sensitive nub. Searching fingers trailed up along my inner thigh, stopping just short of the throbbing flesh at the apex.

"Please—"

"Please, what? How do you want me to please you? Like this?"

The teasing fingers ran up the length of my cock, and my hips surged upward helplessly at the mischievous touch.

"Nnngg!" *I buried my fingers into thick blond hair, pressing my chest closer to the teasing lips. My legs fell apart, giving the hand stroking my aching cock easier access.* "Ah, David! I love you!" *The confession spilled effortlessly from my lips, as though I'd said the words a thousand times.*

"Do you, Tim? Do you really love me?"

"Yes!" *I gasped as the fingers around my arousal tightened their grip. My entire body shook as I strove toward release.*

"Then how could you kill me?"

My eyes flew open and my mouth gaped in a silent scream as I saw the rivulet of blood trickling from the ragged hole in the middle of David's forehead. I shook my head in speechless denial, but I could feel the gun in my hand, still warm from being fired....

I woke with a start, my gaze frantic as I tried to figure out where I was.

"Hey, hey! Easy, now," David murmured reassuringly as he pushed me back down.

Rubbing at my eyes to dispel the remnants of the disturbing dream, I gratefully sank down until my head once again rested in David's lap. "Where are we?" I asked.

"Still in Oklahoma," David replied, glancing toward the driver. "What do you say, Doc? How much farther are we going to go? It's already morning, and it's been over two hours since we split from the hospital."

Father Paul looked back and nodded when he noticed I was awake. "How are you feeling, my boy?" After making a brief check of the IV bags, he turned his attention back toward the road. "Looks like those are finally done."

Both the bag of blood and the one holding the glucose solution were flat. "Can I take the needle out?" I asked.

"Not yet," he replied. "I'll take care of it once we're settled."

"And when will that be?" David inquired for the second time.

From where I was lying, I could see between the front seats and out of the windshield. I noticed the motel sign at the same time as the others. "How about there?" I suggested.

"Yes," Father Paul agreed. "That will do nicely." He pulled the car into the small lot and drove it around back, out of sight of the window opening onto the reception area. After turning off the engine, he angled his body until he could see his passengers. "You two wait here until I get the keys. Someone may come around asking about three men traveling together. There's no sense letting the receptionist see all of us."

"Feeling better now?" David asked after Father Paul had gotten out and closed the driver's side door behind him.

I nodded. "Yes." I sat up and watched Father Paul round the front of the building. "I'm sorry."

"Sorry for what?" David's tone revealed his confusion.

"For dragging you into this. If you had never met me, you'd still be safe in Lubbock." I hunched my shoulders and looked down at my hands, my fingers clenching into fists. "You shouldn't be out here running for your life. You don't deserve that," I finished under my breath.

David sighed. "Look, kid. I'm not saying you're wrong that I'd still be living a boring-ass life in Lubbock if not for you. But do you seriously think I regret any second we've had together?"

I glanced over my shoulder. "But at least you'd have been safe."

David gazed at me steadily. "What's safe? Sleepwalking through my days, having nothing more pressing to worry about than the next resupply shipment?" His expression grew pensive. "When I met you, I realized what I had been doing wasn't living. I was merely existing."

I stared longingly at the corner of David's mouth as it curved up into a self-mocking smile.

"You taught me that, Tim," David continued. "And for that, I'll always be grateful."

"But…." I paused, not wanting to even think it, let alone say it. "What if you get hurt trying to protect me? I'll never forgive myself."

"Whatever happens, it won't be your fault. No one is to blame here except for General Woodard and Coleen Talbot and all the insane people who think you're nothing but some lab rat for them to exploit." David placed a warm hand on my shoulder. "Hell, back there in that lab, you nearly got yourself killed trying to save my life." I felt a reassuring squeeze. "I know you would never do anything to hurt me."

I only barely managed not to flinch as I turned back to watch for Father Paul, my incessant memory of shooting David stubbornly refusing to be ignored. I exhaled in relief when I saw my creator returning. David helped me out of the car, mindful not to let go of the IV bags as he followed.

Father Paul held up a key attached to a rectangular piece of wood. "We're in 102." He studied the numbers on the nearby doors. "Looks like it's this way." He ducked into the car and pulled out the pile of borrowed clothes before locking the doors with the remote. "One more thing," Father Paul muttered as he popped the trunk. "Ah, yes. Good girl." He came up with a large first aid kit still wrapped in plastic. "Any doctor worth her salt is always prepared for emergencies. Okay, let's go," he said, letting the trunk lid fall shut.

I shamelessly took advantage of David's body heat as he helped me to the motel room. The thin shirt I was partially wearing provided little defense against the cool early morning air, and I didn't have to fake the fine shiver that ran over me. The fact that I was at all affected by the chill was proof that I still hadn't quite returned to my peak state, though I was recovering by the second. The room was near the end of the row on the side of the motel where we had parked. Father Paul unlocked the door matching the number on the key and went in ahead of us.

"What a dump," David groused as he escorted me inside.

"It will serve for now," Father Paul stated pragmatically.

I could understand David's misgivings. The room was carpeted with a dingy, rust-colored shag carpet, which matched the equally hideous drapes. The walls were painted an uninspired beige, echoed by the spreads covering the two double beds. My nose wrinkled as I caught the faint whiff of cigarette smoke that seemed to permeate the air.

"You could do with a relaxing shower, my boy. But first...." Father Paul set the first aid kit on the small desk. It was situated to the left of a four-drawer dresser, atop of which sat a small television set. Pulling out the desk chair, he nodded toward it. "Have a seat and let's see to your arm. David, could you get me a towel from the bathroom?"

I sat as ordered, aware of David's every movement as he returned with the towel and dropped down onto the bed nearest the door to watch. The more pleasant part of the dream I'd been having in the car lingered as vividly as the nightmare it turned into. I could still feel David's hands roaming over my body, and the ghostlike sensation made me shiver.

"Did I hurt you?" Father Paul asked, mistaking my reaction. He had removed the tape and was sliding the needle from my arm.

"No," I answered succinctly, remaining silent as my creator finished his work.

Father Paul wrapped the needle in thick surgical tape and dropped it into the nearby trash can. He finished off the task by covering the site of the injection with a Band-Aid from the kit. After retrieving a bottle of iodine, he poured it liberally over the site of the slash he'd inflicted on me. The towel he'd placed under my arm caught the yellowish red runoff. "Another few hours," he remarked, "and I can take those stitches out." Gauze held in place with more tape followed before Father Paul stood back to admire his handiwork. "There. Soon, you won't even be able to see the wound."

"So he's completely recovered?"

Father Paul looked over at David. "Yes," he replied. "Well, for now, at least."

David's brow furrowed in confusion. "What do you mean, 'for now'? I thought you said the blood and B12 infusion would fix him."

Father Paul sighed and walked over to the other bed. Pinching the bridge of his nose with his fingers, he sat heavily on the squeaky mattress. I was fully aware for the first time how old and tired my mentor looked.

"I'm afraid the injection was only a temporary measure. As I told you, Tim's condition is chronic. Eventually his B12 levels will drop back into hazardous territory, and we'll have to go through all of this again. Unless…."

"Unless, what?" David clenched his jaw. "You said we'd talk about this later. Well it's later. Enough with the vague hints already!"

I found myself sharing David's exasperation.

"There is a way to fix you permanently," Father Paul said, staring directly into my eyes. "But it will be very dangerous."

"Explain," David demanded.

I was grateful for David's insistence, as my own voice seemed to have deserted me. In all the time I'd known about my genetic defect, I'd never even considered there might be a cure. If it was true, then not only would I be free of the general, but the chance I'd be able to live a long, normal life would be more than just a fantasy. I could stay forever with David, if he would let me. My mind reeled at the unimagined possibilities.

Father Paul's gaze radiated an odd mix of intensity and exhaustion. "The Facility was the central home for the TM project, but it wasn't the only location. Talbot didn't think it wise to house all of the project's activities in one place, so she set up a secondary headquarters not far from Scott Air Force Base in Illinois, just across the river from St. Louis. While I was in charge of the genetic side of the house, there was a separate team dedicated to developing various performance enhancing drugs, should they prove necessary." A look of discomfort crossed his face. "The drug trials were due to begin about four months ago."

"Right after you helped me escape," I calculated.

"Yes," Father Paul confirmed with a nod. "While I made you as perfect as I possibly could, Woodard and Coleen were interested in learning if you could be… improved. I was very much against the entire notion, knowing the drugs would likely do more harm than good, but they weren't overly keen to listen to my advice by that time. I had already proven too partial to you for their liking."

"But if the drugs the other team made are unsafe," David interjected, "how can they help cure Tim?"

Father Paul threw David an approving glance. "It so happens that, while I couldn't stop the team's work completely, I was able to give them a side project to work on. Woodard objected at first, but I convinced Coleen it was wise to prepare for any contingency. If ever the time came when Tim was sent on a long-term mission, he might have difficulty accessing a supply of the stopgap medication. In such a situation, a more permanent solution would be necessary. While neither she nor Woodard would ever have used it except as a last resort, it does exist." Father Paul looked fondly at me. "I made certain of that."

"And it's at this place in Illinois?" David pressed.

"Yes."

"It can't be easy to get to," I said, finally calm enough to join the discussion.

Father Paul shook his head. "No. The lab is located deep within a sublevel of a hidden base and is maintained under heavy guard, as you might suspect."

"Great, so all we have to do is sneak into a tightly guarded military installation, break through several levels of high-tech security, and steal a top secret developmental drug." David let his head drop back against the wall behind the bed. "Sounds like a piece of cake."

"You don't have to go." I drew on all of my training not to flinch at the incredulous glare David pinned me with. "Father Paul and I can steal another car, so you can take Dr. Marcus's back to Lubbock. You don't have to stay," I repeated, trying to project an insistence I didn't feel. The thought of David walking away from me hurt more than I had the capacity to express, but deep down I knew it was the right thing to do. There was no sense in letting David get any more involved in the cloak-and-dagger drama of my life. Not when it could all too easily get him killed.

David pressed his lips into a stubborn line as he stared at me. "I thought we already talked about this. Whether I stay or go is my decision." He clenched his jaw. "Hell, I could have left you at that damn hospital if I'd really wanted to, but I didn't."

"Why didn't you?" I asked softly, genuinely curious though I was also secretly hopeful.

"Because…." David looked askance at Father Paul, who had closed his eyes as though trying to give us what little privacy he could. "Because I care what happens to you," he continued softly. "You didn't ask to be born into this freak show. You came to me, stayed with me, because you wanted to know what it was like to be normal, right?"

I nodded silently.

"Then you deserve to know what that really means. You deserve to be happy, to live your life without being afraid every moment might be your last because of some cruel disease." David's gaze sharpened as he glanced toward the scientist, not trying to hide his anger. "If there's a way to heal you, to help you to achieve your dream," he added, turning back to me, "then I'll do anything I can to see it done."

David's face blurred, and I marveled at the stinging sensation as tears filled my eyes. David had said I deserved to be happy, but I couldn't imagine why. I'd never done anything to earn it. Even my attempt to help Bobby had ended in disaster. Why did David care so much about me? It didn't make any sense.

"Now, hop into bed and get some rest." David tossed me a tired smile. "It's a long, boring way to Illinois."

I sniffed self-consciously as I rose from the chair. I still felt weak, my energy reserves drained by my body's efforts to repair itself. But I could feel the transfusions doing their job. After a decent stretch of sleep, I would be back in top shape, at least for a while. A gentle snore caught my attention, and I glanced over at my mentor. Father Paul was sitting half propped against the wall, fast asleep, his head dangling so his chin brushed against his chest.

David settled himself onto the other bed, scooting down until his head lay on the pillow. I walked over to Father Paul and knelt on the bed so I could lower him to a more restful position. Once I was satisfied that he was comfortable, I turned and crawled in the other bed next to David.

David's eyes opened in surprise. "I thought—" he sputtered.

In lieu of answering, I simply inched closer and rested my head on his shoulder. The tension that had lingered in my body eased away when David's arms finally wrapped around me.

"Good-night, kid."

Ignoring the sunlight that gave lie to the euphemism, I closed my eyes and willed my subconscious mind to avoid the nightmare that relentlessly dogged me.

THIRTEEN

WHEN DAVID woke, he was rock hard. He could still see flashes of the dream he'd recently been enjoying. Tim had been very eager—and very naked—writhing beneath him as he buried himself again and again in Tim's welcoming heat. But when he opened his eyes, David realized he didn't only have the dream to blame. Tim was sleeping pressed against him, the curve of his ass fitting perfectly against David's groin.

"God," he whispered to himself, moving back to put some much-needed space between them. The quiet oath turned into a soft groan when Tim reacted to the sudden coolness against his backside by sliding farther toward his erstwhile source of heat. Once he'd regained his former position, his buttocks nestled snugly in the hollow of David's hips, Tim sighed contently and settled back down. David gave up and draped his arm around Tim's waist. He tried to banish the dream from his mind, but his body continued to lodge a protest at being denied what was right in front of it.

Shifting his head slightly, David glanced over to the dingy curtains blocking the motel room's windows. Sunlight poured through the narrow slit separating the two halves, but it wasn't the bright light of midday. The clock on the nightstand between the tables was angled away from him, but David guessed it was getting on to late afternoon. He considered waking Anderson and Tim. It probably wasn't a good idea to stay in one place for too long. They weren't all that far away from Magnum, and he didn't know how far Woodard had spread his search net. But all he ended up doing was closing his eyes again to better enjoy the feel of Tim's body lying next to his.

Tim wasn't looking for sex, he told himself. It was obvious he merely wanted comfort, which was something David could definitely understand. The events of the previous fifteen or so hours had been harrowing to say the least. David still couldn't believe Tim had managed to survive being shot at nearly point-blank range. His hand was resting near the healed wound, and his thumb unconsciously began to drift back and forth over the spot where the bullet had pierced Tim's side. A sense of panic threatened to overwhelm him at the thought of how close he'd come to losing Tim all over again. He wrapped his arm more firmly around Tim's body in an effort to reassure himself.

He was still trying to process the fact that Tim was there, not just in his arms, but in his bed at all. When Tim had gone to make Anderson more comfortable after he'd fallen asleep sitting up, David had simply assumed he would want to sleep next to his father figure. He'd had to forcibly prevent a sappy grin from taking over his face when Tim had chosen to join him instead. Although he couldn't deny how happy the gesture had made him, right then David wished Tim had been a bit more standoffish. He wasn't sure how long he lay there, the throb of blood pulsing through his aching flesh marking off the endless seconds. He moaned with gratitude when he finally heard Anderson stir on the other side of the room.

"Hey, Doc. You awake?" David wasn't sure whether he was asking out of curiosity or desperation. Turning his head toward the other bed, David saw the scientist's silhouette as he sat up and glanced at the glowing clock.

"Mmmm. It's after four o'clock." Anderson scratched at the back of his head. "We need to get moving. Is Tim still asleep?"

"Hey, kid." David spoke softly into Tim's ear. He was glad Anderson hadn't yet turned on the lamp and couldn't see him all cozied up with his de facto son. "It's time to wake up. We have to go."

Tim took a deep breath and opened his eyes, transitioning from deep slumber to full wakefulness in an instant. When Anderson finally clicked on the light, Tim seemed to realize just how close he was to David. His sheepish expression and the resulting color that bloomed in his cheeks were entirely too fetching. David quickly pushed himself upright, hoping it wasn't obvious he was running away from the urge to press his lips to that enticing blush.

"I hope you two slept well. I fear it may be a day or so before we have the opportunity to enjoy such comfortable accommodations again."

David stared at Anderson, searching the man's features for the sarcasm he suspected had accompanied that statement. When the scientist simply returned his look steadily, David nodded in salute, impressed by Anderson's ability to keep a straight face. If only he had such a gift. David predicted he might need it before this was all over.

"Where are we headed?" Tim asked. "Straight through to Illinois?"

Anderson shook his head. "No. We need to make preparations first. As you so astutely put it, we'll be infiltrating a tightly guarded military installation. I can guarantee you, it won't be easy." He slid off the bed and walked over to where he'd dumped the pile of clothes they'd taken from the hospital. "But right now we should get something to eat. And I need to make a phone call," he added as he disappeared into the bathroom.

"Call who?" David shouted after him. Receiving no answer, he glanced at Tim. "Any ideas?" Tim shrugged unhelpfully. "Well, I guess we'll find out soon enough. Are you feeling better?"

He congratulated himself for sounding so casual, considering the difficulty he was having taking his eyes off the length of exposed legs peeking out from beneath Tim's shirt. The kid must have taken off his jeans at some point while David was sleeping. He was glad he hadn't realized it while they were lying together in bed. He'd never have been able to control himself if he had.

"Yes. I'm hungry, though."

The familiar statement brought a smile to David's lips. How many times had he heard those very words during the months they'd lived together? Keeping a growing teenager fed and watered had been a Herculean task. Feeling suddenly nostalgic for those lost, halcyon days, he reached out and ruffled Tim's dark hair, smiling when Tim predictably wrinkled his nose in adorable protest.

"We'll take care of that as soon as we get out of here."

A few minutes later, Anderson returned, his gray hair damp from his shower. He was wearing the second change of clothes he'd borrowed, the first folded neatly beneath his arm. "It's all yours, David. I want to take a look at the cut I gave Tim before he gets in."

David took the offer eagerly, having no desire to get another look at the jagged wound. Once he was behind closed doors, he gave himself over to the conflicting emotions running through him. He was desperately worried this whole escapade would end in disaster. From what little he'd learned of the general, David knew the man would never stop looking for them. Anderson and Tim were being uncharacteristically naïve, he thought. Even if they had managed to destroy all record of the TM project—as unlikely as that seemed—there was every possibility Woodard would continue to hunt them purely out of spite. And David couldn't even begin to fathom how much of a problem that Talbot woman might prove to be. If what Anderson had told him was the truth, she had as much invested in the project as Woodard, if not more.

David took off his clothes and stepped into the shower stall. The water pressure was pleasantly strong, and he closed his eyes as the steamy flow poured over his head and down his body. He hadn't been lying when he'd said he'd do anything to help Tim gain his life and his freedom, but he feared he was in over his head. What did he know about any of this military crap? He'd joked about the difficulty of sneaking into the base in Illinois, but the very thought scared him to death. If Tim and Anderson hadn't gotten him out of the Facility, he knew he'd have died there. He highly doubted Woodard would have ever let him go. More likely, the only way he would have left that place was in a pine box.

Which is how he'd probably end up if he joined in this insane raid, assuming they were able to avoid the general's people long enough to reach the base in the first place. When he realized Woodard had already tracked them to the hospital, he'd thought it was all over. Next time they were discovered, they might not be so fortunate in their escape. And as for the undetermined plan to break into the other installation, Anderson had admitted it would be dangerous. An understatement if there ever was one. David was well aware of his limitations. He wasn't superpowered like Tim. And who the hell knew what Anderson was truly capable of? If he went in there, he knew he might not ever come out again. He wanted to do his best for Tim, but how far was he really willing to go? Was it worth his life?

An image of sleepy brown eyes gazing up at him from a sweetly blushing face flashed in his mind. David sighed in resignation as his recently quiescent cock instantly went from zero to aching. Next time Tim took it upon himself to molest David in his sleep, he refused to be responsible for his actions. *Right, like I'd ever force myself on him*, David chided himself.

Reaching down, he took hold of his cock, determined to rectify his raging problem before the others became suspicious of why he was taking so long in the bathroom. It didn't take much exertion, as keyed up as he was. The reality of waking up next to Tim blended seamlessly with the dream of Tim accepting his driving thrusts with breathless enthusiasm. It took only a few strokes before he was a spent, trembling mess. Resting his head against the tiled wall of the shower, David watched blearily as white fluid dripped through his fingers and disappeared lazily down the drain.

When he was reasonably dry and dressed, David opened the door onto the main room. Tim brushed past him with a shy smile, nearly undoing all of his earlier efforts. Wincing as his cock stirred with tired interest, David noticed the front door was open. He looked outside and saw Anderson rummaging in the open trunk.

"Looking for something?" he asked as he joined the scientist.

"This," Anderson replied. He straightened and held up a screwdriver.

Glancing into the trunk, David saw the open toolbox sitting tucked into the back right corner. "Was Dr. Marcus a Girl Scout in her previous life?"

Anderson chuckled. "I'm not certain whether they share that particular motto with their male counterparts. However, I have always known Ruth to be an extremely resourceful woman."

"So what do you need the screwdriver for?" Looking closely, David saw it was a Phillips head.

In lieu of responding, Anderson moved over to the car sitting in the parking space two lanes to their left. David's interest turned to flabbergasted disbelief when the scientist crouched down and began to detach the other vehicle's license plate.

"What the hell are you doing?" David hissed. He looked around frantically to check if anyone was watching the misdemeanor in progress.

Anderson grunted as he forced the last rusted screw loose and pulled it out. "Whatever I can to throw Woodard's hunting dogs off our scent. Help me up."

David found it difficult to reconcile what he was witnessing. Anderson was an elderly man who obviously had bad knees and had trouble standing on his own. But at the same time, he knew enough to do something David wouldn't have thought of in a million years. Though David burned with questions, he understood now wasn't the best time to assuage his curiosity about Anderson's increasingly mysterious past. He watched silently as the scientist similarly removed the plate on Dr. Marcus's car and replaced it with the one he'd stolen. He was finishing up when Tim came out of the room. The kid watched without comment as Anderson tossed the original license plate into the trunk of the Civic, and David grudgingly accepted he was the only ignorant yokel in the group.

"I brought these," Tim announced, holding up the bloody bandages that had been wrapped around his arm and the two IV bags. In his other hand was the wrapped needle he'd fished out of the trash.

"Good," Anderson said with a nod. "We'll burn all of that when we're out on the road. David, did you leave anything in the room? We don't want anything to give away that we were here."

"Just my other set of clothes. I'll grab yours too, kid." David returned to the room and did a swift but thorough check. He'd learned the trick after numerous hotel stays with his mother, who had always been paranoid she was forgetting something at the end of a vacation. The memory hit him hard in the gut, and David experienced an acute bout of homesickness. Suzanna had been so happy when she'd left the two of them after her visit over a month earlier, thrilled that her son had finally found someone to love. He wondered what she would say if she could see him now, a fugitive on the run. Thinking about his mother would only depress him, David decided. Pronouncing the room clean, he walked back outside.

"Don't you need to return the keys?" he asked when he saw Anderson and Tim were already sitting in the car.

"Behind you," Anderson said.

David turned around and saw a locked box affixed to the wall one door over from the room they'd just left. The box had an elongated notch cut out of the top, and the words Return Keys Here were painted on the side in fading red letters. Relieved none of them would need to interact any further with the front desk staff, David settled himself in the backseat, trying not to feel disappointed Tim had chosen to ride shotgun.

The sun was riding low in the sky when Anderson pulled the car up to a service station a few miles away from the motel. "David, would you mind filling us up? I need to find a pay phone." He took the car's original license plate with him when he left.

David resisted the urge to ask about the secretive call for a second time. When he returned to the car after paying the attendant, Tim had already put the nozzle in the tank. David joined him where he was leaning against the side of the car. Tim glanced at him but didn't seem to be in a talkative mood. David gladly obliged, leaving each of them to ponder his own thoughts. His mind stubbornly turned back to the dream that refused to leave him alone, though he suspected Tim's nearness had something to do with that. Tamping down his errant libido, David found himself enjoying the companionable silence after a while. As they watched the digital numbers on the pump count up the gallons and dollars, David couldn't help but wonder what was going through Tim's head. Was he nervous about what lay ahead of them? Or, given what he'd been trained to do, did he even register the probable danger?

Anderson returned without the plate as Tim was replacing the nozzle in its holster.

"Everything okay?" David asked, unable to resist probing a little.

"I'll explain soon. Right now, I don't know about you, but I'm starving."

David was annoyed at the brush-off, but his empty stomach forestalled any argument. Neither he nor Tim had eaten the meal David had brought for them the night before, forced to flee from the hospital before they'd gotten a chance to do so. If he'd known what was going to happen, David might have held off on the heart-to-heart they'd had and taken the opportunity to eat instead. Fortunately, Anderson didn't make them wait for long. He went only a few more miles before stopping at a roadside diner.

The homey décor instantly reminded David of the diner in Farwell, Texas, where he'd taken Tim for their first meal together. At the time, he'd had no clue what to do with his unexpected passenger. David wondered if he wouldn't have been better off simply taking Tim to the police like he'd initially planned to do. *No.* Every fiber of his being shouted the answer as the kid glanced back at him, his expression revealing that the significance of the location hadn't been lost on him. David smiled, encouraged when Tim mirrored the gesture. *No way in hell*, he decided. Missing out on the time he'd spent with Tim was unthinkable, no matter how things had ended up.

A surly blonde in a bubblegum pink outfit seated them. The young woman didn't look any older than Tim, and she clearly resented having to serve her loser customers rather than simply hanging out with her friends. She tossed three menus down on the table in front of them, rising out of her ennui long enough to give Tim a thorough once-over before disappearing into the kitchen. David couldn't blame her. His guess on Tim's size had been off, and the jeans he'd given Tim were just a little too small. They hugged the kid's gorgeous ass almost indecently. Tim, who was sitting on David's side of the booth, was oblivious to the flirtatious waitress. He wasted no time diving into the menu after Anderson told him to order whatever he wanted.

"You need to keep your strength up," the scientist insisted, gazing at his creation fondly.

David perused the selection as well, though his mind was on other topics more intriguing than food. "Are you going to tell us about that phone call now?"

"In a moment." Anderson took his time looking over the diner's offerings, and David rolled his eyes, wondering if the man was being deliberately maddening.

The young waitress reappeared as suddenly as she'd left. "Here's some water for you," she announced, setting the glasses down with enough force that some of the liquid sloshed over onto the tabletop.

"Whaddya wanna order?" David stared at her as she popped a wad of gum in a really annoying way.

"I'll have the spaghetti and meatballs, and a cup of coffee," Anderson replied. "What about you, my boy?"

"A bowl of the clam chowder. Hamburger, medium, with cheese and a fried egg. A side of fries, and a large glass of milk." Tim kept his gaze on the menu as he rattled off his impressive order.

The girl popped her gum as though to punctuate the silence when Tim finally finished, her eyes rounded in amazement as she wrote it all down. "What about you?"

"The hot roast beef sandwich," David said. He hid a grin when Tim's expression grew thoughtful as if to say he wished he'd ordered that too. "I'll take fries, also. And a diet cola."

To her credit, the waitress repeated their order verbatim before she went off to place it. David tapped his nails on the table, but Anderson merely sipped at his water until the girl returned with their drinks. After taking a fortifying sip, the scientist leaned forward, his body language indicating he was finally ready to talk.

"I called an old friend of mine, Mitch Larson. He used to be attached with the project years ago, but he left some time before Tim was born."

"Left?" David asked. "Why?" He glanced over at Tim, who looked like this was news to him as well.

Anderson shifted on his seat, the expression on his wrinkled features unreadable. "Mitch didn't agree with the way the project was being handled. When he found himself at odds with the general and Coleen, he requested a transfer. We've managed to keep in touch."

David exhaled sharply in surprise. "And they just let him leave?"

Anderson gazed at him coldly. "We aren't a cult, David."

"You sure as hell could have fooled me," David mumbled under his breath.

"Why did you call him?" Tim inquired, dragging the conversation back on topic. He had to wait for an answer as the waitress returned with his chowder. Tim inhaled it, his mouth seemingly inured to the temperature of the steaming bowl. David winced, his tongue aching in sympathy.

"Mitch owns a fishing cabin west of Medford near Salt Plains Lake. Have you ever been there?" Anderson turned a curious gaze on David, his irritation apparently forgotten.

David shook his head. "No, my folks never came out this far west. My dad used to take me camping at Bernice State Park when I was a kid."

"Hmm. Well, Mitch retired a while ago and moved to Arkansas. Fortunately he was home when I called and agreed to let us stay at the cabin. He should be able to meet us there in a couple of days."

"That's nice of him," David commented, "but why get him involved?"

Anderson paused as their food arrived. The waitress was slightly more careful with their plates than she'd been with their drinks, and the only casualty of her careless haste was a fry that slipped from David's plate onto the table. The scientist spoke as he swirled marinara-coated noodles around his fork. "It's not as if we're going to be able to knock on the front door and ask politely if they'll let us access the experimental laboratory. We're going to need weapons," Anderson said softly, "and lots of them."

David had been about to take a bite of his sandwich, but his appetite instantly faded at the practical observation. Only the knowledge that he needed to eat something made him force himself to continue. He grimaced as he chewed, the fragrant, juicy meat tasting like so much sawdust.

"And your friend can get us everything we might need?" Tim asked between bites, his own appetite unaffected by the grave subject matter. "He has access to that sort of ordnance?"

David silently thanked Tim for posing the very question he wanted answered.

"Yes, and let's leave it at that for now."

Groaning with irritation, David ruthlessly tore at his roast beef sandwich, knowing they weren't going to get anything more out of Anderson right then. "One of these days, you're going to have to explain yourself, old man."

Anderson raised an eyebrow, his brown eyes lighting with an irritating twinkle. "Is that so? I thought I already had, David."

David ate to keep himself from saying something he might later regret. He didn't trust Anderson, but for now they needed him and his unexpected font of knowledge and skills. Instead, he watched Tim pounce on his food. Feeling a sense of déjà vu, David let his gaze linger on the pink *O* of Tim's lips as he sucked his milk through a straw. The last time he and Tim had been in a diner like this, the sight of Tim using a straw had been enough to make him almost come in his pants. And that was right after they'd first met. Now he latched on to the welcome distraction to keep from dwelling on where they were headed next.

David wasn't sure what he'd been expecting, but somehow the talk of guns made everything feel more real. Weapons meant they would be shooting at people. And, more importantly, those people would be shooting back. As David continued to look at Tim, he found himself thinking of something other than what Tim could do with those plush lips. How much was he willing to risk for the kid's sake? Was he really prepared to kill? Was he prepared to die? Tim had tried to offer him an out, and for the first time, David sincerely considered taking it. Maybe he should just run back to Texas and try to salvage what he could of his life. After all, he didn't remotely resemble a soldier. But if he did leave, would he ever be able to live with his cowardice?

"Are you okay?" Tim mumbled the question around his burger, but his expression was full of genuine concern.

David mustered up a smile, hoping it didn't look as forced as it felt. "Yeah, I'm fine." *So much for total honesty*, he thought darkly before drowning his doubts in fried potatoes and carbonated chemicals.

"REPEAT THAT, Lieutenant." Woodard shoved a finger against the ear not pressed to the radio, trying to drown out the noise of the hundred-odd refugees from the Facility clamoring behind him. He shot an annoyed glance at Cooper, who was currently booming out directions to the harried lab techs who had survived the TM unit's sabotage.

They had arrived en masse at Cannon Air Force Base and were busy imposing themselves on the original occupants. The base's commander had been none too pleased to see them, but an official document bearing the president's signature had shut him up quick and in a hurry. It was a good thing Talbot had given him the forged orders in case of emergencies. Not even the yahoo currently sitting in the Oval Office knew about the TM project. Woodard and the other founders had discovered long ago that it was best to avoid unnecessary interference from squeamish, pansy-ass politicians.

"I said, we tracked down the fugitives, General." Farley's deadpan tone cut through the background drone.

"Excellent." Woodard smiled, pleased to have such good news so quickly. Farley had jury-rigged a portable receiver and had set out as soon as she'd received the relayed tracking signature from Talbot. The radio beeped, indicating that someone else was trying to get in on the call.

"This is Talbot. I want an update, Lieutenant. Immediately."

Woodard bristled at the usurpation of his command but remained silent. Without Talbot's help, they'd have lost valuable time waiting for replacement tracking equipment. Best to let her have her moment of glory and then move on to more important things. Like breaking Paul Anderson into a million pieces with his bare hands.

"Yes, ma'am," Farley replied. "I was just telling the general that we tracked down the unit. Unfortunately, it must have detected the implanted transmitter. We found it destroyed in an emergency treatment room at a hospital in Magnum, Oklahoma."

"Shit," Woodard swore, waiting for the reserved storm that wasn't long in coming.

"This is on your head, General." Talbot's voice was glacial, a reliable indicator of her fury.

She might be a harridan, but she wasn't unattractive for her age. Just once, Woodard wanted to see what she would look like if she showed her temper. "How do you figure that?" he asked, baiting her for his own amusement. It was better than giving in to his own anger at having been so easily outmaneuvered.

"I warned you. Paul is far too clever to fall into such a clumsy trap. It was you who ordered the lieutenant to surround the escapees with a show of force, was it not? He probably saw you coming a mile away."

Woodard ground his teeth, trying not to let his resentment at being dressed down like a raw recruit show on his face. "I assure you, Ms. Talbot," he spat, "I won't make the same mistake twice."

"See that you don't, General. I would suggest using a more indirect approach next time to catch Paul off guard."

"Agreed."

Talbot was silent for a long moment. "You know where they're going, don't you?"

"The base in Illinois," he answered.

"Paul will have no other choice if he wants to keep his precious creation alive for longer than a few weeks."

"I'll make sure he never gets there."

"I wish I shared your confidence, General. If Paul finds a way to destroy the secondary base, all of his research will be lost forever. Without that information, the TM project will die with him."

Woodard noted she apparently didn't consider keeping Anderson alive as a viable option. That was perfectly fine with him. Even so, he didn't want to give her the satisfaction of correctly predicting his failure. "It won't come to that. My people will secure the unit and eliminate the good doctor and Conley, if he's still traveling with them, long before they can reach the Mississippi. But, if it will make you feel better—" Woodard smirked. "—I'll take personal responsibility for ensuring the security at the base is adequate."

Talbot's disgust was audible. "Adequate is not good enough. Make it seamless, or I will find someone who will."

"Farley, you have your orders," Woodard barked the instant Talbot broke the connection. "You're not to come back here until you have secured the TM unit. Is that understood?"

"Yes, sir."

"Contact me as soon as you have another lead." Disconnecting the call, Woodard let his gaze wander over the controlled chaos. *Fucking Anderson*, he thought darkly. That bastard might have evaded him this time, but he'd be damned if it happened again. The TM unit was his, and he didn't like it when people took his things without asking. "Cooper," he shouted, "find out where the rec facilities are in this dump. I feel like pounding on something."

The sergeant's grin promised violence as he marched off. Woodard cracked his knuckles. There was nothing like delivering a good old-fashioned beatdown to improve one's mood.

FOURTEEN

I SMELLED the water before I saw it. It held the scent of vegetation and life, and underpinning it all, a hint of salt. The Civic's suspension fought bravely as the car jerked down the gravel-covered road leading to the edge of the lake. A grove of tall scrub blocked our sight of anything beyond the road in front of us, but I eventually caught a glimpse of the cabin sitting back in a clearing as the car rounded a bend. After Father Paul had driven a few more yards, Great Salt Plains Lake burst into view. Since my experience of nature was limited to the desert I'd traipsed through after my first escape from the Facility, I was transfixed by the sight of so much water spread out before us.

I was out of the car the moment Father Paul slowed the Civic to a halt at the end of a narrow footpath that provided passage between the cabin and the lake. Heedless of the loose rocks beneath my feet, I jogged toward the beach, stopping only when I stood right at the edge of the water. The silvery expanse rippled gently as a warm breeze blew over the surface. The angle of the late afternoon sun set the lake ablaze in stunning hues of red, gold, and orange. In the distance, the sheer faces of stratified cliffs rose up out of the water before softening into sloped hills covered with a verdant blanket of trees and brush.

"It's beautiful, isn't it?"

I nodded at David's observation, my gaze never straying from the splendid scenery. I focused my attention on the dark specks floating far out on the water, my sharp vision winning against the sun's glare as the shapes resolved into swimming birds. When David stepped closer to better share the view, the spicy scent I had come to associate with him wafted past my nose, rising over the smells of nature. I breathed deeply, surreptitiously basking in David's closeness.

"My dad used to take me camping a lot. Trying to make a man out of me, I guess." David let out a guffaw. "I enjoyed our trips, even when he made me wake up at the crack of dawn to fish or hunt. I never get tired of looking at gorgeous settings like this."

"Tim, come help me set up in here."

I spun around at Father Paul's request to comply, though I resented having the moment interrupted. Although hours had passed since we'd shared a bed in that dingy motel room, I could still feel the sensation of David's arousal pressed against my ass. Feigning sleep, I'd tried to get as close to him as I dared, but his reluctance had been palpable. I'd heard every moan and sigh as David had released his tension in the shower, but he had refused to look at me when he'd finally emerged. Not wanting to make him uncomfortable, I had deliberately chosen to give him space while we traveled to the cabin, though I'd longed to feel his arms wrapped around me again.

I took a closer look at the cabin as I headed toward it, leaving David standing alone on the narrow strip of beach. The dwelling was fashioned of white birch and had clearly been built by hand. Although the logs had obviously been chosen for their uniformity, each was a slightly different size. The same type of wood had been used to create a wraparound porch, which surrounded the cabin on two sides, as well as the railing that bordered it. The windows and shingled roof lent an air of modernity to the structure, but, on the whole, it perfectly fit my notion of what a log cabin should look like.

"Ah, there you are, my boy," Father Paul said as I stepped through the front door.

I found myself standing in a spacious living area. The floor was covered here and there with area rugs, the earth tones of the rugs echoed in the drapes covering the windows. A sofa with plush cushions and two matching chairs were situated haphazardly around a birch table likely fashioned from the same wood as the cabin's exterior. I located my mentor in a small kitchen off to the side of the main room. The kitchen was equipped with a simple cook range and compact refrigerator, and he was emptying the bags of groceries we'd purchased at the last town onto a large foldout table. As I walked over to join him, I noticed a set of stairs leading to a loft.

"There are two beds up there, if memory serves. Plus the sofa down here, which pulls out into a full bed."

"I'll take the sofa," David said, following me into the kitchenette. "Why don't you and Tim take the beds?"

I busied myself emptying the bag I'd grabbed, trying to hide my disappointment.

"Thank you, David." Father Paul pressed a fist into the small of his spine. "My back is not appreciative of all the driving I've done the past few days."

"I'll take over, if you'd like." David moved to take the last bag, his arm brushing against me as he worked.

"Yes, maybe that would be for the best. At least until we're closer to the base."

I carried the perishable items over to the fridge. Once I'd stored them, I searched around for something else to occupy me.

"Why don't you look for sheets to make up the beds?"

Gratefully accepting Father Paul's suggestion, I darted up the stairs. At the top, I paused and took a deep breath, telling myself David wasn't deliberately trying to be hurtful with his standoffishness. I knew he was still attracted to me, but for some reason he was holding back. It was an uncomfortable replay of the way he'd treated me when we first lived together. Though I supposed his current reluctance made sense. Things couldn't help but be awkward between us given everything we'd just gone through. Other than that brief moment together in the hospital, David and I hadn't really had the chance to talk. Not to mention he knew I had spent months lying to him. I couldn't expect things to simply go back to how they'd been before. I had no alternative but to respect David's choice.

After a few minutes of searching, I located the linen closet. The sheets were a bit musty, but they were clean. An idea struck, and I gathered enough linens for the two beds and the sofa into my arms before heading back downstairs. Father Paul and David were still busy in the kitchen, though they had moved from the unpacking stage to laying out what we'd need for dinner.

"I'm going to air these out on the porch," I announced.

Father Paul looked up from the package of pasta he was studying. "Ah, good idea. Mitch said he hasn't been here for ages."

I could feel David's gaze on me as I retreated outside, his eyes full of the same mixed messages he'd been broadcasting ever since we'd left the motel. Longing and distance. Advance and retreat. Staring at me heatedly one moment, and then pretending to ignore me the next. I didn't try to fight the frustration that welled up within me. While I understood David's ambivalence, I didn't have to like it. For my part, I was more than willing to pick up right where we'd left off. My feelings hadn't changed. If anything, they were stronger now that I was aware how much David was willing to sacrifice for me. Even after I had effectively stolen his life, he was still prepared to risk everything to keep me alive and out of the general's clutches. I hadn't thought it possible for me to love David any more than I already did, but I was happy to have been so greatly mistaken.

I draped the sheets over the porch railing and used the rocks I found lying between the cabin and the beach to weigh them down so they wouldn't blow away. Night was rapidly approaching, and the sudden drop in temperature had caused the wind to pick up. Satisfied the linens weren't going anywhere, I went back inside to find dinner preparations well underway. I spotted the box of plastic utensils and paper plates we'd bought and began to set them out on the table.

"You don't think we bought too much?" David asked from where he stood in front of the stove, sautéing a package of ground beef. He threw Father Paul a questioning glance. "How much money did Dr. Marcus give you?"

"Enough for now, but you're right to be cautious." Father Paul removed the pot of spaghetti from the stovetop and took it over to the sink to drain. "I'll ask Mitch to give us a bit of a loan."

"How much is 'a bit'?"

"Several thousand should see us well on our way to Illinois and, hopefully, beyond."

David froze, the spatula in his hand dangling precariously over the hot skillet. "This guy will just give you several thousand dollars because you ask him?" He turned off the burner and leaned his hips back against the countertop next to the range. Crossing his arms over his chest, he stared at the scientist intently. "I don't know any former coworker who would do something like that for me. I think it's time you came clean with us, Anderson. Who is this guy, and why is he so willing to help us? Was he Army? Someone Woodard screwed over for a promotion or something, and now he wants revenge?"

David looked quickly in my direction as though trying to gauge my reaction, but I was equally in the dark. I stood silently beside the fully set table, waiting for my creator to respond.

Seeing he was outnumbered, Father Paul sighed and set the pot in the sink. "Mitch is CIA. Or, rather, he was before he retired."

David's forehead wrinkled in confusion. "CIA? I thought you said he was attached to the project?"

"He was. He acted briefly as a liaison between the agency and the team at the Facility back when the government was taking a more public role in its existence."

"Why did it stop?" David asked. "Seems like the whole damn lot of you could have used more oversight."

"That was partially Mitch's doing." Father Paul braced his hands against the edge of the counter, his posture conveying his weariness. "Like I told you, he disagreed with the way the project was progressing and requested a transfer after working with us for just over four years."

"What made him leave?" I asked.

"Yeah," David added. "Four years seems a long time to suddenly get cold feet."

Father Paul grimaced. "Mitch had fallen in love with one of our surrogates, the one before Karen, in fact."

"But you said some of them died...."

Father Paul seemed to age ten years in mere seconds. "Yes, David. Some of them died. Or, more precisely, all of them, except for Karen and two others out of the fifteen women we impregnated."

I blanched in sympathy with David's look of stunned disgust, my stomach instantly queasy at the reminder of my lost "mother" and all the women who had preceded her. "That's when he decided to leave the project?" I pressed.

Father Paul nodded slowly. "Yes, but Mitch still was cognizant of his duty to maintain the project's top-level security status. He convinced his superiors the project was a failure and had been discontinued. Only a few in the Pentagon know the truth. Mitch stayed with the agency for years afterward, but when he became eligible for early retirement, he took it." The scientist exhaled heavily. "I suppose he was tired of living with all the secrets."

"And he never told anyone?" I asked.

"No." Father Paul laughed humorlessly. "He told me once that he still feels some sense of duty to country, even after everything he'd seen during his career."

"Jesus." David visibly shook off the horror that had paralyzed him and glared at Father Paul suspiciously. "If he left the project on bad terms, how did you two remain so close? It's not like your hands were clean in everything that went down. Those women died because of what you did to them." The sharp accusation cut through the tense atmosphere.

"David—" I began, feeling like I deserved to share some of the guilt.

Father Paul forestalled me with a raised hand. "No, my boy, he's absolutely right. I'm as much to blame as anyone." His eyes were full of shadows as he returned David's angry stare. "You're correct, David. I knew Mitch before we worked at the Facility. I, too, was in the CIA for some time before Coleen and I dedicated ourselves to the TM project."

"Son of a bitch." David turned away in disgust and relit the burner under the skillet. He mashed at the ground beef with short, furious jabs as though he was trying to kill it rather than cook it. "Go ahead. We're all ears."

"You were CIA?" I asked hesitantly, feeling off-balance. These new revelations were coming far too quickly for my comfort. I was swiftly realizing how much I didn't know about the man I'd always considered to be my father. "But you're a geneticist. What did they want with you?"

Father Paul turned the tap on to run cold water over the pasta. "They recruited me nearly thirty years ago. The intelligence community was deeply concerned about the unrest fomenting in the Middle East, especially the vicious forms of terrorist activity that were sprouting up." He turned off the water and watched the residual drops fall from the tap into the pot. "Many of the weapons being used over there were chemical in nature. Certain sectors of the government were interested in how those chemicals were affecting their victims on a genetic level. Some of the research was with an eye on how to minimize the effects of the weapons, but there was a special unit assigned to discover ways to make them even more virulent."

"Let me guess," David interjected. "You worked in the latter group." The skillet clattered as he slid it over to a cool burner and turned off the flame for a second time. I stepped closer to him, seeking the reassurance of his presence while putting some distance between myself and Father Paul. I realized I was afraid to hear his answer.

"Sorry to disappoint you," Father Paul answered, his expression shuttered, "but no. My superiors offered me the opportunity, but I refused." He reached into the sink and grabbed the pot by the handles before unexpectedly slamming it back down into the stainless steel basin. "I had a child, for God's sake! I would never have been able to live with myself if I'd been a part of something that might make someone else's child suffer." Taking a deep breath, he let it out slowly, his anger going with it. His entire body seemed to shrink in on itself. "Instead, I focused all my efforts on alleviating the suffering those dreadful weapons caused. I was tasked with traveling to the hot zones to gather samples and examine the victims. The agency assigned Mitch to protect me. We went on over a dozen trips together and became very good friends."

David stared at Father Paul in consternation. "I don't get you. How could you have gone from trying to do so much good to…." He paused and glanced over at me. "I mean," he continued, speaking carefully, "how did you go so far off the rails?"

"I lost my son." The scientist dropped his gaze toward the floor. "And with him my soul. She blamed me, you know. Coleen blamed me for Cody's death."

"How were you at fault?" I abandoned my position next to David and moved to my creator's side. I raised a tentative hand and placed it on Father Paul's shoulder, relieved when I received a grateful though subdued smile in return.

"Many of my missions were based out of Israel. Coleen was convinced Cody was targeted specifically because he was my son, that the terrorist groups were aware of my activities." His shoulders slumped beneath my hand. "I've never been able to say with any certainty that she was wrong."

"Father Paul…," I began, wanting to offer comfort but having no idea what to say.

"But how would that have even been possible?" David frowned. "I mean, it's not like Cody was walking around with a 'My Dad Works for the CIA' sign around his neck."

I started when Father Paul growled in irritation. "No, of course he wasn't." I let my hand fall away when he suddenly turned and bent down to open a floor-level cabinet to the left of the sink. "But I wasn't thinking very rationally at the time." He stood back up with a colander in one hand and a small pot in the other. "Here, use this for the sauce," he said, handing the pot to David.

"And I'm guessing your ex-wife never saw reason." David opened the jar of pasta sauce he'd placed on the counter and dumped it into the pot. He shook his head as he put the pot over a low flame. "You two make a hell of a pair."

Father Paul smiled grimly. "I can't disagree with you there."

"So how did you end up working for Woodard?" David asked.

"Mitch actually heard about the project first and mentioned it to me. He meant it to be more a bit of gossip than anything, but in my state of mind at the time, I made it my business to learn everything I could about what the project developers were planning. I wanted—no, needed—to be involved in something that would focus more directly on eliminating the growing threat of terrorism. When I discovered who was in charge, I offered my services to Woodard directly. Coleen and I had split up by then, so I didn't learn until later that she was working with the group financing the research." Father Paul gazed up into my face. "I might have gone into the project for selfish reasons, but I can't regret what came of it. My miracle child."

I blinked against the sting of tears when he cupped my cheek with a gentle hand.

David cleared his throat, interrupting the poignant silence. “Yeah, well, dinner’s almost ready.” He looked behind him at the table. “When is your friend due to arrive? Should Tim set a fourth place?”

Father Paul shook his head. “No, it will take him a little time to gather everything we’ll need. He probably won’t get here for at least another day.” He took a deep breath and straightened, his expression schooled into neutral lines. “We should take advantage of this time to rest up. Woodard won’t know about this place, so we don’t need to worry about being found anytime soon.”

The meal passed in a fairly relaxed atmosphere despite the lingering undercurrent of tension. Father Paul paid David back for his nosiness by questioning him thoroughly about his life before moving to Lubbock. I noticed David skipped all mention of his childhood and his parents, focusing instead on his years at Texas Tech and UT Austin. He told a particularly amusing story about an encounter he’d had with an embarrassingly persistent and extremely drunk girl at a bar at the Cactus Café near the UT campus. Apparently she’d thought David was the best thing since sliced bread, and he didn’t have the heart, or bravery, to tell her he was gay. He’d ended up chaperoning her for the rest of the evening and seeing her home that night.

“We stayed good friends after that, even when I finally came clean to her.” David chuckled wryly as he pushed away his empty plate. “She even set me up with the first guy I dated in college.”

I toyed with the remains of my spaghetti, trying to pretend I wasn’t jealous of this mystery student. I wanted to know everything about David. It wasn’t fair that so much of our individual lives had passed before we’d met. I excused myself and went to retrieve the linens I’d left airing out on the porch in order to hide my discomfort.

“I’m going to turn in,” Father Paul said when I returned. He pushed his chair back from the table and stood. “Thank you for all your help with the meal, David.”

“No problem. I’m used to fending for myself.”

Taking a set of sheets from me, Father Paul gave us a yawning wave and headed for the stairs. I dumped the rest of the linens on the sofa and helped David carry our dirty dishes over to the trashcan. "Are you going to wash out the pots?" I asked.

"Not tonight. I'll stick the rest of the food in the refrigerator. We can eat off it while we're here."

I lingered in the tiny kitchen, hoping David might invite me to share the sofa bed in spite of his earlier insistence that I sleep in the loft. That day in the motel had been my first real opportunity to rest in what seemed like forever, and being in David's arms had made it all the more satisfying. But I didn't know how to get past the wall of caution he had built around himself.

"Um, I brought down enough sheets to make up the sofa." I scuffed the toe of my borrowed sneakers against the linoleum. "We could…," I began, my voice so quiet I could barely hear myself.

David smiled tiredly at me. "Thanks. I appreciate it." He stretched his arms to the ceiling, the movement pulling his shirt free from the waistband of his pants. I stared greedily at the flash of exposed skin. "Why don't you head on up? Might as well get some sleep while you can."

With that, David moved over to the sofa and began to pull it out. I watched him for a moment, struggling to find a reason why staying down here was the better option. "Okay," I said finally, giving it up as a lost cause. "Good-night."

"Night, kid."

I paused at the bottom of the stairs as David began to fit the sheets over the foldout mattress. Disappointed, I trudged up the stairs to face a long night sleeping alone.

FIFTEEN

DAVID CURSED for the umpteenth time as his foot slipped off yet another moss-covered rock. After reassuring himself his ankle was, in fact, still in one piece, he looked up to find his companion had disappeared farther ahead along the trail.

"Hey, kid!" he shouted. "Some of us aren't mountain goats, you know." He sighed and eyed the stones peeking out of the dirt path with suspicion. "I told you we needed hiking boots for this."

Tim popped up from behind the tree that hid the bend in the path. He made his way back to where David was taking a rest, skipping nimbly from rock to rock as though to prove him wrong.

"Figures," David grumbled, watching Tim walking toward him with all the grace of a damn gazelle.

"Are you all right?" Tim looked him over carefully, his expression radiating concern. "Did you fall and hurt yourself?"

"No and no." He placed his foot cautiously on the dirt patch between the rocks. "But I'm definitely not wearing the right shoes for this."

Tim perched surefootedly on two stones. "We aren't in a hurry. And you were the one who wanted to go outside."

From anyone else, the reminder would have been a taunt. As it was, Tim was simply stating a fact. Unable to deny it, David pursed his lips and began walking farther along the path, being careful to watch where he stepped. Tim kept pace beside him, ready to assist if necessary. *Be kind to the elderly*, he groused silently.

"I figured we might as well," he said aloud. "If Anderson is right, his friend won't show up until tomorrow at the earliest. We're in God's own country out here." He took a deep breath, savoring the tang of unpolluted air. "Can you think of a better way to pass the time?"

The suggestive nature of his comment must have registered on Tim at the exact same instant. David glanced at his companion, only to find himself falling into a smoldering brown gaze.

"That's not what I—" The aborted explanation was all he managed to get out before he was summarily dragged off the path and deep into the shelter of the tall trees bordering the hiking trail. *Damn, he's strong*, he marveled an instant before Tim backed him up against a huge redwood. A seeking tongue filled his mouth, robbing him of the ability to say anything else.

Tim grabbed a handful of his shirt to hold him in place, not that it was necessary. The last thing he wanted was to go anywhere. Blood abandoned his brain, rushing down to increase the sudden throbbing at his groin. He moaned and wrapped his hands around Tim's waist, pulling him forward until they were pressed together from chest to knee.

"Mmmm," Tim whimpered wordlessly, more interested in using his tongue to spar with David's than to speak coherently.

David spread his legs to bring Tim farther into the cradle of his hips. Tim threw his head back with a hiss as their twin arousals came into firm contact, separated only by the rough denim of their jeans.

"Shh, just relax," he whispered before dipping his head to ply his lips to Tim's neck. He heard the rip of fabric as the frantic grip on his shirt tightened.

"Please, David. I want you!" Reaching up with one hand, Tim buried his fingers in David's hair.

David went willing when Tim pulled his head back to resume his attack on his lips. "Shit," he breathed, more to himself than anything. Wanton images flooded his heated mind. Tim stripped naked, his tawny skin exposed to the silent hush of the woods. Tim pressed against a tree as David plowed into him. Tim's beautiful face flushed, his lips parted, red and swollen, as he screamed his climax for only the woodland creatures to hear. The possibilities were staggering, and the mere thought of everything they could do together almost made him come in his pants.

"That's it, baby," he breathed, sliding his hands down Tim's sides until he was within reach of the button holding the kid's skintight jeans closed. Tim was so eager, he was practically humping his leg. He undid Tim's pants and delved inside to find the tempting hardness waiting between those slender thighs.

Tim gasped as David took hold of his erection. "Ahh! Yesss!"

Knock, knock, knock. Overhead, a woodpecker rapped on the tree they were leaning against.

Working Tim's length slowly, David leaned back far enough to watch the ecstasy build on his face. "Come on, let go for me." Under any other circumstances, he'd have been ashamed by how ridiculous he sounded, but he was far too caught up in the sight of Tim coming apart in his hands to care.

Knock, knock, knock.

Ignoring the annoying bird, he sucked gently on Tim's lower lip, feeling fluttery, heated pants against his face as he brought the kid ever closer to release.

"Nnngh! David, I'm gonna—"

Once they got back to the cabin, he would find some way to get rid of Anderson so he could spend the time appreciating his young lover properly. But for now he was focused on giving Tim the most amazing hand job he could dish out. "Yeah, baby, you're almost there. Just a little bit further. You can do it."

Tim let out a desperate keen, and he thrust his tongue into Tim's mouth, moving it in and out in a foreshadowing of what he was planning once they had some less felony-inducing privacy. It wasn't as though the woods were deserted—at any moment, they might be discovered by some other group of nature lovers—but the risk was worth it for this intense, primal experience. He moved his hand faster, swallowing every loud moan that spilled from Tim's lips. The end came suddenly as Tim yelled into his mouth, his release coating the hand working him so diligently….

Knock, knock, knock!

"Fuck!" David found himself on the floor next to the sofa, his head aching from where he'd banged it when he rolled off the makeshift bed. The knocking sounded again, this time at the front door of the cabin. Holding a hand to his throbbing head, he glared at the door, debating whether it would be more prudent to take care of his raging hard-on now or answer the summons and frighten whoever was standing on the other side with it. The clatter of footsteps on the stairs leading up to the loft ended his dilemma.

"Someone's at the door," Tim said, stating the obvious. He glanced at David curiously, no doubt wondering why he was lying on the floor instead of on the perfectly comfortable sofa bed. "What happened? Are you all right?"

The question too closely recalled the dream David had been so summarily dragged out of. "Just answer it." He waved Tim toward the door while scrambling for a pillow to hold over his lap.

Tim looked at him for another moment before moving to obey. David took the opportunity to climb back onto the sofa, grateful Tim was wearing his clothes from the day before and hadn't come downstairs in the underwear he'd probably slept in. A memory of Tim sleeping in the nude the first night he'd spent under David's roof threatened to make his problem even worse. David took a deep breath and wiped a hand over his face, trying to clear away the cobweb remnants of the dream. It was clear his libido hadn't yet gotten the message that he and Tim were taking things slow.

"Didn't you hear me knocking?" a gravelly voice demanded. "Humph. You must be Paul's science project."

The tactless observation instantly cured David of the lingering effects of his dream. He rose from the sofa and moved to where Tim was blocking the way of the man standing just outside the front door.

"Well, freak, aren't you going to let me inside?" the newcomer asked gruffly.

"That's enough, Mitch," Anderson said before David could spit out a sufficiently pithy reply on Tim's behalf. The scientist came gingerly down the steps, his movements stiff, though he looked well rested. He'd spent the previous day puttering around the cabin while Tim and David had gone for a hike. That much of the dream had been true, though it had ended in a far more PG manner than David's overly imaginative mind had conjured.

Anderson stepped around them and went to meet his so-called friend. David had his doubts about anyone who could be so intentionally cruel to Tim. If Larson and Anderson were as close as the old man had claimed, then he had to know how much the scientist cared about his creation. David stood behind Tim in a tacit show of support, but when the kid stepped aside to give Anderson some space, his face was completely devoid of expression. David shot Larson a venomous glower and placed a reassuring hand on Tim's back. Larson looked through him dismissively before turning his attention back to Anderson.

"Paul, it's been a long time." He looked the scientist up and down. "Heard you went and got yourself killed."

Anderson smiled tightly. "I nearly did, though it was for a good cause." He angled himself so he could see everyone at once. "Mitch, this is David Conley. And I believe you've already met Tim."

"Since when does it have a name?"

"Tim is not an 'it,'" David growled.

Larson glanced toward him briefly. "And what's with the civvy?"

Anderson frowned disapprovingly at his former colleague. "I will ask that you be civil, Mitch. I know you're capable of that much, or has retirement robbed you of manners entirely?"

Larson engaged the scientist in a staring contest for a long moment before bursting out in a laugh. The look of amusement transformed his entire demeanor from grizzled toughness to boyish charm. David blinked in amazement at the abrupt transformation. For the first time, he began to understand how this man could have successfully worked as a spy. Larson appeared to be near General Woodard's age—somewhat younger than Anderson. He was tall, standing a couple of inches over David, and had a stocky build that was only beginning to run to fat. His hair was brown underneath a liberal sprinkling of gray, and his eyes were a faded green that nevertheless sparkled with awareness and intelligence. All in all, he gave the impression of someone David might want to have a beer with but wouldn't want to meet in a dark alley.

"Okay, Paul, you win. I'll be nice to your pet soldier." Larson moved past Anderson unceremoniously and headed for the kitchenette. "You can tell me all about what the hell is going on while we eat breakfast. You were damn vague when you called me."

Anderson followed in his friend's wake. "I thought it for the best, seeing as we're being hunted by our former boss."

"Ah," Larson answered. "How is that overbearing son of a bitch?"

"Do you want me to fix breakfast?" David asked, deciding he might as well make himself useful.

"No need." Larson held up a large plastic bag filled with Styrofoam containers. David's nose twitched from the delicious smell of greasy food. "I figure you three have probably been living off the same rations for over a day. I stopped at a place right outside the park limits I like to go to when I'm down here. Breakfast is on me."

In no time, they were all settled around the table, which was now laden with containers full of pancakes, scrambled eggs, sausage, bacon, and seasoned potatoes. Another plate held the half loaf of wheat toast Larson had included with the feast. David had put on coffee, and it was ready by the time Larson and Anderson had set out all of the food. He noticed Tim hadn't said a word since he'd opened the door. Glancing at him worriedly, David nudged him with his foot.

"Get some food while it's hot," he said softly.

Tim continued to watch Larson warily, but complied with the suggestion. For once, David was glad Tim followed orders so automatically.

"Okay, Paul. Spill," Larson said before stuffing a forkful of pancakes into his mouth.

David listened with half an ear as Anderson caught his former colleague up to speed about the eventual success of the TM project, Tim's escape and subsequent recapture, and their more recent breakout. While the old man talked, David kept his attention on Tim, noting how he was picking at his food. His face was a mask, but David guessed Larson's reaction to him was bothering him more than a little.

"Conley, was it?"

David looked over at Larson when he heard his name. "That's right."

"So you're the one who sheltered *Tim* after Paul sent him out into the big wide world, huh?"

David didn't miss the sarcastic emphasis Larson placed on Tim's name. "I am," he confirmed through clenched teeth. The man was doing them a huge favor, letting them hide in his cabin and bringing them supplies. He figured it probably wouldn't be politic to punch the jerk in the mouth.

"Bad luck for you, getting mixed up in all of this."

Tim's chair screeched against the linoleum floor as he abruptly pushed back from the table. "I'm going to eat out on the porch." After grabbing his plate and his mug of coffee, he disappeared through the front door.

David clenched his hand into a wishful fist as he pinned the ex-CIA agent with a glare. "Watch your mouth, Larson. You have no right to talk about Tim like he's some damn inanimate object. He has feelings like any human being!"

"Human being?" Larson scoffed. "That's not a person. It's a fucking experiment that shouldn't even exist."

"You sound like Woodard, Mitch." Anderson spoke softly, but David could hear the icy undertones. "I never pegged you as being so closed-minded." The scientist stood and walked over to the window overlooking the porch. He moved the curtain aside, his expression softening as he caught sight of his protégé. "Tim's genome might have been created in a lab, but I realized from the moment of his birth that he's not merely the weapon we designed him to be. He's deadly, without a doubt. But Tim is capable of so much more." Anderson glanced at David. "He's proof of that."

Larson frowned. "What do you mean?"

David figured where Anderson was going and wasn't sure he wanted to expose either Tim or himself to the former agent's scorn. But he didn't know Larson as well as Anderson did, so all he could do was follow his lead. The scientist waited until David nodded, giving him tacit permission to continue.

"David and I talked a great deal after the general brought him back to the Facility along with Tim. And what I learned was simply miraculous."

"And what was that?"

Anderson smiled. "I learned Tim is capable of that most profound of human emotions. Love."

Larson looked confused for a brief instant before his puzzled expression morphed into one of disbelief. To David's surprise, the large man's look of incredulity held only surprise, not disgust.

"In love? With him?" Larson asked, pointing at David. "Bullshit. You designed a killing machine, Paul. It wasn't supposed to be capable of having feelings. Wasn't that the whole point?"

Anderson gazed sadly out of the window. "See for yourself if you don't believe me."

Following Larson as he rose from the table, David stood behind Anderson but found his view blocked by the former agent's wide shoulders. Larson's heavily creased eyes rounded in surprise.

"Well, I'll be damned," he breathed.

"What is it?" David asked, concerned.

He shoved his way to the window next to Larson and saw Tim sitting with his back against one of the porch railing's posts, his knees pulled to his chest. He was looking down at his plate, which sat untouched on the porch next to him, his cheeks shiny with tears. David didn't bother wasting his time bitching at Larson. He knocked against the man hard with his shoulder as he rushed toward the front door. Tim didn't acknowledge him when he stepped out onto the porch.

"Hey, kid. You okay?"

Tim wiped away the wetness on his left cheek and then stared at his fingers, looking bemused at the proof that he'd been crying. His eyes were huge when he finally glanced up. "Yes," he replied, his voice husky with emotion. "I don't know why I'm feeling this way. I'm not injured."

"Maybe not physically, but Larson said some pretty harsh things." David sat down next to Tim and bent his legs so the outsides of their thighs were touching. "Plus, he's Father Paul's friend," he added, making sure to call the scientist by the moniker Tim had bestowed upon him. "If one of my dad's friends acted so mean toward me, I'd be pretty upset about it too. It's perfectly normal."

"It is?" Tim inquired hesitantly.

Sometimes David forgot how new Tim was at negotiating the volatile landscape of human emotions. "Yeah. Completely." They were both silent for a moment, only the chirping of birds and the omnipresent lapping of water against the nearby shoreline breaking the quiet. David playfully nudged Tim's shoulder with his. "You want me to kick his ass?"

Tim's gaze flew toward him, his pretty features radiating shock at the unexpected suggestion. Suddenly Tim laughed, having apparently gotten the joke, and David felt warmth spread in the region of his heart. "No, you don't have to do that," he said, refusing the offer with an amused shake of his head.

"Okay, then," David said, chuckling, finding Tim's delight contagious. "Why don't we finish our breakfast inside?"

Tim looked undecided for a moment, but he soon gathered up his plate and stood. David followed closely behind as Tim walked back into the house. Anderson and Larson were still standing in front of the kitchen window, speaking with low intensity. They looked up immediately when David and Tim came into the kitchen. Larson squared his shoulders as Anderson fixed him with a pregnant stare.

"Look, Tim," he began, this time without attaching any double meaning to the name. "I should apologize. I didn't realize everything you've been through since I left the project. Paul was right to get you out of there when he did. General Woodard would have turned you into a soulless monster if he could have." The corner of Larson's mouth turned up in a smile that was really more of a grimace. "I'm glad he didn't succeed."

Tim nodded in silent acknowledgement of the apology, but David wasn't ready to let it go so easily. "You should have never blamed Tim in the first place. No kid ever asks for the situation he's born into."

"Look, Conley, I'm admitting I was wrong. Okay?" Larson moved his head from side to side as though to relieve the tension in his neck. "The TM project had such promise when it started. I was pissed at how it devolved into a horror show."

Anderson stood leaning back against the curtain covering the window, his arms folded across his chest as he watched Larson squirm. "If you have a problem with anyone, Mitch, it's with me. I'm sorry about Samantha. More than I can ever properly express." He looked down at the floor. "I know how you felt about her."

Larson's blunt features twisted with an expression of profound pain. Samantha must have been the surrogate Anderson had mentioned earlier. David felt a swell of sympathy for the former agent.

"I loved her," Larson grated, "and you took her from me, Paul. You fucking took her from me!"

Tim tensed, his gaze fixed intently on Larson as though preparing to protect his creator from a perceived threat. David wrapped his hand around Tim's arm and squeezed, hoping to reassure him that Anderson wasn't in any physical danger. He couldn't speak to the old man's emotional well-being. To his relief, Tim relaxed, though his attention never wavered from the confrontation going on in front of him.

"Yes, I did," Anderson replied baldly. Larson growled and clenched his jaw, but to his credit, Anderson stood his ground before the menacing display. "I know I can never right the wrong I have done you, Mitch. That is my cross to bear. But I will do my best to take down the organization behind it all, and for that, I need your help."

David stared at Anderson in disbelief. He was amazed at the man's sheer audacity in admitting he was to blame for killing his friend's lover, and then turning around and begging Larson's help in waging his private war. And yet, David wasn't at all surprised when the former agent blew out a heavy breath and nodded.

"You know I will, you crazy son of a bitch." Larson bared his teeth. "Besides, how can I put this all on you when I'm the one who kept quiet about the TM project even after I transferred out? I could have leaked the whole damn thing, but I didn't. I will have to live with *that*." Larson turned suddenly and stalked toward the front door. "Come on. It's high time I showed you the stash of toys I brought for you."

Tim stayed close to Anderson as they followed Larson outside, obviously trying to keep himself positioned between the ex-CIA agent and his mentor. Larson had parked his SUV next to Marcus's Civic and was standing next to the open rear doors. Anderson smiled reassuringly at Tim and moved to join his friend. Tim's expression darkened, but he didn't interfere.

Anderson bent over to look at whatever Larson had stowed in the back of his car. After a moment, he whistled and raised his head to glance up at Larson, eyebrows lifted in surprise. "I'm impressed, Mitch. This is quite a haul."

David reached them a step behind Tim, and his heart rose into his throat when he saw what Larson had hidden beneath the rear floor mat of the SUV. Tim reached into the trunk and pulled out a rifle, the matte black finish lending the gun an industrial aspect. David felt uneasy at how at home the deadly weapon seemed in Tim's hands. The rifle was one of three that were laid out in a bag beside an assortment of handguns, grenades, knives, and boxes of ammunition. And that was only what David was able to recognize. He also noticed two black duffel bags and a smaller forest-green bag sitting among the arsenal.

"What's in there?"

"Laser sights, silencers, and a few electronic gadgets you might need." Larson swatted David's hand away as he went to reach for one of the bags.

David laughed sharply, the noise sounding uneasy and unnatural to his own ears. "What, no bulletproof vests?"

"Sorry," Larson said. "I didn't have any body armor lying around, and Kevlar isn't going to help you against the rounds Woodard's goons will be packing." He shot David an assessing glance. "You ever use a gun, Conley?"

David shrugged. "Well, every summer my dad—"

He broke off when Tim ejected the magazine from the rifle and examined it briefly before replacing it with a hard snap. Unzipping one of the duffels, Tim retrieved a long metal cylinder and swiftly attached it to the end of the barrel. He raised the weapon to his shoulder and aimed at a tree at the edge of the clearing that fronted the cabin. Without a word, he fired off a half dozen rounds, each one hitting the tree dead in the exact same spot. Lowering the gun, Tim looked it over and gave a nod of what David's brain distractedly recognized as approval.

Larson was equally impressed, if his slack-jawed expression was anything to go by. "Hell, kid. You're the real deal, aren't you?" He shook his head. "Gotta hand it to Woodard. The man knows how to train soldiers."

"Where did you get all of this?" David asked, gesturing weakly toward the deadly cache.

"Keep it up at my brother's place."

David blinked at Larson. "Your brother's place? What, he's fine with you hiding weapons in his garage?"

"David—" Anderson said warningly.

"It's okay, Paul. He couldn't know, and he's right. Samuel would have been pissed to know I had all of this shit in his house." Larson grinned at David. "I moved in with my brother, Samuel, up in Arkansas after I retired from the Agency. He died a few years ago. Massive coronary at fifty-four. Jerk never did take care of himself."

David was horrified at his insensitive remark, understanding too late why Anderson had attempted to caution him. "Larson, I'm sorry—"

The large man waved away his apology. "Don't sweat it. Anyway, he left me his place in his will. He wasn't married, and he didn't have any kids, so I guess I was the logical beneficiary. Our parents are long gone."

Once again, David suddenly felt sorry for Larson. The man was completely alone in the world. David might not have any siblings, and he hadn't spoken to his father in years, but he was close to his mother. And he had Tim, or he had once. Putting a stop to that line of thought, David watched as Larson began to zip up the bags holding what he'd euphemistically called "toys." It was no wonder the former agent had been so torn up about losing the woman he'd fallen in love with. If things had been different, maybe Larson would have been able to enjoy the rest of his years with the ill-fated Samantha.

"This will do nicely, Mitch. But we're also going to need explosives."

Tired of feeling so out of his depth, David struggled not to react to Anderson's matter-of-fact request.

Larson nodded. "Yeah, I figured. Unfortunately, I forgot to pack C4 in my trunk," he said with a bark of laughter.

David failed to see the humor in the situation. "Is that really necessary?" he asked, dismayed at the prospect that explosives might play a role in their as-yet-to-be-determined plans.

Anderson shrugged. "They could come in handy as a means of distraction… or in a more direct way."

Larson scratched at the back of his head. "I've kept in touch with several useful contacts. It will take me at least five or six days, but if you can wait, I can get you the materials."

"I know what we need. A stop at a hardware store should suffice."

They all stared at Tim for a long moment, though David was the only one expressing any surprise at his suggestion.

"I keep forgetting what, or rather who, you really are." Larson shook his head. "Didn't know you had such an eye for making pretty boys, Paul," he added with a lewd grin.

"I had my reasons," the scientist returned without inflection.

Bristling, David clenched his jaw and burned a hole into Larson's back as the larger man turned to shut the trunk. "Are we done here?" he asked peevishly.

Larson ignored him. "Take my car," he offered. "I'll drive the Civic back to my place."

"There may be an APB out on the stolen plates," Anderson cautioned.

"Then I'll make sure to drive at the speed limit." Larson paused before reaching out and pulling Anderson into a tight hug. "It was good to see you, Paul. Even though you're the biggest bastard I've ever had the displeasure to know."

Anderson's grin looked only somewhat forced. "Surely I'm not worse than Woodard."

Larson laughed. "True enough, or than that ex-wife of yours." It was the first time he had mentioned Talbot. "Is she still mixed up in all of this?"

Anderson sighed. "Unfortunately. I'm certain she wants me dead even more than the general does."

"I don't envy you. Coleen was a real looker, but damn, what a ball breaker she turned out to be." Larson shifted awkwardly as though dithering over what he wanted to say. "Cody broke her, didn't he?"

"Yes."

Larson nodded at the terse response. He glanced at Tim and pursed his lips. "I don't know what to make of you yet, but you keep this guy out of trouble, you hear?" Without waiting for Tim to respond, Larson turned and headed for the sedan, obviously deciding David wasn't worth any parting words.

Larson exchanged keys with Anderson and drove off without any fanfare. The scientist stood in the clearing long enough to watch the dark blue car reach the end of the access road and turn out of sight. David wondered what must be going through Anderson's mind after the uncomfortably revealing meeting. But whatever distress Anderson might have been feeling, none of it showed on his face as he turned back toward the cabin.

"We have what we came here for," he said as he reached the porch. "We should also get going. It's doubtful Woodard's people could find us here, since the general has no idea Mitch and I kept in touch after he left the project. But we shouldn't press our luck."

David glanced uneasily at the SUV. "Are we really going to drive around with all that stuff in the back?"

"I don't see as we have much choice," Anderson replied. He stopped inside the front door and turned to look at David. "I hope you aren't under any illusions that what we're about to attempt will be simple. Believe me, we will likely need everything Mitch has brought us when it's all said and done."

"Yeah, I get that," David answered testily. "It's just—"

"*Have* you ever fired a gun before, David?" Tim asked, repeating Larson's question in a less taunting manner.

David felt a moment of embarrassment that Tim so easily guessed the root of his uneasiness, though he was glad he could at least save some face. "Sure. Like I was trying to say, my dad took me hunting almost every summer from the time I was twelve until I… left for college." He hadn't mentioned his difficulties with his father to Anderson during their time in captivity and didn't want to get into it right then. "We only used double-barreled shotguns, though. I wasn't a bad shot, but I don't have any experience with this military-grade stuff."

Anderson nodded, his demeanor blessedly free of judgment. "It will take a while to clean up and pack everything we'll need to take with us. The spaghetti is still good, so I think we should take some for the road." He looked knowingly at his protégé. "Tim, why don't you show David the finer points of how to use the assault rifles? We might not have the chance later to get him up to speed."

David raised a skeptical eyebrow. "What do you mean, 'we'? Don't tell me you're some kind of expert marksman too."

Anderson merely smiled cryptically and disappeared into the cabin.

"He's a very good shot," Tim said matter-of-factly.

David sighed. "Of course he is. Probably learned while working for the CIA."

"That would be my guess."

"I was kidding," David deadpanned. Tim looked at him blankly. "Never mind. So, where do you want to do this?"

Tim tilted his chin to the lines of trees in back of the cabin. "There shouldn't be anyone over that way. The main hiking trails are on the far side of the beach."

The mention of hiking immediately brought to David's mind the dream that had landed him on the floor that morning, aching and horny. "Yeah, okay," he said in a choked voice. Tim glanced at him curiously, but he shook his head dismissively and waved a hand toward the trees. "After you."

Tim rummaged in the back of the SUV and took out a couple of boxes. "These are the magazines for the rifles," he explained. He tossed them at David, who scrambled not to drop them, before retrieving the bag holding the guns. David fumbled one of the boxes as he tried and failed not to stare at the way the denim of Tim's borrowed jeans pulled across his ass when he leaned into the open compartment. Grabbing two different models of rifles out of the trunk, Tim slammed the rear door of the SUV closed with his foot and headed for the dense growth beyond the cabin. David trudged behind, wondering what he was letting himself in for.

They walked for a good ten minutes until they reached a small clearing. The location was far too reminiscent of David's nighttime fantasy for comfort. Clearing his throat, he looked around as though he were actually interested in the scenery.

"Nice and quiet out here," he tossed out.

Tim nodded. "We shouldn't be disturbed. We'd be in trouble if the park wardens caught us shooting, since we don't have a permit for these." He stopped next to a tree and leaned one of the rifles against it. The deadly black casing appeared even more unnatural in contrast to the soft brown of the Chinese pistache. Tim turned to David and held out a hand. "Let me have the one that says 5.56."

David glanced down at the boxes and handed over the one with the correct label. "That's the type of ammunition?"

"Yes." Tim opened the carton and pulled out a magazine. Setting the box on the ground, he held up the remaining gun and the cartridge. "This is a Sig 516. The other one is a Colt M4." Tim looked at David expectantly. "Do you know how to load the magazine?" He waited patiently as David took the rifle and the clip from him.

David shrugged. "Nothing too fancy is required to load a double-barreled shotgun. So, no."

"Here." Tim moved closer until he was standing next to David. "You just slide it into the receiver." Taking the weapon and the cartridge, Tim demonstrated, chambering the magazine into the receiving slot with a single smooth motion. "To take it out, pop the release here." He pressed a finger against the lever situated immediately behind the cartridge, and it fell out into his hand. "Now, you try it."

"Like this?" David tried to copy Tim's actions, but his first attempt ended with him missing the magazine receptacle. "Doing this blind is harder than it looks," he said with a sheepish smile.

Tim returned the smile, and David felt himself begin to relax. Ever since Larson's arrival, Tim had been in what David internally thought of as "robotic mode," save for his brief breakdown during breakfast. He was relieved to see some emotion on the kid's face, and even more so, to see one that didn't involve tears.

"Don't try to do it without looking." Tim tilted the Sig so David could see the opening in the rifle's undercarriage. "The clip fits in right there."

David's second attempt was a success and earned him an even brighter smile from his impromptu tutor. "So how do I shoot it?" He held the stock awkwardly under his arm and placed his finger on the trigger.

"No," Tim said quickly. "Place the butt against you, like this." He repositioned the gun so the flat part of the piece extending from the back of the weapon was pressed into David's shoulder.

"That feels even weirder," David complained. Tim smirked at him, and David found himself enraptured by the never-before-seen expression. Resisting the urge to kiss the teasing grin away, he tried to get used to the feel of the rifle in his hands. "So how do I aim?"

Tim pointed to a spot midway along the top of the stock where a piece of metal curved up on either side. "If we had a scope or sight, it would go here. Father Paul's friend said he brought a few."

David lowered the Sig and studied Tim closely. "Are you feeling better now?"

Tim stared at him in confusion for a moment before his expression cleared. "You mean with what Mr. Larson said about me?" Tim lifted a shoulder in a shrug. "I can't help how he feels."

The mix of maturity and adolescent insouciance brought a smile to David's lips. "You're right, you can't. All you can do is prove to him that you're worthy of his respect." He chuckled. "I think you went a long way toward that when he saw how well you handled one of these." David gestured with the Sig. "Figures. You military types are all the same," he teased, a grin taking any potential sting out of the taunt. Tim laughed, the sound going instantly to David's cock. He groaned and forcibly dragged his mind out of the gutter. "So you were showing me how to use this thing?"

Tim moved the weapon back into its former place against David's shoulder. "Look along the barrel through where the sight would be. Keep both eyes open," he instructed when David closed one of them. "Since you're not using a sight, you don't want to reduce your depth perception. Now," he continued when David complied, "aim at that tree and slowly squeeze the trigger."

David felt pretty confident until the trunk that splintered was the one to the right of where he was aiming. "Shit."

"That's okay," Tim replied encouragingly. "Try it again, and this time, relax."

Two more attempts resulted in one more shattered tree trunk, though again, not the one he was aiming for. The second shot ended up somewhere out in the woods, never to be seen again.

Lowering the rifle, David pursed his lips in disgust. "Maybe I should stick to driving the getaway van," he quipped.

Tim shook his head. "No. I believe I see the problem." He motioned for David to raise the gun back into position. "This time, don't jerk so hard on the trigger. It's making the barrel move to the side. The trigger is pretty sensitive. A gentle squeeze will do."

"I think I understand," David replied as he looked along the sightline.

"Square your stance a bit more. Here, like this."

Any confidence David had gained vanished as Tim moved to stand directly behind him. The lithe figure radiated heat that seemed to flow past the inadequate barrier of David's clothes. He immediately began to sweat, both from the excess warmth of the body standing so close to his and from the instant revving of his libido into high gear.

Apparently oblivious to his student's turmoil, Tim wrapped his arms around David to cover his hands on the gun. "Spread your feet a little," he instructed, kicking David's feet apart with his own. "Now, look down the sightline and squeeze the trigger."

David sincerely tried to pay close attention to what Tim was saying rather than to how tightly he was now pressed against his back. Not that he succeeded too well. A bead of moisture coursed down from his temple as his cock pushed painfully against the confines of his jeans. Yet, somehow, he managed to nail his intended target, the pistache losing a layer of bark to the powerful 5.56 round.

"There you go," Tim praised. "That was perfect."

David was about to thank him when he noticed the telltale bulge pressing against his butt. It simultaneously did him a world of good and put him in a world of hurt to know he wasn't the only one affected by the close contact. When he turned around, Tim was gazing at him with sparkling eyes full of pride. His cheeks were flushed pink, and his lips were parted in a pleased smile. He looked eminently fuckable, the impression only enhanced by the way he shifted his gaze down to stare at David's mouth.

So many tree trunks, so little time. The dream came flooding back in excruciating detail, reminding David of how similar their present circumstances were to his flight of lustful fancy. Ever since they'd fled from the Facility, he'd been worried about coming on too strong, about forcing his own feelings onto Tim when all the kid wanted from him was help and acceptance. But right then he had no doubt that, if he were to press Tim against the nearest tree and rip off his clothes, he wouldn't be turned away. Far from it. And yet, the old hesitancy reared its prudish head—would it be right to give in to his emotions or should he be the adult and not rush into anything? It wasn't like this was the ideal time to rekindle their romance. They were running from a group of very determined military goons and were planning to break into a place that was probably teeming with highly trained soldiers who wouldn't quibble at shooting first and asking questions never.

"David," Tim whispered before licking his lips nervously and sending every high-minded thought straight out of David's head.

Grabbing Tim's arm, David began to pull him into a kiss he was certain would set the forest around them on fire.

"Tim! David! Are you out here?" The voice rang out from the direction of the cabin. "We need to get going."

The remaining inch between their lips might as well have been miles. "Fuck," David swore. He closed his eyes, not sure whether he wanted to thank Anderson or to beat the shit out of him.

"David," Tim murmured again, his husky tone indicating that he was more than willing to ignore the scientist if David was.

"Later," David rasped. Clearing his throat, he turned in the direction from which they'd come. "Father Paul is right," he said. "It's time to leave." He slung the Sig over his shoulder and headed out of the clearing with Tim's gaze burning into his back.

WOODARD'S MOUTH twisted with distaste as he stepped out of the Jeep. *How the mighty have fallen*, he though acidly. Part of him was amused to imagine Anderson and his companions having to resort to such filthy accommodations. But the emotion was a distant second to his aggravation that it had taken the search team so long to catch up with the escapees after losing them in Magnum. Not wanting a repeat of that debacle, he'd decided to oversee the reconnaissance of the hotel personally. It wasn't a significant detour from his route to Illinois where he was headed to supervise the preparations he'd hoped wouldn't be necessary. Given that Anderson had yet again gotten the jump on them, however, it appeared more and more likely he wouldn't be able to avoid going to the secondary base as Talbot had requested.

"Sir." Lieutenant Farley was waiting for him at the door leading to the motel's reception area.

"I don't appreciate how long this took, Lieutenant," he growled. "I gave you this detail because I expected more from you."

She didn't flicker an eyelash at the dressing-down. "Without the tracker, we were forced to resort to more time-consuming methods. I figured they would seek a room somewhere, but it was impossible to anticipate how far they would travel before stopping. Unfortunately, there are numerous hotels and motels in this part of the state."

"I need results, Farley, not excuses." Woodard noted the distinct lack of a civilian presence in the motel's parking lot aside from a skinny, frightened man who was standing in the doorway frantically drawing on a cigarette as he stared at the large gathering of uniformed soldiers. He pointed to the man with his chin. "Is that the manager?"

"Yes, sir."

"Did he give you anything useful?" He didn't wait for her to respond before deciding to get the information straight from the horse's mouth. The whites of the manager's bulging eyes gleamed obscenely in the sunlight as Woodard approached him with the lieutenant following close on his heels. He scowled in revulsion, the manager's terrified expression reminding him why he hated dealing with civvies. Standing a safe distance away in case the man suddenly pissed himself, he attempted to arrange his features into something less intimidating.

"This is Mr. Parsons," Farley said by way of introduction.

"Mr. Parsons," Woodard echoed, pretending he gave a shit. "I hear you have some knowledge concerning a trio of fugitives we're looking for."

"N-no," the manager stuttered. "Like I told the lady, I didn't see three guys together. Only an old man by himself."

"Describe him," Woodard snapped.

Parsons glanced uncertainly at Farley. "I already told her—"

Woodard struggled to tamp down his exasperation. "Tell it again." He took a deep breath and curved his lips in an approximation of a smile. "I only want to be sure you saw the man we're looking for."

"Um, he was old," the manager repeated unhelpfully. "Gray hair, brown eyes. Maybe in his mid-to-late seventies?" Parsons shrugged. "I ain't so good at telling people's ages."

The description fit Anderson, but Woodard wanted to make sure they were on the right track. "Did you see the vehicle he arrived in?"

"Nah." He must have parked it around back before going to check in. "And I never saw no ID or nothin'," the manager added, anticipating what he thought would be the next question. "He paid cash."

"Of course he did," Woodard grated. He'd never taken the scientist for such a fool as to give himself away so easily, not that Anderson had had any identification to use, having fled from the Facility with nothing but the clothes on his back. He must have gotten the money from that Marcus woman. Talbot had told him her ex and the Indian doctor were friends, but interrogating her had gotten them nowhere. Farley had wisely chosen to broaden her search rather than waste time being more forceful in interrogating Marcus. Woodard pressed his lips into a tight line. He'd figured Anderson hadn't had time to ditch Marcus's car before reaching the motel, judging by when the register said he'd checked in. But he wasn't pleased with the manager's inability to definitively confirm whether Anderson had, indeed, been there. Before he could think of another line of question, he looked over at the sound of tires squealing as a Jeep pulled hurriedly into the lot.

"General, we found something!"

Woodard headed toward the two soldiers who had just arrived, Farley once again in tow. The man was talking into the radio installed in his Jeep while his female partner jogged over to meet them. The woman was holding a white, rectangular piece of metal with numbers and letters embossed into the surface. Curiosity piqued, Woodard studied the dirty license plate.

"Sir, we found this in a gas station about a mile and a half up the road. Jones is calling it in right now." She looked back toward the Jeep as the other soldier tossed the radio receiver onto the seat.

"The plates belong to Dr. Ruth Marcus," her partner called out.

Woodard clenched his fist. "So he didn't ditch the car, just its tags." On a hunch, he looked around the lot. His gaze focused on a shit brown Mazda that was conspicuously missing its plates. "Who owns that car?" he asked the manager, pointing toward the rusted vehicle.

The man shrugged. "I don't know. It's been sitting there for a few weeks now." He turned his head to spit. "Guess the owner abandoned it. I should probably get it towed or somethin'."

Woodard glared at him. "You do that." He cursed under his breath. Without knowing the number of the license plate Anderson stole, putting a notice out to state law enforcement would be basically useless. "Keep looking for the Civic, Lieutenant," he ordered. Woodard spun back toward his own vehicle, satisfied they'd done all they could here.

"Dr. Anderson has probably ditched the car by now, sir," Farley cautioned as she kept pace with him. "Searching for it might be a dead end."

Woodard paused to glare at her. "We don't know that for certain. You have your orders, Lieutenant. And if you do find the car abandoned, we'll go from there."

Farley's hesitation was evident only from the sudden narrowing of her striking green eyes. "Sir, the farther they get, the larger an area we have to cover. I don't have the personnel to conduct a thorough radial search."

"We both know where Anderson is going," Woodard growled, spearing her with an icy glare. "He may make a detour or two, but you can bet he's headed to the secondary facility. Concentrate your efforts along the northeast corridor between here and the base. And don't forget the other part of the equation—Conley. The file we put together on him said he's from Oklahoma. Use what we know about him to narrow down the possibilities."

Farley's gaze hardened with a determined glint. "Yes, General. I won't let you down."

Woodard stared at her for a long moment. "See to it that you don't, Lieutenant. I won't stand for failure. Not when it comes to something this important." He had barely turned away before she was barking out orders to her team. Woodard dismissed her from his thoughts as he walked back toward his vehicle. The long miles to southern Illinois would give him plenty of time to ponder all the ways he would torture Anderson once they found him, before he finally gave the bastard the mercy of death.

SIXTEEN

FOR THE fifth time in as many minutes, I caught myself staring at the way the sun picked out the gold strands in David's hair. He was driving, and Father Paul had naturally claimed the front seat, so I was relegated to the back. I stretched my legs out and sat with my head resting against the passenger side window. My position gave me an excellent view of David's profile, and I watched him through lowered lashes. There certainly wasn't anything else to distract me. North central Oklahoma was flat and dull, and the monotony gave me too much time to let my mind wander. It always ended up back in the same place.

The sensation of being pressed flush against David's back, my erection wantonly giving me away, was just as strong as it had been when we'd left the cabin hours ago. And David had been equally affected, if the intriguing distortion that had bulged out the zipper of his jeans was any indication. I couldn't help but wonder what might have happened had Father Paul not interrupted the shooting lesson. Maybe I could have finally overcome David's reticence to rekindling our physical relationship. Now that I knew how it felt to be with him, I didn't relish the return of the frustration I thought I'd seen the last of the night General Woodard had crashed in and ruined it all.

I sighed and shut my eyes to the tantalizing view. Even as dull to emotional clues as I often was, I knew it wasn't the time to push, not when we had so many other things to worry about. But if we survived this—when we survived—I promised myself I wouldn't let David go without a fight. I'd grown incredibly fond of him during the months we lived together, though I hadn't had the emotional vocabulary to express the sentiment at the time. But when I thought he might die at the hands of our young friend's self-loathing father, I'd realized how deep my feelings went. I had been terrified David would turn me away after I'd found the courage to confess my love. Instead, he had given me more than I could have dreamed possible.

"You weren't serious, were you?"

David and Father Paul had been chatting aimlessly for a while, but I tuned in to the conversation at the sudden tension in David's tone.

"What you said about us needing explosives. I mean, seems to me Larson gave us plenty to work with." David glanced at the rearview mirror as though he could see the weapons hidden in the back of the SUV. His gaze met mine briefly before he glanced away nervously. I couldn't tell whether his skittishness was due to the topic or what had almost happened between us in the woods.

"I'm afraid I was. We'll need more than guns." Father Paul looked up from the map he'd picked up at our last gas stop and glanced at a passing road sign. "We should be able to get everything we need in Springfield. I'd rather make sure we're not close to any major towns while Tim does the actual fabrication." He looked back down at the map. "If we keep east on Route 60, we can pick up the interstate. It will take us straight through to Missouri."

David threw a quick glance at the map before turning his attention back to the road. "You mean I-44?"

Father Paul hummed in affirmation. "That's right, you grew up in Oklahoma, though you never said exactly where. Are you familiar with this area?"

"You know," David said quickly, "it would make more sense to head up to Kansas and then cut over into Missouri from there to pick up I-44. See?" he added, pointing to a sign hanging over the road about a quarter of a mile ahead. "We can take US-169 north from here through South Coffeyville."

I stared at David, noting the sheen of perspiration forming on his skin. His face had lost some of its healthy ruddiness, and his knuckles showed a hint of white from the tightness of his grip on the steering wheel. Though I wasn't necessarily the best judge, it wasn't hard to deduce that he was extremely uneasy about something.

Father Paul's brow wrinkled in confusion. "That doesn't make sense. I'd say something about two points and a straight line, but I'm sure you already know that. We lost quite a bit of time waiting for Mitch. There's no point in giving Woodard more opportunity to prepare for us than he's already had." He turned to give David his full attention. "Is there something you want to tell us?"

"Do you honestly think the general knows we're headed to the Illinois base?" David asked. "I mean, it's a pretty crazy plan when you stop to think about it—"

"David." Father Paul's tone was soft but insistent.

I met David's glance in the rearview mirror for a second time. Father Paul was right. David was hiding something, though I couldn't imagine what had him so distressed. I stared back, hoping my expression was as encouraging as I intended.

Seeing he was outnumbered, David slumped in the driver's seat and thumped his head back against the headrest. "It's nothing, really. Just…."

"Just, what?" I prompted softly. This time he turned his head for an instant to look back at me directly.

"My folks live in Vinita."

I looked out of the window in time to see a sign indicating that Vinita, Oklahoma was a mere thirty miles away. David's odd behavior suddenly made complete sense. I vividly remembered a disturbing incident I'd witnessed in David's store between a high school baseball player and his obnoxiously disappointed father. The man had been livid at his son's lack of prowess on the field, and he'd taken it out on the mortified teen in an ugly and very public way. After David had politely read the man the riot act, he'd told me about his difficulties with his own father. I hadn't understood the full context at the time, but now I knew he had been referring to the poor way his father had reacted to him coming out as gay. David had mentioned he hadn't been back home or seen his father since leaving for college over thirteen years before. While I had fond memories of David's mother after her visit to Texas a couple of months earlier, I had no similar positive thoughts to associate with the paternal half of his parentage.

"That's convenient," Father Paul said, noticing the same sign I had seen. "We'd be wise to save money on room and board while we can. I promise you, David, we won't impose on them for long. Woodard surely knows who your parents are, though I doubt he'd expect us to actually seek them out. Still, it wouldn't do to expose them to any unnecessary danger." He nodded to himself. "Yes, a night or two at the most, then we'll be on our way."

"Father Paul," I interrupted before my mentor could warm too much to his impromptu plan. "I think we should take David's advice if he thinks going north would be the better option."

The rearview mirror reflected David's pained look back to me, but he simply shook his head and sighed. "No, kid, he's right. I'm just being an idiot." He moved his shoulders awkwardly as though trying to stretch them. "Besides, it will be good to see Mom again."

Father Paul stared at David curiously. "Clearly I'm missing something."

"I'm, um…." David shifted uneasily in his seat. "I'm not on the best terms with my father."

Father Paul blinked, his eyes rounding with surprise. "Oh. I do apologize, David, for my presumption. If you think it best we don't go to your parents', then, of course, I understand."

"It's not like they won't let us in. Or, at least my mother will." David's expression was unsure as he glanced quickly at Father Paul. "Are you really sure it's safe, though? I don't want to bring any trouble down on them."

"I've done all I can think of to throw Woodard off our trail," Father Paul replied. "I can't be 100 percent certain I've been successful, of course, but if we don't stay too long, it should be safe enough for now. It would be a waste of resources for Woodard to try and stake out every possible place we might stop between Greer and St. Louis. No, I'm sure he's focusing his efforts on intercepting us in Illinois."

"Gee, that's comforting," David quipped. He was silent for a long moment, but when he finally nodded, I could tell he'd made a decision. "Okay, we'll do it your way, Doc." His lips curved up in the semblance of a smile. "It will be nice to sleep on a real bed again, and my mom is an amazing cook."

There was no further conversation as the miles closed between us and Vinita. David turned on the radio after a few minutes of silence, and the twangy sounds of country filled the car. I wondered what Suzanna would say when she learned the truth about me. I had no doubts she would persuade me to tell her everything. I'd been subjected to her unique form of subtle interrogation at our first meeting, and I'd likely fare no better this time than I had then. Especially now that the genie of my emotions had been permanently let out of the bottle. Suzanna was as much to thank for that as anyone. She'd offered me the addictive experience of motherly warmth, and I craved the prospect of feeling it again.

David's father, however, was a complete unknown besides what I'd been told. And what I'd learned didn't make me inclined to look upon the man favorably. Still, I told myself, it was best to reserve judgment until I could form my own opinion. It had been a long time, after all, since David had left home, and I knew better than most how much a person could change.

Forty minutes later, David pulled up in front of an unassuming split-level bungalow. Tan-colored vinyl siding contrasted pleasantly with brick-red trim around the doors and windows, the dark color echoed in the garage door. A porch stretched back along the right side of the house. A profusion of flowers was planted in a carefully arranged border around the modest, neatly manicured lawn. The extent of the property was demarcated from its neighbor with a row of dark green hedges. I could easily imagine Suzanna being responsible for the homey and welcoming effect. I wondered what David had been like, growing from a child to a man in this unassuming place.

"Looks like we caught them at home," Father Paul observed, nodding toward the silver four-door sedan parked in the driveway.

"Yeah," David mumbled, "that's great."

I followed David and Father Paul as they got out of the car. The sound of the SUV doors closing must have caught the attention of whoever was inside. I saw a curtain twitch in the window immediately to the right of the front door. The door swung open a second later, revealing a short plump woman with graying blonde hair and stunned blue eyes.

"David?" she breathed.

"Hiya, Ma." David raised a hand in response, his lips quirking in a sheepish grin.

Suzanna's hand flew up to cover her mouth. She stared at her son like she was seeing a ghost. "My God, David! I've been trying to reach you for weeks. No one at the store knew where you were. I even called the police!" Tears streamed down her rosy cheeks. "Where have you been?" she yelled, her voice a mixture of worried anger and profound relief.

David rushed to her and pulled her into his arms in lieu of answering. She clung to him tightly, sobbing into his chest. "I'm sorry, Ma," he said so softly even I had to strain to hear. "It's a long story, but I promise, I'll tell you everything."

He leaned back far enough to gaze down at his mother's ravaged face, his features twisting with guilt. I felt a thousandfold worse for having contributed to both mother and son's distress.

David glanced past her into the house. "Is Dad home?"

"No." Suzanna shook her head. "He went out with Larry and Frank to the bowling alley. He won't be home for a while." She wiped away the tears staining her face and seemed to notice for the first time they weren't alone. Her expression fell into shock for a second time when she saw who David was with. "Tim? Is that you?"

"It's all my fault, what happened to David." The words fell from my lips before I could censor them, but as I'd discovered back during our first encounter, lying to this woman was the last thing I ever wanted to do. Part of me was relieved I would finally be able to lay that particular burden to rest, even though it meant exposing her to things she was better off not knowing.

Lines of confusion furrowed her formerly smooth brow. "What on earth are you talking about? And who are you?" she added, directing the last at Father Paul.

"My name is Paul Anderson, Mrs. Conley," he replied. "I'm Tim's creator, for lack of a better word," he explained, taking his cue from me to be completely honest.

"Ma, let's go inside. It's not safe to stand out here on the street."

She looked up at her son with a glint in her eye that demanded answers, but she wisely yielded to his request. "Come on in, all of you. I just took a pie out of the oven."

"What kind?" I asked. The warmth of her smile seemed to drain all the tension of the past few days out of me.

"Blueberry," Suzanna chuckled. "I see some things haven't changed since I last saw you, Tim. Still a bottomless pit?"

I shrugged, not at all apologetically. "Yes, ma'am."

"I told you about that."

She accompanied her soft rebuke concerning my habit of addressing her formally with a tap on my forehead as we followed David into the house. I smiled shyly as I waited for her to close the door behind Father Paul. I noted my mentor watching our exchange with pleased interest.

Suzanna wouldn't let us speak another word beyond telling her how big of a slice we wanted of the piping hot dessert she'd set to cool on the top of the stove. Once we were settled with pie, bowls of vanilla ice cream, and glasses of ice water, she took a chair for herself, sitting close to her son.

"All right, someone had better tell me what's going on right this instant." She glared at David. "How could you simply up and vanish like that without a word to anyone? Do you have any idea how worried I was?" She sniffed, blue eyes so much like her son's shimmering with fresh tears.

"What did the folks at the BBW tell you?" David asked.

I listened raptly, equally curious to learn what David's employees had made of our disappearance.

"I spoke with your manager, Patricia Tipton. She was beside herself with worry when I called. She said she hadn't seen you since the night of some incident at Bobby's house." Suzanna glanced at me before looking back at her son. "He'd told her that you two saved him and his mother? What's that all about?"

David shook his head. "A story for another time. What else did Patricia say?"

Suzanna frowned. "That's all. I guess she spoke to Bobby when he called in the next day to ask if he could take a week off work. Apparently he'd tried to reach you and couldn't. She told him she'd ask you when she saw you, but she never did." She glared at David, her patience obviously beginning to run thin. "So where were you?"

"We were taken prisoner," I said bluntly as David dithered over how to respond.

Nonplussed, Suzanna blinked at me. "Taken prisoner?" she echoed, her voice growing shrill. "By who? For what?"

I could think of no other way to explain than to be completely direct. "By the military research division in charge of the project that created me."

Suzanna looked to her son, a hesitant smile forming on her lips as though she was waiting for him to let her in on the joke.

David returned her gaze steadily. "He's telling you the truth, Ma."

She gaped at him for a moment before spearing Father Paul with a glare. "And you? Who are you really?" she demanded. "You said you were Tim's 'creator,' but what in the hell does that mean?" David choked at her use of profanity, but an irritated glance from her shut him up. "How are you involved in all of this?" she said, returning to her interrogation.

"Well," Father Paul replied, "to be precise, I designed Tim's genome to express specific traits."

"What sort of traits?" Whatever confusion Suzanna was experiencing at the scientific jargon, she hid it well.

"Superior strength and agility. Enhanced sensory perception. Superior mental acuity. In other words, Tim is—"

"Perfect," David finished. I felt myself blush under the weight of his stare.

Suzanna frowned. "I don't understand. Why would anyone do such a thing?"

"To create an invincible breed of soldier, Mrs. Conley. Tim was designed to be the perfect weapon."

"My God," she whispered.

"But Father Paul helped me escape," I said, not wanting Suzanna to think of the scientist as the bad guy in all this. "That's how David found me."

Understanding dawned on her face, though it did little to alleviate the horror in her gaze. "He said you were a hitchhiker he'd picked up."

"Yes," I affirmed around a mouthful of pie.

Suzanna sat back heavily in her chair, barely reacting when David put an arm around her shoulders.

"Are you okay?" he asked.

"Tim, you said the people in charge of you captured you?" she inquired, ignoring her son's obviously pointless question regarding her mental state. "Both of you?"

I nodded. "They wanted to use David as leverage against me to…." I sought the best way to phrase it. "To assist with my retraining."

Suzanna stared at me for a long moment. "Do I want to know what that means?"

I dropped my gaze to my pie in silent response.

"Right," she said. "So, how did you escape? I take it you were with them," she added, glancing toward Father Paul.

"Tim got us out," David explained. "All of us. Plus, he destroyed the place where we were being held."

Technically the computer did it, I thought, but I figured the clarification was unnecessary.

"I'd say I understand, but I don't. Not really." Suzanna rested her head against her son's shoulder. "Even so, all I need to know right now is that you're safe." When no one spoke, Suzanna closed her eyes. "Except you're not, are you?"

"Not yet," David confirmed.

"We're heading somewhere to hopefully finish this once and for all," Father Paul said vaguely. When Suzanna looked at him searchingly, he shook his head. "It's best you don't ask any more questions. We were hoping we could stay here for a day or so before continuing on our way."

Suzanna shot upright, dismay etched on her face as she looked up at her son. "You're leaving so soon?"

"Sorry, Ma, but we have to. The people who took me and Tim are still looking for us." David tenderly pushed back a strand of hair that had slipped across her forehead. "If we stay too long, they might find us here, and I would never willingly put you and Dad in that kind of danger." He turned to look out of the kitchen window through which the late afternoon sun spilled into the room. "Speaking of Dad, when do you expect him back? Any chance he'll be gone for a few days?"

Suzanna gazed at her son in mild reproach. "No, David. He should be back any time now. You know he doesn't like to eat dinner out."

I had noticed the pots sitting on the stove burners, which were turned on low heat to keep the food warm. Despite the large piece of pie I was steadily working through, the aromas coming from the pots made me salivate in anticipation.

"Great," David said, wincing when his mother smacked him on the arm.

"Don't be like that," Suzanna reproached. "You can't avoid him forever."

"I can try," David mumbled under his breath.

Suzanna ignored him, visibly willing herself to deal with the situation as normally as possible. "You're all welcome to stay here as long as you like. David will show you to the spare bedroom, Dr. Anderson," she said, making an educated guess as to the scientist's correct title.

"Please, call me Paul."

She nodded. "Okay, then. Tim, I'm guessing you want to sleep with David?"

"M-Ma!" David sputtered.

"What?" Suzanna smirked. "You two are still together, aren't you?" she asked, a hint of warning in her tone.

I stuffed my last bite of pie into my mouth to hide what was becoming a permanent blush. Suzanna had been encouraging of David's and my budding relationship since the moment she'd accepted I wasn't trying to fleece her son out of everything he owned. Apparently she was still firmly on the David-and-Tim bandwagon.

Suzanna stood and began gathering up our plates. "Go on, while I finish getting dinner ready. And David," she added as she turned toward the sink, "I want you to talk to your father the moment he gets home."

I shared a glance with Father Paul. "Should we tell him the truth about why we're here?"

"Oh, good heavens, no!" Suzanna looked back at me with a horrified expression. "My husband isn't the most understanding of men," she said for Father Paul's benefit. "I think you being here, David, will probably be enough of a shock for one visit."

Her son nodded in agreement. "Yeah, that's for sure." David pushed back from the table, signaling it was time to follow our hostess's instructions. "Come on. I'll show you where everything is upstairs."

I waited for David to lead the way, watching with mild envy when he paused to brush his lips across his mother's upturned cheek. I pondered the imminent return of David's father, concerned how the unavoidable reunion would play out. While I'd wanted to give the man the benefit of the doubt, Suzanna's warning had me rethinking that strategy. It seemed we would need to exercise all due caution around the absent Mr. Conley.

"What should we tell your father?" I asked as David passed me and headed into the living room.

"Hell if I know," David replied testily.

Beyond the entrance foyer, the house led into a carpeted living room that took up nearly the entire first floor except for the kitchen. The cut pile matched the cream-colored walls, and the space was interrupted by a couch and several chairs in contrasting black leather. A step up led to a den furnished with an overstuffed sofa and love seat, all upholstered in an identical motif of tiny geometric patterns. A large television was mounted on the wall within easy view, and inset bookshelves broke the monotony of the walls at regular intervals. Beyond the living room was a staircase, covered in the same cut-pile carpet.

Father Paul brought up the rear as David led us up the stairs. "I take it from what your mother said that you haven't been home for some time. You hinted that you and your father had a falling-out," he added gently.

For a moment I thought David wasn't going to answer, but when we reached the top floor, he finally spoke.

"He's not too keen on the fact I like men."

"Ah," Father Paul said at the spare explanation. "How old were you when you came out to your parents?"

David sent him a narrowed-eyed glance, but Father Paul merely returned it evenly. "My mom had known for a while, but when they caught me making out with a classmate in my room one day after school, I had to come clean with Dad too." He let out a humorless laugh. "It was so stupid. Like either of them had ever respected a closed door before. I don't know why I thought that time would be any different. Anyway," David continued as he stopped in front of the open door nearest to the stairwell, "after I left for college, I never came back. You can sleep in here, Doc. I hope it's not too feminine for you. My room is—or was—the next one down, and my folks have the master bedroom at the end of the hall. The three of us can share this bathroom." He pointed to a door opposite the bedrooms. "Mom and Dad have their own en suite."

Father Paul looked briefly into the guest room and nodded in amusement at the floral, chintz-themed furnishings. "Thank you, David. This will do nicely. But Tim raised an important point. We really should figure out what to tell your father when he arrives."

David sighed and dragged a hand over his face. "I don't know," he said tiredly. "Maybe you could say you're related to Tim?"

After a moment's consideration, Father Paul nodded. "Mmm. Yes, that might work. I'll give it some more thought. Whatever I say, just follow my lead."

"Fine."

I had never heard David sound so bad-tempered. Unsure what I should do, I waited until he gestured for me to follow him to the door farther down the hall. He showed me into a room that was plainly a time capsule of an earlier period in his life.

"Damn," David swore, shaking his head. "She didn't change a thing since the last time I was here. Except for that," he added with a wry chuckle, pointing toward the ridiculously large giraffe sitting in a corner of the room. I had won it for Suzanna at the county fair during her visit to Lubbock. "I'd wondered where she put Bertie."

"How old were you when you left home?" I asked.

"Eighteen."

Only a year younger than I was now. I didn't know how a normal boy my age might decorate his room, so I was fascinated by this glimpse into David's past. There wasn't anything too unusual. The furniture—bed, desk, dresser—was typical for a student's bedroom, and the bed sheets and curtains were a nondescript dark blue. There were, however, a couple of posters taped to the wall adjacent to the bed. I crossed the room to take a closer look.

"Football?"

"Yeah," David answered, moving to stand beside me. "I was a fan of Oklahoma State from the time I was a little kid. But when I went to UT and discovered what a good team looks like, I finally accepted how much they actually sucked. Of course, that wasn't the only reason I enjoyed going to games." He stared at the poster absently. "It wasn't until I was in high school that I understood exactly why I liked having pictures of ripped football players next to my bed." David sat, the ancient mattress springs audibly protesting his weight. "I was on our school team for a while, though I still can't say whether it was because I appreciated the game or for, well, other reasons."

I watched as David bent over to reach under the bed, straightening a moment later with a small metal box in his hand.

"She left this here too." He exhaled on a tired-sounding laugh, shaking his head in apparent amusement.

"What is it?" I asked.

He glanced up at me with a raised eyebrow. "You mean to tell me you never… no, I guess you wouldn't have, would you?"

"Wouldn't have what?"

"Kept a box of treasures like most teenaged boys," David replied with a wry smile.

I tilted my head to the side curiously. "What kind of treasures? You mean money?"

David chuckled. “Not exactly.” He removed the lid. “When my dad found these, he threatened to burn them, but Mom must have rescued them and put them back under my bed.”

The tin held nothing more insidious than a dozen or so glossy magazines. I didn’t understand why David’s father would have found them objectionable until I noticed each issue had a well-built, nearly naked man on the cover. “Ah, I see,” I said.

“Yeah. These didn’t exactly improve my dad’s opinion of me.”

I sat gingerly on the bed next to David. “Is he really that bad? Do you think he might not let us stay here? Or….” I was reluctant to suggest it, but it had to be said. “Do you think he might turn us in?”

David shook his head. “I don’t know. I hate to think my own father could do something like that, but, well, it would probably be best if he doesn’t find out what we’re really doing here.”

I wanted to discuss what we should say, but our time suddenly ran out. I stood and walked over to the window as I heard a car pull up.

“David!” Suzanna called from downstairs. “Your father’s home!”

When I turned back, all the color had drained from David’s face. Closing his eyes, David took a deep breath.

“Showtime.”

SEVENTEEN

DAVID STOOD and walked to the door of his room, reluctance in every step. Tim joined him and placed a reassuring hand on his back. He mustered up a grateful, if tired, smile. "I promise not to freak out," he quipped as they moved out into the hallway.

He wasn't at all certain he'd be able to keep his vow. He was feeling decidedly queasy at the prospect of seeing his father for the first time in so many years. And to think, under any other circumstances, having Tim in his bedroom would have been a dream come true. If he'd met Tim when they were the same age, David knew nothing his father could have threatened would have broken them up. While it had taken a lot for him to reconcile the differences in their ages after he discovered Tim returned his feelings, he suspected a teenage romance between the two of them would have been the stuff of legend. Not that it ever would have happened, considering what Tim was. Which begged the question, how in the hell was he going to explain the reason for this surprise visit to his father?

Anderson was waiting for them in the hall and frowned when he heard David's weak attempt at a joke. "Are you sure you're okay?" He looked carefully into David's face. "You look a little green around the edges."

David grimaced at learning that he looked as bad as he felt. "Don't worry, I'm not going to throw up. At least not in front of my dad." He saw Tim and Anderson exchange a meaningful glance and tried not to bristle at the doubt stamped on their faces.

Suzanna stood at the bottom of the stairs, her hands clenched together in front of her. Her attention was fixed on the front door, and it opened right as the three of them reached her. A tall man walked into the house, and David started at the unanticipated feeling of longing that came over him as he watched the newcomer. *Dammit*, he swore to himself. He had missed the old man after all. There was no denying their relationship. Although he had his mother's general coloring, in all other ways he was the spitting image of his father. The older man's hair was mostly silver with only hints of its original medium brown showing through, and his eyes were gray instead of blue, but there was no doubting who he was. It was like looking into a mirror, a fact David had long resented.

"Suzanna? Who owns that SUV parked in front of the house?" The man closed the door, keeping his back to the living room as he toed off his sneakers. "I told Earl our curb isn't part of his damn driveway. Guess I'll have to have another word with him in the morning."

"Hank," Suzanna said, cutting off her husband's speculative chatter. He turned and froze when he caught sight of the three men standing behind her. "Look who came home to visit," she added with a weak smile.

David felt his entire body vibrate with tension as he met his father's stunned gaze. A sudden pain stabbed through his head as the knotted muscles in his neck caused an instant migraine. Right then, a warm spot materialized at his side, and David could sense Tim's nearness. From the corner of his eye, he saw the kid was staring intently at his father, his expression dangerous, as though he was reacting unconsciously to an observed threat.

"Hey, Dad. Long time no see." David tried to keep his tone steady for Tim's sake, but even he could hear the tightness in his voice.

Suzanna's face was pinched, her fingers knitting together in agitation as her husband remained standing by the door, silently staring at their son. "Hank, aren't you going to say something?"

Hank shifted from shock to fury so quickly, David registered the abrupt change like a punch in the gut. He felt like a helpless teenager all over again, quaking under his father's enraged glare as he committed yet another supposed offense. The glint in Hank's steely gaze was unnerving as it raked over David from head to toe in evident disgust. He clenched his teeth furiously, the muscles bulging in his jaw as though he were forcibly swallowing the worst of the vitriol he was preparing to spew. His meaty fists, which had once seemed so intimidatingly large, were held stiffly at his sides. Though his father had never hit him, not even when he'd admitted his orientation, David could still remember the ragged hole one of those fists had left in the kitchen drywall as a result.

David realized he was trembling as his father stalked toward him. Something primitive and childlike deep inside of him wanted to retreat even as he noticed for the first time that he had a couple of inches on his father, not that it made him feel any better. But when Tim touched his arm, standing at his side like a protective sentinel, his presence gave David the strength to hold his ground when Hank got right up into his face.

"Hank—" Suzanna said warningly, anger beginning to overtake the anxiousness in her expression.

"Where on God's green earth have you been, you ungrateful little shit?" Hank spat. "Your mother's been worried sick, wondering where you were. And here you come, just waltzing up in my house like nothing's happened." His voice lowered to a growl as he jabbed a finger repeatedly into his son's chest, punctuating his rant. "You have got some nerve."

David racked his brain for a reasonable explanation, feeling like a deer in the headlights of his father's glower when he came up blank. "Um," he hemmed, desperately trying to think of something. Anything. "I—"

"Oh, Hank," Suzanna interjected hastily, "that was all nothing but a silly misunderstanding." She laughed with only a touch of nervousness as she walked up and grabbed David's hand to pull him close to her side and away from her husband. "David was taking a road trip. Seeing some of the nature reserves, didn't you say? Fishing and whatnot?"

David stared down at her blankly as he struggled to keep up. "Uh, yeah."

Suzanna grinned, but her eyes told him he'd better play along or else. "Patricia, that lovely manager at the BBW, she plain forgot about it and thought David was in New Mexico for one of his franchise meetings. You remember me telling you he goes there a few times a year for those. Well," she rushed on, "when I called his cell phone and couldn't reach him, and then he wasn't at the hotel in Albuquerque where he usually stays, I was simply beside myself with worry." Suzanna smacked David hard on the arm. "Next time you're going someplace you don't get cell service for a couple of weeks, you'd better tell me yourself," she admonished. "I shouldn't have had to call Patricia to find out where you were."

The bullshit his darling mother was spewing was nothing short of genius. David watched as the all too plausible tale completely drained the wind out of Hank's sails. His father frowned but seemed at a loss about how to contradict his wife's hasty explanation. "Hmmmph," he mumbled under his breath.

David recognized the sound. His father had a bee in his britches and wasn't ready to give up just yet. Casting around for a new target, Hank glanced at the two strangers in his living room. David could tell the moment he latched on to them, because he visibly worked himself up into a renewed state of irritation.

"And who in the hell are you two?" Hank's expression when he looked at Anderson was belligerently curious, but when he saw Tim, it changed into something ugly.

David cursed under his breath and rushed to head his father off. "They're friends of mine. They went with me on my trip."

"Friends, huh?" Hank sneered at Tim. "Yeah, I'll bet he is. Is that right, boy? Are you *friends* with my son?"

Even Tim couldn't miss the blatant connotation. For once, David was grateful for Tim's ability to maintain a world-class poker face.

"Yes, sir," Tim answered calmly.

Hank shook his head. "Unbelievable," he said, turning to glare at his son. "Are you sleeping with boys, now, like some goddamned pedophile? How dare you bring your underage whore into my house!"

"Hank!" Suzanna sounded utterly mortified.

David exploded. "Dad, not one more word!"

"Mr. Conley, my name is Paul Anderson," the scientist offered smoothly, holding out his hand toward Hank. "Tim is my nephew. I invited him to visit me up in Missouri, and David was kind enough to suggest we make a road trip out of it. Tim is in school down in Lubbock and has been working at David's store since the beginning of last school year." He bestowed a blandly pleasant smile on the man regarding him with simmering indignation. “I can assure you, the relationship between David and my nephew, who is an adult, as a matter of fact, is perfectly acceptable to me.”

David had to give Anderson credit, but Hank wasn’t to be so easily derailed.

“To you, maybe,” he spat, “but not to me. I want all of you out of my house.” He pointed imperiously toward the front door. “Now!”

“Hank,” Suzanna said quietly, moving to stand directly in front of her husband. She barely came up to his shoulder, but the rage emanating from her seemed to increase her diminutive stature a hundredfold. “This is my home too, and David is my son. This is the first time he’s stepped foot in this house in over ten years, and I’ll be damned if I let you turn him away because you’re being so fucking pigheaded!” she ended in a shout.

All four men stared at her in varying degrees of amazement and disbelief. David could not think of a single time in his thirty-one years of living he’d ever heard his mother drop the F-bomb. Apparently, neither could his father. Hank stared down at his wife, his eyebrows raised in shock as his mouth opened and closed soundlessly. After an excruciatingly long period of silence, he finally managed to find his voice.

“Suzanna, I will not indulge *your* son and his deviant lifestyle under my roof!”

She exhaled in disgust. “Hank, just go on to bed. Clearly you’re overtired. I can’t think of any other reason you’re having a tantrum like a spoiled two-year-old.” She looked up at him with her lips pursed in annoyance. “I am going to enjoy a nice dinner with David and his friends. If you don’t want to join us, that’s fine. I will talk to you about this later.” Having said her piece, Suzanna whipped around and disappeared into the kitchen.

David determinedly ignored the weight of his father’s glare as it bore into him. Realizing his son wasn’t willing to go another round, Hank swept past his visitors and stomped up the stairs in an eerie impression of the toddler Suzanna had accused him of emulating. The instant his father was out of sight, David sagged in relief.

“I hope I wasn’t too presumptuous, David.”

He glanced at Anderson with a tired smile. “No, I appreciate you coming up with that story. Are you sure you and my mother didn’t get together beforehand to brainstorm?”

Anderson chuckled. "That was all her. I simply followed her lead."

"Are you boys eating dinner, or do I have to drag you in here?"

David felt his energy returning as he heard his mother's dulcet tones bellowing out from the kitchen. When she'd come to visit him in Lubbock earlier that summer, she apologized for not standing up for him more when Hank had come down so hard on him. It was obviously a vow she'd made in earnest and intended to keep no matter how difficult it might be. David hated that he was once again causing friction between his parents, but he couldn't help the warmth that had filled him as he'd watched his mother defend him so tenaciously.

Suzanna was ready for them when they filed into the kitchen. She handed David a stack of plates, Tim a handful of silverware, and Anderson, who was easily fifteen years her senior, a set of cloth napkins. "David, you know what to do. I'm serving in five minutes."

He smiled despite himself before turning to the others. "You heard the lady." He hadn't set the table in this kitchen since he was eighteen, but he remembered clearly how she liked it to be done. Under his tutelage, his troops—one amused and the other bemused—had the job done well before the deadline.

Dinner was beef stroganoff with fresh picked green beans. It was his favorite dish, and if David didn't know any better, he'd have sworn his mother knew he was coming. Nearly every bit of ill will he'd ever felt toward Anderson vanished when the man took it upon himself to engage in an almost one-sided conversation that nevertheless made it seem that the four of them were having a lively dinner. Suzanna, for her part, responded graciously, smiling and nodding when appropriate, although her gaze bounced ceaselessly between David and the stairs, which she could see from where she sat.

"Mom," David asked finally, "is Dad going to eat?"

She looked at him with relief, as though grateful for being given permission to discuss the conspicuously absent master of the house. "I'll take him up a plate later, even though he probably won't appreciate it, the crotchety old bastard."

David chuckled softly, appreciative of her attempt to make light of the situation. But her efforts were futile at best. David had long wondered what would happen when he and his father again met face-to-face. Now that he knew, he wished he had stayed far, far away. His father would never understand he hadn't chosen to be gay, that he hadn't chosen to be such a massive disappointment. But he'd hoped, after all this time, that his father might have stopped hating him for it.

He suddenly realized that the youngest member of their party hadn't made a sound since they'd sat down at the dinner table. David glanced over at Tim and sighed as he watched the kid mechanically shovel Suzanna's excellent stroganoff into his mouth like it was nutritious slop he knew he should eat but wasn't interested in actually tasting. Ironically, the sight of Tim's mindless appetite killed his. For his mother's sake, he managed to swallow a few more bites before setting his fork down on his plate and pushing away from the table.

"It's been a long day, and it's still my turn to drive. I'm going to head up to bed so we can get an early start in the morning."

Alarm shone in Suzanna's eyes as she looked up at him sharply. She grabbed his arm, keeping him in his seat. "What do you mean, Davy? You're not really leaving that soon, are you?" Her voice wavered with incipient tears. "You just got here!"

David groaned. He let his head fall backward until he was looking up at the ceiling. "Come on, Ma. That's not fair."

"Fair? What's not fair is how I was worried about you for so long. And now that I'm finally seeing you and Tim again, you're already trying to run off."

She was good, David had to give her that. Not only was she piling on the guilt for his recent disappearance, she'd brought Tim into the mix, reminding him of how close they'd grown during her visit to Texas. Tim was staring at Suzanna with a mixture of surprise and barely concealed joy, and David could almost hear what he was thinking. *She wants me here. She still likes me.* David knew Tim would leave if he asked, but he couldn't do that to the kid, not after everything Tim had gone through after his recapture.

"All right. All right." David held his hands up in defeat. "We'll stay until the day after tomorrow. But then we really need to go." He looked directly into his mother's eyes, trying to impress upon her the seriousness of the situation. "I mean it. It's not safe for you and Dad if we stay too long." He counted the reluctant nod he received as a victory, though Suzanna was clearly unhappy with the timetable he'd laid out. "Good. Now, I really am tired. I'll see you in the morning."

"David," Suzanna said before he could stand. "Hank doesn't hate you. I know you think he does," she continued before he could interject the automatic denial that sprung to his lips, "but it's not true. Your father is stubborn and set in his ways, but if you keep trying, you two can work this out. I have to believe that." Her smile was tremulous as she gazed up at him with watery eyes. "I want my family back together."

David wanted to reassure her, but he couldn't. He still smarted from the vitriol Hank had spewed at him. In some ways it had been worse this time than when he'd been a kid. Back then, he'd been nothing but a boy in his father's eyes, but now he was a grown man. Discovering that his father still had so little respect for him hurt more than he'd thought possible. Although he didn't want to disappoint his mother, he couldn't agree with the reconciliatory fantasy she'd spun in her mind. He stood and leaned down to press a kiss to her cheek.

"Good-night, Ma."

Suzanna let him go without further protest. After trudging up the stairs, David made his way down the hall toward his room, keeping his gaze firmly away from the closed door to the master bedroom. His mind on his bed, David didn't realize he'd been followed until a foot inserted itself between his door and the jam, preventing him from closing it. Startled, he turned around in time to see Tim slip into the room behind him.

"You're already done with dinner?" he asked as Tim closed the door.

Tim nodded. "I wasn't all that hungry."

"Is that right?" David replied, his lips quirking upward at the obvious lie, except there was no hint of teasing in Tim's gaze. Tim merely stared at him, devoid of expression. Still, David could guess what was stewing beneath the otherwise placid exterior. He lifted a hand and cupped Tim's cheek. "I'm sorry, kid."

Tim blinked at him. "For what?"

"For my dad. I'm sorry he was so horrible in front of you and toward you." David sighed. "You didn't deserve that. You are *not* a whore, and he had no right to call you that."

Tim's gaze wavered for a moment, telling David he'd supposed correctly. But when he finally looked up again, his expression was unexpectedly mulish.

"You don't have to apologize to me. That was nothing compared to what he said to you." Tim inhaled sharply, his expression veering between uncertainty and agitation. "I hated that he was being so mean, but I didn't know what to do. I just wanted…."

"Wanted what?" David urged, unable to look away from the myriad of emotions chasing themselves over Tim's face.

"I wanted him to stop hurting you. I wanted to protect you." Tim stared at him intently, his brown eyes shimmering.

"Don't worry about it, kid." David smiled wryly. "It's not your job to protect me. Not from my dad, at least."

"But it is! It is my job."

David started at the unexpected outburst, blinking in surprise. "What are you talking about?"

Tim made a sound of frustration low in his throat. "I should be the one to protect you, because I—I love you, David."

Do you?

The image of Tim glaring at him as he put a bullet between his eyes flashed through David's mind on the heels of the errant thought. But before the doubt could firmly take hold, a warm, lithe form draped itself against him. Any protest he might have made was lost beneath the urgency of the lips that latched on to his. David struggled between desire and caution, but in the end he feverishly returned Tim's embrace and allowed himself to believe that maybe, just this once, love really was enough.

EIGHTEEN

THE MOMENT David kissed me back, my entire body melted. All the stress and anxiety that had been building up in the days since our improbable escape drained away. Soon there was nothing left but blind need.

"I love you," I repeated on a gasp when David momentarily released me. His warm lips traced a path over my jaw, stopping to nibble at the tender lobe of my ear. "I love you," I said again on a moan.

"Tim," David breathed, "you don't have to—"

"No." I pulled away and took David's face between my hands. "You asked me before at the hospital if I had been honest when I told you I loved you. I want you to know, to truly believe, that I was telling you the truth. It wasn't love at the beginning, not when I didn't even know what the word really meant. But it's like I tried to tell you before. After you woke me from that nightmare about my mother's death, that's when I knew it was more than just protection or sex I want from you." I pulled David gently toward me until our foreheads were touching. "For the first time, I understood that all I truly wanted was for you to hold me." My eyes drifted shut as I remembered the profoundness of that realization. "I simply wanted you to love me."

When I opened my eyes, all I could see was a sea of vivid blue. David's gaze held an undercurrent of wariness he couldn't completely hide, and it hurt. But I was determined to erase it, to earn back his trust. I'd used all the words I could think of to convey my feelings. Lifting to my toes, I pressed myself fully against him, letting my actions declare whatever had been left unsaid.

David groaned as our bodies lined up, the matching bulges at our groins meeting through the inconvenient barrier of cotton and denim. "Wait," he rasped. "I gotta lock the door."

Wrapping my arms around his neck, I sucked on David's lower lip, holding on as he backed the few steps to the door. I refused to break our kiss, and he had to grope blindly for the latch. We fell against the wood with a loud thump when I thrust my hips forward in a frantic search for friction.

"For the love of…," David breathed. He sagged, and I could feel the quiver that went through him. "Take it easy, kid. We have to be quiet. My dad is right next door." He barely got the warning out before I thrust an intrepid tongue heedlessly into his mouth.

"I don't care," I whispered when I finally let him up for air. "Let him hear. I love you, and I refuse to be ashamed of that." David looked back at me with pained uncertainty, and I felt a stab of regret for being so inconsiderate. While Hank's opinion of me meant less than nothing, I knew David was not similarly immune. "I'm sorry," I said. "That was thoughtless of me. If you don't want to do this here, I understand."

David shook his head. "No, you're right. We have nothing to be ashamed of, but…."

"No point in making him hate us any more than he already does," I filled in.

"Right, but make no mistake. I do want this." David smiled, running his fingers into my hair. "I want you. We just have to keep quiet. Can you do that?" He leaned over and pressed his lips into the hollow below my jaw. He swept his heated tongue over the vulnerable flesh, and I moaned despite David's admonition. "Can you hold back while I'm fucking you?" he murmured teasingly, easing his thigh between my legs.

"Nnngh!" I cried out, already failing to satisfy the condition David had imposed.

"You're going to have to do better than that." He looked down at me with a raised eyebrow, the pleased expression on his face belying his mock reprimand.

"S'your fault—"

My response was swallowed up as I pulled David's head down into another kiss. He chuckled at the peevish accusation, though the sound was muffled by the press of our lips. I felt myself being lifted and wrapped my legs around David's waist. The room seemed to float past me, my attention entirely focused on the tongue sparring with mine and the ache rapidly intensifying between my legs. The air left my lungs when I landed on the bed, David's large body falling heavily on top of mine. I reached beneath his shirt and dragged eager hands up his back in a clumsy attempt to pull it up and off.

David moved to help, not breaking the kiss until the last possible second. Tossing the shirt over the edge of the bed, I craned upward to find his lips again. But he evaded me and returned the favor by lifting my shirt away from my body. I raised my arms to help him whisk it over my head. Instead, he eased down so he could nibble over the skin he had exposed. I inhaled sharply as he played his lips softly over the quivering muscles of my stomach. His tongue traced a line down to the waistband of my jeans and then back up again, sucking and teasing until I could barely catch my breath. The playful kisses moved upward over my chest, and I trembled in anticipation until he finally reached my pebbled nipples, laving them with an attentive tongue.

"Ahhh!" I cried, my body trembling in response to the incredible sensation.

"Shhhh." David shushed me softly without lifting his head from his self-appointed task.

I slapped my hand over my mouth to muffle the traitorous exclamation. "I'm sorry. It's just…." *It feels too good!*

I was embarrassed to speak the words out loud. I could withstand levels of physical punishment that would reduce the average person to screaming insanity. But the mere touch of David's lips was enough to leave me a trembling mess of nerves and want. Torture I could handle, but the pleasure he was giving me threatened to overwhelm me completely. It had been so long since we'd been together, I'd nearly forgotten how much I loved this. The restriction of my jeans was suddenly unbearable as the throbbing between my thighs intensified. Arching my back, I pressed myself closer to David's mouth in a silent demand. Nimble fingers undid the fastening of my jeans, but I couldn't work up the brainpower to offer thanks. The only coherent thought in my mind was *more*!

"You like that?"

I could only moan in response as David bit down with slowly increasing pressure on the sensitive nub until he won another ecstatic whimper. The sensation was intense, my body processing the feeling as pleasure when anyone else would have registered pain. My moans grew more frantic, and David must have misinterpreted my cries, because he eased up and sucked on the sensitized flesh, earning a genuine sob of protest.

"Shhh," he murmured. "I've got you." He batted my hands away from where they were fumbling with my jeans. I obligingly lifted my hips so he could strip me. As he pushed the jeans lower to bunch at my ankles, he licked at the nipple he'd previously neglected. "Should I do the other one?"

"Yes," I whimpered, digging my fingers into his thick blond hair to hold him in place. "Please. Do it!"

"Hey," David murmured, sounding amused. "Don't rip my hair out."

I bit my lip as sharp teeth again closed over my flesh in a delicious threat. After toeing off my jeans, I spread my knees apart so David could settle deeper in the cradle of my thighs. Apparently not content with that, he reached a hand through the slit in my borrowed briefs and wrapped his fingers around the throbbing cock hiding within. I instantly lost any shred of ability to stay quiet. My shout of approval rang out loudly as David gently stroked me from root to tip. My eyes flew open, but I saw nothing as blood rushed from my head to swell my erection full to bursting. When I finally regained the ability to focus, David was hovering over me with a playful scowl.

"What did I tell you?" he admonished, his hand never letting up. He seemed thoroughly undeterred when I responded with yet another appreciative outburst. He resisted the tug of my hands trying to bring his head down for another kiss. "You want the whole house to know what we're doing?"

The fact that David's mood had improved and that it was because of me filled me with a sense of pride, but the emotion quickly took a back seat to the riotous needs of my aching body. I was far beyond being able to explain how little I cared what anyone else in the house might be thinking right then. Drawing on my enhanced strength, I brought our lips together, relying on the contact to effectively smother my gasps. David humored me with a muffled laugh, seeking out my tongue with his own and engaging it in a playful battle. My hips worked helplessly in time to the hand stroking over my length. My eyelids fluttered shut and white flashes began to appear behind them, sparking in the resulting darkness.

"Unngh, I'm going to come," I warned, feeling the pressure building as the sac at the apex of my thighs drew up in preparation. I wanted to wait, to hold back until David was deep inside of me, but I couldn't. It had been too long, and I loved him too much. "Help me," I begged, unable to say what I was pleading for.

I barely registered it as my briefs suddenly vanished. Next thing I knew, my legs were locked around David's shoulders, and my cock was being drawn into a cavern of wet heat. There was no stopping the sob of pleasure as it escaped my lips, seeming to rise up from the very place where David was determinedly using his mouth to drive me insane. I grabbed blindly at the pillow pressing against the side of my head and dragged it over my face to stifle my screams.

David cleverly swirled his tongue around my length, licking me from root to tip and leaving no inch untouched. My body clenched in dismay against the emptiness as I trembled at the teasing scrape of teeth. I longed for David to fill me, to take me and claim me until no one could deny that I was his and he was mine. The pillow barely muzzled my desperate shouts as he eased his way up to the tip of my cock with a hard suck. My fingers clenched tightly around the pillow as my eyes crossed behind my closed eyelids. The impending rush began simultaneously at the soles of my feet and the top of my head, spreading rapidly throughout my body until the twin torrents of sensation focused in my throbbing cock. My release crashed over me in a wave. A muffled whimper was all I could manage as I flew apart into a million pieces.

I came down slowly, my body twitching involuntarily as David drank every drop I spilled before drawing away with one last, long pull. Lying bonelessly against the bed, I couldn't even muster the energy to remove the pillow from over my face. I moaned helplessly at the soft tickle of his tongue gently licking me clean. The mattress dipped beneath me, and the pillow abruptly disappeared. Sucking in a deep breath, I blinked and looked up hazily at David's tender smile.

"I missed you," he murmured softly before bending low to lick slowly into my mouth. I groaned as I tasted myself. As he pulled back, I breathed deeply, savoring the tang of our mingled sweat. "I missed this. Every night I was in that cell, I thought of you, of how much I wanted to hold you in my arms." He leaned in for an even deeper kiss, but suddenly let out a hiss when I reached down to grasp the bulge pressing against the zipper of his jeans. "Tim—"

"Fuck me," I urged breathily. David groaned at the suggestive vulgarity, the sound turning into a moan as I squeezed his arousal through the unforgiving denim. I felt my own length twitch in sympathy and knew it wouldn't be long until I was fully hard again. "Take me, David." I captured his lips in a deep kiss, breaking off only so I could whisper against his mouth. "I want to remember how it felt when you finally made me yours. I want to feel you so deeply inside of me I'll never forget again." I lifted my head up for another kiss. "I want you to know that, no matter what your father thinks of you, I will always love you."

The playfulness left David's face, replaced by a yearning so intense it took my breath away. The time for teasing was over. I moaned as he devoured my lips with focused desperation. I whimpered in protest when the body covering mine lifted away, until I realized he was scrambling at his waist to tear off his jeans. Instead of helping, I concentrated on exploring the sensitive ridges on the roof of his mouth with my tongue, relishing the shiver I received in response.

"Your shirt—" David groaned.

I responded quickly, ripping it over my head and tossing it blindly to the side. At last we were both fully naked, pressed together skin-to-skin from head to toe. I tilted my hips so his heavy cock slipped into the crease of my ass. He took the hint, thrusting forward reflexively in a mimic of his ultimate intentions.

"Wait," David rasped, raising his head to drag in a deep breath. "I don't have anything, no lotion, or lube, or—"

Whatever he had been about to add remained unspoken as I raised my hand to my mouth and laved the broad side of my tongue over my palm, wetting it from the heel to the tips of my fingers. David stared at me, the heat in those beautiful blue eyes lighting a fire in my belly and spurring my spent cock back to throbbing life. Reaching down with my sopping hand, I took hold of his erection and spread the improvised moisture along his thick length.

David dropped his head forward until his face was hidden in the crook of my neck. "I swear, kid. You're going to be the death of me."

I moaned as David's groan vibrated against my neck. "Never," I promised. "Not if I have anything to say about it." Over and over I stroked, stoking the fire just as thoroughly in myself. I mouthed his shoulder both to taste his skin and to stifle my own helpless moans. "I promise," I gasped. "I'll keep you safe. No matter what."

David began to work his hips, sliding his cock in and out of the circle of my grip. I tightened my hold, wanting to give him the most pleasure, but he suddenly captured my hand and held it above my head.

"No, not yet," he breathed. "Not until I'm inside of you. Now turn over," he growled before swooping in for another hard kiss.

I obeyed the instant I was released, burying my face in the pillow beneath my head. I had only a moment to relax before David's hard thickness breached the muscular barrier of my hole. I yelled into the pillow, ecstasy flooding through me as he filled me with his hard cock. The slight sting of pain from the less than ideal lubrication was nothing compared to the burning joy that swelled in my heart.

For an instant I felt my happiness war with an equally intense rage, my entire being railing against the fate that had nearly stolen this away from me forever. But the dark emotion could not stand long before the light permeating every corner of my soul as David claimed my body. I shouted my desire and my love, hoping by turns that the hateful man in the next room remained oblivious and that he heard every passionate cry. I flushed with heat when David's thrusting cock found my prostate, making my entire body shake as though I'd been jolted with a current of pure electricity.

"Ahhh! David!" My neck arched helplessly, lifting my head from the pillow as I cried out. I instantly regretted my moment of weakness when the sound of my voice reverberated against the walls. "I'm sorry," I whimpered.

"Don't be," he growled. "Let him hear. I don't give a fuck." Bending so he was flush against my back, David gripped my hips with bruising force and drove forward, forcing another shattered cry from my lips. "You're mine, and I want everyone to know it."

Acquiescing to the urgent demand, I gave myself up to the sensation of being filled, overwhelmed, claimed… loved. My desire poured from me in a string of passionate cries, and my hands threatened to tear the sheets to shreds as my fingers dug into them with all of my prodigious strength. I soon lost the ability to discern one thrust from the next, until I could feel nothing but David demanding ownership of every piece of my heart and every inch of my body.

We could still run away together, I thought feverishly, simply disappear and forget about Father Paul's crazy plan to save me. I was deathly afraid something would happen to David and that I would lose him all over again. Nothing was worth the risk compared to this, not even my desire for a long life. All I needed, all I wanted, was to be with David for however long I might have left. The very thought of spending the rest of my days just like this, willingly at the mercy of my lover's demands, sent me over the edge.

My climax tore through me without warning, my cock spilling its pleasure into the hapless covers beneath me as my body clenched rhythmically around its ardent invader. David was only a second behind, his own shout echoing against the walls of his childhood bedroom. His cock emptied its burning heat into my waiting depths, milked by the very orifice it had plundered until it yielded every last drop.

I collapsed onto the bed with David lying heavily on top of me, the resulting silence broken only by the sound of our ragged breaths as we inhaled and exhaled in perfect synchronicity. I felt broken, my body refusing to respond when I attempted to snuggle into the heat of his body. Fortunately, he seemed to hear my unspoken request and somehow managed to maneuver the two of us so we were lying beneath the bedsheet instead of on top of it. He pulled me into his arms, nestling his spent cock against the curve of my ass. I shivered when he pressed soft lips in a tender kiss to the nape of my neck.

"I love you, Tim," David whispered, saying the words for the very first time since the night our lives had been ripped apart.

I blinked against the sudden sting of tears. The sun had long since set, and the only light came from the street lamp shining weakly in through the window. Utterly spent, I slid rapidly toward sleep, but as my consciousness faded, a haunting image invaded my nascent dreams.

The gun was heavy in my hand as David stared at me with pleading fear. My finger trembled on the trigger, but an insidious voice shouted in my ear, demanding me to eliminate the threat. I shook my head, refusing to believe David could ever be my enemy. Yet the voice gave me no peace. "TM 05637! Shoot him!"

Unable to resist, I squeezed the trigger, wondering how I would ever hit anything with my hand shaking so badly. The scene played out as it had many times before, and I cried out as the gun barked its deadly report. But this time I noticed it, the oddity I'd always seen but had never understood. Right before I pulled the trigger, David's face slipped out of focus, shimmering as though it were sinking beneath the spreading ripples of a pond. The bullet hit before his features sharpened once more, but for the first time, I didn't know whether the man I'd shot had really been David at all....

Gasping, I opened my eyes to stare into the darkness, heart racing. The dream lingered, leaving me astonished at its implications. Maybe I hadn't harmed David in those horrible simulations. But if it wasn't David, then who had I killed? Though my victim's identity remained a mystery, the realization that I might not have betrayed the man I loved was sweeter to me than anything. I clung fervently to the possibility with desperate hope.

"I could never hurt you," I whispered, praying I wasn't simply deluding myself. David's chest moved reassuringly against my back with deep, even breaths. I grasped the arm wrapped around my waist and held it close. "I won't let anything happen to you," I vowed quietly. "I swear it." The night was a silent witness, and soon I joined David in an exhausted, yet restful sleep.

NINETEEN

DAVID WOKE up slowly, feeling more rested than he had in far too long. He looked down at the soft caress of warm breath on his skin, smiling when he saw Tim lying against him, face buried in his chest. Tim's sooty lashes fanned across his cheeks, the pinkness of his slack lips making him look even younger. Pushing away the niggling of guilt he felt whenever he considered the difference in their ages, David turned his thoughts to more prosaic concerns.

"Tim," he said quietly. "Hey, kid, I need to get up for a bit."

"Mmmnnn" came the negative response.

David chuckled. He pressed a kiss to the top of Tim's head, breathing in the warm, sleepy scent of him. Tim didn't so much as stir when David ran a caressing hand down his arm, and David allowed himself a moment of prurient smugness. He was perfectly fine attributing Tim's present lethargy to his prowess in bed. After a few hours of rest, they'd come together again, only this time the frantic urgency was gone. Taking the opportunity to simply explore each other, they'd kissed and touched endlessly, sharing the very air they breathed until they'd each come apart once more. While Tim had been just as eager, their second encounter had seemed different somehow. Tim had been almost clingy, like he was trying to reassure himself that David was really there. Not that David had minded one bit, but he couldn't help but wonder at Tim's neediness.

His stomach rumbled, adding to the prompting of his full bladder. "Let me go get us something to eat." While he wanted to take complete responsibility for the kid's exhaustion, he suspected Tim's disease was at least partially to blame. "I'll bring you breakfast in bed, how's that sound?"

Tim murmured an incoherent response, but David took it as permission when the arms wrapped around him loosened enough for him to sit up. Smiling, David pressed his lips to Tim's forehead before slipping out of the bed. Early morning sunlight poured in weakly through the window, but it was enough to allow him to find his hastily discarded clothing. Forgoing underwear, he pulled on his jeans and T-shirt, leaving his shoes where they were. Maybe he would ask his mother to wash the few items of apparel they had brought with them before they got back on the road.

The door to his parents' room was open when he stepped out into the hall, closing the door of his room behind him as softly as he could so as not to wake Tim. Anderson was apparently still sleeping, if the silence coming from the guest room when he passed by was any indication. After making a quick detour to the bathroom, David jogged lightly down the stairs, remembering how Suzanna had always scolded him for thundering down them like a "herd of wild elephants" when he was a teenager. The light was on in the kitchen. Expecting to find his mother making breakfast, David swung into the room with a smile of greeting on his face.

"Morning, Ma—"

Hank looked up from the newspaper he was reading, a mug of coffee in his hand. He was sitting at the table, the dirty plate pushed off to one side holding the remnants of his recent meal. David stopped short as his father speared him with a cold gaze.

"Where's mom?" he asked after clearing the nervousness from his throat.

"She left a while ago. Said she had to go to the store." Hank jerked his head toward the stove. "There's food if you want it."

His father's tone was neutral, but David could sense the nastiness simmering beneath the surface. Unwilling to get into a battle on an empty stomach, he detoured to where the bacon and eggs his mother had so thoughtfully prepared were waiting. The silence was deafening, broken only by the clink of the fork he used to pile up a plate for him and Tim to share and the occasional rustle of Hank's newspaper. David was just finishing up and ready to count himself lucky at getting away unscathed when his father decided to drop the tranquil façade.

"I could hear you. Which was the point, wasn't it? To humiliate me in my own home?"

David took a deep breath and squared his shoulders. "Heard what?" he asked, though he was perfectly aware of what his father was talking about.

The chair Hank had been sitting in scrapped across the floor. David could feel the weight of his father's glare, but he somehow managed to keep his composure as he turned to meet it, leaving the plate safely sitting on the counter. Hank was on his feet, his chest heaving with the rage that had turned his face beet red.

"I heard you, goddammit! You and that… boy, having sex. Under my roof!"

David thought he could almost see steam coming from Hank's ears. For a brief moment, he felt a surge of concern about what effect the strain was having on his father's sixty-three-year-old heart.

"Dad, calm down."

"Don't you tell me to calm down!" Hank's large hands curled into fists where they were braced on top of the table. "You know how I feel about that sort of deviant behavior, and yet you did it anyway out of spite. How could you be so disrespectful to me? To your mother?"

"You leave Mom out of this," David fumed. "Unlike you, she accepts me for who I am. Plus, she knows full well how I feel about Tim."

"And how is that?" Hank demanded.

"I love him!" David's shout echoed loudly in the spacious room. "We've been through a hell of a lot recently," he added recklessly, "and we wanted to be together. To remind each other that, despite everything that's going on, we'll always be there for each other. That we deserve to be happy, the same as any other couple." David sucked in a breath, trying to regain his composure before he said more than he should about their so-called road trip. "Dad, I am a grown man. I do not need your permission to have sex with my boyfriend. That has nothing to do with you. Trust me, when I'm with Tim, you're the last person I'm thinking about."

Hank stared at him, his expression a mixture of disgust and bewilderment. The latter surprised David, as did the explanation behind it.

"Is this my fault, David?" Hank asked suddenly. "Did I do something wrong when you were growing up?" He shook his head in confusion. "I simply do not understand how you turned out like this. How I failed you."

"Oh, come on." David looked up to the ceiling as though seeking divine assistance. "Really, is that what you think? That my being gay is because of you?" Slouching back against the edge of the granite countertop, David folded his arms defensively across his chest. He'd never spoken with his father about his sexual orientation before without having abuse hurled at him. He almost couldn't believe that now, after so long, they were finally having this conversation. "Dad, that's utterly ridiculous. I'm gay because I was born gay. You didn't *do* anything to make me this way." He sighed. "That's what you've never been able to accept. This is not a choice. I didn't wake up one day and decide I was going to be attracted to men."

Hank winced, his discomfort with the topic palpable, but David pressed on. "Do you know when I first figured out how I felt about guys? I was nine," he continued, not waiting for a response. "You remember my best friend, Stan Rhyner? Well, I didn't realize it then, but I was completely in love with Stan in the fierce way only a little kid can be. And then a new kid started at our school, and he and Stan ended up on the same Little League team. You had me in peewee football, so entire weekends would go by when I knew Stan and the new kid were hanging out without me." David stared absently at the tiled floor, his lips curving into a sad smile as he recalled the bittersweet memory. "I was so jealous, I made myself sick once thinking about them together. And then, the next school year, Stan moved away—"

"And you were inconsolable," Hank finished. He had turned away and was gazing out of the window when David glanced over at him. "I never could figure out what had you so upset. I thought it was simply nerves about starting fifth grade, though that didn't make sense. It's not like you had changed schools or anything."

David nodded. "So now you know. How could I have decided to be gay when I was nine years old?" He clenched his jaw when his father didn't respond. Pushing away from the counter, he turned back to the stovetop to retrieve his plate. "Look, I don't expect you to understand or accept me after all this time, but I wanted you to know the truth for what it's worth. I never did any of this to hurt you." He started toward the opening separating the kitchen from the living room. "I'll let Tim and Anderson know we're leaving right after Mom gets back." David paused and glanced over his shoulder at his father. "Thanks for not kicking us out last night."

When he reached his room, David found Tim awake, sitting on the bed while he chatted with Anderson. Tim broke off what he was saying the instant David appeared and scrambled off the bed to meet him.

"Are you okay?" Tim asked, taking the plate. His brown eyes reflected apprehension over whatever he could see on David's face.

"Yeah, kid. I ran into my father downstairs, is all." Tim's expression darkened, so David smiled to reassure him. "Really, everything's fine." He looked up at Anderson. "Sorry, I didn't know you'd be up, or I would have brought you something to eat too."

"Don't concern yourself," Anderson replied. "I'm not overly fond of eating right after I wake up. I'll get something later." He nodded toward his protégé. "Tim and I were talking about how we need to discuss our plans going forward."

David sat on the bed, scooting back until he could lean against the wall. Tim joined him, sitting close to his side so their arms were touching as he picked up one of the forks. David was amused by Tim's ability to show affection while maintaining his single-minded focus on stuffing his face. "I told my dad we'd leave right after my mom gets back from wherever she went. Shopping, I think."

Anderson nodded. After closing the door, he walked over to the desk and lowered himself into the padded chair sitting in front of it. "I'll keep this short, then. Mitch gave us most of what we'll need for the actual infiltration."

"You mean besides the guns?" David asked.

"Yes. He also provided us with an electronic sequencer. It will get us past nearly all of the coded locks we'll encounter," he elaborated when David stared at him blankly.

Tim looked up from the plate. "What about guards? The Facility always used guards as backups to the electronic security."

"Hmm, you're quite right," Anderson acknowledged. "Fortunately, the security at the Illinois base isn't nearly as tight as it was at the Facility. It was only ever meant to be used as a research lab, not for locking away anything as sensitive as you, my boy."

David poked at the cooling eggs thoughtfully. "Do you really think it will be that easy? Simply a matter of slipping past a few doors?" He sighed. "I don't mind telling you, I'd love if that were the case."

Anderson smiled at him wryly. "I'm afraid it's unavoidable that we'll encounter some resistance. Mitch didn't give us those weapons for nothing. And while the guard presence won't be as heavy, the lab itself will most certainly be under close surveillance. I have no doubt we'll be expected, though we have the advantage of choosing our own timetable. And if we are careful enough—and clever enough—we should be able to minimize interaction with the base's personnel."

"You mean by creating diversions," Tim volunteered.

"Precisely," Anderson affirmed, his expression lightening with a genuine grin. David could tell the old man was pleased at his creation's astuteness. He still had trouble thinking of Tim as something the scientist had made, finding it far less disturbing to think of Anderson merely as a doting father. "You mentioned you would be able to fashion some explosives." Tim inclined his head, his mouth occupied with demolishing what was left of the bacon. "Good," Anderson said. "We can place them at strategic points on the external doors to accomplish both that and to ensure our path of escape." He looked pensive for a moment. "We'll need to think carefully about how many devices we'll require. Our resources won't be unlimited."

David rescued the last two pieces of bacon before they too disappeared into Tim's belly. "What about the lab? Can we use the sequencer to get into it as well?"

"No," Anderson replied succinctly. "That lock requires a keycard for entry. We'll have to steal one. Our best bet would be to borrow one from a lab technician."

"And what happens to the tech?" David frowned doubtfully, not liking what Anderson was implying.

The scientist met his gaze calmly. "Don't worry. Our theft should not lead to harm. If we do this right, neutralizing our target will not require lethal force, I assure you." Anderson's eyes became unfocused as he suddenly looked off to the side. "I only hope the drug is still in the outer lab where it was being kept the last time I saw it."

"Outer lab?" Tim asked.

Anderson nodded. "Yes, there are two rooms. The outer area is where the team runs its experiments and where the less sensitive drugs are stored. The more highly classified materials are kept in the inner room. Most of the experiments were stored in the outer part of the lab. The inner section was used only for research considered especially dangerous and, thus, requiring extra security."

David was puzzled. "What sort of research?"

"Synthesized viruses."

The blunt response sent a shiver along David's spine. "For biological warfare," he said, stating the obvious conclusion.

"Precisely," Anderson said. "As I said, that's not what we're looking for. The drug we need for Tim should be in the primary storage area, which is fortunate, since the lock for the inner lab is hardcoded for biometric identification."

"You mean a fingerprint?" David asked, interpreting the technical jargon.

Anderson nodded. "In this case, yes. It would be impossible to access the inner section unless we cut off someone's thumb and took it with us."

David swallowed at the gruesome imagery and ended up coughing as his bite of bacon went down the wrong way. Tim helpfully slapped him on the back.

"Do you have access?" Tim asked. "You used to work there, didn't you?"

"At the time, yes, I did. But my clearance has most certainly been revoked. The only ones with the necessary access will likely be the general and Coleen. So let's hope it doesn't come to that, shall we? I should also tell you," he continued, glancing at Tim, "in addition to the drug that will fix you permanently, my boy, there should also be a supply of the pills you were taking before."

"The blue ones?"

Anderson nodded. "If anything should happen and we can't retrieve what we're after, those will keep you going for some time. And, I swear to you," he added, staring intently at his protégé, "I will figure out some other way to cure you if I have to."

DESPITE DAVID'S promise to Hank that they would leave shortly, it was nearly evening before Suzanna returned home. She wouldn't say what had taken her so long, but from the searching glances she gave him and his father, she had probably hoped giving the men in her life some enforced alone time would do some good. David almost felt guilty for spending most of the day holed up in his room with Tim, using the excuse of getting as much rest as they could to avoid precisely what his mother had tried to facilitate. He could tell she was disappointed when she learned he and his father had barely spoken to each other during her absence.

"Well, I can't say I'm surprised," she grumbled as she unpacked the bags of clothes she'd purchased for them while she was out. "You're both so blasted stubborn. At least, when you leave here, the three of you will have something else to wear besides those thrift store rejects."

David smiled and dropped a grateful kiss onto her cheek. "Thanks, Ma."

She patted his face. "You're welcome, sweetie. I got you guys some toiletries too, and backpacks to carry everything in." Suzanna paused suddenly, and David watched her with increasing worry as her expression slowly crumpled.

"What's wrong?"

Straightening her shoulders, Suzanna sniffed and hastily dashed away her tears. "It's nothing. I'm being silly."

He took her hands in his and turned her to face him. "Come on, Ma, talk to me. What is it?"

"Oh, Davy." The tears returned quickly once she abandoned her enforced self-control. "It breaks my heart to see you two like this." He didn't need to ask who she was referring to. "Your father and I won't be around forever, and I would hate to think about you losing him with this—this misunderstanding festering between you."

David sighed. "I'd hardly call it a misunderstanding."

"That's exactly what it is. He loves you, David, and you love him, but neither of you will give the slightest inch enough to tell each other." Suzanna glared at him with watery eyes as he dropped his hands from her cheeks and turned away.

"We talked some this morning," he said defensively, "but he didn't have anything new to say. Except that he thought my being gay was somehow his fault." David shook his head at her gasp of surprise. "Trust me, it wasn't productive." He began to gather up the clothes and supplies. "Thanks, again, for all of this. It's late, so we'll need to leave first thing in the morning." Her anguish tore at his heart. Dropping everything back on the kitchen table, he drew her into his arms. "It'll be fine, Ma. I'll try to come back once everything with Tim is settled." When he looked down at her, she was staring out of the screen door leading to the porch.

"Please, David. At least promise me you'll tell him good-bye before you go."

David groaned inwardly, but he nodded, unable to deny her request. "Why don't I do that now, then? We'll probably go at first light, and I don't want to wake either of you." He gave her a brave smile and was glad when she gathered herself enough to return it. It vanished the moment he turned away and headed for the porch door.

Hank was gazing out at the sunset, puffing away on a pipe. David inhaled deeply as he stepped out onto the porch, savoring the sweet aroma of the tobacco his father favored. He'd always loved that smell. Even now he associated it with pleasant memories of happier, simpler days when his father had been his hero and he'd been the apple of Hank's eye.

"Dad, I wanted to tell you good-bye in case I miss you tomorrow. We'll be leaving pretty early." Hank didn't reply, and David was about to leave when he caught a glimpse of his mother watching them expectantly from the kitchen. Setting his jaw, he turned back and moved over to his father's side. "I'm thinking about taking another vacation this time next year. Maybe we could go back to Bernice and camp like we used to. Or, we were just at Great Salt Plains Lake. It was very nice. They have pretty good fishing from what I saw."

"Will you be bringing that boy with you?" Hank didn't take his attention away from the growing darkness of the sky as he spoke.

Gritting his teeth, David managed to refrain from saying something he'd regret later. "Yeah, I'd like to. I think Tim would enjoy it, having both of us show him the great outdoors."

Hank tapped his pipe against the railing, sending the tobacco into the flowerbed below. "Then, no, I'll pass. I thought I made myself clear." He threw David a speaking glance before turning toward the house. "I want no part of the way you've chosen to live your life. When you're ready to come to your senses and apologize to me and to your mother, maybe then we can talk."

David gripped the railing tightly as he heard the screen door bang shut behind him, his jaw clenching with the struggle to swallow the pointless retort that ached to break free. He didn't know why he'd even bothered. No matter how much his mother might wish it, there was no getting around the impasse between him and Hank on this particular topic. After so long, he was ready to simply let it go for good. It hurt too much to keep trying. The porch door scraped softly against the jamb as it opened again. David didn't wait for Suzanna to speak.

"I tried, Ma, like you asked me to. I really tried."

"It's me," Tim said tentatively.

Turning around, David watched the kid step out onto the porch. "Did you hear any of that?" Tim's expression told him everything he needed to know. He held out his hand and pulled Tim toward him once he had grabbed hold. "I still want to take you camping. And this time, no high-powered assault rifles are allowed."

Tim tried out a smile, but it died quickly on his lips. "I'm sorry, David."

"Don't be. It's not your fault." He wrapped his arms around Tim, standing so Tim's back was against his chest. They remained quiet as they took in the last of the sunset, and David decided Tim's ability to simply be was yet another thing he loved about him.

Tim stiffened an instant before David also heard the rumble of an approaching car. At first he didn't think anything of it, but when it pulled into his parents' driveway, his stomach twisted into a hard knot. "You don't think—" he began, halting when Tim held up a hand for silence. The vehicle's doors creaked open and slammed shut. David's anxiety increased when he heard the front door open, followed by the sound of his father's voice.

"May I help you?" Hank asked.

"Good evening, sir." The speaker was female and authoritative. "We're US Marshals, and we're searching for a trio of escaped criminals. We've had reports they were recently seen in this area."

David didn't resist when Tim pulled him down until they were crouched below the rail, hidden in the shadows the house cast onto the porch. It was just as well, he figured, since his legs no longer seemed interested in supporting him. "Fuck," he hissed. "Is it them?"

Tim held a finger to his lips before creeping to the edge of the porch closest to the front of the house and leaning over to peer around the large bush planted at the corner. David did the same, and as he stared through the sparse foliage—his father had promised to remove the scraggly bush for years but had never gotten around to it—he saw two figures wearing marshals' jackets. Standing next to the woman speaking to his father was her brawny male partner. Both of them were wearing the type of hats favored by state troopers, so he couldn't get a clear view of their faces.

"The fugitives are all men. One is over seventy, with a medium build, gray hair, and brown eyes. One is in his early thirties, approximately six feet, blond, blue eyes. And the third is barely out of his teens. Brown hair and eyes, swarthy complexion."

It is them! David thought frantically, answering his own question. *Shit! How did they find us so quickly*? He broke out in a cold sweat. The woman had given his, Tim's, and Anderson's descriptions perfectly. There was no way Hank wouldn't know who she was looking for. She chose that moment to angle her head toward the porch light, and when David finally saw her face, he wasn't at all surprised to see the female soldier from the hospital parking lot in Magnum. Huddled next to him, Tim's lithe body was a coiled spring, ready for action. David feared their adventure was doomed to end right then and there. It would only take a word for Hank to give them all up.

"They are wanted for destruction and theft of military property," the woman explained. "The FBI has issued a high priority search notification to all local law enforcement from Arizona to Michigan. They are extremely dangerous, and it's critical we apprehend them as quickly as possible. Any information you could give us would be greatly appreciated."

"Three men, you say?" Hank was still holding his pipe, and he tapped it against his chin. "No," he said after a long moment, shaking his head. "I haven't seen anyone like that. Sorry I couldn't be of more help to you."

The woman stared at him, her expression loudly proclaiming that she knew he was lying through his teeth. David couldn't help but share her astonishment, gawking as he watched his father calmly return the woman's incredulous gaze.

"Sir, let me remind you that these are wanted men. Any attempts to conceal them will be met with the full weight of the US government."

Hank's pleasant demeanor evaporated in an instant. "And let me remind you, I am a citizen of these United States. I will not be harassed on my own property. I already told you, I haven't seen anyone like you described." He glared at the female "marshal."

"Sir! You can and will be prosecuted if you persist in obstructing our investigation—"

"You can't come here and threaten me without so much as a warrant. I'm an American, goddammit. I know my rights!" Hank stepped into the woman's space, throwing her partner a look for good measure, as though daring him to object. "I said, I haven't seen them. Now get off my property before I call the police and have you arrested for trespassing." He went back into the house and slammed the door in their faces without another word.

David fidgeted anxiously until the fake marshals had returned to their car and driven away. The instant they were out of sight, he sprang up from his hiding place and dashed inside, Tim hot on his heels, only to find his father waiting for them in the middle of the living room. Suzanna was standing in the kitchen doorway, her hand pressed flat against her chest and her face white as a sheet. David eased around her and went to meet his father, his steps slowing as he met Hank's steady regard.

"Dad," he said hastily, glancing quickly toward Suzanna before dragging his gaze away from his mother and back toward Hank. "I can explain—"

"Explain what?" Hank folded his arms across his chest. "Those officers came here looking for criminals, and I know my son is not a criminal. He may be many things, but never that."

David blinked, his throat tightening on the words he wanted desperately to say. "Dad—" he managed before his father interrupted him again.

"Just tell me, David, are you in trouble?"

After a moment's hesitation, he nodded. "Yeah, I am. We all are."

Hank glanced at Tim. "I'm guessing this has something to do with you."

"It's not his fault," David interrupted.

"I asked him, David, not you."

Tim nodded. "Yes, sir. Your son is in danger because of me, but I'll make sure nothing happens to him." The earnestness in Tim's dark gaze took David's breath away. "I owe him my life."

Artifice or not, Tim's emotional appeal was powerful. Not even Hank was completely immune to Tim's engineered perfection. David saw his father slowly succumb, though he visibly fought to retain his animosity toward his son's lover. Finally Hank simply exhaled sharply and pinned David with a look that defied him to lie.

"It's not drugs or anything, is it?" Hank asked.

Not the illegal kind anyway, David thought as he shook his head.

"And you didn't kill anyone."

Swallowing loudly, David was glad he could answer truthfully, at least for now. "No. There's some bad people after Tim, and Anderson and I are just trying to keep him safe."

"Hmph. That sounds like a load of bullshit, but I'm trusting you, young man." Hank glared briefly at Tim. "And you too, David." Hank held his son's gaze. "Don't make me regret it."

"Thank you," David said, unable to order his thoughts into anything more profound right then.

"Whatever else I may think of you, you're still my son." Hank turned and started up the stairs, his shoulders slumped and his steps weary. "If anyone comes asking again, I'll make sure they never know you were here. Eat some breakfast before you go in the morning."

David stared sightlessly at the staircase until a gentle hand fell onto his arm. When he glanced down at his mother, Suzanna was crying again, but her face was radiant with joy. "Don't say I told you so," David murmured as he pulled her into a tight hug. He felt lighter than he had in years, as though a great weight had been lifted from his shoulders. "That's all I ask."

"No promises," she said, the words muffled against his chest.

Smiling, David closed his eyes and rested his cheek against the top of her head.

"I'M SORRY, sir." Farley's voice crackled over the radio. "Conley's parents' house was a bust."

Woodard gritted his teeth. "You and I both know he must have gone there, Lieutenant. Hell, he might even still be there. What about the car parked in front of the house? Did you run the plates?"

"Yes, sir. It's registered to a Samuel Larson."

Woodard shared a glance with Talbot, who was standing in his makeshift office at the new base. She raised her manicured eyebrows, apparently as surprised to hear that name as he had been.

"That must be Mitch Larson's brother," she offered.

Woodard nodded. "Larson is a known associate of Dr. Anderson," he said into the phone. "I want you to get back there and search that house yourself."

Farley was hesitant when she replied. "But, sir, Conley's father did have a point. If we try to go in there without a warrant and he contacts the LEOs—"

"I don't give a damn if he calls every local law enforcement mook in that Podunk town. Search that house, now!"

"Belay that order, Lieutenant Farley." Woodard glared daggers at Talbot, but she merely ignored him. "You were right to exercise caution. It wouldn't do to invite any unnecessary attention into the nature of what we're looking for." She spared him a pointed glance. "I'm glad someone remembers this operation is to be handled with complete discretion. Continue to search along the projected trajectory, Lieutenant. That will be all." She turned away as Farley voiced an acknowledgement and ended the call.

"You know, Talbot," Woodard spat, "I tolerate a lot of shit from you, but if you ever dare contradict me in front of my own fucking people again, I'll—"

"You'll what?" she asked calmly. "Thank me when I prevent you from making yet another attempt to screw up this mission? You're welcome, by the way, for perhaps saving your pet lieutenant's life. The TM unit is dangerous. Even if Farley and her detail had found it and cornered it at the house in Vinita, they likely wouldn't have been able to handle it alone. Let the unit come to us where we'll be more equipped to deal with both it and that traitor, Anderson." Talbot turned away and began to walk slowly around the lab. The technicians who worked there were busy with their various experiments, but several kept throwing her nervous glances. She moved over to one particular rack of vials and picked up a glass tube filled with a yellow-orange liquid. "Relax, General. Soon this will all be over."

Woodard marveled at her composure, even in the face of everything that had gone wrong since the TM unit broke itself and the others out of the Facility. He never would have guessed it would take this long to find the escapees, but he had obviously underestimated Anderson's resourcefulness. "Do you seriously believe they'll be foolish enough to come here?" he asked. "I'd think this is the last place Anderson would want to be. He has to know we'll be waiting for him."

Her smile was chilling, and he shivered despite himself. "Oh, yes," she replied coolly. "I assure you he will." She held up the vial and shook it gently. "After all, we have something he needs if he's going to save his beloved monster."

TWENTY

I CAUGHT myself glancing at the clock yet again. Sighing, I tried to focus instead on the solution of nitric acid and hexamine I was vigorously stirring. As Father Paul had predicted, the large hardware store in Springfield yielded all of the materials I needed to fashion a batch of plastic explosives, as well as a remote detonator. I had completed this procedure dozens of times during my training and could perform the steps blindfolded and half-asleep if necessary, as I'd been forced to do on more than one occasion. Still, I was glad David had stepped out to go find food for the three of us. Even though he was well aware of what I was by now, it still made me uncomfortable to think of him witnessing firsthand the awful things I was capable of. But David had been gone for longer than I thought the food run should have required, and I was getting worried.

"Relax, Tim," Father Paul said through his facemask. Both of us had our mouths and noses covered to protect us from the noxious fumes generated by the fresh batch of nitric acid. "He'll be fine. This town is more than large enough to hide us safely for the time being. And this motel is beyond nondescript." He fell silent for a moment as he watched me manipulate the toxic materials. "How are you holding up, my boy?" he asked finally.

"I'm fine," I answered. "A little tired, but the hamburger David said he'd bring back should provide sufficient B12 to keep me going for a while."

"That's not what I meant." Father Paul pointed to the large metal tub of water and crushed ice sitting at my feet. "Twenty minutes are up."

I stopped stirring and carried the glass container over to the tub. Carefully, I poured the mixture into the frigid bath. All there was to do now was wait for the RDX crystals to solidify. "I don't understand," I said when I had finished.

"I gather from what happened at David's parents' home that you two have, well, worked out your differences, shall we say." Father Paul chuckled at the color that bloomed across my cheeks just visible above the mask at the subtle tease.

I pursed my lips ruefully as I pulled the cloth from my face, feeling overheated. Clearly I needed to work harder on controlling my reactions to emotional stimulus. "David still loves me," I confessed. Merely saying the words suffused me with remembered heat. It had been nearly two days since we'd come together in the quiet darkness of his childhood bedroom. Yet I swore I could still feel David deep inside of me, moving against me, holding me tight. The lingering sensations had kept me company nearly every moment since.

Father Paul's gaze was steady as he removed his own protective mask. "But? I sense one in there somewhere."

I stared down at the tub, watching absently as the deadly white crystals slowly titrated out of the solution. "I killed him. David, that is. Or, at least I thought I did."

His eyes widened with surprise. "Why would you say that?"

I glanced at him. "You know about the simulations they used to reprogram me." It wasn't a question.

The confusion cleared from my creator's face. "Ah, yes. And they used David's brainwave patterns to inject him into the scenarios." His expression saddened. "I never imagined that's what Woodard was planning. I'm so sorry, my boy."

"Every time, during each mission, they tried to make me hurt him. But I didn't. I couldn't. At least until…."

"Until?" Father Paul prompted.

"Until I had to do it to save you. David was going to shoot you. He did shoot you, and so… I shot him." All of the doubt I had tried so desperately to foster in my own mind began to disintegrate before the terrible memory. I looked at my creator, silently begging for forgiveness. "I killed him."

"No, Tim." Father Paul shook his head firmly. "It wasn't real. You did nothing of the sort."

"You weren't there." I backed away from the bed where he was sitting and spun around until I was facing the desk where I'd situated the various equipment I needed to make the explosives. "All of those other times, I was able to resist the suggestion they tried to plant in my mind. But that time, that one time, I couldn't. They ordered me to kill him, and I did."

Father Paul appeared next to me and placed a comforting hand on my shoulder. "Tim, I highly suspect they drugged you in addition to running you through the simulations. As you grew stronger, the team discussed using powerful mind control substances to rob you of your free will if you ever became unmanageable. Woodard would have definitely resorted to them when you proved so recalcitrant. And yet, you still managed to fight them off." He gazed at me intently. "If I've taught you nothing else, my boy, it's not to believe anything where the general is concerned. Now tell me everything you remember."

I related the events of that fateful simulation in excruciating detail as though I were being debriefed, the rote recitation allowing me time to rein in my distressed emotions. "And then I pulled the trigger and shot him through the head," I concluded, my throat tightening despite my efforts to remain detached.

Father Paul tapped his finger against his lip, his gaze roving searchingly over my face. "You're leaving something out. Tell me."

Hesitating, I debated whether to share my suspicions about what had happened at the end of the simulation. The more I thought about it, the more I came to believe the conclusion I'd reached was nothing but wishful thinking. Still, it wasn't in me to avoid a direct order, especially not from Father Paul.

"Right before I pulled the trigger, David's face seemed to go out of focus. Almost as though—"

"Your brain refused to accept what was happening and compensated by manipulating the parameters." Father Paul smiled as I looked at him in confusion. "It's precisely as you said, my boy. You didn't shoot David. You couldn't have, not even under the influence of all those mind-bending drugs Woodard pumped into you. And do you know why?"

I shook my head.

"Because you love him. It really is that simple." Father Paul patted my cheek.

I didn't fully understand, but having him confirm my suspicions was a great comfort. I inhaled deeply, feeling like I could breathe freely for the first time in a long time. But knowing the truth and the reason behind it only added to my concerns. If my feelings for David were as strong as Father Paul believed—and I knew deep in my heart that they were—how could I in good conscience saddle the man I loved with someone like myself? Someone who was perfectly capable of killing in cold blood? A piece of ice cracked in the metal tub, drawing my attention back to the explosive material I had recently finished making. The sight of the crystallizing RDX solidified my resolve. No matter how ordinary I pretended to be, I wasn't, and David deserved better than someone who knew how to create deadly weapons out of items found under the kitchen sink.

"After this is all over, I need you to help David get safely back to Texas."

Father Paul's expression was unreadable. "And where will you be?"

"Away from him." I began to clean up the items on the desk. Once the RDX had fully formed, I would need space to begin combining it with the lecithin and heavy grade mineral oil that would serve as the moldable plastic to hold the explosives. "It's for the best."

"The best for whom?" Father Paul asked softly. "For David? Or for you?" When I didn't answer, he hummed under his breath. "Somehow I don't think David will be overly appreciative of your thoughtfulness."

DAVID BANGED on the motel door with his foot. His arms were laden with bags of greasy cheeseburgers and french fries, and he struggled not to drop them while balancing the holder filled with three large soft drinks. He smiled his gratitude when Anderson answered, and pushed past him into the room, managing to deposit his burden on a desk before he lost his grip. "Thanks." He began to rummage through the bags and pulled Tim's food out first. "Okay, kid. Fresh beef, right off the grill."

When Tim didn't rush to grab his share of the spoils, David looked over at him, noticing for the first time the air of depression that surrounded him. He watched Tim uncertainly, not sure whether he should say something. His hesitancy seemed justified when Anderson gave him a subtle headshake at his inquiring glance. David thought he knew what was bothering Tim. The prospect of what they were planning would leave anyone feeling a bit uneasy. But as they ate amid the background noise of some police procedural show on the room's pathetic twenty-four-inch television, Tim seemed to slip deeper into his funk. After there was nothing left of the takeout meal other than a few stray fries and the dregs of their sodas, David decided to speak up.

"Hey, kid," he began. Tim was sitting on one of the two double beds, and David had stretched out next to him as they ate. "You feeling okay? You look a little, I don't know, blue." David smiled, hoping he'd maybe simply misinterpreted Tim's mood. After all, the kid wasn't the easiest person to read. His smile faded when Tim looked over at him morosely. "What is it?" he prompted. He racked his brain for what could have upset Tim enough for him to show it. "Did, uh, something go wrong with the explosives?"

Anderson chuckled softly, and David shot him a confused glance. The old man merely shook his head and rose from the desk where he'd sat to eat. He dumped his trash in the bin located beneath it and stretched his arms into the air. "I think I'll catch some shut-eye. We're only about five hours out from the base, even if we avoid the interstate." His amusement dampened as he shuffled over to the bed farthest from the door. "This will be the last time we have to rest before… well, before whatever is going to happen happens."

David sobered even more at the reminder. *Right*, he thought. By this time tomorrow, Tim would be free of his manufactured disease and, hopefully, from the general's clutches. Or, he added grimly, they might all be dead. David hated to admit that the latter was the far more likely outcome, despite Anderson's confidence that they could pull this off.

"Sounds like a good idea," he said to no one in particular. When he turned to Tim, the kid looked even more miserable, if that were possible. "Hey, what's going on with you?" he asked, remembering that his earlier question had gone unanswered.

"I know I've said it before." Tim spoke softly, whether to avoid disturbing Anderson, who had lain down and was already beginning to snore, or because of his mood, David couldn't say for sure. "But I'm truly sorry for dragging you into all of this."

David shook his head dismissively. "And like I told you, I want to help. If anyone is to blame for me being involved, it's Woodard. Not you."

Tim looked down at the dingy mud-brown comforter covering the bed and plucked at a loose thread with his fingers. "Maybe, but all the same, I wish you had never gotten mixed up with all of this. Or with me."

David balled up his empty wrapper and tossed it onto the bed next to him before sitting up. "Hey, look at me." He placed his hand beneath Tim's chin and tilted it up until the kid was forced to meet his gaze. "Were you lying when you said you love me?" His eyes widening in denial, Tim shook his head as vigorously as David's fingers would allow. "Good," David replied, "because I meant it when I said I love you." He ran a thumb over Tim's cheek, watching raptly when long, sooty lashes fluttered in response. "If you believe me, then you have to know I'd much rather be here, at your side, than to think about you facing this without me. Okay?" he added with a gentle smile.

Instead of returning the gesture, Tim took hold of David's free hand and clasped it between both of his. "I can't stop thinking about what your mother said. About how worried Patricia was and how Bobby was looking for you."

"Looking for us," David corrected.

Tim raised a dismissive shoulder, as though he was skeptical at the notion that anyone back in Lubbock was concerned for him. "You have people who care about you, David. It's not fair to them, or to you, to keep you away from them. You should probably just go home—"

David pressed the pad of his thumb against Tim's full lips, interrupting what was clearly a rehearsed speech. "At the risk of sounding unforgivably clichéd, wherever you are is home to me." His voice deepened with emotion, and his heart began to race as he lost himself in fathomless dark eyes. "Lubbock is simply a place where I live. The BBW is nothing but a store I happen to own. Patricia, Bobby, and Bill," he continued, referring to his second-shift manager, William Hurley, "they're my friends, no doubt about it. But they're not you." David shifted closer to Tim. "They're not who I think about when I first wake up in the morning, or who I dream about after I've dropped off to sleep at night. I haven't fallen in love with any of them." He stared into Tim's eyes, willing the kid to believe him. "I'm in love with you."

Tim's eyelashes fluttered against David's cheeks as he leaned in for a kiss. Saying the words aloud wiped away the uncertainties that had lingered in his heart ever since Woodard showed him that blasted simulation of Tim shooting him. So what if Tim had killed him in some twisted, manufactured game. None of it had been real. David knew deep down Tim would never intentionally hurt him. The only thing that mattered was the way Tim had struggled so viciously to protect him when they were first captured. All he needed to remember was how the kid had fought so bravely, armed with nothing but his fists, feet, and skill to break them out of that nightmarish laboratory. And there had been nothing fake about his heartfelt response as they made love surrounded by the remnants of David's forgotten youth. David couldn't deny how much it had hurt to see the utter coldness on Tim's face when he'd pulled the trigger, but he told himself to get the fuck over it. It had been nothing but a meaningless lie.

Tim's lips glistened temptingly when David finally pulled back. He grinned when Tim blinked at him in hazy confusion.

"I'm sure Patricia and Bobby are just as worried about you. I don't think you realize how much you mean to them." David chuckled. "I know for a fact Patricia thinks of you as the little brother she never had. And as for Bobby, hell, he worships the ground you walk on. So no more talk like you don't matter to anyone, because you do. You matter to them, and you sure as heck matter to me." The haunting uncertainty on Tim's face made David want to wring Woodard's neck with his bare hands. He knew he was fighting against a lifetime of conditioning, of Tim believing he was less than human, but beneath the doubt, he could see a nascent glimmer of hope. "*When* we get back to Lubbock," David emphasized, "I know they'll be relieved and thrilled to see you again. Okay?"

Tim gazed at him with a rapt solemnity that was almost painful to behold. "I swear to you," he whispered fervently, his voice husky with emotion, "I will make sure no one ever comes hunting for us again. When this is all over, you'll have your life back. I promise."

David took the vow to heart, knowing Tim would do everything in his power to fulfill it. He made his own silent pledge that he would take Tim back home with him no matter what. While it didn't lessen his trepidation of what they were about to face, the unspoken pledge gave him something to strive toward. All he wanted was for them to spend the rest of their lives together, nothing more and absolutely nothing less.

"You know," David said, smiling to lighten the tension, "we'll need to come up with a good cover story for why we disappeared. Something the folks back in Lubbock will buy." He laughed, encouraging Tim to join in the levity by nudging him with a friendly elbow. "Any suggestions?"

The kid was adorable as he pursed his lips, earnestly considering the puzzle David had presented to him. "Mmmm," he hummed, the sound perversely reaching straight into David's shorts as he found himself staring at Tim's luscious mouth. "Maybe we could say that I kidnapped you and held you hostage as my sex slave."

Tim's delivery was so deadpan it took several seconds before David fully appreciated exactly what he had suggested. His mouth fell open as he stared at Tim stupidly, unable to comprehend that the kid had made such a deliciously naughty joke. "Um, w-what?" he stammered.

Tim simply smiled at him. "Father Paul said we should get some sleep." After planting a glancing kiss on David's slack lips, he flopped down onto the mattress.

A tug on his shirt caught David's attention, and he shook off his shock long enough to settle down on the bed next to Tim, who was still visibly amused at having left him speechless. Tim instantly arranged them to his liking, burying his face in David's chest and entwining their limbs such that escape—if David had so desired for whatever reason—was impossible. Sighing, David tried to ignore the throbbing that grew predictably between his legs at Tim's nearness. *Sex slave? I'll show him who's a sex slave.* His overheated brain proceeded to conjure explicitly detailed fantasies, and David groaned, enjoying every minute of the delicious torture. If Anderson wasn't on the other side of the room, he'd show the kid every last one of them. As it was, he had to resign himself to a blissful, if fitful, rest. Wrapping his arms around Tim, David pulled him closer, equally determined to never let go of his precious find.

TWENTY-ONE

FRETTING. I engaged in the new exercise the entire way between Springfield and St. Louis. Adjusting the frequency of the impromptu transmitter I'd rigged to act as a remote detonator was easily accomplished and provided me with little distraction from my increasing edginess. I kept dwelling on everything that could possibly go wrong, and there were almost too many contingencies to contemplate. As we finally rejoined the interstate at I-55 and motored across the Mississippi by way of the Poplar Street Bridge, my fretting began to turn to panic.

I found myself staring at the back of David's head as Father Paul sped us toward the Illinois border. What if this was the last time we ever saw each other? Though I'd willingly give my life for David, my stomach clenched with nausea at the mere thought that we might be forced to part. What frightened me wasn't the mission but the prospect of losing him forever. Ironically, dealing with the entirely unwanted sensation of dread occupied me as we weaved through East St. Louis. I didn't take note of our surroundings until we had bypassed Fairview Heights, sticking to the freeway in the interest of speed over stealth. Soon, Father Paul exited the freeway at Route 158. By the time Scott Air Force base loomed into view off to our left, I still hadn't gotten a grip on my unruly emotions.

"The compound is located about a mile and a half beyond SAF," Father Paul elaborated as he turned left where Route 158 joined Route 161. The sun had just dipped below the horizon, and he turned off the car's headlights as he suddenly veered right off the main road. Before either of his passengers could question the seemingly rash maneuver, the tires found a narrow dirt road.

"Good thing you were the one driving," David observed. "I'd never have seen that turn-off."

"Which reminds me." Father Paul pulled a folded piece of paper from his pocket. "I made this while you two were still sleeping." When David and I had awakened earlier in the afternoon, Father Paul had apparently been up for some time. He'd had food waiting for us and had repacked our belongings into the backpacks Suzanna had given us. "It's a rough sketch of the base's layout. The place is a labyrinth. If we get separated, you will never find your way." He handed the map to David, who studied it carefully while I glanced at it briefly over his shoulder, committing it to memory.

David whistled. "Wow. You did this in, what, a couple of hours? I'm impressed," he added before pocketing the map.

Deep breaths, I said to myself, unable to concentrate enough to participate in the conversation. I could have gone my entire life without this particular emotional experience. Still, I didn't have to wonder at the source of my anxiety. It wasn't the hastily made explosives packed as tightly as we could manage in the trunk. I was confident in my skills on that front. No, the cause was sitting in front of me in the passenger's seat. It was insanity to think David would be able to handle himself during the infiltration. He was a civilian, not a soldier. The moment the car came to a halt, I voiced my decision.

"You should wait here in the car, David. If the operation goes badly, we'll need access to a secure means of escape."

He turned to look at me incredulously over the headrest. "You're kidding me with this, right? I thought we already figured it all out. He's the lead." David jabbed his thumb at Father Paul. "You're the offense. I'm the one who makes sure no one is sneaking up on our tails."

My mentor's expression was understanding but firm as he looked at me through the rearview mirror. "He's right, my boy. It will take all three of us to make this work."

"I don't trust that he'll be useful if we run into real trouble." I ignored the flash of hurt that crossed David's face. If it took me being a jerk to keep the man I loved out of harm's way, so be it. "You, at least, have had training," I added, returning Father Paul's gaze with a pointed stare. "Except for me showing David how to load and fire the Sig, he's completely green. He'll be a liability, and you know it."

"I'm sorry, Tim." Father Paul's tone indicated that the discussion was over. "If anything happens to compromise you, we'll need David as backup. We all go or none of us does."

David's eyes had gone flat and cold during the exchange. "That's settled, then? Good." He faced forward to look out at the rapidly darkening view, the muscles in his jaw visibly clenching.

I ached to apologize, but my fears kept me silent. It had been difficult enough having nightmares about the simulation of David lying on the floor of Father Paul's lab, shot and bleeding, without witnessing it in real life. I was tempted to wrap the seat belt around David's wrists and tie him to his seat, but without Father Paul backing me up there was nothing more I could do. Father Paul's caution was likely warranted. The previous day's burger was already wearing off, and my body was feeling the effects of the resulting vitamin deficiency. Cursing my manufactured infirmity, I took a deep breath and resolved myself to the fact I couldn't shield David from the danger we were preparing to face.

"All right," Father Paul said, "the base is on the other side of Route 4. We'll have to cross it on foot. The security system includes sonic detectors, so the car's engine will set off the alarms." He opened his door and swung his feet to the ground. "The equipment will be heavy, but we must bear with it."

David and I followed suit and joined him at the rear of the car. Father Paul pulled a dark hat over his gray hair and handed another one to David before opening the trunk. He distributed the three duffel bags stowed within between us before retrieving a smaller backpack.

"You take the explosives," I suggested, trading the bag containing the RDX for the one my mentor was carrying. "They're lighter. Just be careful not to drop them."

"Naturally," Father Paul replied drolly. He eyed the bulge in my pocket, verifying I had the detonator. David hefted his bag without comment, taking a second to likewise cover the bright blond of his hair. We had picked up straps from a sporting goods store on our way out of

Springfield, allowing us to sling the bags crosswise over our shoulders instead of having to carry them in our hands. It would make the going much easier.

I opened my duffel and examined its contents. I was carrying a Colt M4 with extra ammo, which meant David had the Sig 516. Since David had zero familiarity with the Colt, giving him the Sig was the best option… except for forcing him to stay behind. David darted a glance at me before looking away, and I sighed. Since it was inevitable we were all going together, I might as well clear the air.

"I'm sorry," I muttered. "I didn't mean to insult you. I only—"

"Wanted to keep me out of trouble," David finished. He smiled wanly. "Yeah, it's okay, kid. I appreciate the sentiment, but like the man said, we're all in this together."

The curve of his lips softened into something more genuine, and I felt some of the tension lodged in my stomach dissipate. I nodded, unable to find the necessary words to express everything I was feeling.

At a gesture from Father Paul, we set out. We had timed our arrival so dusk had begun to fall in earnest, lending us the cover of darkness. Unlike the desert landscape around the original Facility, the level farmland surrounding the Air Force base was unchallenging. It also provided little cover, and I was grateful for the onrush of night.

Our destination came into view after half a mile. The installation was as featureless as its predecessor, though it boasted a more aboveground profile. It had been built to resemble run-down barracks with twelve identical, ramshackle structures arranged in a staggered formation of three rows of four buildings each. A fence surrounding the buildings had all but fallen down in several places, lending support to the fiction of neglect the designers had intended to foster. The area was mostly deserted, but a few shadowy figures moved between the buildings, indicating a minimal guard presence.

"Do you know which building the lab is in?" David asked, voicing the question running through my mind. "Or do we have to search each one of them?"

"Yes, I do, and no, we don't," Father Paul answered succinctly. "These structures are merely a front. As with the Facility, the compound is situated primarily belowground. Only one of the buildings houses the true entrance. The rest are false fronts, and trying the wrong door will trigger a general alarm."

"Which is the correct one?" I inquired.

"The structure in the middle row, second from our right," Father Paul replied.

I studied the layout for a moment before nodding absently. "We'll need to draw attention away from the building in case the situation gets hairy once we're down below. Is there any way to reach the underground bunker from the other buildings?"

Father Paul shook his head. "No. Only the true entrance provides access to the base."

"Good. Follow me." Keeping low to prevent being seen by the guards, I ran toward the far left side of the group of fictitious barracks. I heard scuffling sounds behind me and was reassured that Father Paul and David were keeping pace.

I crouched next to the wall of the leftmost building in the first row. The phony door was around the front of the structure to our right. The night was essentially moonless, only a thin crescent betraying the natural satellite's position. Light spilled out from fixtures hanging over the doors of each barrack, but they did little to push back the enveloping darkness. I made quick work of positioning one of my impromptu explosives against the wall. We had spent the afternoon before leaving the motel encasing the RDX in putty, so all I had to do was press it firmly against the brick for the bomb to stick fast. Arming the receiver was the work of seconds, and my remote explosive was ready for use. A quick glance as we darted to the second building told me that our presence had gone undetected. I repeated the procedure on the long back wall of the structure in the third row.

"Two of these will make a sizable bang," I whispered. "No point in wasting any more of them here."

"Then it's time to make our way inside." Father Paul looked meaningfully at the bags David and I carried. "Might I suggest that we arm ourselves first."

I laid the bag I was carrying carefully on the ground, and Father Paul reached in to retrieve one of the handguns Larson had provided, a semiautomatic Ruger SR40. It didn't have the magazine capacity of the rifles, but at fifteen rounds per clip, it was still a formidable weapon. As my mentor pocketed several extra clips, I glanced over at David. He was fumbling with the Sig, trying to insert one of the cartridges, his face noticeably devoid of color even in the limited illumination.

"Follow our lead, David," Father Paul suggested, "and you'll be fine."

David finally managed to get the clip properly seated. Wiping away the sheen of sweat that dampened his upper lip, he returned Father Paul's gaze. "Yeah, okay. I'm sure as hell not planning to wander off on my own."

Extending my senses, I could hear David's elevated heartbeat. Despite my concerns, I couldn't help feeling proud of his bravery. Besides, he looked pretty sexy holding the rifle. I noticed I was starting to get hard. Blaming my condition on the adrenaline seeping into my system in preparation for the impending mission, I forced my attention back to the matter at hand. I peered between the buildings to gauge the wisdom of approaching our target directly.

"We need to go back the way we came. It'll take more time, but we're less likely to be detected if we come from that direction." There was no disagreement, so I led the others back around the darkened perimeter. After long minutes of crouched running, we arrived at the outermost barrack in the middle row, on the side of the compound opposite of where I'd placed the RDX. There were six guards on patrol, and after watching for a short while, I discerned a pattern to their movements. "They're walking the paths between the buildings so there's always a pair of them watching all the internal access points. We need some way to draw them away from the entrance."

"What about the bombs?" David asked.

"No," Father Paul said before I could reply. "We don't want to show our hand too soon."

Movement from above caught my eye. I looked up and pointed. "There," I said, using my finger to indicate what I'd seen. A black shape wheeled overhead in lazy circles some distance away, the buzzard obviously looking for its last meal of the day. "Do you have the sequencer ready?" I asked Father Paul.

He nodded, comprehension dawning on his face, and pulled the small device from the smaller bag he was carrying. Spying a suitable rock,

I quickly targeted my quarry and let the missile fly. It struck true, and the bird let out a loud squawk of pain as it plummeted to the ground.

"What the hell was that?" a voice said from the space between the two columns of buildings nearest where we were hiding.

"Sounded like a bird," another voice answered, "but we should check it out."

Right on cue, the guards ventured out into the surrounding landscape, leaving the pathway unwatched. We darted over to the door Father Paul had identified as the true entryway into the compound. Sequencer in hand, the scientist used it to bypass the code on the electronic lock. David stared nervously in the direction the guards had gone, watching for their return.

"Like I said, it wasn't nothin' but a dying bird."

"Well, something must have hit it for it to just fall out of the sky like that."

"Maybe, but right now, I don't give a damn. Let's get back to our post. We can take another look when our shift is over, if something hasn't carried it off by then."

I heard the men returning, but Father Paul had the lock open before the guards caught sight of us. He ducked inside, and I herded David ahead of me before closing the door, leaving no trace of our passing.

"Shit, I can't see a thing."

David's curse was apt. The entryway was completely devoid of light, but it took only a moment before my pupils compensated. As they dilated to their maximum extent, a faint glow far below where we stood became visible, as did the way to reach it.

"We're at the top of a flight of stairs," I said softly.

"You can see?" David exhaled in a whistle. "Incredible."

"I think this might be a good spot for another diversion," Father Paul murmured.

I placed the explosive at the edge of the door more by feel than sight. If nothing else, it would serve to blow the door open should we need a quick way out. "Hold on to me," I ordered once I was finished. A hand landed on my shoulder while another felt for mine. Squeezing David's hand in my own, I started down the stairs, going slowly so neither he nor my creator lost their grips.

The light brightened as we neared the bottom. Given how long it had taken us to descend, I guesstimated we were over a hundred feet underground. At the bottom of the stairwell, a long hallway stretched off to either side. There wasn't a soul in sight, the security seeming to be even more lax than Father Paul had predicted. Still, I refused to let myself be complacent. Somewhere in this subterranean labyrinth was the key to my salvation along with my deadliest nemesis.

"Which way?"

"Left," Father Paul said in response to David's query. "The lab is situated on the far side of the building. The main door is the only way in, and the room is surrounded on its remaining sides by concrete and earth. The center of the compound is where the offices and living quarters are located."

I stared down the corridor in the opposite direction. I couldn't see anything, but goose bumps rose up inexplicably on the back of my neck.

"What's wrong?" David asked, following my intent gaze.

"Nothing, except—"

"Except what?" David pressed.

"It's too quiet." I exhaled, frustrated with myself and my uncharacteristic paranoia. I was far more accustomed to relying on my physical senses. This odd premonition I was experiencing was extremely unsettling. "Never mind," I insisted. "We should keep moving." The click of the safety disengaging on my Colt bounced off the bare walls, and I was relieved when I heard the others follow my example.

The rubber soles of the tennis shoes David's mother had bought us allowed us to move silently along the concrete flooring. Two left turns and three rights found us at the mouth of the hall fronting the lab. Father Paul glanced around the corner toward the door. "One guard. Damn it."

"What?" David breathed. "Only one sounds good to me."

"Except he won't have the card key we'll need. Only the lab techs and execs have those." Father Paul sighed. "We'll have to double back and find a more likely target."

I knelt beside Father Paul so I could likewise see into the adjacent corridor. I was concerned about the guard's presence for another reason. Specifically, I wondered why there was only one man. Father Paul had said the lab would be heavily secured compared to the rest of the base, but that didn't seem to be the case. The discrepancy didn't do anything to alleviate my suspicion that something was very wrong. Yet, when a female figure in a white coat suddenly came into view from the far end of the hall and began walking toward the entrance to the lab, I didn't hesitate.

"There."

The single word was the only warning I gave to my companions. The technician froze as she saw me dashing toward her. The guard had been watching the woman's approach and barely had time to react to her expression of alarm before I was on him. Tackling the larger man to the floor, I delivered a sharp blow to the guard's head with my elbow, rendering him unconscious. The technician's eyes widened in fear when I looked up at her from my crouched position.

"Don't worry, my dear. We simply need to make use of your key."

The woman risked glancing away from me at Father Paul's reassuring tone. "Dr. Anderson?" she asked uncertainly. "You're alive?"

"It would appear so," he replied with a kindly smile. He walked slowly toward the technician, the Colt lowered and his posture slumped to appear less intimidating. The effect was somewhat ruined by David, who followed behind nervously, his knuckles white where he gripped the Sig.

"I-I think I need to report this," she stammered. "General Woodard told us how you helped the TM project break free a few months ago." She looked down at Tim, realization spreading across her mousey features. "You're it, aren't you? The TM unit."

"Tim is a he," Father Paul said, "not an it. Now, Simone, do be a dear and let us have your access card. There's no need for you to alert anyone and no need for anyone to get hurt." His voice deepened on the latter, and she didn't miss the implied menace in his words. Her hand shook as she pulled a credit card-sized piece of plastic from her coat pocket and handed it to her erstwhile supervisor. "Excellent," he crooned, all traces of intimidation gone in an instant.

I kept my attention on the technician as Father Paul slid the card into the reader situated to the right side of the door. The light on the reader flashed green, and the door slid open.

"Fuck me."

Whipping my head around at David's groan, I felt my entire body tightening, my muscular and endocrine system revving into high gear. The door opened onto a large room, brightly lit with florescent lights and covered floor to ceiling with bleached white Formica. The room's spaciousness, however, was dwarfed by the dozen soldiers standing at attention in a loose arc formation. They carried an impressive array of arms and sported body armor that matched the camouflage pattern of their fatigues. In front of them, the general smirked in satisfaction. He was dressed as I had always seen him, casually wearing his uniform, arrogantly eschewing the armor his men wore. Other than the sidearm at Woodard's hip, he didn't appear to be carrying any weapons. To his left, an older woman with piercing light green eyes stared at us, distaste etched on her handsome features.

"I have to hand it to you, Talbot. You called it exactly on the nose." Woodard sneered. "I swore you didn't have the balls to try something like this, Anderson, but I guess I was wrong."

"Compassion," Talbot said, staring coldly at her former husband, her thin lips quirked slightly in amusement. "It always was your downfall, Paul. Though I can't say I blame you for your single-mindedness. Even when everyone else at the Company wanted to abandon the TM project as a wasteful money sinkhole, I was determined to keep it going." Her expression darkened. "For Cody, you understand. But you took it a step beyond duty, didn't you? You made yourself a new child to replace our son," she spat. "I knew you would do everything in your power to ensure the TM unit's survival. So," she continued, spreading her hands before her, "where else could you go but here?"

The corner of Father Paul's mouth quirked up. "Your clever mind was the first thing that attracted me to you, Coleen. Did you know that?" He shrugged. "Of course, that was back when you still had a heart." His expression was dispassionate as she glared at the pointed taunt. "I see you've done some rearranging since the last time I was here." His gaze flitted about the room, plainly searching for something.

"You won't find it, Anderson." Unconcerned with the domestic dispute unfolding before him, Woodard crossed his arms over his broad chest, appearing completely pleased with himself. "Not that you'll have the chance to get a closer look. Take them," he ordered to the men arrayed behind him.

Six of the soldiers moved forward simultaneously. I snapped my gun up to attention, noting in my peripheral vision that David had quickly followed suit, the gritty determination on his face making up for his amateurish stance. Concerned about the amount of firepower arrayed against us, I stepped in front of my mentor protectively, knowing his handgun wouldn't do much against the soldiers' body armor.

"Ah, ah," Talbot scolded. "You don't want to use those in here. There are all sorts of nasty chemicals in these vials." She gestured gracefully with one hand toward the walls. Glass tubes were arranged in neat rows in the locked cases that covered nearly every available inch of space. "I doubt you're feeling as sacrificial as these two, are you, Mr. Conley?"

She glanced at David. He blanched but remained silent, his aim unwavering. I felt another surge of pride at how well he was keeping it together in the face of such overwhelming odds. But not impossible ones. Already a viable plan was forming in my mind for how to get us out of this. We likely wouldn't be able to retrieve the drug, but keeping David and Father Paul alive was now my paramount objective.

"I can take them," I said softly. "It's in my pocket," I added, referring to the detonator, grateful Father Paul was so close behind me he would be able to retrieve it without being seen.

Father Paul exhaled gustily, not liking the situation but obviously seeing no alternative. "If you must," he whispered in response.

"On the count of three," I instructed.

Talbot's voice rose over the tense atmosphere. "Did Paul ever tell you why we got involved in the TM project?" She regarded me pointedly as she spoke.

I was amazed that she was addressing me as a person, but refused to let myself be distracted. "One," I mumbled through clenched teeth.

"Our son, Cody, was killed by terrorists." Her features grew pinched, her expression conveying genuine sadness. "It was a needless tragedy, one which could have been prevented if only the insurgents responsible had been dealt with before they could unleash their hatred on a group of innocent students."

"Coleen," Father Paul interjected abruptly, "don't do this."

"Two." I kept my focus on the task at hand, hoping Father Paul would do the same. Besides, I really didn't want to hear a repeat of the story about his long-lost son. I'd already accepted my subordinate place in my creator's life. Shutting down the nascent resurgence of jealousy, I stared fixedly at the soldiers, keeping them in my line of sight.

"Never again, we promised ourselves," Talbot continued. "Didn't we, Paul? We were so dedicated to the project that we gave the ultimate gift, our ability to create life, to avenge the one that was taken from us. Our very own DNA."

"What?" David breathed, seeming to realize what was coming before I could process everything her revelation implied.

"Thr—"

"Now, Tim, was it?" Talbot interrupted the last of my countdown. "Be a good boy, and listen to your mother."

The words reached into my brain and squeezed, driving away all free will, all memory, all sense of self. A keening cry reached my ears, but I registered it only in the abstract, not as sound my own vocal cords had produced. I was no longer the human called "Tim." I was no longer a human at all.

It was a tool, a weapon, and it had been triggered to fulfill its primary mission—to follow orders. Lowering the rifle as the noise faded away, it stood at attention and waited for instructions.

"Tim!" David shouted, his voice shrill with shock. "What the hell are you doing?"

Talbot smiled benignly. "Whatever I tell it to."

"Coleen," Dr. Anderson growled, "what did you do to him?"

She raised an eyebrow at her former husband. "Only a tiny suggestion I had implanted in the unit's mind while it was being reprogrammed. I thought taking the precaution might come in handy for precisely such a circumstance as this. TM 05637," Talbot said, coldly dismissing the scientist from her notice.

"Ma'am," it replied in a clipped, precise tone.

"Be a dear and take the good doctor prisoner. Oh, and while you're at it, kill Mr. Conley."

TWENTY-TWO

DAVID STARED at Tim, torn between feeling gut-wrenching pity and being scared shitless. Those beautiful brown eyes he adored so much were staring at him without an ounce of recognition. All he could see on Tim's impassive face was the intent to fulfill the fatal command. David almost couldn't blame the kid for shutting down, not that he'd done it willingly. It must have been awful to have learned the identity of his biological parents in such a terrible way. Whatever David had thought about Anderson's ex-wife before, he absolutely hated her now. How could she be so heartless to her own child?

But whatever Tim might be feeling was clearly trapped along with the last vestiges of his free will. The mindlessly submissive soldier Tim had tried so hard to bury was fully in control thanks to whatever that cold-eyed bitch had done to him. His expression was all the more frightening for its utter blankness. Even back when they'd first met, he hadn't been this detached. Back then, he'd at least pretended that he understood human emotions, though they had obviously not come naturally to him. But now there was nothing behind Tim's eyes but death. David's death.

"H-hey, kid," David stammered, his throat dry as Tim trained the Colt toward him. Somewhere, in the part of him that wasn't terrified, he could appreciate the irony of the situation. Just when he'd managed to convince himself the simulation Woodard had shown him was nothing more than the general's sick fantasy, here they were, acting the damn thing out for real. He held his own weapon at his side, pointing the barrel unthreateningly at the floor as he raised a beseeching hand. "You don't want to do this. It's me."

Tim held the rifle steady on his target, finger on the trigger. But the shot never came. For some reason Tim was hesitating. David allowed himself to inhale as a sliver of hope broke through his dread. Maybe he'd actually get out of this alive.

"That's right, kid. You don't want to shoot me."

A fine shiver began at Tim's feet and traveled up his body, as though something within him were fighting the order he'd been given with every fiber of his will.

"TM 05637," Talbot barked, "I told you to kill him."

Tim's gaze narrowed as his trigger finger twitched. David could feel his heart attempting to jump into his throat.

"Tim, please," he begged. "We promised we'd go back home together. Don't you remember?" Shoving down his fear, David forced himself to move closer to the motionless figure. "We can see Bobby and Patricia. And my mom said she'd come to visit. I know you want to see all of them again. Put down the gun, and I swear, we'll get out of here and head straight there, just you and me."

"TM 05637!"

A fine sheen of sweat popped out on Tim's forehead, and David saw a glimmer of life behind the frozen mask of his face.

"Tim," David pleaded, his voice cracking with urgency. "I love you. I don't want to lose you, not like this. Please, come back to me."

"Do it now!"

Talbot's screech was nearly overcome by the shot that rang out, deafening in the close confines of the lab. David jerked, waiting to register the searing pain of the bullet ripping through his body. But after a moment of sheer panic, he realized he was unharmed. He stared at Tim's colorless face, but the kid wasn't looking at him. Instead he was looking at the woman who had just revealed herself to be his mother. By the time David turned toward her, the disbelief on her handsome features had already begun to melt away. She slid to the floor, blood pooling beneath her from the gaping wound in her chest.

"I'm sorry, Coleen. I truly am."

David looked around at the voice and found himself staring at the still-smoking gun in Anderson's hand. The scientist was gazing down sadly at his ex-wife's body.

"Like I told you," he said, "I'll do anything to protect our son."

"You son of a bitch." Woodard appeared almost impressed, though he had his sidearm fixed firmly on his former associate. "I didn't think you had it in you. She was a pain in my ass, sure enough, but don't think I'm going to thank you for that. And I'll be damned if I'm going to let you walk out of here with my weapon again." The general glanced at Tim. "TM 05637," he barked.

"Y-yes, sir." Tim spoke the words as though they were being forced out of him, still clearly under the control of Talbot's implanted suggestion. David could tell he was struggling valiantly against it, but he wasn't sure how much longer Tim would be able to resist.

Woodard's smile reflected grim satisfaction at his realization that Tim was also receptive to his commands. "Change of plans," he said. "I want you to take both of them out, Conley and Anderson."

The scientist switched his attention to his protégé and regarded Tim with a fixed gaze. In a blur of motion unbelievable for someone his age, Anderson suddenly dashed forward. He reached into the pocket of Tim's jacket and pulled out the detonator.

"Anderson!" Woodard shouted. "What in the hell—"

Anderson hit the button before the general could draw a bead on him. At the same moment, Tim directed his Colt upward and fired off a volley at the ceiling. The bombs they had planted as they made their way to the lab went off in rapid succession even as .223 rounds shredded the florescent lights to powder. The explosions were deafening, shaking the floor beneath their feet and causing more than one person in the lab to fall to the ground. Ignoring Talbot's previous warning, Woodard cursed and returned fire, as did several of his soldiers. David grunted, barely managing to maintain his hold on the Sig as something crashed into him and knocked him to the ground. He shot blindly in the direction of the muzzle flashes of the enemy weapons and heard the answering staccato of the Colt coming from slightly above his head. The Ruger sounded as well, but the emergency lighting came on in time for David to see it clatter to the floor along with Anderson.

Though Tim didn't call out, his face reflected his horror. David was relieved to see the kid's expressive capacity had returned to normal, even as he discovered the source of Tim's distress. The soldiers and Woodard had begun to abandon the lab the instant the shooting started, but someone had gotten in a lucky hit. Tim continued to lay down cover fire, encouraging the stragglers to get the hell out while they could. Only when the three of them were alone in the lab did Tim turn toward the fallen scientist, frantically pulling Anderson's clothes off to find the site of his injury.

"No," Anderson wheezed, "there's no time."

Tim ignored him and continued to rip at Anderson's clothing until he revealed a chest wound eerily reminiscent of the one the scientist had inflicted on the Talbot woman. Tim's mother. David was still trying to wrap his mind around that astonishing revelation. Blood bubbled up to Anderson's lips as he struggled to breathe, and David didn't need a medical background to know the bullet had pierced his lung.

"I can save you," Tim said doggedly. "I won't let them take you from me again."

"It's too late." Anderson coughed, expelling more spittle tinged with bright red. "I need you to listen to me now. The drug you need is in a vial labeled 'Ambrosia.' You can see, even in this light. Tell me if it's in this room."

Reluctantly, Tim dragged his gaze away from the scientist and did as asked, carefully scanning the rows of vials in the glass cases. The firefight had shattered some of the cases, but most of them and the vials appeared to be intact. "No," he said after a moment, shaking his head. His pupils were unnaturally wide to accommodate the dimness of the emergency lighting, and David felt another stab of amazement at what Anderson had created. "It's not here."

Anderson fought to draw in a breath. "Damn," he grated. "It must be in the smaller lab. Do you see the door?"

"Yes," Tim replied. David followed Tim's gaze to the narrow opening on the far side of the room.

"No need for subtlety now. Shoot out the lock and find the drug—" The scientist broke off as a wracking cough assaulted him, his features twisting in agony.

"Okay. And then we're leaving. All of us." Tim's expression was closed off, and he clearly refused to consider any alternative.

Anderson shook his head. "No. I'll only slow you down." His smile was gruesome as blood coated his lips, but his love for Tim shone from his eyes. "It's funny, isn't it? Here we are again, back where you started on your adventure."

David wondered what that meant, but didn't want to interrupt. This moment wasn't about him. It was between the newly revealed father and son. He watched Tim's expression crumple as tears formed in his dark eyes.

"Like I told you then," Anderson wheezed, "I did all of this because I love you."

"I love you too," Tim said, his voice full of conviction though it was raspy with the effort to hold back his grief.

Anderson's smile broadened, the effect only slightly ruined by an underlying grimace of pain. "I'm grateful you finally know what that means. I thank you, David."

"Me?"

"You taught my boy what love is. That should have been my job, but I failed, as I did at so much else. It was you who broke Tim's trance, by reminding him of what is important." Tim keened softly as the scientist suffered through another round of coughing. Speaking was clearly taking great effort, but he wouldn't be deterred. "I told Coleen the truth. Giving you the life I always wanted you to have is worth any sacrifice. After all, I'm your father, my boy, and a father should do right by his child. Now you can have the life you always should have had if you hadn't had such horrible parents." Anderson turned his head slightly and glanced at the dead woman lying on the floor several feet away. "It's a shame Coleen never understood that."

David heard low voices coming from the hallway. "I think Woodard is coming back, probably with reinforcements. We need to get out of here."

"Father Paul," Tim whimpered, "please don't make me do this. Don't make me leave you here."

"Save yourself. That's the last order I'll ever give you." Anderson reached up with a trembling hand and cupped Tim's cheek. "But as your father, not as your creator." The hand fell suddenly, and he was gone, his eyes remaining open to gaze lovingly on the last thing he'd ever see.

Tim bent over the body, finally giving in to his anguish. David wanted nothing more than to pull the kid into his arms and console him, but this was neither the time nor place.

"Tim, we need to find the drug and get out of here."

Tim sat up slowly as though weighed down by his grief. He dashed away the moisture on his cheeks with the back of his hand and nodded in silent reply. David followed close behind when Tim finally stood and headed for the inner room. But before they could go more than a few steps, he heard a faint clattering noise. A shade faster than David could react, Tim stopped cold and swung around to the door leading into the corridor.

"Hold your breath!" he yelled.

David caught only a glimpse of a small cylinder a split second before thick, choking smoke filled the room. The smoke stung his eyes and filled his lungs, robbing him of both sight and breath. All he was left with was sound, which resolved into a hail of loud, angry voices. Something grabbed the scruff of his jacket and dragged him bodily across the floor. With the working remnants of his abused, oxygen-starved brain, he knew it had to be Tim. He didn't struggle, and soon they were both in the hall, free of the effects of the smoke bomb.

"Thanks," he hacked, trying to clear his lungs. His eyes continued to water from the acrid fumes, and he could barely discern the formless shapes rushing into the room they'd just vacated. "But we lost our chance at getting into the lab."

Tim helped David to his feet. "We'll worry about that later." He kept his voice low, using the sounds of the soldiers hunting them to mask their presence. "Right now we need to regroup. Let's get back up top."

"What about the drug?" David insisted. "We can't just leave without it." Even though everything had gone to shit, they'd risked their lives for a reason, to save Tim's. Failure meant his inevitable and untimely death, and David refused to give up so easily. Nor, he knew, would Anderson want him to. The shouting grew louder, and David realized the soldiers were headed in their direction.

"Come on," Tim said, coming to the same conclusion. He led the way farther down the corridor until they came across a closed door. After kicking it in, Tim dove inside, pulling David along with him.

David tried to breathe quietly, but it proved a challenge when his heart was trying to crash through his ribcage. Tim had shut the door behind them and had his ear pressed against it, listening for signs they had been discovered. David realized they were in a storage closet, the mundane janitorial items sitting on the shelves threatening to make a bubble of hysterical laughter break free from his lips.

After several interminable minutes, Tim's shoulders relaxed. "We're clear."

"Okay, so how do we get back in there?"

Tim shook his head. "We don't. It's too dangerous right now."

"Then when?" David pressed, his lips tightening into a frustrated line. "Not to sound cliché, but failure is not an option here."

His head bowed, Tim stood motionless for what seemed like an eternity. When he finally looked up, David knew he'd reached some internal decision.

"The mission is over," Tim announced. "I'll get you someplace safe so you can make your way back home."

David growled in frustration. "Damn it, kid, we already had this conversation. Either we go together, or I don't go at all."

"But—"

"No buts. We won't fail, not after everything we've been through." David refused to be swayed by Tim's beseeching gaze. He had already made up his mind. There was no way in hell he would stand by and watch Tim die, watch the life slip out of him because of the disease that had been forced on him. Any sympathy he'd felt toward the recently deceased scientist rapidly disappeared. It was Anderson's fault Tim was in this position, and the selfish bastard had the nerve to leave the kid to face this on his own. But David was determined to see this through. He never wanted Tim to be alone again, not if he could do anything about it. "Now," he urged, "what do we do?"

Tim stared at him silently as the seconds ticked by, wonder dawning on his face in view of David's implacability. His full lips curved into a shy smile for an instant before he was, once again, all business. He dropped to his knees and began to rummage in the small duffel bag Anderson had been carrying. David hadn't noticed it until right then, and he was amazed Tim had been able to think clearly enough to grab it as they frantically evaded the smoke bomb.

"I detonated all of the explosives I planted before, but I can rig a few on the fly to use as grenades."

"That sounds dangerous," David opined before tossing Tim a grin. "I like it."

Tim mirrored the expression, his smile somehow both beautiful and deadly. "The explosion should stun anyone standing in the hall long enough for us to reenter the lab. Hopefully the door is still unlocked. Father Paul has…." He stumbled over his mistake. "The card key he stole is in the lab." *With the body*. The caveat remained unspoken.

David rushed past the awkward pause that fell between them. "How many bombs can you make? Maybe we can blow the door if we need to."

"Three. And, yes, that will work if necessary. But it risks damaging the vials in the lab, so we'll use it only as a last resort." Tim's hands flew over the deadly materials, and in a few minutes, he was finished.

David shook his head as he studied the newly fashioned explosives. "I don't think you'll ever cease to amaze me, kid."

Tim smiled again, the expression looking entirely at home on his face. "Let me check whether the coast is clear." After stuffing the bombs into the duffel, he pulled the door open the barest inch. He closed it an instant later, his jaw working as he clenched his teeth. "There are six men between us and the lab. I could take them out, but it will take time and call attention to our position."

"What if we went around the other way? Came at the lab from the opposite side? Wait," David said abruptly before reaching into his pocket. "I still have the map Father Paul drew." Tim stood close behind his shoulder as they studied the map together, his breath warm where it caressed the side of David's neck. *You've got to be joking*, David scolded his body as it reacted as it usually did to Tim's nearness. This was so not the time to be having impure thoughts, for the love of Christ. Ignoring his inconvenient hormones, he pointed to a group of lines with his finger. "This is where we are now, right?"

Tim nodded. "And here's the lab," he confirmed, noting the label Anderson had given the boxlike shape. He placed a finger beside David's and moved it along a line to the right and then up at a bend. "This is the way we came in. Look here, there's a bisecting corridor," he said as he pointed to a horizontal line midway between their current location and the stairs where they'd entered. Tracing farther along the middle passage, Tim came to the other side of the map. "If we cut through here, we can do what you suggested."

"Okay, so how do we clear the hall in front of the lab once we get over there?" David scratched the back of his head. "A grenade?"

"No. I'll set one of the bombs here, in this room. It will divert their attention away from us when I detonate it."

David nodded. "Yeah, I gotcha. So, are we ready?"

Tim placed the explosive with the swiftness of long practice before hefting the duffel holding the explosives and peering out the door. "There's enough smoke remaining in the hall to give us cover. Let's go."

Silently, they made their way back into the corridor. David could see the soldiers blocking their path, but only because he was looking for them. He didn't know how they could stand to breathe in the chemical remnants hanging in the air, but when he noticed the misshapen silhouettes of their heads, he realized they were wearing gas masks. As Tim had anticipated, the guards didn't see them as they moved away down the hall. The central corridor was right where Anderson's map had indicated it would be, and David sent up a silent word of thanks to the man's ghost. He'd go back to being angry at the scientist once he and Tim were out of danger. As he followed Tim along the corridor, David felt a small niggle of concern in the back of his mind at how easily this was going, but stopped the thought before it could fully form. No point in jinxing everything. In the next instant, he was cursing himself for even that thought. They were nearing the end of the bisecting hallway when a handful of figures rounded the far corner directly in their path. Four of them were large men, but the last was a slim female, her black hair shoved under a hat that matched her fatigues.

David had only an instant to recognize the woman as the same whippy brunette he'd seen both at the hospital in Magnum and at his parents' house before Tim abruptly backed him into a wall. Tim was firing at their assailants before David had even properly registered the danger.

Once his brain finally kicked into gear, he raised the Sig and added its firepower to the mix.

"Get on your stomach and stay there!" Tim shouted. He dashed to the opposite wall, shooting the entire time.

David dropped flat on the floor as instructed, though he wondered what the hell Tim was doing. He was confused only for a moment before he comprehended the sense behind Tim's maneuver. By covering a wider path, they could more easily keep the soldiers pinned. Staying low made them a more elusive target. The soldiers took refuge in the corridor they'd appeared from. They popped their heads around the corners occasionally, firing blindly. With icy precision, Tim alternated his suppressive volleys with carefully aimed shots. It was the same as when they'd played Whack-a-Mole at the county fair what seemed a lifetime ago, only the moles were people and the rubber mallets were bullets. Tim proved as proficient at this game as he had at the more innocent version. Two screams were cut short as rounds from the Colt found their marks.

The woman must have grasped that they were at a stalemate at the same time David did. "Conley! TM 05637!" she shouted over the roar of the assault rifles. "Cease fire! If you surrender peaceably, I promise you won't be harmed."

Yeah, right, David thought darkly. It didn't take a military genius to figure out she was simply buying time until reinforcements arrived to attack him and Tim from behind. Tim had apparently reached the same conclusion because he never let up. David kept up shot for shot, but after another minute, his gun fell abruptly silent. Cursing, he fumbled at the zipper of the duffel slung over his back. He was reaching for a clip when the concrete floor exploded into shrapnel mere inches from his head.

"Jesus!" Ducking away from the lucky shot, David sat up and scrambled back frantically.

"David, are you hurt?" Tim called out over the noise, his tone pinched with worry.

"No, I'm okay! Just switching out a clip…. ARRGGG!" Pain burned through the meat of his calf as a bullet pierced him. "Fucking hell!"

"David!"

Tim's pitch had gone up an octave, his cry imbued with fear. Through his agony, David saw all the color drain from Tim's complexion. In the next breath, Tim surged to his feet and raced toward the shooters, emptying his own magazine as his shots gouged holes into the walls. One found a human obstacle, and the man dropped to the ground, his head boasting a new orifice. The remaining two kept well out of range, but that didn't help them once Tim was within arm's reach.

David wasn't a complete stranger to the pain of being shot. But compared to this, his previous injury had been nothing more than a flesh wound. He gritted his teeth, trying not to black out as waves of agony spread up from his lower leg. He shook his head in a desperate attempt to remain conscious. Concern about Tim's seemingly reckless action helped somewhat, and he was able to muster his swimming vision enough to see the kid grab the last man standing and drive his head into the wall with one powerful thrust of his arm.

The woman jumped into Tim's path, her weapon aimed toward him. He knocked the gun out of her grasp with a precise cross-body chop and reached for her, but she stopped him with a hasty kick to his knee. He grunted as she forced the joint to hyperextend, but whatever damage she'd caused didn't slow him down for long. He grabbed her by the throat and hauled her farther out into the corridor. David winced at the rough handling, but another stab of pain in his leg reduced his capacity for sympathy. Still, the woman surprised him when she dug her fingers into Tim's hand, apparently triggering a pressure point. Tim's fingers went lax, and she twisted his hand around, forcing him to turn so she could drive his arm high up along his back. But, while her skill was impressive, she was no match for Tim's bioengineered strength. Ignoring the ache he must have been feeling in his arm, Tim drove both of them backward, slamming the brunette into the wall. She let out a moan as the air was forced from her lungs, though she never relinquished her hold.

"Give up," Tim said, his voice strained under the pain of having his arm nearly dislocated. "I don't want to have to kill you."

"As if you could," she growled. In the next instant, however, she doubled over as a sharp elbow dug into her stomach.

Free from the aikido lock, Tim spun around, his fingers extended to deliver the same blow he'd used to level Woodard when they escaped from the Facility. The woman swept her left arm up and out, deflecting the blow. Gasping to regain her breath, she shifted away from the wall and hopped back to put some space between them. Before Tim could react to her maneuver, she placed her booted foot over his sternum and pushed him away with a forceful shove. She reached behind her back and came up with a wicked, serrated-edge knife. The sight of the weapon filled David with panic, and he shoved aside his pain enough to retrieve the spare clip he'd been going for before getting shot. Slamming it into place, he looked up in time to see the brunette take a vicious swipe at Tim's stomach. Tim jumped back, but she pressed her attack, not giving him the chance to retaliate.

"Tim! Hit the floor!"

Tim obeyed instantly and, whispering a quick prayer that he didn't miss, David triggered a burst of firepower from the Sig. The woman jerked as the bullets riddled her body. She dropped like a marionette with severed strings. Blood and adrenaline pumping, David felt a brief respite from his wound as his limbic response briefly overrode his nervous system. Tim rose to his knees and stared down at the woman for a long moment as though to reassure himself she wouldn't be getting up again. Apparently satisfied, he hurried back to David's side. He fell to his knees, his gaze frenziedly seeking the source of David's injury.

"Guess I can't tell my dad that lie again." David felt giddy from pain. The memory of his father asking him whether he was in trouble for killing someone grabbed hold of him and wouldn't let go.

"Where are you hurt?" Tim asked sharply, refusing to indulge his mental lapse.

"My leg," he grated out. He hissed when Tim lifted his torn pants away from the bloody mess of flesh. "Ugh, that looks awful." He felt woozy from the sight of the blood seeping from his wound, as well as from the loss itself.

Tim ripped the arm of his jacket off, the seam giving away easily before his forceful tug. Taking a clip from David's open duffel, he used it and the fabric to fashion a tourniquet in order to slow the flow of blood. It hurt like hell, but David didn't complain, knowing Tim was probably saving his life.

"Thanks," he said, favoring the kid with a weak smile. Tim was understandably pale, but he was also sweating. David had never seen him sweat, except for when they were having sex, and he'd always attributed that to heightened emotion. The incongruity worried him far more than Tim's complexion. "Are you all right?"

"My reserves are getting low," Tim muttered. "I can feel it."

David blanched. "You mean your B12 reserves?" He remembered how helpless Tim had been before they'd gotten him a transfusion, but that was after Tim had been shot. Surely the fight with that female soldier hadn't taken so much out of him as that, though it did explain how she'd been able to hold her own against him. The lack of the drugs Tim usually took to help offset his symptoms must finally be catching up with him. "Can you make it to the lab?" David asked anxiously.

Tim nodded, but his exhausted expression and labored breathing contradicted the reassurance. "But I can't carry you. Not all the way there." He met David's gaze forlornly. "If more of the general's soldiers find us, I don't know if I'll be able to protect you."

The decision wasn't hard to make. "Then leave me here," David urged. "You can come back for me," he continued as Tim violently shook his head.

"No." Tim's features took on a mulish cast. "Don't ask me, because I won't do it."

David guessed Tim was vividly caught up in the recent memory of having to abandon Anderson's body. Trying to change the kid's mind would be worse than pointless. "Then we stick to the original plan." He took a deep breath and gathered his legs beneath him. It hurt like a motherfucker, but with Tim supporting some of his weight, he managed to stand on his own two feet.

"Are you sure you can make it?" Tim asked worriedly.

"Not like I have much choice. Whether it's to the lab or the exit, either way I have to walk there." David hoped his grin was encouraging instead of merely pained. "So let's go."

With Tim's help, they maneuvered past the fallen bodies. David studiously ignored the brunette's vacant eyes, which stared sightlessly toward the ceiling. He had never killed anyone in his life, but he didn't have the luxury of freaking out about it right then. Tim must have read his mind because he reached up and grabbed his hand.

"I'm sorry you had to do that, but thank you. In my current condition, I might not have been able to beat her. She was very skilled."

David was thankful for the reminder of why he'd pulled the trigger. "Glad I could help," he said, squeezing Tim's hand back. He frowned as Tim tensed beneath the arm David had wrapped around his shoulder. "What is it?" he asked when Tim suddenly turned to look over his shoulder back the way they'd come.

"What I was afraid of. The firefight drew attention to our location." He pulled David around the corner into the cross hallway. "Do you think you can run?"

David shrugged, trying not to think too hard about how much it would hurt. "If the alternative is getting captured, sure," he replied, hoping he was telling the truth.

"Then when I say run, you run." Tim took out one of his homemade bombs and set the detonator. "Once I arm this, we'll have fifteen seconds before it goes off."

The voices grew louder until even David could hear them clearly. The soldiers approaching their position must have seen the bodies of their comrades, because their tone became more strident.

"They can't have gotten far!" someone shouted.

Booted feet pounded down the hall toward them.

"Any time now, kid," David prompted with nervous humor. Tim pushed a button on the tiny electronic device he'd buried in the mold next to the RDX.

"Go." He threw the bomb into the corridor while David focused everything he had on running as fast as he could.

Though weak, Tim was still able to support him partially as they dashed away from the impending explosion. The hall they were rushing down formed the last side of the rectangle they had been traversing on their way back to the lab. It was half the length of the last corridor, and they had nearly gone the entire distance when the bomb detonated. Fire, smoke, and the screams of dying men rang out behind them, but they dared not stop.

"The lab is around the next corner," Tim said, reaffirming David's understanding of where they were. "I'll trigger the bomb I planted in that anteroom to clear the path." Tim held the detonator in his hand, but froze when he checked to see what was between them and the lab.

Sucking in ragged gulps of air, David was struggling to remain standing against the agony burning in his calf. It was a moment before he noticed Tim hadn't triggered the explosive. "What is it?"

"No one's there." Tim sounded uncertain.

"Maybe they all went to investigate the fight." David shrugged, pain overriding his caution. "Whatever. Don't look a gift horse in the mouth." He caught the glance of confusion Tim threw him and remembered that he had gaping holes in his knowledge when it came to idioms and pop culture references. "Never mind. We might as well go now while we can."

Tim nodded, clearly hesitant but willing to be convinced. They moved slowly, both out of prudence and to accommodate David, but the way remained unimpeded. When they reached the lab, it was deserted except for the soldiers who had fallen during the first confrontation, and, of course, the bodies of Talbot and Anderson. If Tim was fazed by the sight of his dead parents, he didn't let it show. He lowered David to a sitting position on the floor immediately inside the lab.

"Guard the door," he said before heading toward the lab's inner room.

Bracing himself against the doorjamb, David kept watch over the corridor. His brow furrowed when Tim suddenly veered away from his goal and headed for one of the locked cases mounted on the wall. "What are you doing?"

"Those blue pills," Tim said, pointing to a bottle sitting on a shelf in the case mounted on the lab's right side wall. "They're what Father Paul gave me when he helped me escape the first time. Their effect is limited, but they'll alleviate my symptoms, at least for a while."

David winced when Tim smashed the glass with the side of his bare fist. He shared the relief that lightened the kid's expression when he retrieved the container. Those pills could make the difference between life and death for them both. If they were discovered again, Tim needed to be at full strength if they were to have any hope of escape. With the pills secured, Tim returned to his original objective.

"Maybe you should take one of them now." As he voiced the suggestion, David lost sight of Tim. It was a second before he realized it was his vision, not Tim, that had briefly disappeared. He glanced down at the makeshift tourniquet and blanched. The cloth was soaked dark with blood, having probably slipped during the run. That was the last clear thought he had before slumping weakly to the floor.

"David!"

He pried his eyes open enough to watch Tim start back toward him. "No," he rasped. "Get the drug." Tim looked like he wanted to argue, but the opportunity was stolen by the clomp of boots heading quickly in their direction. "Shit," David swore. He'd completely failed in his duty as sentry. He lacked the energy to even move out of the way as Woodard appeared in the doorway, flanked by a large contingent of pissed-off flunkies.

"You are resourceful, TM 05637," the general began, "I'll give you that. I'll have to congratulate myself on training you so effectively once I've taken care of that unfortunate independent streak of yours." He moved into the lab, ignoring David as he stepped over him. Half of the soldiers entered behind him, fanning out to cover Tim from all sides. One of them remained close to the general, a hulking behemoth of a man with graying hair and eyes narrowed in a permanent glower. He appeared to be similar in age to his superior, if not slightly older, but there was no question which man was in charge. "Sergeant," Woodard said to his shadow, "relieve Mr. Conley of his weapon. We don't want him hurting himself any worse." He sneered down at David, gaze darkening with malicious glee as he took in the severity of David's injury. The large man obeyed the order without comment, pulling the Sig out of David's lax grip.

Tim had brought his rifle into firing position the instant the soldiers entered the room, but the hopelessness of the situation was lost on no one. They were completely outmanned and outgunned. David was terrified Tim would still try something foolishly heroic and get himself killed.

"It's not worth it," Woodard said, echoing David's thoughts. "You stand zero chance against all of us, TM 05637. You're beaten. Accept it."

"Help David. He's lost a lot of blood." Tim's brown eyes were intent as he stared at the general. "Promise me that you'll help him, and I'll come quietly."

The general's bark of laughter was barely deserving of the name. "This all sounds very familiar, doesn't it? Begging for your boyfriend's life," he sneered. "And just like the last time, you are in absolutely no position to bargain, you little piece of shit." Woodard sneered. "Let me tell you how this is going to go down. First, you're going to drop the gun. Then, I'm going to shoot lover boy here in his fucking head while you watch." He unholstered his sidearm and pointed it at David. "And when that's done, I'm going to take you back to New Mexico to see the Facility's research team. That's right, everyone happily survived your sabotage attempt. They're going to pump you so full of burundanga, you won't remember how to find your own dick. Your memory will be completely wiped, and you will be reprogrammed to my specifications. But make no mistake. If you put even one foot out of line ever again, I will end you."

As the general issued his ultimatum, panic twisted Tim's increasingly haggard features, though David suspected it wasn't his own safety he was concerned about. Woodard's expression radiated disgust as he witnessed the kid's helpless suffering. There hadn't been time for Tim to take one of the blue pills, and he was visibly weakening by the second. David's heart wrenched at how tired Tim looked, even as he struggled to accept that he was about to die.

"There was a time," Woodard growled, "I thought the life experiences you'd gained on the outside might actually help you during missions. But now I realize they were nothing but a liability. You are a weapon, TM 05637, a tool in my shed to be used whenever and however I see fit. You think you're in love? Well, let me tell you something. Love is a bitch." He bared his teeth in a vicious grin. "Now, say good-night to your boyfriend."

The gun loomed in David's vision, the seemingly inevitable certainty of his death all consuming. He was weak from fear, pain, and the loss of blood, yet he was still able to hear Tim's soft voice.

"Close your eyes, David."

Then there was nothing but ear-shattering noise as the blast tore through the wall separating the lab from the storage room where Tim had planted the first of his impromptu bombs.

TWENTY-THREE

I WASTED no time. The instant the explosive went off, I took the container of pills from my pocket, dumped a few into my hand, and slammed them into my mouth. To shorten the time it would take for my body to break down the chemicals in the tablets, I chewed them to dust and swallowed them dry, wincing at the revoltingly bitter taste. I felt like a little child all over again, whining to Father Paul about how much I disliked my weekly dose of the life-giving medicine. I could feel my vitality returning before the debris from the detonation had even begun to settle. The effects of the pills might be temporary, but all I cared about was the present. The future would take care of itself, so long as David lived to see it.

David, I thought frantically. Squinting, I quickly located his prone form through the haze. Before I could get to him, though, I first had to deal with the soldiers who, despite the ferocious explosion, were already climbing to their feet. I wouldn't have expected any less from anyone under Woodard's command. They were formidable in appearance and were armed to the teeth, but I wasn't like anyone they had ever faced. The debilitating weakness had vanished completely, and I was in top form.

I didn't bother trying to retrieve the Colt, which lay beside my foot. Pivoting sharply on my heel, I turned and dove toward the man standing behind me. I grabbed the soldier and spun him so his back was flush against my chest. A choke hold around his neck kept him pinned in place. Using the larger man's body as a living shield, I commandeered my captive's gun to disable the man to my right, the trapped soldier covering my left side from attack. I aimed to maim, not to kill. Not that I expected them to afford me the same courtesy. Nor did I believe they would let something as insignificant as killing a comrade stand in their way. Sure enough, the soldier's body jerked against me as he was pummeled by friendly fire. I didn't let go, incapacitating the two men standing on the opposite side of the room with a sweep of gunfire before turning my attention to the ones on my left.

I glanced around quickly and saw that Woodard and the sergeant—Cooper, I recalled—were still on the floor. I hurled the dead soldier toward the nearest enemy figure. The unsuspecting man collapsed beneath the heavy body, clearing the way for me to deal with the remaining three soldiers. The fallen man recovered more quickly than I had anticipated. He pushed his dead comrade off and sat up, the bullets from his weapon tracking unerringly in my direction. I flung myself to the side, firing as I went. I hit the man in the right flank, and he screamed in agony as the shot tore through his body armor and ripped cleanly through his abdomen. The wound was most likely fatal, and I briefly felt regret at ending his life in such an agonizing way. The immediate threat neutralized, I regained my feet and started toward David, only to find myself dead in Cooper's sights.

"The general may think he wants you alive, but he and I both know you're far too dangerous." The sergeant regarded me with a flat, lizard-like gaze. "So this is where you die."

David was staring at me, his blue eyes wide with fear as he registered my predicament. Our gazes met briefly, understanding passing rapidly between us. "Not today," I replied, sounding more confident than I felt. This would depend on split-second timing, and I hoped David was up to the task. I tossed my stolen weapon toward him at the same instant Cooper fired. I dodged to the side but was a nanosecond too slow. Fire burned in my left shoulder as the shot missed its intended target, my throat, by inches. I hit the floor hard, gritting my teeth at the jarring impact.

Cooper readjusted his aim, preparing to finish the job, but David scrambled for the weapon I had thrown toward him. Shouting with adrenaline and pain, he jammed his finger on the trigger. The rifle spat death in an upward arc as he aimed for Cooper's head. Bullets riddled the large man from his left ankle and up his leg and side, not stopping until his graying hair was dripping with bits of bone and brain matter.

The wild shots ended at the ceiling of the lab, chunks of drywall and plaster raining down on us from above as the rifle went silent. Woodard had regained his senses moments before, and his gaze fell on Cooper as he looked up from beneath the protective cover of the arm he'd flung over his head. The general stared at the ravaged body of his second in obvious disbelief, seemingly unable to comprehend that there was nothing left of his loyal subordinate except a heap of motionless flesh. He twisted his head to spear David with a glare of pure venom.

"You fucking bastard! You're a dead man, Conley," Woodard growled, climbing to his feet before turning to look through the door leading to the corridor. "Get reinforcements," he shouted to the men he had wisely stationed out in the hall. "And find Farley!" Hearing no response, Woodard frowned. From where I stood, I could see the bomb had taken care of his reserve troops, collapsing a section of the hallway ceiling and blocking their access to the lab. The general realized it a moment after I did if his murderous snarl was any indication.

I spared a moment of thanks for the superior reinforcements the builders had installed in the lab's structural foundations. "She's dead," I said, guessing this "Farley" person was the woman David and I had encountered earlier. The general's stunned look prompted me to add, "I'm sorry."

"Farley was a soldier. She knew the meaning of loyalty and duty." Woodard's shock quickly turned to fury. "She was worth a hundred of you!"

"Maybe so," I replied, "but either way, she's gone, and so is Sergeant Cooper. You're all alone, General."

A moan from David drew both my and Woodard's attention. Whatever reserves of energy David had dredged up before were utterly depleted. His face was completely drained of color, and his head listed wearily to one side.

"So are you," Woodard sneered, aiming his sidearm at David's head.

I wasn't about to give him the chance. Lightning quick, I lunged at him. My foot slammed into his wrist, sending the gun flying. Woodard let out a howl of pain and spun toward me, his face dark red with fury, but I whirled out of reach faster than he could track. The pills had done their job thoroughly, boosting my energy and enabling my body to swiftly mend my injuries. Still, my opponent's combat skills had been honed by years of practice and hard-earned experience. Instinctively, Woodard brought up his hands, grunting as he used them to grab hold of my leg before my follow-up kick could find its target. Flipping his hands over, he forced me to turn facedown to prevent my knee from dislocating.

The maneuver might have worked on anyone else, but I wasn't just anyone. Catching myself on my hands before my face could find the floor, I sprang into a handstand. I slammed my foot into Woodard's chest, forcibly breaking his hold. My body followed through on the somersault, and I landed gracefully on my feet as he stumbled backward. I spun to face him and rushed forward, intending to smash my fist into his face, but he regained his balance in time to block the incoming punch. He used my momentum against me to score a hit in my solar plexus with a rock-hard fist. I grunted, the air whooshing out of me under the assault to my diaphragm, but I didn't let the momentary lack of oxygen slow me down. Already bent over from the force of the blow, I dropped into a crouch and spun in a circle with my leg extended, intending to sweep Woodard off his feet. He jumped clear with a grunt.

"Don't try using my own moves against me, you little punk!"

Woodard arced his foot toward my face but missed as I rolled forward until I was under his guard. Ramming my fist upward, I aimed a devastating blow at the vulnerable flesh between his legs. He howled as the attack struck his privates with crushing force. I stood quickly, my body already poised to deliver the finishing strike. I lifted one foot, and bending my knee, I began to pivot on the other to strike out at the general's head with an incapacitating side kick.

"Look out!"

I couldn't fathom how David had managed to remain conscious, but I saw the dull flash of the steel blade of a bowie knife at the same moment the weak cry of warning reached me. Staggered by the pain radiating out from his injured groin, Woodard had fallen back against the wall adjacent to the lab's main door. But the maneuver had put me in perfect throwing range. Flipping the blade so it was in his hand, he bared his teeth in a triumphant growl and drew his arm back to hurl the weapon. Summoning every ounce of speed my enhanced body possessed, I darted toward him and grabbed his hand before he could let fly with the knife. Woodard's ice-blue eyes widened incredulously as my iron grip held him immobilized, the sound of his gasping breaths an audible indicator of the strain he was under.

"I don't want to kill you, General," I said, my breathing steady despite my recent exertion. "I don't want to turn into the thing you wanted me to be." I moved our joined hands downward, pressing the knife inexorably closer to Woodard's heart. "But I won't let you destroy everything I love. You've already taken enough from me." I didn't turn to look, but I could almost sense Father Paul's body lying behind me, stiff and cold. "Let me go. Let us both go," I added, keeping sight of David in my peripheral vision. "Do that, and I'll let you live. Just promise me you'll never come after us again."

Woodard's scowl morphed into a vicious grin. "You think you can escape your own nature so easily?" He arched his neck, thrusting his head closer to me. "You're a killer," he hissed. "That's all you'll ever be, and he knows it." Woodard cut his gaze slyly toward David. "He'll spend his entire life in fear of you, wondering when you'll decide you've had enough of pretending you're no different from anyone else. When you'll decide you've had enough of him."

"He knows that will never happen," I replied. David and I had no more secrets from each other. He knew what I was capable of and loved me anyway. But a shiver tripped forebodingly down my spine at the abstruse hint. I knew the general was up to something, but what?

"Is that right?" Woodard sneered. "Then why don't you tell him, Conley. Tell him about how you saw him shoot you over and over again."

"Shut up," David rasped feebly. "It wasn't real, you bastard. I know that now."

I jerked as though I'd been electrocuted. They could only be talking about one thing. "The training simulations. You showed him?" I choked, my constricted throat permitting nothing more to pass than a horrified whisper.

"I did," Woodard replied, unrepentant. "I wanted him to know what you really are. I wanted him to see for himself how you murdered him on my orders."

"But I didn't." I took a deep breath, my shock fading as the memory of the simulation rushed back to me at last in full detail. "You ordered me to kill David, but I didn't."

"Bullshit." Woodard frowned. "I saw you do it, and so did Conley."

"No," I said. I stared closely at the general's face, and the truth hit me like a freight train. "It was you."

"What?" Woodard spat.

I shook my head, feeling almost giddy. "Even after you resorted to drugging me, even when I couldn't stop myself from pulling the trigger, it wasn't him I was shooting." I narrowed my gaze as confusion flashed in the general's glacial eyes. "Right before I fired, David changed into someone else. He changed into you." Woodard's confusion disappeared and fear hastily took its place. "It was you I killed, every time," I said slowly, wanting to make sure he understood. "But not this time." I backed away, putting space between us. "Leave us alone. That's all I want from you."

Woodard slumped against the wall, his entire body conveying defeat. Maybe now, at last, he would accept that I was far more than a weapon he could control. I was my own person with my own thoughts and hopes and dreams. And, most importantly, I knew what it meant to love. I spared Woodard one last glance before I dismissed him from my awareness. All I cared about right then was getting David to safety. My shoulder was healing rapidly, thanks to the pills, but I had exerted myself greatly during the past few minutes. I could feel the temporary fix wearing off faster than I was used to. I wondered if the pills weren't as potent as the ones Father Paul had given me before. Maybe they were an earlier version, not that it mattered. I had plenty of them, nearly a hundred if my quick, visual guesstimate was anything to go by. They would keep me alive for at least the next few years, and after that… well, I'd worry about the future when the time came.

I knelt at David's side. "I'll carry you out of here, and then we can go find help. Just hang in there a little while longer."

David's gaze slid toward the door leading to the inner lab. "We still need to find that medicine."

"Not now," I replied. "Reinforcements could arrive from elsewhere in the base. All we need to worry about is getting out of here. The pills I found will hold me for a long while yet."

David seemed too tired to argue. He nodded. "Okay.… No!"

I didn't bother asking what was wrong. The astonished terror on David's face told me all I needed to know. I stood and whirled around, but the general was already on me. The knife slid into my gut up to the hilt. Woodard backed away, his features twisted in a manic grin, only to find himself directly in the path of a hail of bullets.

"Motherfucker!" David shouted as he emptied the rest of his clip until nothing remained of the general but shredded flesh, shattered bone, and gushing blood. When the only thing coming from the rifle was the clicking sound of the spent magazine, David tossed the rifle away. His eyes were stretched in horror as I dropped hard to my knees beside him. "Tim! Shit!" I felt David's hands flutter helplessly over the knife hilt sprouting from my side. "What do I do? Tell me!" he shouted hysterically. "What do I do?"

I felt the warm track of the tears as they spilled down my cheeks. They fell onto my lips, leaving a salty residue behind. *Why*? I wanted to beg the universe for answers, but all I could do was gasp at the burning agony in my gut. It wasn't fair. Father Paul would have been so proud of everything I planned to do with the new life I'd been given so miraculously. I would have been the best friend, the best lover, the best person I knew how to be. David and I could have been happy together. But one man and his irrational hatred had stolen it all away.

"David," I whimpered, "I'm sorry—"

"Shut up!" David glared at me. "You can heal from this, right? I just have to take out the knife."

I groaned as he lowered me carefully to the floor. "No." I moaned at the tormenting flare of pain in my side. "The pills I took aren't strong enough. I won't… recover from this." More rivulets of moisture welled in my eyes and traced hotly down my face.

"Stop it. Just stop it!" David growled. "I will not let you die!" His own eyes were swimming with tears, the muscles in his jaw clenching resolutely. "Not after all of this. I'll be damned if I let that bastard take you from me."

I could only lie there as David pushed himself to his feet, sweat beading his face as he struggled against the throbbing of his injured leg. I knew he was probably running on nothing but pure adrenaline to be able to get up at all. The ceiling seemed to move overhead, and I realized he was dragging me across the floor in the direction of the inner lab. Closing my eyes against the sudden dizziness, I sensed David leave my side an instant before I heard odd rustling sounds. When I was able to open them again, he was standing over me, his face flushed red from his exertion.

"What are you doing?" I croaked.

David reached down and grunted as he lifted a hand to the bioscanner next to the door. I followed the hand down to the attached arm and then farther down to its owner. I blinked when I ended at Talbot's stiff body.

"She was lighter." That was the only explanation David gave before he pressed her thumb to the scanner. The door slid open, and he sighed with relief. "Okay, come on."

I found the strength to smile as David dragged me into the smaller room. If I weren't so busy bleeding to death internally, I'd have probably find his stubborn tenacity unbearably sexy.

"Ugh," David groaned when he let me go. "Please tell me someone stashed some fucking morphine in here."

The joke fell flat as I couldn't muster the energy to laugh.

"What was that stuff called again?"

"Ambrosia." Breathing as deeply as I could, I focused my attention on the rack of vials sitting on the counter at the back of the room. Fortunately, the blast hadn't disturbed anything in here thanks to the thickness of the door separating the inner and outer labs. "Help me sit up."

David looked at me uncertainly. "What if that… thing rips something in you?"

"Too late to stop it now." I spasmed at a vicious twinge as my contrary flesh tried futilely to heal around the blade. "Help me," I demanded.

Reluctance oozing from him, David complied, gingerly raising me into a sitting position. He flopped down behind me, propping me up against his chest. "Okay, now what?" he asked, panting heavily from the exertion.

"Let me take a look." Stretching out with my enhanced vision, I focused all of my remaining concentration on the rows of vials. The room was dim, still illuminated by only the backup systems, but I could see every word as though it were a bright, sunny day. "There. Second row from the top. The one with the yellow-orange liquid." I grunted in pain when David eased me back down. "And look for a syringe."

David winced and hobbled over to the vial, favoring his injured leg, but in moments he had it in hand. His forehead wrinkled as he examined its contents. "This stuff looks weird. I hope it's safe." He glanced down at me. "Though I guess it doesn't really matter at this point." His rueful smile did nothing to mask the anxiety etched into the lines of his face.

"No, not really," I responded, trying to mimic the forced levity.

"Syringe," David muttered. "Syringe. Maybe in here…."After a short search through the drawers built into the counter, he came up with a narrow cylinder shrink-wrapped in plastic. "Got one!" He hurried back to me as quickly as he could. "Okay, now what?"

I studied the vial, wondering if the oddly colored substance truly held my salvation. I would simply have to put my faith in Father Paul one last time. "You'll need to inject me with the serum."

David goggled at me. "What? You want *me* to give you a shot?" The grayness in his complexion from the pain in his leg was overtaken by a sickly greenish hue. "I don't think I can," he mumbled, looking decidedly nauseated by the very idea.

"You have to. I can't do it by myself." I gazed up at him beseechingly. "Please. I trust you. Just, you know, stick it in."

David returned my weak smile queasily. "Okay, since you asked so nicely." He unwrapped the syringe and poked the needle through the stopper sealing the vial. "Don't we need alcohol or something? That's what the nurse always does at my doctor's office when she gives me a shot." He spoke fast, not even trying to hide his nervousness.

"If this doesn't work, an infection will be the least of my problems." I paused as pain stabbed at my side. "If it does, then you'll need to take the knife out right away before my body heals around it. The blood in my abdomen will flow out through the wound, and I'll be okay." I stared into David's frightened eyes. "You can do this. Ready?"

"Y-yeah. Here goes."

I barely felt the needle as David jabbed it into my arm. My lover was a man of hidden talents, I thought idly. And then I couldn't think of anything as sensations the likes of which I'd never experienced overwhelmed me. Ice froze my flesh. Fire burned along my nerves. Knives dug into my muscles. The sensation of the blade sliding out of me as David pulled it free was nothing but a trivial distraction in comparison. A harsh noise assaulted my ears, and it was only when my throat began to ache that I recognized the sound as my own screams.

"Tim!" David's cry was barely audible beneath the din. "Tim! Are you okay? No, please! What have I done?"

I wanted to answer, but I couldn't. The intolerable agony shrieked through my entire body, rendering me a writhing mass of unspeakable anguish. With my last coherent thought, I said farewell to David and tried not to hate Father Paul for consigning me to this unending hell.

And then, as abruptly as it had begun, the assault on my senses ceased. Where there had been only torment, now there was stillness. Warmth spread through me in the wake of the receding pain, and I inhaled deeply, feeling as though I were taking my first breath. It took me only a moment to realize that I felt better than I ever had in my entire life. I was whole. Perfect. Unstoppable. My eyes had shut on their own accord in the midst of my transformation, and when I opened them at last, the first thing I saw was David's beautiful, grief-stricken eyes looking down at me, reflecting a crystal clear image of my face as I gazed back up at him in wonder.

I reached up and buried my fingers in his thick hair, pulling his head down until we were an inch apart. "You saved me," I murmured before pressing our lips together in a gentle kiss.

David gave into the embrace only for a moment before breaking away. "What the hell happened?" he asked, his voice unsteady. "I thought you were dying."

"The serum, it fixed me." Warmth seeped over my stomach, and I glanced at the wound to watch as the blood, which had pooled dangerously inside my abdomen, ran free.

"You're still bleeding," David said worriedly.

"No. That's old blood. My internal injuries have already healed." Even as I spoke, the last of the blood trickled away, leaving nothing but a red stain behind to mark its passing. The wound immediately began to close until all that was left was a shiny line of new skin.

David gaped. "Unreal." He looked up at me. "And what about your condition? What did Anderson call it?"

"Addison–Biermer anemia," I supplied absently, more interested in studying all the subtle nuances of David's expressions I could discern using my heighted vision. I was absolutely certain I'd never seen anything more beautiful in my life than the play of the emergency lighting in his golden hair. "Cured, I think. Only time will tell, but I'm feeling pretty damn good."

David blinked at me, visibly relaxing for the first time. "That was awfully colloquial of you." His grin was followed by a hiss as his leg protested all the demands he'd recently put on it. As though remembering how tired he'd been before adrenaline had kicked him into action, David collapsed on the floor next to me. "Ow. I don't know about you, but I need a hospital."

I examined David's leg as gently as I could. "The bullet passed through." I sacrificed the other sleeve of my jacket and resecured the makeshift tourniquet. I turned my attention to the rack of vials once more, my jaw set in frustration. In the next instant, my eyes widened as I remembered something I'd seen in the outer lab. "Hold on a second," I said before hopping nimbly to my feet, no hint remaining of how close I'd come to dying.

Before David could ask me where I was going, I ran into the outer lab, praying what I sought hadn't been destroyed by my makeshift bomb. Most of the glass cases had been destroyed, but a few opposite the damaged wall were still intact. I headed toward the one I wanted, grateful beyond measure that it had survived. Finally, something was going exactly right. The vial I wanted was sitting on a shelf, tipped over but otherwise unbroken. I grinned broadly, the expression feeling natural on my lips, and hurried back toward the inner lab, my fingers wrapped securely around the bottle of clear liquid.

"Rocephin and EACA?" David asked, reading the label after I retrieved another syringe and returned to his side.

"It's a broad-based antibiotic laced with a coagulant, designed to be administered to those suffering traumatic injuries," I explained, remembering the drug combination from my field medic training. "We can't take you to a local hospital. They're required to report all gunshot wounds to the authorities." I prepared the syringe. "This will help stop the bleeding and prevent any infection. I can suture your leg on the way back to Lubbock. We'll get you something to eat as soon as we can to rebuild your lost blood volume."

David smiled at the suggestion, though he kept his gaze firmly away from where I was positioning the needle at his arm. "I like the sound of that. It seems like you're always sewing me up after I've gotten shot," he said hazily, obviously remembering how I had fixed him up after our encounter with Bobby's father. David winced as I administered the injection. "But don't quit your day job. A nurse you aren't."

"I still have a day job?" I was surprised at how anxious I was to hear his answer.

David returned my gaze as steadily as he could in his woozy condition. "If you want it. I thought I'd made myself clear," he continued. "I want you to stay with me."

"Forever?"

"Yeah, kid." David grinned. "Forever. Or at least until you kill me with sex. Whichever comes first."

Laughter bubbled up from deep within my soul, spilling out without restraint for what seemed the first time in my life. "I'll try to go easy on you," I teased. Kneeling up, I wrapped my arms around David's neck and lost myself for a few timeless moments in a heated kiss. My tongue sought out its playmate, our teeth and lips nipping and soothing by turns. I started to ache once more. This time it was a far more pleasant sensation, though no less urgent. David growled and pulled his head back far enough I could feel his breath brushing across my lips.

“Later. Right now we need to get out of here. I want to get you home before you discover there’s more out there than a small-town store owner.” His tone was playful but weighted with an underlying seriousness. “I mean it, Tim. I don’t want to hold you to anything. Maybe you should see the world a bit. All you’ve ever known is captivity. I don’t want to tie you down or—” He paused, biting his lip. “—or make you remember painful things. It might be for the best if you try to forget about everything that’s happened.”

I had remained quiet while he talked, sheltering my emotions behind a practiced mask of indifference. “Does that include you?”

David shrugged. “Yeah, I guess.”

There was nothing restrained about the next kiss I pulled him into. Words had never been my strong suit. I had been built for action, and I used every seductive technique in my arsenal to stop David from spewing more nonsense. Mindful of his injured leg, I pushed him to the floor and straddled him, taking unabashed advantage of his weakened condition to override his stubbornness. I ground our hips together until he was moaning and digging his hands into my buttocks to hold me in place. I bent over and swept my tongue into his mouth, seeking out every nook and cranny, taking note of what drove him wild and repeating the motion until he was a helpless puddle of need beneath me. I could feel the throb of our matching erections—David’s arousal apparently overcoming the pain of his injury—the pulsating flesh maddeningly separated by the stiff denim of our jeans.

“Jesus, kid!”

His strangled cry was music to my ears. I stilled only when we were both near the point of no return. I could almost taste my release, it was so close, but I would have to be patient until we were in more accommodating surroundings. “Do you understand?” I growled, speaking directly into his ear before nibbling it with my teeth. He jerked his hips, frantically searching for the friction he needed to finish getting off. “This. You. That’s all I want.”

David nodded spastically in defeat. “Okay, whatever you say. Fuck.” He shifted beneath me, clearly feeling discomfort from the pressure of his swollen cock in addition to his wounded leg.

I nodded, pleased at his compliance. “Good. Now we can go.”

It was a simple matter for me to sling David over my shoulder in a fireman's lift and carry him back through the lab. I glanced at Father Paul's still form as we passed by and gave one last silent word of thanks to my creator. The ceiling had fortunately collapsed on the opposite side of the corridor from the way leading to the exit. Picking my way carefully over the rubble left by my bombs, I made my way quickly back to the staircase leading up to the surface. Though littered with debris, luckily it was still intact despite the numerous explosions. I mounted them as swiftly as I dared, ever mindful of my precious burden. Whatever personnel had been spared during the assault must have fled, because the area around the phony bunkers was abandoned. I felt a twinge of doubt about leaving the base without somehow destroying it completely, but if anyone had survived, I didn't want to impede any escape or rescue attempts or hinder any efforts to secure the dangerous biological agents still down in the lab. I meant what I'd told Woodard. Never again would I take a life, not if there was any other choice to be made.

I pondered for a moment that the Company might decide to send someone else after me, that it might be wiser if David and I remained on the run. But with the general, Father Paul, and Talbot gone, there was no one left to carry on with the project even if anyone were mad enough to even attempt resurrecting it. They had been the heart, mind, and soul of the TM project. Without Father Paul, no one had the technical know-how to recreate my special genetic code. And Talbot had admitted she'd been the driving force at the Company. No, the TM project was dead, and I was reborn.

David was sweating profusely from the pain in his leg by the time I got him settled in Larson's SUV. It would be an uncomfortable ride back to Lubbock, but once there I could take care of him properly.

"God, I really need to get back to work," David said, probably more to distract himself from his discomfort than anything else. "And we really do need to figure out what to tell the folks at the store. That I had a hunting accident might work. I can hardly say I was shot breaking into a military installation while committing treason."

I huffed in amusement. "We can work it out during the trip." I'd placed David in the backseat so he could stretch out and prop up his leg, and after getting behind the wheel, I turned around to meet his gaze. "I bet Bobby will want to hear all about it." I felt a sudden longing to see my young friend.

David read my expression easily. "Why don't you call him once we find somewhere to rest and tell him we're on our way home."

I nodded. "I'd like that. You okay back there?"

David smiled wryly. "I'll survive, according to you. But wait a second. Since when did you learn how to drive?"

"I watched you and Father Paul long enough that I figured it out. I think," I added teasingly at his continued skepticism. A laugh worked its way unbidden from my chest, and I basked in the happiness bubbling up inside of me. I almost couldn't believe it was all over, but it was. I was free, and I was going home with David where I belonged.

"What is it?" David asked, looking at me curiously.

I gazed out of the back window past his head, seeing not the featureless expanse of plowed fields, but the image of a much-beloved face. "My father once told me, 'Man lives to die.' But I believe that man's real destiny is to love and to be loved in return." I looked back at David and gave him a dazzling grin. "I think that's what it means to be human."

Don't miss how the story began!

To Be Human

By Pearl Love

TM 05637 was created to be a killer. Genetically engineered for superiority, he was facing a life of missions, blood, and death until his creator decides to set him free. On the run from those holding his leash, he is found by David Conley, an ordinary store owner who stumbles upon a remarkable find. Renaming himself "Tim," TM 05637 sets out to discover what it means to have a normal life.

Through his friendships with a young boy dealing with a nightmarish family life, and David's mother, who decides Tim is perfect for her son, Tim slowly discovers his humanity. Even more importantly, David teaches Tim about the power of love. But General Woodard, leader of the project that created Tim, threatens their happiness with his determination to bring his evasive quarry permanently to heel.

As the search net closes ever tighter around him, Tim must find a way to thwart his pursuers so he can stay with David and live out his dream.

http://www.dreamspinnerpress.com

PEARL LOVE has been writing since she was a kid, but it was the pretty boys who frolic around in her head who finally convinced her to pursue it seriously. She's a Midwest transplant who currently thrives in the hustle and bustle of the nation's capital. A jack of many genres, she enjoys just about any type of story, so long as in the end, the boy gets the boy. Pearl is the proud mommy of two bunny rabbits and a ridiculously large stash of yarn and knitting needles.

You can contact Pearl at pearllove925@gmail.com.

Visit her website at http://pearllovebooks.com;

Facebook: Pearl Love (pearllove925@gmail.com);

and Twitter: pearllovebooks.

PEARL LOVE
BURNT
OFFERINGS

'Til
DARKNESS
Falls
PEARL LOVE

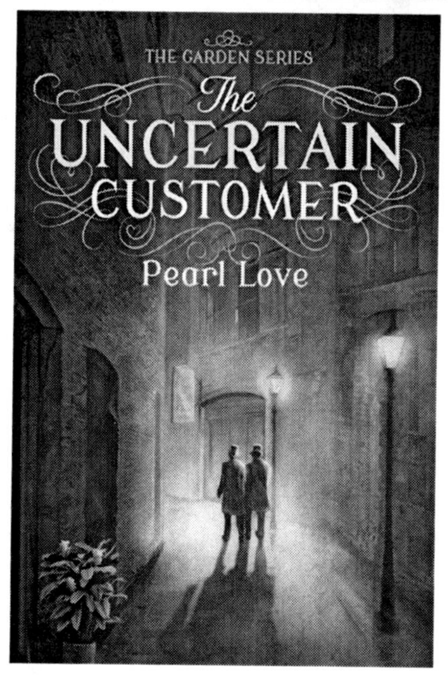
THE GARDEN SERIES
The
UNCERTAIN
CUSTOMER
Pearl Love

CPSIA information can be obtained at www.ICGtesting.com
Printed in the USA
BVOW04s1038310315

394091BV00006B/21/P